This book to be returned on or before the last date below.

SURPLUS STOCK

lease return to LSS/Bib Services
OLD on completion of the loan

08. MAR 07.

21. MAY 07.

23. NOV

09

12. SEP

30. SEP 11.

M   A3023227

Chandler, G.

Savage tide

OLDHAM METRO

Also by Glenn Chandler

The Sanctuary
The Tribe
Killer

Burning Poison
(non-fiction)

GLENN CHANDLER

SAVAGE TIDE

NEW ENGLISH LIBRARY
Hodder & Stoughton

A CIP catalogue record for this title is
available from the British Library

ISBN 0 340 82876 5

Typeset by Palimpsest Book Production Limited,
Polmont, Stirlingshire

Printed and bound in Great Britain by
Clays Ltd, St Ives plc

Hodder and Stoughton
A division of Hodder Headline
338 Euston Road
London NW1 3BH

For Robert Love and Diana Tyler,
who both did so much

PART ONE

I

Steve Madden was having one of the worst nights of his life. He was sitting in his car at one o'clock in the morning, looking at those blue and yellow curtains again. He knew every inch of those curtains, every angular idiosyncrasy of the pattern. Sometimes he felt he was staring at a maze from which there was no escape, where you just kept going round and round futilely until your brain seized up, like some laboratory mouse. Sometimes he felt like that. Like he was going round and round with no hope of escape. He wondered who had chosen the pattern. Not Clara, that was for sure. She had too much taste. Not Clive, either. He had too little imagination. Madden reckoned it must have been a joint decision, a compromise. When Clara had lived with him, she would never have chosen such appalling curtains. Then *that* scared him. *Joint decision.* The thought of them doing things together, choosing things, perhaps holding hands like star-crossed lovers as they picked out items in the furniture store. Going home and taking simple pleasure in the things they had bought. Like he used to do with Clara.

The light was still on in the room so Madden knew they were both up. He had given up smoking years earlier but now, to try and ease the pain, he lit the odd cigarette and savoured it. There was nothing like digging up an old forgotten pleasure to help you get through a difficult period in your life. He sank back into the warm contours of the driving seat and blew the smoke at the windscreen, watching it mushroom back at him. Tonight it didn't help. Nothing helped. The pain was acute tonight, like a fist turning in his stomach, grinding his insides to pulp. A demon inside, gnawing at his guts. It ate and it ate, and in the end he did the vomiting. It had no mercy, it didn't sleep. It was there when he woke up and it stayed with him throughout the day and it went to bed with him at night. It was here now, in the car with him, as though it had become an old friend he couldn't shake off.

He should have got over it by now. Like he had got over his mother and father when they'd died. But that's what parents did. They died. You mourned and either absorbed their things or got rid of them. They didn't move along the street and keep reminding you of your pain. You didn't push your trolley into theirs at the supermarket and feel your grief surge up again. You didn't see them holding hands in the corner of a restaurant or a local pub. At least when people died they went off to a place from which they could no longer inconvenience or physically or emotionally hurt the people they left behind. Clara had only moved along the road. To the Marina. He had to pass it three or four times a week. She still did her shopping at Safeway down St James's Street, where Madden did his and saw no reason why he should find somewhere else, other than the obvious one. Her gallery, Avida Art, was up in the fashionable North Laine area and he couldn't walk past it without feeling he had to look in. Brighton was big but it wasn't so big that you could lose yourself or hide away, like you could up in London. Brighton was bohemian, a little bit larger than life, and the people who lived there grew with it. Being anonymous in Brighton wasn't an option.

And he still had some of her things.

Paintings, mainly. Pictures he had begged her to leave because he couldn't bear for her to go out of his life completely. It was easier to break up with somebody you hated. To break up when you were still in love, that was a life sentence. Madden hadn't forgiven her, but neither had he learnt to hate. And worse, he hadn't mourned. Mourning wasn't just feeling down and sorry for yourself, it was a whole host of practical things like clearing out wardrobes and cupboards and throwing away the past and deleting her first faltering efforts to write *I love Steve and will love him for ever* on the new PC and expunging her mobile number from your phone. It was about abrogating the past. Pretending that twenty-two years of your life had been a waste of time and that the rest, the best part of your life, started here. All of which depended, of course, on there being a new life ready to start. At forty-eight, Steve Madden wasn't so sure he wanted to begin again. The past lay heaped around him like baggage at an airport while he waited for a flight out, a flight that never came.

Of course, there had been other women in his life since. But what angered him was that none had been the same as Clara. He had projected his anger onto them. Somehow it had been *their* fault, not his. All they had done was remind him how good Clara had been. How dare one person take that away from you – the simple pleasure of enjoying another?

The lights went off. Something lurched inside his stomach, as though it was the demon gearing up to put him through more hoops of agony. The lights going off signified only one thing. They were going to bed. Clive had been Clara's accountant. Did accountants make love, or did they just square the balance sheet? Madden conjured up an image of her sliding into bed next to him, that skinny but sexy body entwining him, her cool and delicate pea pod of a mouth planting itself on his lips, the tingle of electricity passing from her to him. Clara was never voluptuous, she was too slight for that. Instead, she had kept the agility of a nineteen-year-old student, which was how old she had been when he had first met her. Sex had never been just sex with them, it had been fun. An adventure followed by orgasm. Now all those precious minutes of foreplay and teasing were Clive's. He couldn't get the picture out of his head. Clara straddling him with her long milky-white legs, bent over him like some tigress bent on devouring him, her lightly freckled arms wrapped around his head while she found the zones of his body that responded to her mouth. Did accountants have zones? Madden could only assume that Clive did. He couldn't see anyone going to bed with Clara and not experiencing what he had experienced. And then there was the final release, when Clara would take him inside her and move her hips like no other woman had done before or since. No one but he deserved to enjoy that.

To help him cope, he had read books on jealousy. They all seemed to have been written by professors and human-behaviour scientists and social-study experts who lived lives a million miles removed from what he was going through. It all stemmed from insecurity, they said. Wanting something as a child and having it taken away from you. They advocated reaching back into your life to find the moments that made you feel insecure. Madden had reached back but had found nothing, like searching a well and discovering it empty. The trouble was, he hadn't had an insecure life. As a child, he'd been loved. Up until his divorce from Clara his life had been as perfect as any man could hope it to be. So much for cod psychology Method Number One.

Believe in yourself, they said, become autonomous. Trust yourself as a real person. Let go and become unique. Succeed as an *individual*. Madden believed in himself, there was no problem in that. When you felt as much pain as he did, you couldn't do anything other than believe in yourself. He was there, he was suffering, therefore he existed. He tried to think of himself as a special person, as a *unique individual*. But humility always overcame his vain attempts to become narcissistic and self-assured. Another fail.

It's a natural emotion, they said, don't deny it. When your partner leaves you for somebody else, it's natural to feel jealous, hurt and angry. But was it so natural a year after the divorce? It hadn't been a messy divorce. They had both agreed it for the sake of staying friends. It had been, all things considered, a very civilised separation. But then the problems had started. Actually, the problems had started a long time before, otherwise they'd still have been living together. Madden was still in denial about these. He didn't think he'd been irrationally jealous of her, he couldn't accept that he'd made her life unbearable, he couldn't believe that the rows and the arguments were his fault entirely, caused by a possessive streak that he could not control. But then, that was only natural. You had to blame somebody else so you could at least feel a little bit holy. Clara had told him his jealousy was unfounded, that her accountant Clive was no more than a good friend. Then she had moved in with him. That was worth a few points for Madden in anybody's score-keeping. Knowing was at least better than not knowing, having his suspicions confirmed at least enabled him to have his blast, to take the lid off the pressure cooker of his emotions and throw it at her feet. She went, and the pain eased. Now he hated Clive with a loathing that bordered on the psychotic, but still loved her with all the commitment of a martyr. And his obsession with them had grown. She suddenly had a new life. He didn't. That was the problem.

So much for the experts. Now the little green demon of sexual jealousy needed feeding nightly. Clearly, it didn't read the same books.

Madden stubbed the cigarette end in the ashtray, started the engine and drove home. Another hour of his life wasted, another hour spent in self-imposed torment. He knew those things but was powerless to do anything about them. Like addicts everywhere, he wanted to get off the wheel, but it never stopped turning. He'd considered therapy but was too proud to go for it. Therapy was surely for losers, people who had lost control of their lives, people who had given in. What was he supposed to say on the psychiatrist's couch? That he couldn't sleep at nights because he couldn't stand the thought of his ex-wife sleeping with another man? Then the psychiatrist would come out with Tell Me How Insecure You Feel About Yourself. Be Unique. Be An Individual. What You Are Feeling Is Only Natural. He had been there. Done that.

An urban fox streaked across Marine Parade, reddish brown like engine oil and its motion as viscous. It disappeared into a garden, where it too had a secret world. Madden's mobile rang. He answered it as he drove.

'Steve Madden.'

'Dad, it's Jason.'

'How are you, son? Good to hear from you.'

The lift, the sudden lift. When you were down, you hoped for these things. Often they were just little things, but they mattered. They mattered a hell of a lot. When you lost the ability to dig down deep inside yourself and find reasons to be happy, it was often other people who brought you out. He hadn't seen Jason for two months and had missed him. Jason was up in London, doing an art history degree, for what reason Madden couldn't fathom as the boy didn't have the talent of his mother. He was also working in a bar to finance his studies.

'I'm in Brighton. I'm at the station. I came down on the last train. Can I stay the night?'

'Course you can. I'll pick you up. Just stay where you are.'

'That's all right, dad, I'll walk.'

'I won't hear of it. I'm in the car, anyway. Just finished work. Heading home. It'll only take me a few minutes. You eaten?'

'Dad, it's quarter to one in the morning.'

'I'll fix us up some supper.'

Madden smiled as he put the mobile phone down next to him on the seat. He longed for the company. For over an hour his car had been like a prison, a cell in which he had entertained his demon. Now at least he could forget Clara and Clive for a few hours and relate to someone. He would open a bottle of wine or perhaps sink a few beers with Jason, maybe they could even get drunk together. It hadn't happened very often in the past, while Jason was growing up. In fact, he couldn't remember it happening at all, except in his imagination. But now the lad was nineteen and living his own life away from home. It was a father's longing to see his son not just as an appendage to his family but as an individual, an adult to whom he could relate. The phrase *talk man to man* came to mind. There were certain subjects that he couldn't talk about to Jason, of course – such as what he had been doing tonight – because fathers had to be seen as strong and not weak. But there was enough common ground between them, he felt.

In that, he was deluding himself. They had never been close. Jason had always been more attached to his mother. The long and irregular hours that Madden worked, the job that had distanced Clara, had also estranged Jason. They had never talked 'man to man' about anything. But, he felt, all that could change. All it needed was a little effort on both their parts. He knew fathers who got to know their sons as friends, and thought he would like that kind of relationship.

Yes, he was looking forward to seeing Jason as he turned the car off Marine Parade and headed up to Brighton railway station. It was a Monday night, or rather it was early on Tuesday morning, and a fine wet mist was blowing in from the sea. What had quarter to one in the morning to do with having eaten, or not eaten as the case may be? It was then that Madden realised he had not eaten since lunchtime. It wasn't because he hadn't been hungry. He had just forgotten.

He pulled in at a kebab house and bought two kebabs and two portions of chips. One for him and one for Jason. Just in case. The smell of hot roast lamb, salt and grease engulfed the car and, like the aroma of good junk food always did, it comforted.

2

Jason Madden stood in the early-morning drizzle, jacketless, the hood of his light blue sweater pulled up over his head instead. The legs of his baggy beige jeans looked generous enough to contain the week's shopping, and the laces of his trainers trailed on the wet ground. He had a small dark rucksack on his back. Jason had his hands thrust deep into his jeans pockets and stood scouring the traffic coming up Queen's Road for his father's blue Volvo.

Even so, Madden saw his son first. He didn't so much recognise him from his clothes as from his stance. Madden always thought his son stood bowed, like a monk. He was standing in front of the modern, ugly portico of the station. Behind and within was the original station house with its vast glass arching roof, a minor marvel of Victorian architecture and a reminder of the days when the coming of the railway was the making of the modern city of Brighton and Hove. Royalty, Oscar Wilde and Ivor Novello had travelled on the line and made Brighton fashionable. Now it was the thousands of day trippers and holidaymakers who kept the city buzzing. A few of them hung around the station still, either just arrived or waiting to go, it was difficult to tell. Drunks, junkies, drug dealers, all were pretty much in evidence around the main artery into the City that Liked to Say Yes.

Madden pulled up and his son climbed in, throwing his rucksack down between his knees. He tossed back his hood that was damp with rain. He was a handsome boy. Most of his looks, Madden had to admit, came from his mother. That deep auburn hair, his pale face, even his freckles he seemed to have inherited from her.

'Well, this is a surprise,' said Madden.

'I was going to give mum a ring but Clive doesn't like it if I turn up there late. You know how he is.'

Great, thought Madden. *I haven't seen my son for two months and I'm already made to feel second-best.* He decided not to show his chagrin.

'I got us something to eat. Just in case you were hungry.'

'Been working?' asked Jason, smelling the kebabs and chips that lay wrapped in greasy paper on the back seat.

'Yes. Just finished.'

'Got any big cases on?'

One of the advantages of having a Detective Inspector for a father was that conversation was rarely strained. As a young boy, Jason had thrilled to hear his father's stories. Now that he was nineteen it was less of a thrill, more of a handicap. That was part of the reason he had left Brighton. Still, he took an interest in the stories, as long as they involved murder, rape, violence, blackmail, paedophilia, spectacular suicides off Beachy Head and drug smuggling. He didn't want to know about stress or paperwork.

'We've just been dealing with a guy swept away by a freak tide near the West Pier. Never found his body. That was three days ago.'

'Probably at the bottom of the Channel by now,' Jason contributed cheerfully.

'Few weeks ago I was involved in the Chaney case. She was a prostitute, into rough sadomasochistic sex. She set fire to this client's genitals that he'd asked her to cover in butter first. Unfortunately, he died before she could blow him out.'

'Haven't heard of that one.'

'Didn't make the nationals. Not exactly a family story.'

'What's she been charged with?'

'Manslaughter.'

'Poor woman,' said Jason.

'I've got some beer in. Or there's some wine if you fancy.'

'Cool, dad.'

Madden was flattered that something he'd done was cool. He headed for home. Home was Queen's Park, smack in the heart of the city. Madden loved it. He loved it mainly because this was the house he had shared with Clara for twenty-two years. His father had moved down to Brighton from the East End of London just after the war and had set himself up as a tattooist – '*A tattoo artist, son, don't you ever forget that.*' The business flourished and Sid Madden bought the four-bedroom semi-detached Victorian house on the hill for what was then the princely sum of five hundred pounds. Now, thanks to Brighton being the most fashionable place on the South Coast, it was worth two hundred and fifty grand. It was too big for him, really. He had thought of taking in a lodger, but preferred his privacy. Sometimes he felt as though he rattled around inside it, but the view from his upstairs bedroom window down the hill, across the ornamental park to the sea, made it worthwhile.

Jason, as befitted most teenagers in his situation, was singularly unimpressed with a house from which his parents had broken up and in which his father seemed desperately in need of company. Jason had moved out and moved on.

Madden put the paper parcels containing the chips and kebabs on a glass-top table in the lounge.

'Tuck in,' he said. 'You look in need of a feed.'

'Don't take this personally, dad, but I had a meal just before I came down here. I couldn't eat a thing. Sorry.'

'That's all right. You don't mind if I do?'

'You go ahead, dad.' Then, 'Didn't you eat tonight, then?'

'Didn't have time. Too busy working.'

Too busy sitting in the car outside Clive's place, feeling sorry for myself and wanting your mother back.

'Beer or wine? Which is it?'

'I'll have a beer, thanks.'

'Cook for yourself up in London, then, do you?'

'Sometimes. I eat out a lot.'

'What did you do tonight?'

'Got taken out to a new French restaurant in Chelsea.'

'Oh yes?' Madden took two cans of beer out of the fridge, gave one to Jason. He sat down in the lounge, opened the parcel of kebab and chips and ate with his fingers. 'Posh, was it?'

'Not terribly.'

Madden could see Jason's eyes scanning the place. He could tell what the lad was thinking. Apart from four of Clara's paintings on the wall, the house lacked her touch. In fact, it lacked a great deal more than her touch. It seemed as though when she walked out of that house, the soul of the place slipped out after her. It wasn't so much that it was untidy, it had just become colourless and lacklustre. There were few personal touches. Madden saw no need for personal touches. He slept and ate and drank in the place now and called it home. Apart from a couple of colleagues, he rarely invited anybody back. It was too soon after Clara.

'Have you seen mum?' asked Jason.

'Why should I have seen your mum?'

'I just thought you might. I know you bump into her sometimes at the supermarket. She told me.'

'I try not to bump into your mother.'

They tore the tops off their cans of beer, though not at the same time. Madden was already downing his when Jason picked up his can and opened it without so much as a look or a thank-you or a salutation. On the surface, it seemed cosy, the way he wanted things to be – father and son drinking beer together at one o'clock in the morning. The way things ought to be. But deep down he knew there were barriers there, barriers that were going to be hard to overcome.

Jason blamed him for the break-up and there was little that Madden could do to change his son's opinion. Madden contemplated the whole course of the marriage, from its halcyon beginnings to its tragic end. A policeman's life was part of it. The pattern was ingrained, almost threadbare. Long hours, too much alcohol, too little time spent caring for the things that had once been important. Then there had been his affair, not a serious thing but enough to drive a wedge between them, with a female colleague, no longer in the force. He had tried to make up after that, but Clara had found her own wings, and new friends. The more they drifted apart the more he tried to cling on. He became jealous of her new friends, began to accuse her of having lovers. He had no right to accuse. One night it all exploded. She left him. Make-ups and break-ups followed but in the end it was beyond salvaging.

Out of the dust came Clive. And a son who had seen most of it and formed his own opinions and would always be closer to his mother. It was difficult to repair that with two cans of beer. He tried, nevertheless.

'Cheers, son,' he said.

'Cheers, dad.'

'I'll make up your bed for you. It'll be nice, having you back in your old room.'

'Dad, I came down because I wanted to tell you something. Mum knows, so it's no great secret. But I don't see any reason why you shouldn't know too. It's no big deal, actually.'

'Know what?'

'I'm gay.'

Madden felt as though he should have known. As a parent, you picked up all sorts of signs. As a detective, you were trained to look for evidence. He'd suspected as much for a couple of years before Jason had left home but like most fathers he hadn't wanted to face it. You wanted your son to grow up and get married and have kids and give you something to live for. Especially when he was your only son. Clara had wanted another child, a girl, but a miscarriage had dashed those hopes. After that she became terrified of pregnancy. They had both pinned their hopes and their aspirations on Jason.

Now, those two words effectively quashed all those hopes. He wondered whose genes had contributed.

'And I've got a boyfriend. He's at Cambridge University. His name's Daniel.'

'Hold on,' said Madden. 'One thing at a time.'

'Sorry.'

'So am I.'

'Why should you be sorry? I'm happy, dad, I'm happy,' Jason

said, piling on the agony he had no idea he was piling on. 'I just wanted us to get it out in the open, that's all.'

'Okay, now it's out in the open.'

'You don't like it, do you?'

'Tonight, of all nights, no. I don't like it. I suppose I was looking forward to a nice chat and you throw this at me. As though I don't have enough to put up with at the moment.'

'What do *you* have to put up with? This is *me* I'm talking about. My life and how I feel and what I want to do with it.'

Already there was acrimony. Madden considered biting his lip, saying no more. But it was difficult. This night made it especially hard. He had looked forward to a chat, a few beers, an hour in which he might forget his problems. Not be saddled with more. Another night he might have coped with this. Why had Jason picked this night of all nights?

There were twenty-five thousand gay men and ten thousand lesbians in Brighton. So they said. He wasn't sure who had gone out and counted them. But in essence you didn't have to. It was reflected in the house prices. His own had doubled in price in ten years, and it was largely because of the pink pound. Or so they said. All those disposable incomes flooding into the city. You couldn't afford to be homophobic in a city like that. Madden didn't consider himself homophobic. He just wasn't prepared for it happening in his own family. What he ultimately wanted was a son he could relate to, a son he could talk his problems out with, a son who would support him.

He didn't know his son.

'We've never talked about my life, dad. How I feel. What I want to do with it. I thought tonight was just a good time to do it.'

You were wrong.

'I mean, that was one of the reasons I left home. I was scared of you finding out. But now I don't want to be scared any more. Like I said, I'm happy. I don't see why I should keep it from you any longer.'

'I'm glad you're happy,' said Madden.

'You don't sound it.'

'How do you expect me to sound? Do you think I've been happy since your mother left? I have to cope with thinking about her living with another man. I had hopes for us all, I had hopes for you especially – getting married, settling down, having children. I really did.'

Jason let out one of those long exasperated sighs that signified a widening gulf.

'And don't give me that sigh, Jason. I know what it's all about. You think you're the only one in the equation who matters.'

'Equation? This isn't about mathematics, dad.'

'Just hear me out. I admire you for coming home and telling me this but please don't think you can just walk in here and I'm going to jump for joy and everything's going to be all right. I need time.'

'How much time?'

'You want to give me a deadline, is that it?'

'I just want to know how much time you need to feel pleased that I'm happy and I'm doing what I want to do.'

'Jason, don't make this difficult for me.'

'I'm not making it difficult for you, dad. You're making it difficult for me. I came down here because I wanted to talk to you. I have problems too sometimes. Decisions I have to make. I'd like to talk about them with you but I can't if you're going to start on all that settling-down-and-having-grandchildren nonsense.'

'Do you think it's unreasonable for a father to want that?'

'It's unreasonable for you to want it of *me*. Because I'm not that way inclined. I'd make a lousy father.'

Like me. Like me.

'It's not been easy for me either, dad,' Jason went on. There were tears in his eyes.

'I can understand that.'

'So try.'

Try to understand me, Jason.

'Maybe it would be better if we talked about it in the morning,' Madden suggested.

'If that's what you'd prefer.'

'It's been a long day, Jason. Not the best day for me.'

Madden wanted to tell Jason what *he* was going through. That this jealousy thing over his mother was not getting any easier. That he was beginning to hate Clive more and more for taking her away from him. That he didn't know how to get off the downward spiral. But he couldn't. The chasm between them was too wide. He wanted Jason to see that he was coping.

'Okay, dad. In the morning,' Jason said, getting up.

'Anything you want?'

'No, thanks.'

Jason took his beer to bed. Madden picked up the unopened kebab and chips and dropped them into the waste bin in the kitchen. Then he turned in.

It had not been a good night. He thought about Clara again. Like a looped tape, the thought of her and Clive went round and round endlessly in his brain. He longed for the day when he wouldn't think about her once, for the morning he might wake up and become aware that he hadn't thought about her for the whole of the previous day. Was it such a tall order to want to get on with your life?

He woke at four in the morning. He tried to think of Jason instead.

I'm happy, dad, I'm happy.

Madden was glad one of them was. He put on the light. Over his bed was a framed photograph of his father standing outside Sid Madden Tattoos in Trafalgar Street, Brighton. The premises were now a retro second-hand clothing emporium, but in his father's day Sid Madden Tattoos had been *the* premier establishment of its kind on the South Coast. In the sixties Sid Madden had had leather-clad rockers queuing up for his needle, and there were always at least half a dozen motorbikes parked outside, as though it were some kind of shrine. His father had lived among Jews and other immigrants in the East End of London throughout the era of Oswald Mosley and the Blackshirts, who would march through the streets with their fascist banners stirring up hatred and anti-Semitism. His father had no truck with such people. 'Let 'em live,' he used to say. Like the rockers who used to patronise Sid Madden Tattoos. They were vilified and hated and feared, but to his father they were all great blokes. He wondered what his own father would have said if he had confronted him with the news that he was gay. 'Let 'em live,' probably.

He rose at six-thirty, put some coffee on, carried a mug of it to Jason's bedroom door and knocked gently. He had never been the kind of father to burst uninvited into his son's bedroom. At least, not since Jason had told him off for it at the age of fourteen. He knew what he wanted to do. Somehow he had to put right what had gone wrong the previous evening. Jason had made a special journey to see him. He had to make the effort to build some kind of a bridge between them before he went back to London.

'Jason, you want some coffee?'

He opened the door gently, looked in. Jason wasn't in the bed. The covers were thrown back and his rucksack was gone.

It took Madden more than a few seconds to realise that his son had got up early and left.

3

His 'ferapy', his father had called it. 'Getting his ferapy'. Every morning of his retirement, Sid Madden had got up early and jogged down through Queen's Park to the seafront where he'd stripped off his clothes, left them in a pile on the shingle, and gone in naked for his dip. Occasionally Steve Madden had gone with his father and joined him in the surf. His old man would swim out much further, though, and he could see him now, his cadaverous body covered in tattoos, his bony yet incredibly strong and sinewy arms churning the water like the paddles of a steamboat. He claimed that it had given him ten more years of life, though the fags and the booze had eventually joined forces to kill him.

Now Madden too saw it as a kind of therapy. About once a week he would brave the cold surf and splash naked into the sea, leaving his clothes in a pile just as his father had done. Brighton at six o'clock in the morning reminded him of Brighton in the winter, when the residents had the city to themselves. The steeply raked beach was deserted. He felt the chill waves rush up to his waist and then rise gently to his chest. The sea seemed as somnolent as the rest of the town, a gently rolling tide that came in with a soft hush and clattered on the pebbles as it withdrew. It was better than lying in bed thinking about Clara. He wondered if he had the stamina to do it every morning.

He hadn't heard from Jason. He had left a message on his mobile phone but he hadn't got a reply. He decided on a course of action. It meant seeing her, but he couldn't help that. He stepped out of the water, enjoying the feel and crunch of his naked feet on the smoothly rounded stones. He had once read that the most popular last request on Death Row was to walk barefoot on the grass on the way to the electric chair. He didn't know how true it was. But there was nothing quite like the feel of wet shingle beneath naked soles. He dried himself. The air was cool, but there was a tingle in it that augured of the day to come. The sun hung like a pale orange disc behind the mist that crept in from the sea and was wrapping itself around the pier.

He wasn't working that day. He went home and made breakfast, two poached eggs and two rashers of bacon on hot buttered muffins. Then he walked into the centre of town, to the North Laine where Clara had her gallery.

The North Laine was full of tourist shops selling the kind of kitsch he wouldn't be seen dead with. If you wanted a string of plum-shaped lights to drape around your conservatory, or a plastic Noddy car radio, or a telephone shaped like a penis resting between two breasts, then fine. To be fair, it also had some of the best bookshops and places that still sold vinyl records and great delis and fine cafés, but the kitsch was what caught your eye.

Clara's gallery, Avida Art, shone out like a beacon. It wasn't the kind of art gallery that intimidated. Clara had gone all out to make sure it didn't. There was a sign on the door that said PLEASE COME IN TO LOOK AROUND and the gallery was dotted with wicker chairs for customers to relax in while helping themselves to small plastic cups of freshly squeezed orange juice. She was a bit of a mover and a shaker in the Brighton art world, mounting regular exhibitions and displaying and selling other artists' work as well as her own.

Madden arrived only minutes after she'd opened up. She was as startled to see him as a deer surprised by a hunter with a rifle. The last time had been at the supermarket when their trolleys had clashed: that had been three months before and an accident. They had been civil to each other then. But the last thing Clara expected was for him to just walk in. It was painful for her, too.

'Hello,' she said.

'Just thought I'd drop by.' He sounded unconvincing.

'That's nice.'

'You're looking good.'

'You too.'

She put on a breezy air, even though it was an act. He deliberately sounded upfront and confident. That was an act too. The first rule of meeting with your ex-wife, or ex-anybody for that matter, was not to show that it hurt, nor to give the impression that you were the worse off. You had to give the impression that you were not only coping admirably but enjoying life. Madden conveyed that impression to the full.

'Never been better,' he said. 'Keeping fit. Still swimming. How's living at the Marina?'

'It's wonderful,' she said, and he thought he detected the slightest hint of a grimace.

'You don't find it soulless? Some people have said that. They find it soulless.'

'No. *I* don't find it soulless.' she said defensively.

She busied herself around her desk, put on a few more lights. She was wearing a lemon-coloured blouse with short sleeves and the sunlight filtering in through the windows sparkled on the tiny translucent hairs on her arms. Madden studied her with a sense of longing. She was still as beautiful as ever and still very much part of him. And yet she was as remote as though she was standing on some other distant continental shelf. He felt a rush of remorse through his blood, anger that he had ever let her go. He instantly regretted everything he had ever done to drive her away. If she were to offer to come back to him now, he wouldn't even take the time to think about it.

'Jason came to see me the day before yesterday.'

'Did he?'

'Did he come to see you?'

'No. I didn't know he was in Brighton.'

'He implied that he goes to visit you more than me. I just thought he might have turned up.'

Clara glanced away, then down at a brochure on her desk.

'No,' she said. 'He didn't.'

'He told me about himself. I didn't know.'

'You didn't know what?'

'About him being gay.'

'Oh. That,' she said.

Clara responded as though Jason had told her he was going on a holiday to Ibiza.

'I've known for some time,' she followed it up.

'Even when we were married?'

'Even when we were married. Come on, Steve, I'm his mother, mothers know these things.'

'Didn't you think of telling me?'

Clara had the habit of busying herself, doing little unimportant things, whenever the big thing was too unpalatable or too problematic to discuss. She was doing that now. He wondered what was so important in her drawer that she had to search for it at that precise moment.

'Clara, I said didn't you think of telling me?'

'I didn't tell you for the same reason that Jason didn't want to tell you. He knew how you'd react. Like you're reacting now.'

'I'm not reacting.'

'Yes, you are.'

'How am I reacting? How do you know how I reacted?'

It sounded clumsy but she knew what he meant.

'I reacted the way any normal father would.'

'Steve, you were never a normal father.'

'Okay, the job meant I was never at home as much as I would have liked to be. But that doesn't make me some kind of ogre.'

'So what did you say to him?'

Madden backed off a little. He pretended to take an interest in a couple of paintings. Actually, they were rather good. One was of a naked couple on a beach. It was faintly erotic. No, it was extremely erotic. He wondered where the boundary between art and eroticism lay. Or art and pornography, for that matter.

'I didn't say all the things to him I wanted to say. I've had time to think about it and I'd like to put things right. Okay, I was a bit upset. It's only natural. He stayed the night but left before I could have a chat with him in the morning.'

'He stayed the night? With you?'

'Yes. Why? Does that surprise you?'

'It does a little bit. He usually stays at the Marina with me and Clive when he comes down. I wonder why he didn't contact me this time?'

Did she have to mention that name?

'He arrived late. On the last train. He said Clive doesn't like it if he turns up that late. Anyway, why shouldn't he stay with me? It's his home. Clive isn't his father. I am.'

He had been searching for ways to feel good about himself. He had just found one. If he could only talk to his son and tell him he accepted him and that he could come and stay with him and talk to him any time he wanted, he would feel even better. What had Jason said? *I have problems too. Decisions I have to make. I'd like to talk about them with you but I can't if you're going to start on all that settling-down-and-having-grandchildren nonsense.*

Well, there wouldn't be any more of that nonsense. He would see to that.

'If you hear from him, will you tell him to come round? I left a message on his mobile but he hasn't come back to me yet.'

'What number did you leave it on?'

He read it out to her.

'That's his old number,' she said. 'He had that phone stolen. Here's his new one.'

Time wasted. Madden punched the new number into his phone. He determined to ring Jason the moment he left the gallery.

'How are you otherwise?' he asked.

'I'm fine,' she said.

'Good.'

'And you, are you all right?'

'Oh, I've never been better.'

It was odd how people who had once been so close and intimate could lapse into the most meaningless and dishonest exchanges after they had split up. It was as though each was terrified to dredge up the past, to talk about something, anything, that mattered. If it hadn't been for Jason's visit, he doubted if either of them would have had much to say. How could he tell her he was still in love with her? That he parked his car to be near where she was? That he was tormented day and night by his loss? And were there things she wanted to tell him?

'I'll see you around, then,' he said.

'Yes. See you.' She smiled.

He left the gallery and walked only a few yards before dialling Jason's number. It was a different-sounding message on a different phone.

'Hi, this is Jason. Sorry I can't get to my phone right now but if you leave your name and number I'll get back to you as soon as I can.'

'Jason, this is your dad. I left a message yesterday on your old phone, I didn't know it had been stolen. Your mother gave me your new one. I just wanted to say—'

What exactly did he want to say?

'—Sorry about the other night, and I missed you in the morning. Next time you're down in Brighton, or I can come up to London, maybe we can have lunch and a proper chat. Okay?'

He hung up, the job done. It was up to Jason now. The next time they met, it would be different. Very different. The next time the boy came to Brighton he would have a place to stay that was not only home but that would feel like home. He would see to that.

4

Jason returned his father's call at eight o'clock the next morning, just as Madden was driving into the forecourt of the police station. Some bastard had parked in his space, a car he didn't recognise. You took a few days' leave and they took liberties. What made matters worse was that it was purple. Not just any purple. Bright purple. And it was small and round and very feminine-looking.

'Hi, Jason. Glad you got my message.'

'Sorry I had to get up early the other morning. I had a few things to do.'

'I just wish you'd said goodbye.'

And it had bright yellow upholstery. And a cream-coloured dashboard.

'There just didn't seem any point in continuing our conversation.' Jason was more honest.

'Never mind. Let's continue it soon. What do you say I come up to London one evening and we go for dinner? We can go to that French restaurant in Chelsea you were telling me about.'

Jason sounded as though he was on a train.

Madden pulled into the space next to the purple offender. It belonged to Jack Fieldhouse but that didn't matter. He had crossed swords with Jack Fieldhouse too many times for it to matter.

'Are you on a train?'

'Yeh. Actually, I'm coming down to Brighton today,' Jason replied.

'Even better. Why don't we meet for lunch today? You free?'

'Yes. Course I'm free.'

'Suppose we go to English's Oyster House?'

It was the best restaurant in Brighton. Madden didn't want

his son thinking that he was a complete philistine in the food department. A boy who went to French restaurants in Chelsea deserved such treatment. It was also the place he had taken Clara on the night he'd proposed to her. Admittedly he hadn't been back there since, but only because it wasn't on his culinary axis.

'Cool, dad,' said Jason.

'Okay, I'll book a table for one o'clock. Meet you there.'

'Yeh. See you there, dad.'

'Little purple bastard's French.'

'Pardon, dad?'

'Sorry. Talking to myself. Somebody's parked a little French purple car in my space.'

Jason didn't respond. Perhaps, thought Madden, he thinks I'm losing it.

'See you at one, then, dad.'

Jason hung up. Madden peered in the windows of the purple offender. There were twenty-seven miles on the clock. It looked brand new. Sickeningly new and smug with it.

He went up the three flights to his office. Detective Sergeant Jasmine Carol came up to him with an authority for an observation that needed signing. There was reputed to be regular pot-smoking in the courtyard of a Brighton pub. In the old days, you just waited and watched and pounced. Now you needed separate authorities for binoculars, cameras, practically if you needed to blink. It was all to do with what had been described as the 'collateral impact of an observation'. Innocent people would also be in the line of observation, and their human rights had to be protected.

'Bung it over to the Drugs Squad,' he said.

'Drugs Squad don't want to know, sir.'

Detective Sergeant Jasmine Carol was a result of the force's commitment to recruiting ethnic minorities. She had a Pakistani mother but her father, now dead, had been English. There was little of the Anglo-Saxon to be seen in her appearance, however, Jasmine having taken after her mother in almost every regard. She was as western as western could be, but that hadn't stopped her suffering racial harassment on her way up the ladder. Madden had never harassed her, except on these occasions when he would have harassed anybody regardless of their sex or colour, which came under his heading of equality. He liked her too much. Besides, he had been working with her for just under a year. Jasmine had worked with four other DIs before him, all male, all white, all members of the canteen-culture club, who for one reason or another hadn't found perfect bliss in the relationship. The one reason was the fact that she was a woman, the other was that she was Asian. As far as Madden was concerned, she was a good copper. Bottom line.

'Somebody's parked a small purple French car in my space.' he said

'I know, sir.'

'Do you know whose it is?'

'Yes, sir,' she said.

'Whose?'

'Mine, sir,' she said.

He stared at her for a few moments, quietly observing her spirit of insubordination.

'Come this way, DS Carol.'

He went into his own private office. She followed him and closed the door.

'I wanted you to notice it,' she said.

'Well, I noticed it. I couldn't help but notice it.'

'Last time I bought a car you didn't,' she said. 'I wanted to make sure you noticed this one.'

'Point taken.'

'It's brand new,' she said. 'I just collected it yesterday.'

It matched her clothes, Madden thought to himself. Asians had a propensity for bright colourful garments. Jasmine this morning was wearing a tailored purple trouser suit with a yellow scarf. Her rich black hair cascaded onto her shoulders.

'It's very . . . eye-catching,' he said.

'Thank you.'

'Move it.'

'Yes, sir.'

'Oh, and Jaz – I'm going to English's for lunch today. They don't like mobiles in there so if you need me urgently for anything, contact the restaurant.'

'Is she anybody I know?'

'It's my son. I'm taking my son,' he said dryly.

He only called her Jaz in the privacy of his office or when they were alone together. Most other times he called her Jasmine or gave her her full title of Detective Sergeant Carol. In private, she no longer called him sir. It had all come about since they had slept together shortly after Clara had left him. She had done it out of sympathy, he had done it because he was lonely, and in retrospect it hadn't been the most successful of couplings. Both had woken up feeling guilty. Madden had also woken up to the sobering and frightening thought that no woman could ever replace Clara in his bed. Since then they had slept together again a few times, but each had decided separately that a police-station romance was not a good idea. It was a sad fact that in the modern British police force a woman who got a reputation for sleeping with her colleagues also got a reputation for being a bike. And that didn't help promotion prospects.

It helped that they worked together well. Both were pretty adept at snuffing out any rumours that there had ever been anything, or that there was likely to be anything in the future, or that anything might be imminent that day. Ninety-nine per cent of the time it was business anyway. They played it straight. Nobody spotted the game.

It was a quiet morning. Then, at 11.59 a.m., everything changed.

Jasmine came into his office. She had taken the call.

'A murder in Kemp Town, sir.'

'Not *today*. Not a *murder*.'

'Shall we take my car?' she offered with barely disguised pleasure.

A few minutes later, they were on their way. Kemp Town was nicknamed 'Camp Town' because of the number of gays who lived there. It also had a sizeable student population. Madden knew it well. St James's Street ran through the centre of it, only fifteen minutes' walk from his home. The local Safeway store was where he had met Clara the time before.

Madden hated doing it but he had no choice. What made him feel so bad was that he had done this all his working life. Made arrangements to try and have a normal family life and then had to break them at the last minute. This lunch with Jason had been important, for both of them. If there had ever been an occasion he hadn't wanted to cancel, it was this one. But the job came first. He hoped Jason would understand.

He tapped out the number as Jasmine drove. Madden wasn't sure it was going to do his street credibility much good to be seen turning out for a murder inquiry in a little purple car with yellow upholstery and a cream dashboard in the middle of Kemp Town. He began to have serious reservations. If only it had been anything but bright purple.

'Couldn't you have got a more sober colour, Jaz?' he asked as she drove.

'It was the only colour in the showroom. Don't you like plum?'

'I prefer to eat one, not drive in one.'

'Hi, this is Jason. Sorry I can't get to my phone right now, but if you leave your name and number I'll get back to you as soon as I can.'

Madden left a message, apologising. He said he would ring him that night. They would fix up another lunch soon. The murder looked like a domestic. Domestics tended to get solved pretty quickly. Most people who got murdered were murdered by somebody they knew. It wasn't much comfort if you were on the receiving end, but it was a fact.

'I saw Clara yesterday,' he said to Jasmine.

'Why?'

'I had a few things I wanted to talk over with her.'

'Why do you keep torturing yourself? You'll never get over her that way.'

'Who says I want to get over her?'

Jasmine was the only one who knew about his occasional

night-time vigils. He had told her in a weak moment while drunk. He'd regretted it ever since.

'You don't get over someone you were married to for twenty-two years,' he added.

But thank you for your concern, he thought.

'It's unhealthy, Steve. You'll make yourself ill. You've got to break away, get a new life.'

'You don't get a new life like you get a new pair of shoes or a new suit.'

'Just get out more.'

'I'm trying, Jaz. Believe me, I'm trying,' he said.

Devonshire Place was a run-down street of Georgian terraced houses on a hill that ran up almost at right angles to the seafront. Large houses converted into flats, the stucco peeling off the walls, curtains that definitely weren't Laura Ashley. Most of the flats appeared to be for sale or to let. The property, which was cordoned off, had a first-floor balcony surrounded by black railings from which two girls, one with spiky orange hair and another with safety pins stuck through her nose and lips, gazed down in oddly tranquil curiosity. Madden looked up at them. He couldn't see the point in facial mutilation. He saw too much of it, practised without consent.

The young uniformed police constable who had first been called to the scene looked no older than eighteen or nineteen. He had a fresh face that seemed at odds with his uniform. He also had vomit on his shirt.

'The body's in the first-floor flat, sir,' he announced. 'The place belongs to a George Adams, but he's not at home. The occupier of the flat below was alerted when blood started dripping through the ceiling.'

'You've got vomit on your shirt,' said Madden.

'I was sick, sir.'

'Not at the crime scene, I hope.'

'No, sir. I ran across the road.'

'You'll go far,' said Madden.

The rookie – Madden tried to remember his own first tentative steps in the force – opened the communal door for them.

'It's not a pretty sight, sir,' he said.

'When I go to a murder that's a pretty sight, I'll let you know.'

Madden and Jasmine went into the flat alone. It was a complete shambles. Drawers had been pulled out, their contents tipped out, chair pads ripped open. Three pictures on the wall, depicting muscular naked men, had been slashed. A bust was broken in half. It had been the bust of a boy's head. On a table in the corner were the remains of what once had been a computer. Madden had never seen a computer so pulverised. It looked as though it had been dismantled with about fifty blows from a hammer. The inner mechanism was shattered and smashed all over the table.

They entered the bedroom. Clothes were strewn about. As in the first room, drawers and cupboards had been turned out. The mattress was ripped wide open, exposing the springs.

At the foot of the bed lay the naked body of a young man, on his right side, head twisted down so that his face was pressed to the carpet. His blond hair was wet with the blood that lay in a pool around him. His hands were bound behind his back with a piece of cord. There were dozens of bruises on his body, and more stab wounds than Madden could count. Many were around his buttocks and genital area. Horribly, the penis and testicles had been severed and left lying about three feet from the body. His throat had been cut.

The boy had defecated out of fear. In one final degrading, humiliating act, the murderer had placed the excrement in his mouth.

It was not a pretty sight.

'Has all the hallmarks of a gay sex murder,' said Jasmine.

Jasmine Carol could never resist jumping ahead, thought Madden. He put it down to her youth and enthusiasm. Neither could she resist doing everyone else's job for them. Their job was to gather evidence. Before she left a crime scene, Jasmine usually had a psychological profile of the killer.

'Never jump to conclusions,' he said.

'The flat obviously belongs to somebody who is gay.'

'This George Adams, whoever he is.'

'And you don't sever a penis and testicles unless sex is the motive,' she pointed out.

Where had a good Pakistani girl like Jasmine Carol learnt to say 'penis and testicles' as though she was saying 'bangers and mash'? thought Madden. She never failed to surprise him. He remembered the first post-mortem he had taken her to. Most young police officers, confronted for the first time with a body from which the guts were being removed, felt sick or fainted or at least went off their food. He had seen strapping men dissolve like jelly on mortuary floors. Jasmine Carol went out and had a curry.

In the Chaney case, which they had both recently handled, where Louise Chaney, a part-time prostitute (she was also a dental technician, a fact which continued to boggle his mind), had set her client's genitals alight and then attempted to blow them out but had ended up giving him a coronary, Jasmine had taken an inordinate interest in the type of butter Chaney had used in the preliminary frying. Madden sometimes wondered what kind of upbringing Jasmine had enjoyed. 'A good Hindu one.' she answered one day when he had asked her.

He had an adage. Murders were usually what they seemed. This one didn't seem like anything. The phrase 'sex murder' always gave him pause for thought. Sex was a beautiful thing, or should be. Murder was not. In any form, it was a despicable act. That the two could be lumped together always scared him. In actual fact, he hated the expression. It was too neat, too horrible a phrase for something that lay just beyond his comprehension. No matter how used you became to violence, it beggared belief that one human being could do something like this to another.

Madden saw a mobile phone on the bed. It was switched off. Mobile-phone records were always good for evidence. He wondered why the killer had not removed it. He assumed it belonged to the victim and that whoever had perpetrated the crime had left no clues on it. Nevertheless, the chip would give up its secrets.

And then he looked closer at the body. There was something

about the hair. He realised that it was dyed. Between the splashes of blood, a little bit of auburn remained at the roots at the back of the head.

Madden crouched down on the floor, twisted his own head round and stared at the lad's face. At first the blond hair had fooled him. But not now. There was no mistake.

'Jesus – oh, Jesus,' he said out loud, almost falling backwards.

'Sir?' said Jasmine.

'Sweet Jesus,' Madden cried.

'What is it, sir?'

'I need air. Christ, I need air!'

He turned and left the flat hurriedly. Jasmine ran after him.

'What's wrong?' she called out of the door. Then, forgetting for the moment where they were and lapsing into familiarity: 'Steve? What is it? Tell me.'

The police who were on the scene, the pathologist who was at that moment coming up the stairs, the scene-of-crime officer, the rookie with the vomit on his shirt, the onlookers, all saw Steve Madden stagger out into the fresh air, his hand covering his face.

'Has something happened, sir?' asked the rookie.

Steve Madden ran to the other side of the street where he held on to a gatepost and let out a wail of grief.

Everyone thought that he had lost his cool. Sometimes it happened. A hardened police officer who had seen everything suddenly saw something he couldn't handle and cracked up.

It wouldn't be long before everyone knew the truth. Detective Inspector Steve Madden knew the identity of the victim. He had just cancelled a lunch date with him.

PART TWO

5

Madden thought that the pavement was turning beneath his feet until he realised that it was his head that was spinning. He felt sick enough to faint. And still nobody knew. Nobody came forward. Until Jasmine touched him on the shoulder. He buried his face in his hands, unwilling to face her, reluctant to look at anybody. For a few minutes, he found it difficult if not impossible to take it all in.

They had spoken just that morning.

Cool, dad.

He had left a message on the boy's mobile phone. The phone that was at that moment lying switched off on the bed. Did Jason ever get the message?

'Tell me,' urged Jasmine. 'What is it? What's wrong?'

'Tell me I made a mistake up there!' he cried. 'For God's sake, tell me!'

'What mistake? You just rushed out like you'd seen a ghost.'

'It's Jason!' he told her. And in case she didn't take it in the first time, he said it again. 'It's Jason. I know it is. He didn't have blond hair when I last saw him – but it is him. I – you saw what was *done* to him?'

'Jason? Your *son*, *Jason?*' She found it equally difficult to comprehend.

'I just – phoned him. In the car. You were with me. He didn't answer his phone. I just – cancelled lunch with him!'

'Steve, you've got to sit down.'

She took his arm and led him back towards the car.

'You'd better call in, tell them to send another team,' he advised her in what was an agonising decision to have to make. But there was no other he could have made.

Jasmine called the station. Madden stared at the onlookers. He wanted to ask them what they were looking at. Herded behind crime-scene tape, they gawked with half-open mouths. They had never angered him before – they'd been part of the furniture. Now he wanted to tell them to go away. There was nothing here to look at. Nothing he wanted strangers to see.

'Steve, all you can do is sit down till they come,' Jasmine impressed on him.

Always cool, always professional, Jasmine never let it slip. He eased himself into the passenger seat of her car. She slid into the driving seat and closed the door. She took his hand in hers. This was no time for protocol. She squeezed it tight.

'You're sure you weren't mistaken?'

'Unless Jason has a double – no, I'm not mistaken.'

Jasmine seemed determined to keep him talking.

'What time did you speak to him this morning?' she asked.

'Eight o'clock this morning. He was on the train coming down to Brighton.'

He half expected her to bring out her notebook but she didn't. He suddenly sat bolt upright.

'Jaz, whose flat is that?'

'A George Adams's.'

'Who's George Adams? I don't know him. How did he know my son?' Madden fired off the questions in desperation, surveying the crowd of onlookers. 'Some of these people might know.'

'Steve, you're in shock. You've got to stay here.'

'We've got to find out,' he said.

'We'll find out.'

'I want to know who this guy is!'

Madden got out of the car. He couldn't just sit while there were residents hanging around. While Jason was lying up there, his blood still fresh on the floor. Madden's professionalism took a back seat for a few moments. He reckoned most of the onlookers were locals. He strode up to them, giving them something else to look at, something to consider, a way for once to be helpful.

'Who's George Adams?' he shouted. 'A person called George

Adams owns the first-floor flat there. Does anybody know him? Has anybody seen him?'

His enquiry was met with blank looks and shrugs. A few people, deciding that they didn't want to be elevated from the status of onlooker to witness, drifted away.

'Does nobody know George Adams?' Madden pleaded once more. He became angered at one person in particular. 'You there, walking away, don't. If you know something, please stay.'

Jasmine pulled at his arm.

'Sir, this isn't going to get us anywhere.'

'It might get *me* somewhere.' He shrugged her off.

'Sir, you've got to stop this.'

Her calling him 'sir' suddenly was in no small part due to the arrival of Jack Fieldhouse. At eighteen stone, he weighed in as the heaviest detective in the local force. Jasmine remembered the three miserable months she had been paired with him. In the history of unlikely working relationships, theirs had been the most absurd. He the misogynistic hard-drinking racist bully, she the only Asian woman. She well remembered the first time she had ever set eyes on Jack Fieldhouse. He had studied her from top to bottom and said with a laugh, calculated to endear him to the canteen-culture club, 'Are you really up to this job?' Things had rapidly gone downhill after that. To be fair, he had never insulted her racially, never condemned her sex outright. Jack Fieldhouse knew all about disciplinary proceedings. Knew the limits he could go to. And he skirted along these limits with proficiency.

There were ways of making someone feel useless, of making their life an abject misery, without resorting to racial and sexual slurs. Jack Fieldhouse knew all of them. He'd give her chances, then make sure she fluffed them. He'd give her the lead, then take it away. There were times while she was teamed up with Jack Fieldhouse that Jasmine had felt like leaving the force. But that would only have given him satisfaction.

So she stuck it out.

'You okay?' Fieldhouse's grip was like iron on Madden's arm. It was clear that Fieldhouse didn't really appreciate the true nature or the scale of the crisis. He had just come in response to Jasmine's emergency call.

'No, I'm not okay. That's my son up there.' Madden put him in the picture.

'Hell, Steve!'

Fieldhouse released his grip and strode on to the flat. Madden felt a surge of disgust that somebody like Fieldhouse should take over *his* case. A case where *his* son had been murdered. He wanted to go back up to the room now, to be a part of it.

But there was no way he was going to be allowed to handle this.

Then it struck him. How the last time he had seen Jason he had been more concerned with his own problems than with his son's. He had been going to put that right today. To salve his conscience, to tell Jason that everything was fine, that he accepted how he was. Now he was never going to get that chance. Someone had snatched it from him, violently, brutally. It was a grossly selfish consideration, but he couldn't shake it off. Jason would never know what he'd wanted to say.

Madden had witnessed it a number of times himself. Interviewed people whose relatives had met sudden death. There was always guilt, guilt that had nothing to do with culpability. The burden of a parent whose child had been run over and killed because she was sent down the road to buy a newspaper. A family destroyed for what? The sports page? And then there were the mothers, fathers, wives and husbands who would have said so much had they known that the last time they saw their loved one was to be the very last time. Guilt was such a part of sudden death. When the shock wore off, you thought off all the things you should have done, all the things you never told them, all the wrongs you could never put right.

Madden felt the shock and and the guilt simultaneously.

Maybe it would be better if we talked about it in the morning.

That was what he had said. They hadn't talked about it in the morning. Maybe if they had spoken that night he would now know things that he didn't. Like who George Adams was.

The most unbearable thought of all was that perhaps, just perhaps, if they'd talked, Jason might now still be alive.

6

Detective Chief Superintendent Raymond Millington was so old school that he would not have looked out of place in one. Along with his beetling eyebrows, thinning hair and long aquiline nose, there was a schoolmasterly gaze in his eyes that made many people feel uncomfortable. He had got where he was by being good at his job and knowing the right people – that, and the fact that he had married the daughter of a Chief Constable. He was never seen without a striped tie and a pair of cufflinks. When he sat and listened he linked his fingers and rotated his thumbs. When he spoke he unclenched his hands and spread them in front of him as though he was laying down a decree. It was unnerving.

Madden sat in front of him. He drank from a mug of strong sweet tea.

'I'm deeply sorry, Steve,' Millington said, his words if not his tone painfully inadequate. Madden wondered how he himself would handle a colleague whose son had been murdered. He wasn't sure. It had never happened to him.

'I want to get who did this. Personally,' Madden said grittily.

'I sympathise. But you know I can't allow you to take charge of the investigation. Or even be a part of it. You do understand that, Steve?'

'Oh, I understand that. Sir.' Madden's tone was pungent.

'You'll be kept informed, naturally. All the way. As the investigation progresses. You can be sure we'll do absolutely everything to find who did this. But you can't take part in it.'

'I take it you're putting Jack Fieldhouse in charge?'

'You know his record. If anyone can clear this up speedily, he will.'

Madden knew Fieldhouse's record. It was good. He had solved every murder case he had worked on within forty-eight hours. But he cut corners. Sometimes he cut them so roughly that the corner was no longer there to observe.

'Detective Sergeant Carol will be working with him.'

'That's not a good idea, sir.'

'I know things didn't work out very well last time, but at least they've had the benefit of working together.'

Madden was tempted to ask who it benefited.

'I know your feelings, but you also know I'll tolerate no racial or sexual harassment on this force. I know Jack can be a little . . . abrasive at times, but DS Carol's demonstrated that she can stand up for herself. Besides, she's close to you. I thought you'd want her to be part of this case.'

Madden met his gaze as he said *close to you*. He wondered if Millington knew.

'I appreciate that, sir.'

'Your ex-wife has been informed.'

'I would have preferred to have told her myself.'

'How are things between you?'

'Things aren't between us. She's married to somebody else. That's the end of the matter.'

'I'm told that you've found it difficult.'

'Who told you that?'

'Word gets around.'

Millington mustered a sympathetic smile that concealed the smug reminder that he was still happily married, had been for thirty years, and considered the union impregnable. Raymond and Joyce Millington were part of the South Coast social scene. Their daughter had gone to Roedean, the premier school for girls in the area. Happy Families.

'I didn't think divorce was ever easy.' said Madden.

'When did you last talk to her?'

This was beginning to sound like an official interview. Then he realised that of course he and Clara were in the same position that any parents would be in when one of their children was murdered.

Witnesses and, like everybody else connected to the victim, possible suspects to be eliminated. It was the way things were.

'Yesterday,' he said. 'I called in to see her to talk about Jason.'

'Specifically about what?'

'I just found out he was gay.'

'Did you have a disagreement with him about it?'

'What is this – you think *I* had something to do with it?'

'Of course not. But you know as well as I do the questions that we have to ask.'

Fieldhouse came in at that moment. He didn't so much walk in as lumber in. He pressed his hand on Madden's back, held it there. Madden could smell stale alcohol on his breath. Alcohol from the night before. The man was huge, a giant. He had a belly on him the size of a small car. Madden often found himself pitying the suspects who ended up being questioned by Jack Fieldhouse.

'Christ, Steve, I don't know what to say. Just that we're going to get him. I give you my word. We're going to clear this up faster than any case we've ever handled. This one isn't going to drag.'

'I'm grateful,' said Madden.

'When did you last see Jason?'

'Monday night. He stayed the night with me.'

'What did you talk about? I need to know everything.'

'He told me he was gay. I suppose I'd suspected it for some time but, like fathers do, I pushed it to the back of my mind. He said he had a boyfriend who was at Cambridge University. Called Daniel.'

'Anything else? Do you know who the rest of his friends are?'

'I don't know anything about his friends. I don't know who this George Adams is whose flat he was found in. I know it sounds as though I didn't know Jason – but that's how it was.'

It was hard to say, even harder to admit.

He hadn't known his son.

Madden had interviewed so many people who had volunteered as little. It was frustrating, annoying, when people couldn't tell you what you thought they ought to know. Now there he was, in that same position.

'You didn't ask him anything about the boyfriend? How things were between them?' Fieldhouse quizzed him.

'No, I didn't. It was a surprise to me just to discover he had one.'

'Or how long they'd been together? Or if they were happy? Or if they'd had rows?'

'No, we didn't talk about anything like that.'

'What *did* you talk about, Steve?'

'We talked about very little, if you must know. I wasn't in the mood. Look, instead of talking to me, go out there and find people who *did* know him!'

Madden stared down at his lap. He clenched his fists. Worse than the guilt was having it rubbed into you. Sitting there and admitting that his son and himself had virtually been strangers. But it was true. It was starting to haunt him. If he'd reacted differently that night, talked to the boy, maybe he would know things now. Maybe he would know the name of his murderer. If he'd taken an interest in him instead of throwing him out, circumstances might have changed. Jason might not be dead. If. If.

'We're not blaming you, Steve,' said Millington. 'No one's blaming you. None of us are perfect as fathers. We all know that.'

'I'm blaming myself.'

'DS Carol tells me you'd arranged to meet him for lunch today? Is that right?' asked Fieldhouse.

'Yes. At one o'clock.'

'I played back the message you left him. It was timed at 12.11 p.m. It was a new message so he hadn't played it back. You only got there a few minutes later so it's obvious he was already dead when you left it. That would fit in with the pathologist's findings.'

It was a horrible thought. That Madden had left the last message to his son when his son was already lying there dead.

'When did he die?'

'Sometime between ten o'clock and ten-thirty this morning. Probably nearer ten.'

Two hours after Jason had phoned him from the train. Two

hours of life was all he had remaining. What had happened in that period? Jason's life was a mystery to him. Who had he seen?

'I don't even know why he was coming down to Brighton. It wasn't initially to visit me,' Madden said painfully.

'He lived there,' Fieldhouse told him.

'What do you mean, *lived* there?'

'In that flat. It was somewhere he stayed regularly.'

'But you said *lived*?'

'He didn't live there all the time.' Fieldhouse went on to explain. 'Just some of the time. The flat belongs to a George Adams who owns a pub in London. He's not working there today. We're trying to track him down.'

'You had no idea,' Millington pressed him, 'that Jason had a place he went to when he came to Brighton?'

'No. He usually stayed with his mother.'

'Actually, he didn't.' said Fieldhouse. 'Occasionally he did. But most of the time he slept at George Adams's flat.'

'Where did you get all this from?'

'Just information that we've had supplied.'

'Who from?'

'Look, Steve, why don't you go home? I'll let you know everything as soon as I know it myself. I'll keep you informed every step of the way. That's a promise.'

Madden stood up. He didn't trust Fieldhouse's promises.

'There's something you're not telling me,' he said.

'Steve, don't be ridiculous.' Millington attempted to pour balm over the conversation. 'We all feel for you and we're going to solve this quickly, and you're going to be kept informed. What I can't allow is for your emotional involvement to interfere in the case.'

'Interfere in the case? He was my son!'

'I'd better go,' said Jack Fieldhouse. He pressed his hand on Steve Madden's shoulder. It was like a steam hammer coming down. 'Trust me,' he said.

Madden trusted Fieldhouse like he trusted a leopard in a kindergarten.

'You're suspending me from anything to do with the inquiry into my own son's murder?' Madden put the question to Millington.

'I have no choice, Steve. I can arrange counselling—'

'I don't need counselling. All I want to do is go home, be by myself for a while.'

'You've had a shock and it's only natural.'

'I don't need counselling,' Madden repeated. 'I need to track down the bastard who did this. That's what I need.'

7

Madden did not – could not – go home. There were moments when he considered that Millington might have been right, that he did need counselling. A lot of people who thought they didn't usually did. They were the ones who suppressed it, shoved it all back, tried to pretend that they could cope and instead would have nightmares in years to come. Madden liked to think he was strong enough to get over this without it. He had every reason to feel guilty, to feel ashamed. He was facing up to that squarely, not burying it. He didn't need to be told about trauma being part of the healing process. He just wanted to get on with the job, be a part of it. If there was any healing process, that was it. Neither did he need some psychologist coming along and telling him he shouldn't feel that way.

He did feel that way. It was the first step.

He walked the streets, went up to Hanover. Tourists and day trippers rarely strayed up to that district. He had grown up in Hanover, in a small, terraced Victorian house that was almost unchanged. It was comforting, in a moment of crisis, to step back into the past. His father had moved the family down to Brighton from the East End of London to the tiny terraced house in Washington Street when Steve Madden had been only three, and it was from a back room in that humble abode that Sid Madden had set up the tattooing business that eventually expanded to become famous along the South Coast. Madden remembered playing in these streets. Although many of the old families had moved out, Hanover still embraced him with its community spirit.

He sank a pint in the back bar of the London Unity, the pub that had been his father's local. There was a youth behind the bar whom he didn't recognise. He sat down, spoke to no one. He could almost see his old man, holding court in front of the fire, telling jokes, buying drinks, each of his bare arms boasting a portrait of his mother and the words 'I love Emily'. There was also an older tattoo, a heart with the name Claire, but his father never spoke about that.

A new image had now seared itself into Madden's brain. That of Jason, lying face down on the floor, his body in a pool of blood. The violence had been appalling. All violence was appalling, but what had been done to Jason exceeded anything he had ever witnessed. He could not get the picture out of his head. He kept replaying it, like a videotape, over and over again, until his head throbbed. A few days ago, he hadn't been able to stop thinking about Clara in the same way. This replaced it in his overwrought brain, knocking every other emotion out of him.

Who the hell was George Adams? He sunk his pint and walked out. He went back briefly to the scene of the crime, like a moth drawn to a flame. Fieldhouse was there. So was Millington. Millington told him to go home, that he couldn't do any good there.

'I just had to see it again,' Madden explained.

'Steve, won't you consider sitting down with a counsellor? Talking this through?'

'I don't need to talk it through. Have you found out any more about George Adams?'

'You'll know almost as soon as we do.'

Millington walked with him to the end of the street.

'I never wanted to be a bastard father,' Madden muttered.

'You weren't. And you're not.'

Clara had been informed. He thought of going to see her, but couldn't bring himself to face her. Not yet. He felt responsible. Hell, he all but threw his son onto the street. That was the way it felt. As Madden walked the same streets, not knowing where he was going, or where he was trying to go, he tried to recall every word of their conversation. All he could clearly remember was *I'm happy, dad. I'm happy.*

Finally he went home. Jasmine found him there later that evening.

'Am I glad to see you,' he said.

She gave him a hug and a kiss. He held her for some time too. There was a sweet lemony fragrance emanating from the smooth dark skin of her neck. For a few moments they didn't say anything. He was too pleased to see her to press her immediately for information.

'Sorry,' he said.

'What for?'

'Landing you with Jack Fieldhouse.'

'Oh, that,' she said, as though dismissing it as something of little importance.

'How's he treating you?'

'Like it was my first day as a detective.' She grinned.

'He'll never learn.'

'Luckily I have. I've learnt to show him that it doesn't bother me. That's half the battle. I just do the job I'm there to do and if he doesn't like it and wants to find fault, then it's tough. I've dealt with worse than him.'

'Really?'

She sat down beside him.

'Did I ever tell you about the time I went to visit my cousin Rajid in Bradford?'

'No. Tell me.'

For a few moments it seemed as though she talked for no other reason than to help him forget. If that was her intention, it didn't work. But he was grateful to her for at least trying to take his mind off it.

'It's not a very nice story and I've tended not to tell anybody. But you know how some of the guys are in these multi-ethnic communities – they think every minority is against them. Anyway, Rajid and I had been out to a club and we were stopped by these two constables about two o'clock in the morning. One of them called Rajid a Paki and asked him if it was his car. Rajid said it was and then the other asked if I was his bitch.'

'What did you say?'

'I let them carry on insulting us for a few minutes. They checked Rajid's documents, all the time making aspersions. Then just before they left us I showed them my ID. You never saw two people more apologetic.'

'Did you report them?'

'That's the strange thing, Steve. I didn't. I urged Rajid not to either.'

'Why not?'

'Because I didn't want to make a fuss.'

'Jaz, you had every right to make a fuss. Racist bastards like that.'

'I reckoned they'd learned their lesson. The point is, if I can put up with something like that, I can put up with Jack Fieldhouse. And, hopefully, it won't be for long anyway.'

There was a flicker of something in her expression. It looked like an unwillingness to divulge a piece of information more relevant to their immediate concerns.

'I hope your assessment's right,' he said.

'What have you heard?' she asked.

'I've heard nothing.'

'I didn't know. I wasn't sure. Fieldhouse only shares me with me what he feels I ought to know. It's part of his way of being in control.'

'That's why you came here, Jaz. To tell me.'

'I don't think you're going to like what we found out.'

'Jaz, I want to know. Stop keeping me in the dark.'

'We traced George Adams, the fellow who owns the Brighton flat. He owns another flat, in London's Earls Court. He also runs a pub.'

'Who was he to Jason?'

'He was . . . a kind of a landlord, I suppose you'd say.'

'Come on, Jaz, what do you mean, a kind of a landlord? Either he was Jason's landlord or he wasn't. I want to know what you've found out.'

'Adams let him live there. That's all. And in the flat in London.

Jason moved between them, sometimes staying at one address, sometimes at the other. Depending on—'

'Depending on what?'

'His business,' she said haltingly.

'Business? What business?'

It felt weird. Unsettling. A few hours after finding his son's body he was asking questions of a colleague to enable him to know the boy better.

'What are you not telling me, Jaz?'

'George Adams employed your son as well for a while.'

'Employed? What do you mean? In his pub?'

'No. He didn't have the pub then.'

'Then what, Jaz? What are you not telling me?'

Jasmine knew she couldn't keep it from him any longer. What she didn't know was how he would take it.

'It was a kind of an agency. Jason was working as a male prostitute,' she said. 'Only they don't call themselves that. "Escort" is the expression they use.'

'You mean my son was selling his body for money.'

Jasmine delivered the final blow.

'He'd been doing it for three years,' she said. 'Since he was sixteen.'

8

The Queen's Arms in George Street was packed. It was cabaret night, and one was about to begin. A proportion of Brighton's twenty-five thousand gay men were crammed shoulder to shoulder, waiting for the act to materialise on the small stage.

Madden squeezed his way through, wondering how often Jason had come here, wondering how many people here Jason had known, wondering if his killer was perhaps among them. He found the pile of magazines in the corner. They were free for the taking. He picked one up and leafed through it. Inside were six pages of escort ads, most of them with photographs. All male. Big beefy bodies, skinny kids, some with faces fuzzed out. A mature disciplinarian threatened to devastate bare backsides. Most offered a versatile service. In/out, twenty-four hours. There were mobile-telephone numbers, and some even had websites.

He found Jason. At least, he was almost certain that it was Jason. He was posing in a pair of briefs and his face was deliberately blurred out. It took only seconds for Madden to expel any doubts. That was Jason, even though he wasn't using his real name. He called himself Todd. Nineteen, versatile, in/out, twenty-four hours. There was a mobile number, and a website address.

Music struck up. A drag queen parted the crowd like Moses cutting a swathe through the Red Sea. She climbed onto the stage and began to sing 'Don't you leave me now.'

Madden left.

Outside, he rolled up the magazine and tucked it into his pocket. His own son had been working as a rent boy and he didn't know. He should have known. He should have asked more about his son's life. Even then, would Jason have told him? He was nineteen years old with a policeman for a father. No wonder he blurred his face out and called himself Todd.

Madden wanted to cry but that could wait until he was indoors and alone. He had to shoulder even more guilt now. Millington had said that none of them were perfect as fathers. Madden felt so far down the scale from perfect that it seemed to him that he had done little that was right. And this was the terrible price he was paying.

I'm happy, dad. Look at me. I'm happy.

He blinked tears from his eyes. He wanted to make it up. To hold the lad in his arms. To say something. It was too late.

He had never been into an Internet café as a customer before.

'We're closing in ten minutes,' said the surly kid behind the counter.

'That's all I want,' said Madden. 'I want to look up a website.'

'You came to the right place.' There was a hint of sarcasm.

Madden sat down at a computer. He was not computer-literate. They scared him to Hell.

'Hey,' he said, scribbling down the web address on a piece of paper. 'Can you get this up for me?'

'We do tuition for six pounds an hour,' said the surly kid.

'When I want tuition I'll ask for it. Right now, I just want this website.'

The surly kid brought up a box on the screen and typed in the URL.

'Thanks,' said Madden.

'That's what we're here for.' More sarcasm.

Madden waited about a minute for the website to load. Or did they download? He was never sure. There were more pictures of Jason. He was still called Todd but this time his face was revealed. In one he was naked, lying on a bed, a cocky smile on his face and a lick of hair tumbling over his forehead. In another, he was posing languidly in a pair of jeans and a T-shirt. A third showed him lying on the beach in a pair of Bermuda shorts. It looked like Brighton beach.

The pictures were all of the best quality.

Then came the description of the services he offered. *Genuine nineteen-year-old lad, based in London and Brighton, offers a full and versatile service for the discerning gentleman. I am 5'8", with reddish-brown hair, a wicked smile and a nice personality. I am smooth all over with a nice bum and an eight-inch uncut dick. I prefer to be active and can indulge you in your favourite fantasy, CP, water sports, most colours. You won't be disappointed. Love, Todd.*

Madden found the quit command, but not before the surly kid glanced at the screen.

'Dirty fucker,' he heard the kid say to one of the other customers.

Madden went over to him.

'When I want your opinion, I'll come and get it,' he said, showing his ID.

'Sorry,' said the surly kid.

Madden left the Internet café, thinking back to the time when Jason was just a little boy. He remembered him asking where babies came from and how they were made. Clara and he had sat him down and told him. They saw no point in pretending. The boy was growing up.

He had grown up, all right. Eight-inch uncut dick, CP, water sports. Yes, he had certainly grown up.

Madden got home to find Jack Fieldhouse sitting outside in his car, waiting for him.

'Thought you'd be at home,' said Fieldhouse.

'You think I'm just going to sit at home and wait for you to bring me news?'

'You've found out Jason was on the game?'

'Yes. Jasmine told me.'

'Mind if I come in?'

'Be my guest.'

'Did you never guess? In three years?'

'What do you mean?'

'Did he never say anything, do anything that made you suspicious?'

'Yes, he used to bring his clients back to the house. We used to talk about them regularly over Sunday lunch,' Madden said angrily. 'What do *you* think, Jack?'

'No need to get shirty, Steve.'

'I am *not* getting shirty. I told you, I didn't even know Jason was gay. Seems I was blind to a lot of things.'

Fieldhouse looked around the lounge. Madden had never invited him inside before. There had never been any need. Fieldhouse gazed at the paintings on the wall. Clara's paintings. The ones he should have got rid of but couldn't bring himself to. She was a good artist. She had tried to teach him but he didn't have her eye or her sense of colour. She was still there, in these paintings on the wall. Maybe – Madden had once entertained the thought – she had left them there to give her an excuse to come back one day. It was all part of his not letting go.

'These your wife's?'

'My ex-wife's.'

'Sorry. Your ex-wife's.'

Fieldhouse wasn't sorry. Madden doubted that his colleague had the ability to be sorry for anything. Everything Fieldhouse said was subtly calculated to antagonise. It got him results but won him few friends. Madden was wrong if he thought that recent events might soften Fieldhouse's approach. The man had a bad streak running through him.

'They're good.' he said. 'Very – what's the word? Colour-ful.'

They were of Brighton Pier, Brighton Pavilion, Brighton Beach, and one was a self-portrait. They were colourful. They were also, to his mind, brilliant. But then, he was biased and always would be.

Madden threw the gay contact magazine onto the coffee table.

'You've seen that?'

'We've seen it.'

'There's a website, too.'

'Seen that as well.'

'Had four thousand, two hundred and fifty-seven visitors.'

Fieldhouse sat down, crossed his legs, emitted a slight whistle. 'That's a lot of visitors.'

'The website maybe had that many. How many did Jason have?'

'We've been over his mobile, and we've got the phone company to provide a list of his calls. There were four shortly before he was murdered, all from the same unregistered mobile. They were all missed calls so Jason wasn't picking them up. No message was left except the one you left him. And, of course, we've got the numbers in his phone memory. We're working through those.'

He added, with a touch of boasting, 'You know my record. Forty-eight hours and we'll have him. We're helped by the fact that this wasn't just an ordinary sex killing.'

'The flat was searched,' said Madden.

'That's right. Pretty thoroughly. And the post-mortem – you want the details?' Fieldhouse hesitated.

'I want every detail.'

'Okay. Sorry to have to give you this. But Jason was beaten up pretty badly before he was killed. Some of the stab wounds were – well, not exactly intended to be fatal. Know what I'm getting at?'

Madden knew what he was getting at. He felt sick. He sat down and didn't want to ask the question. He was thinking of the cruellest cut of all. *Eight-inch uncut dick.* He couldn't ask. He didn't want to think about it. It was too much to bear.

'What killed him?' asked Madden.

'The cut to the throat.' Fieldhouse fidgeted, then met his eyes. 'You want any more, Steve?'

'How many times? Was he stabbed, I mean.'

'Twenty-seven.'

He wanted to kill the person who'd done that to his son.

'We found what his murderer was looking for.'

'What was it?'

'It was well hidden. Though it's surprising he didn't find it. It was jammed behind a panel under the bath. We found a bag containing Ecstasy tablets. About two thousand pounds' worth at street prices.'

'Christ.'

'Did you know that Jason was into drugs?'

'Oh yes. We talked a lot about that, too. In between discussing him being a male prostitute and chatting about football results,' Madden said, averting his gaze.

'Don't feel bad. What parents really know what their kids are up to these days? Jason was probably no different from a lot of youngsters. He was a regular at clubs in London, and down here. You know what goes on in these places. Kids getting out of their heads, all love and happiness. It's the way they protest today.'

'Most kids don't have two grand's worth of E under the bath,' Madden argued.

'That's true.'

'Have you tracked the source?'

'Not yet. But it's similar to the batch we found recently. The likelihood is that it came from the Netherlands.'

Madden was having enough problems coping with the fact that his son had been a male prostitute. He didn't want to think of him being a drug dealer. He had met plenty of drug dealers in his job. None of them looked like drug dealers. There was a popular image: the ogre at the school gate, the Rastafarian in his council-house kitchen. Drug dealers looked like ordinary people. They *were* ordinary people. He had recently arrested a fourteen-year-old public schoolboy who'd had twenty Ecstasy tablets in his pocket. He was selling them to his classmates. The boy was regarded as the brightest in his school. That was the way it went. Drugs transcended class, transcended stereotypes.

'What about George Adams, the guy who owned the flat? Couldn't they have been his?'

Clutching at straws.

'Just interviewed him,' said Fieldhouse. 'Says if he'd known Jason was into drugs he'd have thrown him out. Seemed a genuine response. Pathetic individual. Hung up on rent boys, likes to be around them, likes to be a kind of father to them. He used to run a male brothel in London, but recently he just took a cut from Jason's earnings for the use of his flat.'

'He's a pimp,' said Madden.

'Went to prison for nine months for not paying his taxes. Defends himself by claiming that he was saving Her Majesty's Government the embarrassment of living off immoral earnings. For the past year Jason's been finding his own clients, through his advert, through his website, probably through word of mouth as well. Adams says he didn't find clients for him any more.'

'Does he have an alibi?'

'Not a very good one. Claims he was at his London flat. That's in Earls Court. He rents that out to another escort called Ming. Thai boy-stroke-girl, if you get my meaning. Transsexual or transvestite or something like that.'

'Which is it?'

'I interviewed him, I didn't undress him. I don't know. Same thing.'

'Like saying a guy who behaves like a shit is the same thing as a guy who is a shit,' said Madden.

'He knew Jason,' said Fieldhouse, ignoring the jibe. 'Jason worked from the London flat too. He, or she if you prefer it, alibied Adams and he alibied him. Or her as the case may be.'

'Convenient.'

'This Ming had a client about the time of the murder. We're trying to trace him. Adams let him in. If the client can put them both in London at the time Jason was killed, then we can eliminate them. But my feeling is that neither had anything to do with it.'

Madden knew how difficult it was to trace the clients of prostitutes. Most of them didn't use their real names. Most didn't sit down and give out their life stories.

'How many clients did Jason have?'

'About a dozen regular ones. We're trying to put all the pieces of information together to come up with a list of them. But you know what it's like. Then there are the ones he would visit just once, or they would visit him. We've heard about a guy from Liverpool called John. John probably isn't his real name. Nobody else has ever seen him. It's that kind of thing we're up against. But like I said, Steve – there's more to this. It isn't just an ordinary client-prostitute sex killing.'

'I'm grateful for that assessment.'

'It isn't just mine. It's Detective Sergeant Carol's.'

She's changed her tune, thought Madden.

'She's showing a lot of improvement. You've trained her well,' Fieldhouse said grudgingly.

'She's a person, Jack. Not a dog.'

'Never heard that training people was a politically incorrect phrase these days.'

'It isn't. It's the way you use it.'

Fieldhouse shrugged off the criticism.

'Look after her,' said Madden.

'We'll get Jason's killer,' promised Fieldhouse, going to the door. 'Forty-eight hours. That's my record. Or I'll jump off Brighton Pier. That's a promise.'

'I'll hold you to that.'

Fieldhouse left. Madden watched his car pull away. It was only a few more minutes before the phone rang. He picked it up.

It was Clara.

'Oh, God, Steve—'

'I know, Clara.'

'What's happening to us?'

'We've got to get together and talk.'

'Come round.'

'I'll be right there.'

He hung up. It was funny how tragedy could reunite people. He cupped his hands over his face and sobbed. He cried until his face hurt. He thought of Jason sliced up on the carpet. Nobody deserved to die that way, it didn't matter what a person did with his life.

Forty-eight hours, Fieldhouse wanted. Madden would give him that. And no more.

9

The new flats down by Brighton Marina were bright and spacious and airy and had perfect views. Clive Westmacott was chief accountant for a publishing house in London and commuted every day. He wasn't home yet. It was half-past ten in the evening. Madden wondered why he wasn't back, though he was grateful for the fact. He hoped that Clive was shagging his secretary and that Clara would soon find out. He wanted her back. He wanted justice.

'Come on in.' She ushered him into a cool, blue sitting room with bay windows looking out over the Marina. She had been crying too. Her son was dead, and Clive couldn't bother to come home. 'Do you want a drink, Steve?'

'I'll have a beer if you've got one.'

She found a beer. There was a mechanical hum from the fridge as she opened it. Everything was clean, fresh, like a sea breeze. Her paintings were all over the walls. Madden wondered if Clive appreciated them as much as he had done. She took the ring-pull off for him and the beer frothed over. She cleaned it up instantly. It was the sort of flat where you cleaned up spills as soon as they happened.

'I can't believe he's dead. It hasn't sunk in,' Clara said.

'Who broke it to you?'

'A nice woman detective. Asian she was. A Sergeant Carol.'

Madden smiled for the first time that night. *Good old Jaz.* She had to come and see for herself. He was glad she had done it. He'd have hated it if Fieldhouse had broken the news. He tried to think of a police equivalent of having no bedside manner.

'How much have they told you?' asked Madden.

'Very little. I was hoping you could—' She broke off. She clearly did not know.

'You haven't been told about Jason's . . . profession?'

'Profession?'

She didn't know about the advert, the website, Jason's 'profession' – if it could be called that. She didn't know about the drugs.

Madden told her.

'Oh God, Steve, what have we done?'

'We split up and we shouldn't have.'

'If he's been doing it for three years, that means he was doing it when we were still together. I just can't believe that.'

'That he was sixteen and going out selling his body?'

'You're sure there's no mistake?'

'If there is, I'll be the first to tell you.'

The door was open into a room that she used as a studio. It was nothing like the one-room studio in the house that they had shared. Madden glanced in. Clara's studio had once been a chaotic collection of canvases, easels, paint pots, finished and half-finished sketches, rags, dustsheets and pencils. Here, at the Marina, it was orderly to the point of obsession with neatness. It was also much bigger. A large canvas with a half-finished sea painting rested on an easel in front of a wide picture window. During the day the sun bathed the room with light. There was a brass telescope mounted on a tripod. Her art materials were arranged in neat white boxes.

'We weren't bad parents,' she said.

'Somehow we slipped up.' He added, 'When did you last see him?'

'About a month ago. He used to visit us regularly. You knew he had a boyfriend at Cambridge?'

'I know now,' said Madden. 'He also had a flat in Brighton which he used. It belonged to a George Adams who used to run a male brothel in London. Yes, I know, it gets worse.'

He thought of something else. It had only just occurred to him.

'Did Jason ever talk to you about his problems?'

'No. Jason didn't seem to have any problems.'

'What? He was working as a rent boy for three years, and you're telling me he didn't have problems?'

'I'm saying he didn't *seem* to have any.'

'It's just that when he came to stay with me, he said a strange thing. That he had problems too sometimes. Decisions that he had to make. He wanted to talk about them with me but my attitude made it difficult for him.'

'Did it?'

'Are you sure he never talked to you about any kinds of problems? Decisions?'

Clara looked exasperated.

'I told you. He always seemed completely – sorted. He was in love with Daniel, he was happy with everything. I never gave a thought to the fact that he might be unhappy about something because he never showed it.'

She stared at him. The realisation dawned.

'But he did with you?' she said.

'It may be that he was trying to tell me something. Something that he couldn't tell you. I don't know. I wish I'd listened. Something that maybe he could only tell me, his father.'

'Oh God.' Clara turned away.

'I didn't want to listen.'

'You never did,' she said. 'All our lives he tried to speak to you! And you're telling me now that a few nights ago he came and wanted to talk to you and you *turned him away*?'

'I didn't turn him away, Clara. I just couldn't talk to him that night. I was sick to death over you. It was just one more stab in the back. Believe me.'

'Oh, I see – *I'*m to get the blame for it now, am I?'

This was how it had always happened before. A reasonable discussion would turn into an argument, a casting of the blame. The irony didn't escape him that here they were, a year on, ex-husband and ex-wife, standing in the apartment she shared with her second husband and having exactly the same kind of argument.

'I contacted him straight after you gave me his number. I was going to take him out to lunch the day he was – the day he was killed. I was going to . . . put things right.'

'You always did everything too late, Steve.'

Madden walked over to the bay window and looked down at a brightly lit boat with strings of lights like pearl necklaces and people partying on board as it cruised into the Marina. Beyond, a murky pall had settled over the Channel.

'Don't you think I feel bad about that?'

'How could you do it? Ignore him when he wanted help? He was our son.'

'Don't, Clara. Please. I've been through my conscience ten times since this morning. I found his body, for Christ's sake! I saw what was done to it!'

She backed off. She realised that she had gone too far.

'I'm sorry.'

'So am I. I'm sorry and I'm sick and I need us to see this through together.'

'What I said was monstrous and cruel. Forgive me.'

'Didn't I always?' he said. 'I just wish you'd forgiven me a little more often.'

'I ran out of it.' She tried to raise a smile.

'Clive will be home soon.'

'Screw Clive.'

He went over to her and tried to hold her. She slipped gently out of his embrace. It was unkind, unnecessary. But he understood her reasons for doing it.

'Does he know? About Jason?'

'Yes, I rang him at lunchtime and told him.'

'I feel helpless,' Madden admitted. 'The inquiry's out of my hands. If ever there was an inquiry I wanted it's this one. But I know I can't be a part of it. I want to do it for Jason. Okay, I didn't do very much for him when he was alive. Maybe I didn't listen when I should have done, maybe I didn't make the attempt to get to know him. But I want to make up for that.'

'How are you going to do that? asked Clara.

'Tell me about the Cambridge guy. The boyfriend.'

'He's a student, doing literature and French. His name's Daniel Donoghue. They'd known each other about a year. They were in love, Steve. Just like you and I were once.'

'Do you think the problems he alluded to might have concerned Daniel?'

'They might. I don't know.'

'Have you met him?'

'Yes. He brought him down here to meet me one weekend. He was a pleasant boy. Well-spoken. Well educated. A little bit arrogant and a bit self-centred – but then, I suppose that's what comes of going to Cambridge.'

'Did you give this information to the police?'

'Of course.'

'Suppose this well-spoken, well-educated boy found out what Jason was doing for a living?' Madden put the possibility to her.

'I never thought of that. He just – didn't seem the type.'

'If everyone ran to type our job would be easy.'

'I thought you said that drugs were involved?'

'I don't know what's involved. Drugs, sex – it's wide open. Murders are usually what they seem but at the moment this one doesn't doesn't seem to be anything. Whoever murdered Jason went way beyond just trying to find out where he'd stashed a bag of Ecstasy.'

'That I can't believe about him.' said Clara.

'Nor me.'

They gazed at each other for a moment. It was odd how they had come to terms with their son being a male escort, yet the thought of him dealing in drugs was abhorrent.

'You're on the case?' She mustered a faint smile.

'I'm on the case.'

Clive came in. He was a tall, gangly man, balding prematurely, with limbs that reminded Madden of those jointed teddy bears. When he walked his arms seemed to swing along an axis. He was wearing a black business suit and carrying a briefcase that was so full of documents that the clasp was straining. There was something hawkish about his countenance. He was older than Clara, a lot older. Madden wondered what she saw in him. He didn't believe any of the myths about bald men. It was understandable when your wife ran off with her personal trainer – a common scenario, he'd heard – but to lose out to a balding, long-limbed accountant, that was tantamount to an insult.

'I thought you'd be here,' Clive said.

'We had a lot to talk about,' said Madden.

'I'm dreadfully sorry.' He didn't sound as though he meant it. He went over to Clara, put his arm round her and said, 'I really am sorry.' Only then did he sound genuine.

'Steve would like to be on the case officially but he can't,' Clara explained.

'That's reasonable.' Clive looked across at him.

'Why is it reasonable?' asked Madden.

'Your emotional involvement.'

'You don't think I could be emotionally involved and professionally detached, is that it?'

'I'm sure you could be.' Clive shrugged, not wanting to get into an argument. 'It just seems to me the correct procedure, that's all.'

He wound his arm more tightly round Clara's shoulders. Claiming his property. He planted his long legs firmly astride on the cream-coloured carpet in the centre of the floor. Claiming his territory.

'You said you had a lot to talk about. Do you need any more time?'

Madden got the message.

'It's just that I'd like to be alone with Clara at this time. I hope you understand,' Clive said, just in case he hadn't.

He's my son too, you bastard, thought Madden.

'I have every sympathy with what you're going through, Steve. Clara tells me that you even found his body. But I'm her husband now and I don't really like coming back to find the two of you together. Try putting yourself in my place. I hope you understand.'

'Oh, I understand.'

'I think you'd better go, Steve,' she said.

Madden shot Clive Westmacott a withering look.

Clara saw him to the door but Clive's eagle eyes were on them. Madden wanted to grab her and kiss her but that would just have made trouble. He wasn't going to cross the line. She gave him a peck on the cheek.

'We've got to keep in touch,' he said.

'I know,' she answered.

He left. As he walked out of the Marina complex, he wondered what another man might have done. Carried her out of there. Persuaded her to come back. Used every ounce of emotional blackmail in his being. It would have been wrong to use Jason's death in that way. He wasn't capable of it. But in that moment he hated Clive with an intensity that he had never felt before. It almost scared him.

Madden wondered what Clive had been doing in London until late that evening, on the day his wife had rung him at lunchtime and told him her son was dead.

10

'We've got him.'

The words reached Steve Madden's ears thirty-four and a half hours after he had knelt by Jason's body. It was eleven o'clock in the evening. The voice on the other end of the phone was Fieldhouse's. Madden took less than ten minutes to get to the station, breaking the speed limit most of the way. Fieldhouse had promised to find the killer within forty-eight hours and he wasn't even cutting it fine. Madden was glad he wouldn't have the lesser satisfaction of seeing his colleague jump off Brighton Pier.

'Where is he?' were the first words he uttered when he arrived. Then, 'Who is he?'

'Steady on, Steve,' said Millington. 'Step into my office.'

'I want to see him.'

'We're still questioning him. I'm not allowing you to barge in. I'm going by the book – I'm sorry.'

'Show me the part in the book that says I can't see the bastard that killed my son.'

'In good time.'

Madden sat down in Millington's office. It wasn't a time for commendable restraint but he showed it. Jasmine was already there. There was a look on her face that seemed somewhat at odds with the triumphant mood. Madden stared at her. He knew that look. Or rather, he didn't know it. He didn't know it on the face of any officer involved in a major murder inquiry where the number one suspect was in custody and the evidence was piling up. You got to know how it *felt* when a big case was solved, and that feel communicated itself round everybody on the team. Jasmine wasn't feeling it. He wanted to know why.

'It's a name you know,' said Millington.

'Who?'

'Demos Panagoulis.'

'Jesus Christ.'

Madden knew the name, all right. Every policeman in Brighton knew the name. Panagoulis had muscled in on the London club scene, running a security firm that controlled the doors and hence the vast amounts of drugs that were consumed behind them. After one of his bouncers was proved to have supplied a number of double-strength and apparently dodgy Ecstasy tablets to a group of students, one of whom died and three of whom fell seriously ill and had to be hospitalised, Panagoulis's little empire had collapsed. But 'The Greek', as he had been dubbed, hadn't stayed down long. He was currently pushing his way around with some success on the South Coast, with a company called Portcullis Security that, as with his previous outfit, controlled the drug distribution in half a dozen top nightclubs.

He was also homosexual and had once been tried for attempted murder.

'He was a client of your son's,' said Millington.

'Can this get any worse?'

'I'm afraid it does, Steve. From information we've got, Jason was selling his body to Panagoulis not for money but for – well, for drugs.'

'What kind of drugs?' As though it mattered.

'A few tabs of Ecstasy. A line of coke, that kind of thing.'

Madden stared down at the floor, wringing his hands.

'I didn't know my own son,' he said.

'I have three daughters, Steve. All at university. God knows what they get up to. We talk to them about drugs but they laugh and look the other way and make you feel as though you're square and old-fashioned and don't really understand.'

'I should have talked to Jason.'

'Would it have done any good? He was an adult, Steve, he was making his own decisions. You couldn't have stopped him.'

'I might have *tried*.'

'I know how you're feeling. I would feel the same.'

'Do you? My son was a rent boy, he was sleeping with a known villain and getting free drugs in return? That's ten light years away from the kid I brought up. He wasn't an adult, he was still just a boy.'

Fieldhouse barged into the office. Madden had never known him to knock.

'You've told him?'

'I've told him,' said Millington.

'What evidence have you got?'

'You know he was a client of Jason's?'

'I asked you about evidence.'

Fieldhouse dropped into a chair. One of these days, one of them was going to break under the weight of his eighteen stone. A nerve was pulsating under the moist skin of his right temple. The palms of his hands were sweating. It was hot down there in the interview room. Fieldhouse had the look. The atmosphere was electric. Madden felt it surging through him. He wanted this to be it. *He so desperately wanted a resolution.* The first forty-eight hours in any murder inquiry were crucial. There was nothing worse than a case that dragged on for weeks and months without a clue turning up. Such cases were the bane of every detective's existence. He could have added to that, *And of every parent's torment, too.*

'He's been a regular client of Jason's for about a year now. Contacted him through his magazine ad. He says Jason was happy to take drugs off him instead of money,' Fieldhouse explained.

'Who suggested that?'

'He says Jason did.'

'He would.'

'He made four phone calls to Jason's mobile on the morning he was killed. Jason was expecting a call from him because they were due to meet, but Panagoulis couldn't get through. Instead, he kept trying. The last one was made within half a mile of the flat. He admits he got a bit shirty, went round to the flat hoping Jason would have arrived by then. Not the sort of guy who likes to take no for an answer. Seemed to think Jason was there for him and him alone. Says he couldn't get in, there was no answer. He was seen leaving the flat at about quarter to eleven by the girls who lived upstairs. The pathologist puts the time of Jason's death more exactly now at about ten.'

'Did anyone hear the noise?'

'Unfortunately, no. The girls, a Joyce Smith and her flatmate Corinne Burnham, were out all night and didn't come home until quarter to eleven in the morning. That was when they saw Panagoulis leaving. They didn't hear any noise after that. They described him as shifty.'

Madden recalled the two girls on the balcony: the orange hair and the face full of safety pins.

'What about the downstairs neighbour? The one who saw the blood dripping through his ceiling.'

'Stoned out of his head. Musician sort. Had his music on so loud he couldn't hear a thing.'

'So, going by the girls' timing, the Greek waits a further forty-five minutes before he leaves the flat?'

'We're working on the theory that he spent the time searching for the Ecstasy and didn't find it.'

'Hold on,' said Madden. 'If he's paying Jason in drugs, what is Jason doing with a stash of the stuff that he's not supposed to have?'

Fieldhouse gave a deep sigh and shook his head. Millington rocked back in his chair and looked out of the window briefly. Loose ends. There were always loose ends. There were different ways of tying them up. Sometimes you ignored them because they were inconvenient, sometimes you tied them up to make them look pretty. Sometimes you took a hammer and rammed them into the picture to make them fit.

'Perhaps Jason got greedy and stole it,' pondered Millington.

'Wait a minute. First my son's a rent boy, then he's into cocaine and Ecstasy, now he's a thief?'

'It was found in his flat.'

'It wasn't *his* flat,' Madden reminded him. 'It belonged to this Adams character.'

'Steve, I know this is hard for you,' Millington went on. 'You have to face up to the fact that Jason – well, he wasn't the boy you thought he was. The facts are, it was found hidden in the flat he used for sex. Panagoulis paid Jason in drugs for sex. And he went to the flat around the time of the murder.'

'Okay, it's suspicious. But where's the evidence?'

'The Greek didn't have normal sex with Jason,' said Fieldhouse. 'It was pretty kinky stuff. Tied him up, beat him, that kind of thing. Sorry.'

'You're saying it got out of hand?'

'I'm saying Panagoulis's reason for wanting to see Jason didn't have anything to do with sex. It had to do with getting his hands on that Ecstasy. Pure and simple.'

Madden knew that murder was never pure but often simple.

'It was a sexual murder,' he said. 'Jason was naked. If Panagoulis barged in there looking for stolen drugs, you think he would have wasted time getting him to undress? It doesn't add up. Nothing adds up.'

'It's all we've got at the moment,' admitted Fieldhouse. 'And Panagoulis is shit-scared.'

'I want to see him. I'm not leaving until I do.'

'Okay.' Millington gave in. 'But I'm coming with you. And there's to be no physical contact between you, Steve. I'm not having it thrown at us that we let you in there to – well, you know what I mean.'

'What kind of guy do you think I am?' Madden asked.

'You're a father.'

They went down to the interview room. Fieldhouse opened the door. Demos Panagoulis looked up. Madden stepped in and looked into the face of the man his colleagues believed had killed Jason. Panagoulis was short, dark-skinned, with a hook nose and a deeply furrowed brow. His hair was unnaturally curly. He was about forty. And he did looked scared. He looked more scared than anyone Madden had ever seen in an interview room. The sweat was trickling down his forehead in little rivulets, and every few seconds he wiped it off with the palm of his hand.

It was strange, being on the outside of an investigation. Leading it, if Jason had been someone else's son, he would have been thinking exactly the same. Grounds for suspicion. Pretty heavy grounds at that. The evidence would come.

'This is the father of the boy you fucking killed!' Fieldhouse leant across the desk and went almost purple in the face as he shouted. 'What are you going to say to him?'

Panagoulis didn't just look scared now, he was shaking and terrified.

'I didn't kill your son, Mr Madden,' he said. 'I don't know anything about it. He was a good boy.'

Madden tried to picture it. This guy getting his rocks off by tying Jason up and beating him. Jason swallowing the tabs of E he was paid, sniffing a line of coke. Madden wanted to put his hands round the Greek's throat just for that.

'If you're lying, I'll see you dead,' said Madden, shaking.

Millington laid a hand on his shoulder.

'That's enough, Steve. Let's go.'

Madden wanted to be left alone with the Greek. But he knew that wasn't going to happen. Not today, not tomorrow, probably never. Millington was doing it by the book.

Madden was too personally involved.

As he turned to leave, Panagoulis spoke to him one more time.

'Please believe me, Mr Madden,' he said. 'I know nothing about any stolen drugs. What Jason did, he did willingly. I never did anything to hurt him. I swear on my mother's life that I know nothing about his death.'

'You've got a *mother*?' said Fieldhouse.

'Yes, sir. I have a mother.'

'I thought worthless scum like you just floated to the top of barrels. I didn't know you were actually *born*.'

Madden glanced back. He didn't want to say so then, but he believed Panagoulis. He didn't quite know why. He had seen the crime scene and it still did not make the kind of sense he expected a crime scene to make.

'Can I ask a question?' asked Madden.

'Go ahead,' Millington said to him.

Madden leant forward and stared into the Greek's eyes. The Greek stared back at him

'Demos, do you have children?'

'No, Mr Madden,' came his reply.

'Brothers, sisters, anyone?'

'I had a brother. He died of a heart murmur when he was five.'

'Did you love him?'

'I loved him, yes, I did, Mr Madden.'

'I had a son I loved. You took him from me.'

'I did not take him from you, Mr Madden. I swear I did not.'

The Greek's gaze didn't flinch, didn't move away from Madden's own. Even when a bead of sweat trickled onto his left pupil, Panagoulis remained staring at him, without blinking.

'I'm through,' said Madden. He turned and left the interview room.

Fieldhouse slammed the door on the way out.

'What do you suggest we do? Give him a kitten to play with to prove he's nice to animals?' Fieldhouse bellowed.

'The trouble is, you have two motives. Murder for perverse sexual gratification: he gets off on being sadistic and it goes too far, or Jason tells him to stop and he doesn't and he gets carried away. Then there's murder in anger for the return of stolen goods. As far as I know, they don't normally coexist. At least I've never known them to.'

'Better than no motive at all,' said Millington.

'Wrong. I'd prefer there to be no motive at all,' Madden argued. 'Then maybe we could start looking for something inside his head that makes sense. At the moment, this murder doesn't make sense.'

Jasmine was at her desk as they walked back into the office. She looked up at them.

'Detective Sergeant Carol.' Fieldhouse gave her her full title.

'Would you like to give us the benefit of your opinion and experience?'

'I'll do my best, sir,' she replied coolly.

'In your opinion, and based on your experience, tell us what you think. We can put Panagoulis at the scene of the crime about the time of the murder. Not only did he have the opportunity but he had two possible motives. In the light of what you know, do we let him go or do we keep looking for evidence?'

Jasmine glanced from Madden to Fieldhouse to Chief Superintendent Millington.

'I say bang him up, sir.' Jasmine gave the answer he wanted.

Fieldhouse beamed.

'From the mouths of babes,' he said triumphantly.

'I'm not a *babe*. Sir.'

'It was just an expression.'

Like 'You've trained her well' thought Madden.

'There you are, Steve. Your own partner agrees. Take it from me, Panagoulis is the man.'

'I hope you're right,' said Madden, walking out. As he passed Jasmine's desk, she shot him a look that told him everything he wanted to know. She was playing the game from the other side but she was on his.

Murders were usually what they seemed. And this one still didn't seem like anything.

I I

It was raining when Madden got to London. He took the Underground to Earl's Court, tucked up his collar, and merged with the transient tide of humanity he always associated with that part of the city. Not that he came up to London that often. It was mainly work that brought him here, the occasional extension of a case that had begun in Brighton. The last time he had been here was to talk to the parents of a teenager who had been stabbed late at night for his fish and chips and left lying in a pool of blood outside an amusement arcade in West Street. The boy had survived, but the battle in 'Little Beirut', as West Street was known, had been a sad affair. Brighton was a relatively safe and peaceful resort, but there were hot spots and occasional eruptions, more often than not caused by day trippers down from the capital.

It hadn't always been like that. Brighton had an illustrious history in the annals of crime. Back in the 1930s there had been two cases within only weeks of each other where a female victim had been dismembered and stuffed into a packing trunk. One had been deposited at the left-luggage office of the railway station, the other had been discovered at a flat not very far away. Incredibly, the two cases were completely unconnected. In one, the murderer had been acquitted but had confessed years later to a Sunday newspaper. In the other, neither the victim nor the killer were ever identified. Brighton had been dubbed 'Torso City' and 'The Queen of the Slaughtering Places'. Police officers still spoke occasionally of the famous Brighton trunk murders. Equally remarkable was the fact that there were only six such crimes on record in the whole country, so Brighton had the dubious distinction of playing host to far more than its fair share.

Luckily, it had all been a long time ago.

Madden knew he shouldn't be up in London now but if you went through life not doing what you shouldn't do, then you didn't get anywhere. A man had been arrested and was still helping police with their inquiries, as the parlance went. Madden thought he would make one or two of his own. Off the record, of course.

He made his way through the bedsit jungle to a street where every second house seemed to be a run-down hotel. The flat that belonged to George Adams was on the fourth floor of a grey, peeling building, the lower half of which was covered in scaffolding. He rang the bell. A woman's voice came from the intercom.

'Yes?'

'I want to speak to George Adams.'

'He's not here.'

The intercom went dead. Madden rang again. No reply. He somehow didn't expect one. Pimps tended not to open their doors to complete strangers without an appointment. Madden decided not to play the police card. He was there unofficially. As Jason's father. He had to remember that.

Someone came out from the ground-floor entrance and Madden took the opportunity to let himself in. He climbed the stairs to the fourth floor. He knocked at the door of flat number twelve. He heard a shuffling within and the door opened, but it was kept on the chain.

'I'm Jason Madden's father,' he said.

'I'm busy,' said the woman. She looked Thai and smelled strongly of perfume. Madden put her age at about twenty-five. She wore a tight-fitting bottle-green dress that appeared to have been painted on her, and had hair as black as a raven. She had the kind of legs that most women would die for. High-heeled elegant shoes supported equally elegant ankles. They made her look taller than she really was.

'I'm not here officially.' Madden put her at her ease. 'I just want to talk about my son.'

'It's not easy right now,' she answered.

'When would it be easy?'

'You're a policeman, right?'

'Yes, I'm a policeman. But like I said, I'm not here officially.'

'The police were here yesterday,' she said. 'You could come in and wait if you want.'

'I'd like that.'

She took the chain off the door. For the first time Madden sensed something unnatural about her. This had to be Ming. Transvestite, transsexual, he couldn't make his mind up. Fieldhouse clearly hadn't bothered to make the distinction. Madden could imagine Fieldhouse barging in here, looking Ming up and down once, and just wanting to get out. Fieldhouse didn't have too good a record with minorities, especially those that threatened his masculinity.

'I've got a friend with me,' she said. 'You can wait in here.'

She showed him into a room that smelled of cannabis, probably from the night before. There was a long yellow settee that took up one side. He sat down. He'd been in prostitutes' waiting rooms before. On police business, never as a customer. The most remarkable one had been decorated like a jungle tableau with dense bushy ferns and yuccas and sweet-smelling tropical plants, as though Jane (now he came to think of it, that had been her name) was about to swing through it in her loincloth and grab her Tarzan. This one was shabby and plain. The only other piece of furniture in the room was a coffee table on which was an ashtray full of cigarette butts.

But then, he didn't suppose many clients came to admire the decor.

'Sorry to disturb you,' he said, without a hint of apology in his voice.

'Shouldn't be long.'

She closed the door. She was about forty minutes. Madden heard her showing someone to the door. He heard her say, 'Hope I'll see you again.' Then she came back in.

'Sorry about that,' she said.

'I did show up uninvited.'

'Jason told us about you. You're not like I imagined.'

'How did you imagine me to be?'

'I don't know. Want a cup of coffee?'

'No, thanks. I take it that was a client you were showing out.'

'I do have friends as well,' said Ming. 'But yes, if you must know, it was a client.'

Ming sat down next to him. Madden caught just a hint of the male sex but he wasn't sure which part of her body it emanated from. In physical appearance and in voice, Ming was female, one hundred per cent, if too polished and too perfect. In any other circumstances, he would have been attracted.

'I understand Jason worked from here too?' Then he added, 'I do know everything about my son's occupation, if you want to put it that way.'

'It's an occupation.' She shrugged. 'Like any other. Depends how professional you are about it.'

'You class yourself as a professional?'

'I'm a pro,' she joked.

'Excuse my ignorance, but do your clients – well – know what they're getting?'

It was a clumsy way of putting it, but he couldn't think of a better one.

'You mean, do they know they're getting a transsexual?' Ming put it more succinctly. She clearly had fewer hang-ups. 'I advertise as a transsexual. It turns a lot of guys on.'

'I'm sure it does.'

'More than you would imagine.'

She offered him a cigarette. Madden declined it. She lit one for herself and Madden caught in that simple action just a hint of the man she had once been. It showed in the corners of her mouth which she contorted ever so slightly as she blew smoke into the room.

'I really want to know about Jason,' he said.

'What would you like to know?'

'You worked with him?'

'Not *with* him, honey,' Ming corrected him. 'Not in that sense, if that's you mean. Bit like chalk and cheese.'

'What I meant was, did you work from the same flat? This one.'

'I knew what you meant. Sure, we both used this place. Sometimes he'd live up here, sometimes in Brighton. Mostly he was here. This was home to him. He was terrified of bumping into you when he was working in Brighton.'

'Is that why he rarely contacted me?'

'I guess so,' she said.

'You ever meet a client of his called Demos Panagoulis?'

'Most clients don't tell you their names.'

'This one did.'

'Greek. Right?'

Madden had to give her ten out of ten for genius.

'Right.'

'That was one of his Brighton guys. He never saw him up here. I don't think Jason liked him very much but he kept seeing him because he was afraid of him. I told him, if you don't like a client or he freaks you out, just stop seeing him. But he was soft-hearted. A lot of people get hard in this game, but he just stayed Jason.'

'He kept seeing him for another reason.'

'I wouldn't know.' Ming took another draw on the cigarette and put it down. *Definitely a man*, thought Madden.

'Why was he afraid of him?'

'I told all this to the police already.'

'Tell it to me.'

'This – er – Greek – Pappagopolis, whatever his name was, honey—'

'Panagoulis. And please don't call me honey.'

'This guy Panagoulis liked to tie him up. Hit him with a cane, spank him, that kind of thing. Lot of clients want that sort of thing. Jason didn't like it, he preferred giving it, if you know what I mean.'

'Panagoulis was violent with him?'

'Under controlled circumstances. There's got to be some control. Would you like to see Jason's room?'

'Yes, please.'

Ming took him through to a bedroom. There were posters on the wall. UB40, Depeche Mode, Annie Lennox, Westlife. Madden recognised a couple of them. Jason had stuck them on his wall at home and had taken them down the day he left.

On the bed was an Arsenal scarf. Jason had supported Arsenal. In many ways, he'd been a normal boy.

Madden sat on the bed and held the scarf in his hands. He remembered taking Jason to his first match when he was twelve. Father and son, just as things ought to be. There was no hint then that Jason would turn out to be the boy he became.

'You sure you wouldn't like a coffee?' Ming noticed his distress.

'Tea, if you don't mind.'

Ming went away and came back a few minutes later with a mug of pale brown liquid that smelled of perfume.

'Hope you don't mind Earl Grey. It's all I've got.'

She sat next to him on the bed. Madden had tears in his eyes. He hoped she wouldn't see them. She did, straight away.

'Honey, I know how you feel,' she said. 'A man shouldn't be afraid to cry.'

'You know what I wish? I wish people would stop telling me they know how I feel.'

'Sorry.'

Madden played with the scarf, winding it round his fingers.

'How heavily was Jason into drugs?'

'Not heavily. Just – well, you know, the odd joint.'

'I'd rather have the truth.'

'Okay, he'd take a few tabs of E when he went clubbing. Very occasionally he'd take a line of coke. Nothing excessive. He knew how to handle it. He took speed, too.'

'You make it sound almost natural.'

'He wasn't an addict if that's what you mean. He wouldn't touch heroin or anything like that. He just liked to get high when he was with friends.'

'Tell me about his boyfriend.'

'You mean Daniel.' Ming uttered the name with barely disguised contempt. 'He came to the flat here once. Can't say I liked him. He used Jason.'

'How do you mean, used?'

'Jason used to spend lots of money on him. Buy him presents, that kind of thing. Help him settle his bills. He used to take him out to expensive restaurants. That's what I meant about Jason being a bit of a soft touch. I got the impression Daniel was just living off him. Oh, they were very much in love. But you know what they say about love. No romance without finance.'

'That's pretty cynical.'

'But true.'

'Did Daniel know what Jason did for a living?'

'Daniel did a bit of it himself. Course he knew.'

'We're talking about the same Daniel? Cambridge undergraduate?'

'The same one. Lots of students do it to supplement their income. The university doesn't matter.'

Madden remembered Jason telling him about the French restaurant in Chelsea he'd been to on the same night he'd stayed with him in Brighton. He wondered if he'd been taken there by a client. He asked Ming.

'He took Daniel there. Like I said, he was always doing that kind of thing. He'd seen a client that day, made a hundred and fifty pounds, so the first thing he does is treat the love of his life to a candlelit dinner.'

'Guilt?' asked Madden.

'Generosity, honey. That was Jason.'

'You ever get taken out for candlelit dinners?'

'Of course, all the time.' She wasn't lying. 'There are loads of men that want to be seen out with a transsexual. It's fun.'

'What else can you tell me about Jason's clients?'

'Like I said, most don't tell you their names, and if they do they're not their real names. Sure, he had regular guys, but they all had names like David and Paul and Robert, you know what I mean.'

'His ad said he did in and out calls. He must have got to know something about the ones he visited.'

'He did a lot of calls to hotels.'

'What about clients' homes?'

'Sure. I told the police as much as I knew. As much as he told me.'

'How much was that?'

'Jason wasn't that discreet. He should have been. When you do a job like this, you owe it to your clients.'

'So be indiscreet. My son was murdered, remember.'

'One of his regular clients was Roger Dimarco.'

'*The* Roger Dimarco?'

A policeman's life was rarely full of surprises. You saw it all, and after a while it took a lot to shock. But Roger Dimarco's name came as a surprise. The guy was rarely out of the newspapers. A one-time reigning tennis champion at the age of twenty, he had worked his way up over the intervening three decades to become one of the country's most successful entrepreneurs. He owned an airline, an independent television company and a chain of restaurants. 'Mr Clean' was written through him like the word *Brighton* through a stick of rock. He had a house in Tongdean Avenue, said by some to be the Beverly Hills of Brighton and Hove. He had a stunningly beautiful French wife who was photographed with him almost as frequently. Roger Dimarco was rarely out of the society columns.

'Dimarco's gay?'

'Well, he didn't pay Jason to scratch his back, honey.'

Madden put the mug of Earl Grey tea down.

'Sorry, but you don't mind if I leave this?'

'Not to your taste?'

'Right at this moment there's a bad taste in my mouth I've got to shift.'

He got up, holding on to Jason's scarf. He didn't have very much that belonged to his son. In fact, when he came to think about it, he didn't have anything.

'You don't mind if I take this?' he asked.

'Course not.'

He stuffed it into his pocket. It felt good to be taking a little bit of Jason out of this place.

'Where can I find George Adams?' he asked.

'He runs a pub called the Happy Kangaroo.'

'Popular with Australians, no doubt?'

'Lot of them in Earl's Court, honey.'

'I told you. I'd rather you didn't call me that.'

'Sorry. I just call everybody honey. Guess I'm sweet.' As she showed Madden out, she said, 'Jason was a sweet kid. He didn't deserve what happened to him.'

'Nobody deserves what happened to Jason.'

'The person who killed him does.'

'That's all I want too. Justice,' said Madden.

12

The Happy Kangaroo was the sort of place where the sawdust looked just too good to be true and the women's toilet had a sign that said 'Sheilas'. A couple of sorry-looking individuals sat staring at a televised football match of little consequence to either of their lives. Whether they were expatriates or not Madden couldn't tell. Not even the rain could drive much of the population of Earls Court into this dismal make-believe corner of Down Under.

He found George Adams behind the bar. He was younger than he'd imagined, in his forties, with a plump, rosy face, shorn hair, and shirt slashed open down to his navel, revealing a rounded belly covered in soft fluff. He had a ring in his left ear lobe. He looked like a pirate who had been pensioned off rather too early in life.

'I'm Jason's father,' Madden said.

'Pleased to meet you.' Adams extended his hand.

Madden didn't shake it. He'd made up his mind to dislike George Adams and wasn't about to compromise that intention.

'Can we talk privately?'

'Pretty private here.'

'You know why I'm here?'

'Is this police business or personal?'

'Personal.'

Madden had a lemonade. Adams poured himself a half of lager. The two customers who were staring at the football match noisily lamented a missed goal and sank back into their beer-hazed stupor.

'I'm really sorry about what happened to him,' Adams said, and Madden caught a note of sincerity in his voice. 'He was a good lad.'

'Yes, he was.' Madden looked down at the sawdust that was sticking to his shoes, then up at the guy who had made money out of his son working in a male brothel. 'When did you last see him?'

'About a week ago. I came down to Brighton, stayed at the flat. I've given the police all this information.'

'I know you have. As his father, I have rights too. How did you first meet him?'

'You want all this again?'

'Like I said, this is personal.'

'He came to me,' Adams replied, obviously uncomfortable about having to rake it over once more. 'I was advertising for guys for my agency, he came along, said he'd never done escort work before, thought he would like to give it a try.'

'Agency?'

'Yes. Lads of London.'

'Was this the kind of agency where you sent boys out to meet clients, or did they come to visit you?'

'Both.'

'So let's call it what it was, shall we? A brothel.'

'Call it what you want,' said Adams.

'Did you know he was only sixteen then?'

'No. He looked older.'

'You don't ask them for their birth certificates?'

'I did if I was suspicious. I'm not in that business any more, as you can see. I got out. It's pretty stressful. The doctor put me on tablets.'

'I feel sorry for you. Didn't you consider the danger you were putting him in?'

'Mr Madden.' Adams looked at him squarely, unflinching. 'Why don't you consider the danger he was in through doing it on his own?'

Madden resisted the temptation to lean across the bar and punch Adams. It wasn't the way to get answers.

'You started him doing it. By your own admission.'

'I told you. He came to me. Asked for a job. I had twenty boys working for me. I looked after them. When they went with clients

I knew who they were going with, where they were going. Wasn't that preferable to your son doing it on the streets? Where he might be picked up by some pervert? There are a lot of them about.'

'I'd prefer it if he hadn't been doing it at all. There were other dangers I'm sure you're aware of.'

'My boys only ever practised safe sex.' Adams rose to his own defence sheepishly. 'At least, they were told to, and that's what clients were told, too. I supplied them with condoms. If a boy ever got into trouble or the client wanted something he wasn't prepared to do, he could come to me. I'd sort it out.'

'You want some kind of medal for that?' said Madden.

'No.'

'You ever touch Jason yourself?'

Adams prickled at the question.

'No.'

'Is that the truth?'

'That's the truth. I had a lover at the time. He'd have killed me if I'd played around. Believe me.'

'What about more recently? Jason was living in your flat in Brighton, using your flat in London too. What were you getting out of it?'

'Rent,' said Adams. 'He paid me for the use of it.'

'Why him? What happened to your other boys?'

'I went to prison,' Adams said. 'You'll know that.'

'I know that. Non-payment of taxes.'

'Before you criticise me for living off immoral earnings, look at the government,' Adams said sourly, and predictably. 'They were just as guilty. People like me get condemned but the Inland Revenue are quick to take their slice if they get the chance. Where's the justice in that, Mr Madden? When I came out, all of the boys had gone their own ways, some to other agencies, some working for themselves. Jason got in touch with me and said he needed a place to stay. By that time, he'd gone independent, and it was difficult for him to have clients at the bedsit he was living in. So I helped him out.'

'Did you know any of his clients?'

'No. Most of them use false names anyway.'

'What about a Greek guy called Demos Panagoulis?'

'He mentioned him,' Adams said.

'So you did know one?'

'I knew *of* him, that's all. Wasn't a particularly savoury character, from what I heard. Contrary to what you might think, most clients are decent guys. Lots are married.'

'Did you know that Jason got drugs off him in exchange for sex?'

'No, I didn't.' Adams took an empty glass from one of the departing customers and started to wash it up. 'I wouldn't have had anything to do with that.'

'How do you mean?'

He put the glass upside down to dry and turned his gaze up to look at Madden.

'When I ran the agency, if I suspected a boy was doing it for drugs, I would get rid of him. You can go to some other agency I might name, they get their boys straight off the banana boat. Figuratively speaking.'

'Name it.'

'Golden Boys. You won't get any gold out of them. Most of them are from Brazil or Eastern Europe. Some of them can't even speak English. Lot of them are on drugs.'

'And Jason wasn't?'

'I'm pretty sure he wasn't. Look,' Adams said, 'I'm not expecting the OBE for my part in the world's oldest profession, but I ran a decent business.'

'You call renting out kids to middle-aged men decent?'

'They weren't kids. They were young adults. They made the choice, not me.'

The second customer left the bar. It was empty now except for Madden and George Adams.

'Business isn't good,' Adams whinged.

'You don't know anything about two grand's worth of Ecstasy at the flat in Brighton?'

'If I had, Jason would have been out.'

'You ever know Jason to steal anything before? From a client?'

'Never.'

'You would know if he had?'

'If I sent a boy to a client's house and the boy pinched something? There'd be all hell to pay. It happened once with a guy I took on. He helped himself to this client's credit cards. The client complained to me since he didn't want to involve the police because he was married – you know the score. Anyway, I got the cards back and threw the boy out. End of story.'

'Some clients might not complain.'

'You're asking me to tell you if I thought your son was a thief? I'm telling you he wasn't. Jason was honest, probably the most honest boy who worked for me. That's no lie. You don't get very far in this business if you cheat customers.'

'It's a small compensation,' said Madden.

'You spoke to Ming?'

'Yes. She is a he, I take it?'

'He was a he. Now he's a she. He worked for me. When I came out of prison, he was a she. Ming was the lover I told you I had before I went into prison.'

'But not now?'

'I came out of prison and found that my one true love had changed sex.'

'Life's complicated,' said Madden.

'Life's a pig,' moaned Adams.

Madden left the Happy Kangaroo and took the train back to Brighton. He'd gone to Earls Court expecting to hate George Adams but couldn't quite do it. Partly it was because he felt responsible. Jason had been his responsibility. If only he and Clara hadn't split up, Jason might not have ended up wandering around London offering his services to a male brothel. Was he maybe trying to get back at them? Punish them? What drove a boy to do it? If he needed the money, he could have come to him. Or his mother.

I'm happy, dad, I'm happy.

There was a text message on his phone. It was from Jasmine.

It said simply: *They've charged him. Must see you. Urgent. Private.*

At Brighton station, Madden bought a newspaper. Demos Panagoulis had been charged with the murder of Madden's son. No one had rung him to tell him. He felt sick in his stomach, and the bad taste that had been in his mouth since the previous day had just a got a hell of a lot worse.

13

Jasmine was waiting outside in her car for Madden when he arrived home. She looked cut up about something.

'Where have you been?' she asked.

'London. Making inquiries. A one-time brothel keeper and a transsexual prostitute.'

'Does Millington know?'

'I doubt it.'

'There's something you ought to.'

She came in with him. He made some coffee. Jasmine stood next to him in the kitchen. He remembered the last time it had happened. She'd stayed the night. He hadn't slept with a woman since then and was sorely missing the company.

'What evidence clinched it?' he asked.

'A tiny piece of the circuitry board of the computer that was smashed up. No bigger than half a centimetre across. It was found embedded in the sole of Panagoulis's right shoe. It had blood on it. Panagoulis presumably stepped in it. It was Jason's DNA.'

'No other blood on the shoe?'

'He could have wiped it off. The only blood was on that tiny piece of circuitry board that was so sharp it got embedded.'

'And he didn't notice it was there?'

'Presumably not.'

Madden studied her expression. He could see that she wasn't happy.

'What's the problem?' he asked. 'You *do* have a problem with that?'

'The knife hasn't been found,' she said.

'So he threw it in the sea. Off Brighton Pier.'

She threw a file down beside the coffee percolator. Madden opened it. It was Panagoulis's record sheet.

'Read it,' she said.

'I've got a better idea. You tell me what's in it.'

'Demos Panagoulis, charged with attempted murder six years ago. Do you know who he attempted to murder?'

'I thought he was acquitted.'

'The charge was reduced. He served two years of a four-year sentence for G.B.H. instead. The victim was a young bouncer who had stolen five thousand pounds from him.'

'So where's this getting us?'

'Do you know where the money was hidden?'

'Let me guess.' He guessed. 'Under the bath.'

'Behind one of the panels.'

'And we're expected to believe that he goes to see Jason about stolen drugs, beats him up, kills him, turns the flat upside down, rips open the mattress, even smashes the computer to bits – and doesn't look in the one place he'd be almost certain to look first?'

Madden poured the coffee out, sloshed a dash of rum into each. He remembered that Jasmine liked it that way.

'You remembered?'

'How could I forget? Last time I poured you one of these, you spent the night. I haven't forgotten that, either.'

They sat down in the lounge. She drew her knees tightly together. Madden thought they had the best bone structure he'd ever seen on a pair of knees. Other than Clara's. She had the most perfect legs he'd ever seen on any woman.

'Okay, so he manages to wash every bit of blood off his shoe, so thoroughly that forensic find not a trace. But he misses that little piece of circuitry board. Are we talking planted evidence here?'

'I wasn't going to be the first to say it,' admitted Jasmine.

'Say it.'

'I'm working alongside Fieldhouse now. I have to be careful.'

Madden sat down beside her, slinging his arm along the back of the settee so that it rested inches from her shoulders. Although they'd been familiar in the past, there was never any assumption that they would be so again. He didn't want to make demands on her. She had no other commitments that he knew about, except that her family expected her one day to marry a nice Hindu boy. Her mother, who had been born one of the small Hindu minority in Pakistan, had shocked the family and married a non-Hindu; an English landscape gardener. He had died young and she had been taken back into the fold and forgiven. It was Jasmine's mother who was most vociferous about her daughter not making the same mistake.

'Was that what you were doing yesterday? Being careful?'

'Not rocking the boat,' she said.

'You mean if you agreed with me, Jack Fieldhouse would have given you a hard time?'

'Something like that.'

'Traitor.' He smiled.

'It's not easy going against somebody you're working with. Especially someone like him.'

'I hope you'd never be afraid to disagree with me.'

'You're different,' she said.

'Thank you.'

'I wish it wasn't that way,' she said. 'But sometimes you just have to keep your head down in this job.'

'No, you don't, Jaz. In my experience, if you keep your head down people will normally sit on it.'

He took her hand and held it. She didn't pull it away.

'Suppose Jack Fieldhouse *is* fitting up Panagoulis. What reason would he have for doing it?' she said. 'Other than the fact that he's convinced Panagoulis is guilty and is desperate to get a conviction?'

'I've been thinking about that,' said Madden.

'Me too. And I started thinking about who would benefit if Panagoulis is put away.'

And, thought Madden, *came to the same conclusion*.

'Frank Sullivan?' He voiced both their thoughts.

Frank Sullivan was the competition. Rather, Sullivan had *become* the competition. Frank Sullivan had not been content to run a security firm, he wanted to own the clubs as well as control the doors. He had lately expended a lot of energy on the club scene, subcontracting the security operations to a separate company in which he had a financial interest. Panagoulis was already on the way out when Sullivan decided that the South Coast and its sea air were to his liking. There was no love lost between the two. Panagoulis had controlled the doors and the security on a club that Sullivan had owned in North London, and allowed in the Ecstasy that killed one teenager and hospitalised another three. The club had closed down, and Sullivan swore that Panagoulis had done it deliberately out of revenge for the fact that his contract had just been abruptly terminated. As unlikely as that probably was, from that moment on Panagoulis was a dead man as far as Sullivan was concerned. Brighton, where both were to end up, was definitely not big enough for the two of them. In the Sullivan empire, Demos Panagoulis was a turbulent priest, and turbulent priests traditionally met one fate.

'Why didn't he just put a bullet in the Greek's head and let him prop up a motorway bridge somewhere?' asked Jasmine.

Nice thought, Madden mused.

'Bit obvious. He'd be the first person we'd suspect. Even though he hasn't got a record for that. What better than taking advantage of a murder and having your enemy framed for it? On the other hand, if we want to assume Sullivan's really twisted, maybe he had Jason murdered, knowing that Panagoulis would carry the can.'

'You think that's likely?'

'I don't know, Jaz. Everything's possible. Even the possibility that Panagoulis is the right person to charge. I just don't know.'

'You confronted Panagoulis.'

'I did. And he looked me straight in the eye. Even when I told him I'd lost a son. I think he's a coward, Jaz, I don't think he could have done that if he'd murdered Jason and done to him what we saw.'

'That isn't in the book.'

'It's in *my* book.'

'I got you a few other things,' she said.

She put in front of him a list of Jason's other known clients. At the top of the list was Roger Dimarco.

'Dimarco,' he breathed.

'You know about him?'

'I was told about him by Ming, the transsexual Thai. The point is, has Dimarco been told about us? Does he know we know?'

'Fieldhouse interviewed him personally. And discreetly.'

'I didn't think Jack Fieldhouse was capable of doing anything discreetly.'

'Dimarco had an alibi. Didn't want any publicity, naturally.'

'Naturally.'

'Probably didn't want his wife to find out, either.'

Madden knew that prostitute murders were among the most difficult to solve. Clients disappeared into the night like rain flowing down gutters. Men would cover their tracks well to stop their wives finding out. Few people ever came forward voluntarily.

'How good an alibi?'

'His wife. They were on their boat. In the Mediterranean.'

'Convenient.'

He studied the rest of the list. At the bottom were the unidentifiables. A computer operator from Swindon called John who drove a white van. It never ceased to amaze him how often white vans crept into murder investigations. That white van certainly got around. Then there was a balding Scottish schoolteacher who called himself Stuart and would turn up at the London flat with a real tawse, wanting to be flogged with it. An American called Hiram. A coloured businessman who used to turn up in a pinstriped suit and with an attaché case and who wanted no more than a massage with 'extras'. The list was endless. There was even a client who professed to be a Royal footman.

Dimarco was the only client identified by surname apart from Panagoulis. Madden considered it strange that among all the anonymous punters, a high-profile figure like Roger Dimarco should be one of two clients who hadn't bothered to conceal his identity. But then, when you had a well-known face like Dimarco had, how could you conceal it?

He became aware that Jasmine was looking at Clara's paintings.

'Why do you keep them there?' she asked. 'The paintings?'

'To remind me of her.'

'Why do you want to be reminded?'

'Because I still love her.'

'It's not good, Steve. It's not healthy.'

'I know. People keep telling me that. But I can't let go. Even though we're divorced and she's married to another man, I still feel there's something between us. I suppose by keeping her paintings on the wall I keep a bit of her here too.' He added, 'A bit of something that accountant she lives with can't take away from me.'

'You've got to let go, Steve. You can't go through your life chasing memories – you've got to move on.'

'Move on where?'

'Just move on.' She seemed to be pleading with him.

'My son's dead, my wife's living with a guy I'd like to put under a motorway bridge. Where do you suggest I move on to?'

'Anywhere,' said Jasmine. 'Nursing your jealousy and bitterness isn't going to help.'

'I know that.'

'You're still hoping she'll come back to you, aren't you?'

'Yes.'

'Don't martyr yourself.'

'She was perfect, Jaz. You know how somebody can be so perfect that you believe you were made for each other?'

'I never met that person. Yet.'

'I did, and I spent twenty-two years jealous of every other man who looked at her.'

'That's a long time to be jealous, Steve.'

'And when she looked at Clive and ran off with him, it was like – someone just tore me in two. Clara and me were meant to be together. Not them.'

'You *have* got it bad.'

'Is it wrong to hope that Jason's death might bring us back together? Just a bit?'

She stood up and gazed down at him. She took one of his hands in hers and stroked it.

'Yes,' she said. 'It would be wrong to use it that way.'

'Don't worry. I have no intention of doing that.'

Then he summoned up the courage to ask her. 'Would you like to stay the night?'

'Just to help you forget her? That's not the way I want things to happen.'

'You didn't object before.'

'There are times when it seems right and times when it doesn't. This is one of those times when it doesn't. I'm sorry, Steve. I know what you're going through.'

'How do you know what I'm going through?'

'You want a shoulder to cry on. Fine. Cry on my shoulder. I'm here for you. But I don't want to go to bed with you just for you to do that. We tried it once before and it was a disaster, remember?'

'We tried it since. And it was more successful.'

'Steve, you thought about *her*.'

Madden couldn't argue with that. She was clearly more perceptive than he'd realised.

'A woman knows, Steve,' she said.

'Okay.' He swallowed a lump in his throat. 'Maybe some other time.'

She kissed him. It was soft, like a butterfly wing brushing his cheek.

'How long do you think it will be before you come back to work?'

'I think I'm entitled to take a certain amount of compassionate leave. Besides, it's useful to me right now. There are inquiries I can better make as a father than as a detective. You know what I mean?'

'I think I do,' she said. 'Let me know if you need anything.'

'Just keep supplying me with information.'

'You can count on me.'

As Jasmine went out of the door, Madden said to her, 'Sorry if it means you're stuck a little while longer with Jack Fieldhouse. It might be advisable if you did keep your head down for a little while.'

'I intend to.' She smiled.

14

Steve Madden had arranged to meet Lucky Maynard on Brighton Pier at ten o'clock that night. As it happened, Lucky was twenty minutes late. Lucky was always late. It didn't matter. When you had an informer as good as Lucky, you made allowances.

'Hello, Lucky,' he said, playing pinball and not looking at him.

'Hello, Mr Madden,' said Lucky, tackling the penny falls and not looking at him either.

Lucky was a dangerous name to have. Lucky had never had much and it had started before he was born. His mother had smoked and drunk her way through an unwanted pregnancy, and it had left Lucky with less than the full quota of intelligence. He had been brought up in a children's home where no one, apparently, had called him any other name but Lucky. Many things were said of Lucky. The lights were on but nobody was at home. The picnic hamper was short of a sandwich or two. The elevator didn't go all the way to the top floor. Lucky made up for it by being streetwise. What he lacked in the mastermind department, he made up for in cunning. He wouldn't make Brain of Britain but he could drive a car and lose coppers and cover his tracks and those of the villains who had employed him.

That was what made Lucky Maynard so valuable to Frank Sullivan. Madden knew, as everyone else did, though nobody had ever been able to prove it, that Frank Sullivan, behind his respectable businessman's facade, as ubiquitous among criminals of that echelon as the white van was among those lower down the scale, made a lot of money out of drugs and particularly the drugs that were sold nightly in the half-dozen clubs that he owned. Affluent kids with money to spend and energy to burn were his treasured customers. Proving such links, however, had always been more trouble than it was worth. Everybody knew that drugs found a way into clubs. Someone had to profit from them. Sullivan had simply decided on the expedient solution that it was better if it benefited the organ grinder rather than the monkeys. Frank Sullivan gave big contributions to charity, even if it was a bit like a rattlesnake donating its poison to a worthy cause. He hosted big boxing tournaments. He was Mr Big. Mr Impregnable. Drugs money or chemical substances never stayed around him long enough to be traced. He was Mr-Far-Too-Fucking-Clever-By-Half. So long as nobody else died, he reckoned he was safe.

It was also reckoned that Lucky was too thick and would be too frightened to be an informer. Lucky had an air of loyalty about him, like a faithful puppy dog. Lucky saw and heard and never repeated. You could rely on Lucky. There was rarely any need to ask him to leave the room. Lucky was okay. Lucky was lucky.

But Lucky only ever got the titbits. The name of a villain here, a suspicious contact there, an overheard phone call, a conversation. Lucky would never have been privy to any big stuff. Still, the little stuff had proved useful over the years, even though none of it had come near to touching Sullivan. But a few of the big man's contacts had been put away. There were rumours that Lucky was Frank Sullivan's bastard son and that Lucky didn't know it. There were always rumours like that.

'I'm sorry about your son, Mr Madden,' said Lucky.

'Thanks. Got anything for me?'

'Only that he's moving in fast. Within hours of Pana— what's-his-name being charged.'

'Panagoulis.'

'Never was much good with foreign names, Mr Madden.'

'You mean, he's getting his own security company to handle the doors for other clubs that he doesn't own?'

'That's right.'

'For the ones Panagoulis thought he had a monopoly on?'

'Whoever controls the doors controls the drugs, Mr Madden. That's what it's all about.'

'You ever see any drugs, Lucky?'

'Me? I never see drugs, Mr Madden. I smoked a joint once. It gave me a hangover. I've got low tolerance. I've got low tolerance to a lot of things. Milk makes me funny, too. I get stomach cramps if I drink that.'

'You heard anything else?'

'Like what?'

'Like anything else that might interest me.'

'Not about your son's death, Mr Madden. I wouldn't hear nothing about that, anyway.'

'What makes you so sure?'

'That's murder. He wouldn't discuss murder in front of me. You think—'

'I don't know what to think. I'm relying on information.'

'Not murders.' Lucky spoke as though it was some holy grail to which he was denied access. 'I don't get told about murders.'

'How's life treating you anyway, Lucky?'

'In what way, Mr Madden?'

'You lucky in love yet?'

'Love?'

Lucky spoke the word in the same tone as he'd said 'murders'. It was something beyond his grasp, beyond his reach. Something to which he wasn't entitled. Madden looked at him and could understand why. He dressed like fashion was going out of fashion. His long dark hair fell down over his eyes, in need of a comb. He was only twenty-five but he looked older. His nails were grimy. It was possible that he didn't wash, or that if he did, the water ran off him out of fright.

Madden took a photograph out of his pocket and passed it to Lucky.

'Recognise anyone in that photograph, Lucky?' he asked.

Lucky stared at it. The photograph was of a police Christmas function six months earlier. It had been a Christmas that Madden had not enjoyed, the first Christmas after Clara had left him, and though he was smiling in the photo he'd been feeling like shit.

There was nothing worse than being surrounded by happy people when you were miserable.

'Yes, you, Mr Madden,' said Lucky.

'Anybody else?'

Lucky looked a bit closer. From the way he screwed up his eyes, Madden figured that he needed glasses.

'Yes. The guy standing on your left.'

'On my left? Or left of me in the photograph?'

'On your right. Left of you in the photo.'

'Point to him so there's no mistake.'

Lucky pointed. Madden tucked the photograph away in his pocket. Lucky Maynard had identified Jack Fieldhouse. There was no mistake.

'I saw him recently,' said Lucky.

'Where?'

'With Mr Sullivan.'

'Frank Sullivan? Let's make sure there's no mistake about this.'

'There's no other Mr Sullivan.' Lucky looked at him as though he was daft.

'Go on. Where and when did you see them together?'

'He was chatting to him in the back of the car I was driving. I couldn't hear what they said, though. It's one of them limousines with a glass job.'

'You mean a partition?'

'Yeh, that's it. To stop people hearing.'

'When did this happen?'

'Day before yesterday. About half-past ten at night.'

'Thanks, Lucky. Take that for yourself.'

Madden slipped him thirty pounds. Lucky was not a registered informer.

'Two bits of information, Mr Madden – surely that's worth fifty at least?'

Madden pressed an extra twenty into his hand.

'You'll go far,' he said.

'No, I won't. Too stupid.'

'Sometimes stupid people succeed where intelligent ones fall by the wayside.'

'I'll remember that, Mr Madden.'

'Bye, Lucky.'

'Bye, Mr Madden.'

Lucky turned away from the penny falls, not having won anything. A kid with a skateboard tucked under his arm took over from him, fed in a coin, and created an avalanche. He went off with his pockets jangling. Lucky was a dangerous name to have.

Madden now knew that between Panagoulis being arrested and charged, Jack Fieldhouse had met Panagoulis's rival Frank Sullivan in the back of a limo. Sullivan's limo. The coincidence was too great. It was also hard to stomach. When policemen and villains got into bed together, the consequences were often ruinous.

He phoned Jasmine.

'Jaz,' he said, 'you were right.'

'I knew I was. Sometimes a woman's intuition is more reliable than a policewoman's,' she answered.

15

Madden put in a call to Daniel Donoghue, Jason's boyfriend. It was a mobile number, which was all he had. He left a message with an answering service and then hung up. He figured that Daniel would have known Jason better than anybody. The day was to prove him wrong.

Dimarco's house was in Hove. There was an old joke that Hove should be called Hove Actually, because of the number of people who, when asked if they lived in Brighton, protested snootily at such an appalling suggestion. Once Brighton and Hove had been separate towns, joined at the hip. Now they had city status, jointly. Madden didn't know anybody who called the place Brighton and Hove. He couldn't think of any other city in the country with a double-barrelled name. Sometimes he wondered what the point was. It was a bit like calling Birmingham 'the city of Birmingham and Coventry'. People who lived in Brighton said they lived in Brighton, people who lived in Hove lived in Hove Actually. Clara had once referred to them as Hovites and the Brightonista. It made him laugh when he thought of that.

Hove was more residential, quieter, less touristy, parts of it singularly grand. Living there cost two arms and two legs, instead of the single limbs you'd be expected to lose in Brighton. The Tongdean area had a number of millionaires' houses, one of the most palatial of which belonged to Roger Dimarco. It was built along the style of a Spanish hacienda and had a roof garden and swimming pool. Wrought-iron gates in a high brick wall kept out unwanted intruders.

Madden rang the bell in the wall, and waited. He was expected. The gates swung open at a leisurely pace and he drove through.

Exotic plants and mulberry trees lined the driveway up to the house. There was a white Bentley parked outside. He stuck his eight-year-old blue Volvo next to it. He wasn't jealous. Not yet.

The silvery-haired gentleman with the white polo shirt, the black tracksuit bottoms and the too-perfect tan who came out to meet him was not smiling. Madden put Dimarco at about sixty. Yet he was a lean, youthful sixty, a man who had worked to keep his figure. When Dimarco smiled, he revealed an almost perfect, if slightly discoloured, set of teeth. His face was tanned and heavily lined, and he sported a slight beard.

'Mr Madden, I've been looking forward to meeting you,' said Roger Dimarco, soberly. 'Needless to say, I've been nervous about it as well.'

'Me too,' lied Madden.

Dimarco's handshake was that of a man who had done major deals all of his life. This time Madden thought a handshake was in order. He didn't yet know what to make of Dimarco. He didn't want to like him, he didn't want to dislike him. How the hell did you react on first meeting to a man who had paid to have sex with your son?

'Come on through and let's talk. This isn't official police business, I take it?'

'No. Would you rather it was?'

'I'd feel more comfortable. I've got nothing to hide. I told a Mr Fieldhouse everything. Would you like something to drink?'

'No, thanks.'

Dimarco took him up an internal staircase to the roof garden, which overlooked a lawn of bowling-green smoothness, surrounded by perfectly symmetrical flower beds, and a large rectangular swimming pool in which the water seemed impossibly blue. On the edge of the pool a naked young woman was sunning herself. A few feet away from her, a man was sitting with his feet dangling in the water. There was what looked like a bottle of champagne and glasses between them. The woman sported a pair of dark sunglasses and it appeared as though she was looking up at them, curious about his visit.

'My wife,' said Dimarco. 'Don't worry, she knows everything. We have no secrets from each other. That might surprise you.'

'In my job, you learn not to be surprised by anything,' Madden explained.

'Ah. I detect the hardened and cynical cop.'

'My son's been murdered, Mr Dimarco. If I was hardened and cynical, I would have a perfect right to be.'

'I apologise.' Dimarco sounded sincere. 'It was a stupid thing to say. Forgive me.'

Dimarco sat down in the centre of a hammock with a pink-and-purple-striped awning and crossed his legs. Madden eased himself into a canvas deckchair. Plants grew in profusion. The entire roof area was tiled in warm, red terracotta. There was an outdoor jacuzzi. Madden wondered how many other people in Brighton and Hove had roof gardens in which to lounge around.

'Let me tell you about Jason,' Dimarco said.

'That's why I'm here.'

'I read in the paper that someone's been charged.'

'That's right.'

'I was devastated when I heard. I know what you're thinking. I was just a client of your son, but it was more than that. Really it was.'

'How much more?'

'He talked about you a lot to me. In fact, he talked about you so much that I feel I know you already.'

Madden shifted uncomfortably in his chair. The woman by the pool stood up and slipped gracefully, legs first, into the water. The man she was with began kicking with his feet, splashing her face. She cavorted back.

'You said it was more. I asked how much more.'

'I take it you didn't know what your son did?'

'I do now. How much more?'

'I found Jason on his website. He came to the house and we got on rather well. He wasn't one of those male escorts or prostitutes – whatever you want to call them – who hated what he did and just wanted to take the money and run. Do you know what I mean?'

'Explain it to me,' said Madden. 'I never had the need to buy sex.'

'Nor do I.'

'So you got on well? How well?'

'Well, the first time Jason came here, he was bowled over by the house. I don't think he'd ever been to a place like this before. Any nineteen-year-old lad would be. I asked him if he wanted to go out for dinner. We did, and we spent the evening by the pool. He told me his father was a policeman and that his greatest fear was of you finding out.'

'How many times did you have sex with my son?' asked Madden.

'I'd hoped you wouldn't ask such intimidating questions.'

'I'm a policeman. It's hard to break the habit.'

'I saw Jason once a week. On average.'

'How much did you pay him?'

'A hundred pounds a time. There was nothing seedy or exploitative about it, I want you to believe that. What Jason did he did readily.'

'How old are you, Mr Dimarco?'

'What does that have to do with it?'

'I just want to know.'

'I'm sixty-one.'

'Jason was young enough to be your grandson. Doesn't that make you feel ashamed?'

Dimarco leant back, looked up at some passing clouds and looked anything but ashamed. He looked like a man who was used to justifying everything he did.

'Jason told me about clients who were arrogant and unpleasant to him. Guys who wanted to beat him, people who just generally got off on abusing him. There are some pretty unpleasant people about.'

'I know. I meet them daily.'

'I treated him with respect. And he gave me it back. And I am going to miss him more than you can ever imagine.'

Madden noticed that Dimarco's eyes filled up with tears at

that moment. He hadn't quite expected this. He'd met prostitutes in his line of business, he'd met their clients. Loads of them. This was something else. This was Madden's son Dimarco was talking about.

I'm happy, dad, I'm happy.

'You said it was much more. How much more?' Madden pressed him.

'I suppose you could say we became friends. The age difference never really entered into it. He found he could talk to me about things that he—'

'That he what?'

'That he found it difficult to talk to you about.'

'Such as?'

'Everything to do with his life. You and your wife separating – he told me about that – his boyfriend at Cambridge. I took Jason abroad a few times, down to the south of France. I have a house on Cap Ferrat, near Nice. Do you know it?'

'No.'

'We'd go sailing. He was starting to become quite a sailor, I can tell you. I taught him how to handle a boat. He was a great lad to have around.'

Madden felt as though a hollow pit had just opened up in his stomach.

'It ceased to become a financial arrangement, then?'

'No. I still paid him. But it was – different. My wife and I both became very fond of him, he almost became one of the family. We don't have any children.'

'Just as well,' said Madden, turning away.

'I don't really like the tone of that, Mr Madden. Or what you're implying. I'm not a paedophile or a child molester, I've never hurt a kid in my life. I couldn't. Your son just – well, kind of adopted us.'

The pit in Madden's stomach got deeper then. Inside himself he felt the stirrings of something he tried desperately to suppress. He knew this feeling. It was when something you valued was taken away from you. He'd last felt it when he'd learnt that Clara had moved in with The Accountant from the Black Lagoon. Intense jealousy. A seismic shock to the emotions. He'd gone to meet a man who'd paid his son for sex and had discovered instead someone who'd become a surrogate father to Jason.

'I want you to know that he did talk about you a lot.' Dimarco appeared to be aware of Madden's feelings and tried to soften the blow.

'That's very comforting.'

'He wanted to talk to you. About being gay. He loved you but – well – he was afraid of you. It was only natural. You being in the job you're in. It was nothing personal.'

'He could have come to me.'

'I believe he did.'

'How did you know that, Mr Dimarco?'

Roger Dimarco looked vaguely smug.

'He phoned me up the morning you'd had your row. He told me all about it.'

'We didn't have a row. We had a disagreement. It's a different thing.'

'He told me that he'd admitted his gayness to you and you hadn't taken it very well. He was really, really desperate that you should. In fact, I'd encouraged him to tell you. He told me that he couldn't face you in the morning and so he left before you got up.'

'It was the wrong time. I tried to get in touch with him again. We were going to meet.'

'I know. Celestine and I were just leaving for Nice for a couple of days' holiday. He phoned me the day before. Before – he was murdered. He said you'd left a message on his mobile asking to meet him and he was really pleased. I said he should ring you back straight away and I assume he did.'

'He phoned me in the morning. We were going to meet that day,' said Madden.

'I'm sorry. I'm so sorry.' Then, 'You mustn't blame yourself.'

'Mustn't blame myself? That's rich.'

'Jason did appreciate it when you got back in touch with him,' said Dimarco. 'He loved you for it. He was just scared of getting close to you in case – well, in case you found out what he was doing. He dreaded meeting you in Brighton, since you lived so close.'

So that was it. Jason hadn't cut him off. Perhaps he hadn't been such a bad father after all. If he hadn't been a detective and Jason hadn't been working as a male prostitute, maybe things would have been different. It was nothing personal, Dimarco had said.

He hated admitting it but Dimarco's words gave him something to cling on to.

'It seems that you were pretty intimate with Jason. For him to call you up like that.'

'Like I said, we were friends. He could talk to me.'

Madden got up and looked down at the swimming pool. Dimarco's wife was floating naked on the surface of the water. He could see the outline of her breasts bobbing above the surface. The man she was with was now stomach down on a floating Lilo and they were flicking water at each other.

'I wanted to be friends with my son. I wanted him to talk to *me*.'

Dimarco looked away. Madden's words had stung.

'What kind of marriage do you have, Mr Dimarco?' Madden asked.

'A very happy one.'

'If you'll pardon me saying so, it doesn't seem that way to me.'

'We live our own separate lives but that doesn't mean we're not happy.'

'How the other half live,' commented Madden wryly.

'How *we* live, anyway. Celestine is French. She's very beautiful. The kind of wife any man would be proud to have.'

'So why did you need my son?'

'Just my nature,' said Dimarco.

'Did Jason ever talk to you about drugs?'

'Oh God, yes.' Dimarco exhaled deeply. 'He was into Ecstasy. I never touch the stuff and I did try to advise him of the dangers but you know what it's like trying to talk to the young. He took it when he went clubbing and with his boyfriend.'

'Daniel Donoghue?'

'Yes. He used to wax eloquent about its virtues. How it made him feel so happy and free, and how sex was a thousand times better when he was on it – that sort of thing. I told him there was evidence that prolonged use could lead to severe depression but he would just argue saying that was nonsense and that smoking and alcohol were more dangerous. What can you do?'

'What can you do?' Madden echoed.

They sounded like two fathers lamenting their errant offspring at a parents/teachers association meeting.

'Did he talk to you about Demos Panagoulis?'

'Yes. He didn't like him very much but he was scared to give him up. He said the man was violent.'

'Did you know that Panagoulis paid him in drugs?'

'No, I didn't.'

'Doesn't it bother you that the money you paid Jason went to buy drugs? Drugs that might also have killed him?'

'What Jason spent his money on was no concern of mine.'

'He was my son! He was nineteen years old! He was into Ecstasy and cocaine and speed and all that kind of stuff – and you paid him a hundred pounds a week to satisfy your own sexual appetite, knowing that he might kill himself one day?'

Dimarco's face darkened. Up until now, Madden felt, he had behaved pretty civilly. But there was anger boiling up in him.

'Where were *you*?' Dimarco fired back, standing up suddenly. 'I'm sorry to have to say it, Mr Madden, but don't blame me for Jason's lifestyle. At least I talked to him about drugs, tried to warn him. Tried to take an interest. Did you ever?'

'Jason never gave me the chance.'

'Maybe *you* never gave *him* the chance. Don't you come and start taking out on me your own failings as a father because I took an interest in him.'

Madden caught his breath. His fists were clenched. He didn't need anyone telling him about his failings as a father. He knew he had failed Jason. He had reminded himself of it a hundred times. He couldn't bring his son back to life but he could find out who had killed him. He wasn't going to fail Jason's memory.

'I'm sorry,' he said. 'My life's been turned upside down by this.'

'I understand. Meeting me must be hard for you. If it's any consolation, I share your grief. Jason was a friend and a great companion.'

Madden turned his head to the stairway that led up to the roof garden. On it appeared a woman who could have been no older than thirty-five. She had the reddest hair he had ever seen. She wore a large towel wrapped about her but it didn't conceal the pool water that ran in little rivulets down the insides of her thighs. Her eyes appeared so deep that he could have fallen into them. But what was most striking were her eyelashes. He hadn't seen lashes like that since Olive Oyl had blinked at Popeye.

She held the towel about her and looked from Roger Dimarco to Madden.

'Mr Madden, this is my wife Celestine,' Dimarco said.

16

There was nothing so queer as folk, Madden thought, as he gazed at Celestine Dimarco's hauntingly beautiful eyes. They were sitting by the pool. She'd brought him a pink lemonade with lots of crushed ice in it. Her husband had gone upstairs to his office to make a few business calls. Her pool companion had made himself scarce in the house somewhere. Madden was quite glad. To be left alone at a poolside with a woman like Celestine Dimarco was something that didn't often happen to him in his job.

If he hadn't been investigating Jason's death he'd have enjoyed it a lot more. What mystified him was why a man like Dimarco should want a nineteen-year-old boy when he had a wife like this. He said so.

'You're looking at it from a very heterosexual point of view,' she said, in an almost chastising way. Her accent was terrific. Like something straight out of a French movie.

'I know no other way.'

'When I married Roger I knew his predilections.'

'Why did you marry him?'

'Money,' she said. She sat up on the poolside Lilo, drew up her knees and tucked them between her arms. 'Money is power. I like powerful men.'

She tilted her face to the sun. She had a disarming honesty about her. *A great interviewee,* thought Madden.

'Would you like a little champagne?' she asked.

'No, thank you.'

'Do you mind if I do?'

She took a bottle from an ice bucket and refilled her glass. That of her poolside companion stood empty. It was a great life in Hove if you didn't weaken.

'How did you meet?'

'My father was on the board of Air Nice when Roger's company took it over. I took *him* over.'

This woman could have had any man she wanted, Madden thought. *She chose a gay millionaire*. He said so. She laughed.

'He wasn't completely gay. Or should I say, isn't. But it makes men interesting. It makes them vulnerable. And I find vulnerability very sexy.'

'More sexy than power?'

Celestine changed the subject.

'You came here to talk about Jason.'

'I came here to talk.'

'I can't express how sorry I am. He was a lovely boy. And so good for Roger. It must be hard for you.'

'It's not easy.'

'Men make better prostitutes than women,' she said. 'They're far more sensitive. Jason was like that. Sensitive. Kind.'

'I find that hard to believe.'

'That he was sensitive?'

'No. What you said first. That men make better prostitutes than women.'

'Women are bitches,' she said. 'They use men. Men, on the other hand, know what men want. Do I shock you?'

'What shocks me is finding out things about my son that I never knew.'

The champagne looked good. He tried to imagine when he'd have another chance to sit by a pool and drink Bollinger with a woman who looked like Celestine Dimarco. One sip and he reckoned he might forget all about Clara. He weakened.

'Mind if I do?'

She fetched a clean glass from a poolside cabinet.

'I like it when a man weakens.'

'It doesn't happen too often.'

It tasted good. He found himself staring at her legs – long, smooth, tanned creations that belonged in a commercial.

'I'll tell you whatever you want to know.' She blinked at him.

'How well did you get to know Jason?'

'Pretty well. I suppose you're thinking that this is a bizarre situation.'

'I've come across more bizarre.'

'Roger and Jason would go upstairs, do whatever it was they did, come down, we'd all have drinks, go out for dinner. Jason talked about you a lot.'

'I know.'

'He was a very grown-up boy. In a very grown-up situation.'

'Apparently.'

'What happened to him was just too awful.' Celestine turned away from Madden as though she normally kept awful things at bay in her life, and when they intruded she didn't know how to handle them. 'I'm glad you've caught the man who did it.'

'So am I, Mrs Dimarco.'

'Roger cried the night he learnt. I've never seen him cry.'

'I cried for a pretty long time myself,' Madden assured her.

'It was almost as though he had lost a son as well.'

'The last time I saw him –' Madden decided to open up '– he told me he was happy. Was he?'

'What do you think? He had a boyfriend with whom he was very much in love, he had a regular client and good friend in Roger who was good and generous and kind to him. He had a home here he could come to any time he wanted. Roger made that clear. Then there were the trips we all made to the south of France.'

'You all went?'

'We spent a lovely week on the *Heraklion*. That's our boat. Jason even learnt to steer it.'

'And your husband and Jason – they slept together?'

'Yes.' She shrugged as though it was the most natural thing in the world. '*Pourquoi pas?* I too had my partner.'

'The man I saw you with down here?'

'Jacques is French. He comes over from Marseilles a couple of days every week to see me. He's a photographer.'

'What does he photograph?' asked Madden, as though he needed an answer.

'He's a fashion photographer. But he takes lots of other kinds of photographs.'

'What's sauce for the goose,' said Madden.

'Exactement.'

Only the gander's sauce was no more. Madden wondered how it would affect the Dimarcos' lives. Somehow he doubted that it would affect them very much. Roger would probably find a new boy and they would carry on much as before. He didn't consider that an uncharitable thought. It stuck in his craw that Jason had almost – how had Roger put it? – adopted them.

His mobile phone rang. He answered it.

'Mr Madden?'

'Speaking.'

'This is Daniel Donoghue. You wanted to speak to me.'

'Yes. It's overdue. Where are you?'

Donoghue gave him an address in Cambridge, then arranged to meet him outside King's College the next day.

'I'm looking forward to meeting you,' said Madden.

'I'm looking forward to meeting you, too.'

Celestine Dimarco let the towel slip slightly so that it exposed the side of her breast. Madden couldn't tell whether it was deliberate or not. She tossed back her mane of red hair and held her face up to the sun again as though she worshipped it.

'Feel free to cool off with a swim if you want,' she told him.

'I didn't bring any trunks.'

'I can find you a pair.'

'No, thanks. Some other time, maybe. I really must be going.'

He finished the champagne and got up to leave. He felt he had to get away before he started enjoying himself too much.

'Can I say something that might help?' She stood up to see him off.

'Anything that helps I'm ready to hear.'

'You had every reason to be proud of Jason,' Celestine said. 'He was a decent boy.'

Madden left her with only the briefest of smiles.

'It runs in the family,' he said.

17

'Clara?'

'What?'

'Fancy a trip up to Cambridge?'

'I can't,' she said. 'I'm working at the gallery. I could get Paula to step in for me—'

'You've met this Daniel. I'd like you with me.'

'If Clive was to find out—'

'This is family business. Anyway, I've got to talk to you. About Jason's funeral.'

'Okay,' she said.

'That's good.'

At eleven o'clock the next morning they were driving up to Cambridge, a distance of about eighty miles. It felt strange, having her sit by his side again. She was almost a stranger but not quite. His intentions were completely honourable. He wasn't using Jason's murder in that way.

He told her all about the Dimarco ménage.

'I can't believe it,' she said.

'Believe it. Whatever our son was, he was a high-class one.'

'He didn't tell me any of this.'

'How could he? You'd have suspected. A man old enough to be his grandfather and with more millions than we ever dreamed of takes him cruising in the Med. What would you have thought?'

'Sugar daddy,' she said. 'That's the expression, isn't it?'

'Only in this scenario there's a sugar mummy as well.'

'What's she like?'

'Ought to be a law against a woman looking so great. And against a husband not appreciating it.'

'Why are you doing this, Steve? I mean, you've caught his killer.'

'I caught nobody. A man's been charged, that's all.'

'They wouldn't charge someone if they weren't sure.'

'I just want to make sure. That's all.'

'You think they're wrong.'

'Wouldn't be the first time.'

'Oh my God.' It dawned on Clara what he was suggesting. 'Don't tell me that. I couldn't stand it. I was just so relieved they'd caught somebody. And you're saying the wrong person is in custody? I don't want to believe it, Steve.'

'Whatever Jason was, I don't believe he was a thief. I don't believe he had any need to steal two grand's worth of Ecstasy tabs. I don't believe he was a drug dealer, either. Okay, he went wrong somewhere and we're at fault. We have to put it right.'

'We?'

'*I* have to put it right.'

They parked the car in a multi-storey and walked to King's College. A clutch of students cycled past wearing shorts, bells ringing to clear pedestrians and cars from their path. Madden gazed up at the spectacular chapel with its twin Gothic towers that dominated the college. There was something about Cambridge that made him feel inferior, as though the whole city was a club to which you couldn't belong.

'That's Daniel,' said Clara, waving.

Daniel was waiting for them. He waved back and ran across the road to meet them. He was a handsome youth, lean and wiry, with coal-black hair gelled up into a quiff above his forehead. There was something insectile about his face. If Celestine Dimarco had reminded Madden of Olive Oyl with her exaggerated eyelashes, Daniel Donoghue reminded him of Jiminy Cricket. His long freckled neck boasted a little black cord with a rectangular charm hanging from it. He was wearing baggy jeans, chunky trainers, and a black vest. His arms were long and thin, as were his fingers, and covered in freckles. He had almost feminine eyelashes and a perfect set of white teeth.

'Hello, Mrs Madden,' he said, almost shyly.

'Daniel, this is my ex-husband Steve. Jason's father.'

'Pleased to meet you.'

Madden shook his hand.

'We need to talk,' he said. 'Anywhere you suggest?'

'There's a pub by the river.'

'Sounds good to me.'

They walked to the pub and found a wooden table and two benches right by the edge of the water. Punts drifted past occupied by languid students, pictures of indolence. Even the branches of a nearby elm looked laid back. Brighton was never like this. If cities were girls, Madden thought, Cambridge was a lethargic and unconcerned young woman draped across a punt while Brighton was a tart.

'I asked Clara to come along with me, Daniel, because I didn't want you to think this was an official police enquiry.'

'Cool,' Daniel said. 'The police did interview me for about two hours. It was terrible. He was a big fat guy.'

That just about summed up Jack Fieldhouse.

'We're here as Jason's parents. We want to know things. Things you maybe haven't told anyone else.'

'Such as?'

'Will you level with us?'

'I'll try.'

'Jason's drug taking. How extensive was it?'

'He took drugs.'

'Do you?'

Daniel hesitated.

'This isn't a police inquiry.' Clara echoed what Madden had said a few moments earlier.

'That Greek's been arrested and charged.' Daniel looked from one to the other.

'Did you ever meet him?' Madden leant forward.

'Once. When I visited Jason at Brighton. I had to make myself scarce while – well, you know.'

'He was your boyfriend, yet you didn't mind what he did?'

'I wanted him to give it up.' Daniel looked towards the river. 'I asked him to give it up.'

'Was part of the reason he wouldn't give it up the fact that you were doing the same thing?'

Daniel flushed a bright crimson. Clara looked at her ex-husband in surprise.

'I have information, Daniel, that you were working as an escort too. Don't worry. We're not here to moralise. We just want to know the truth. Anything you want to tell us is in complete confidence.'

'My parents would kill me if they found out.'

'They won't find out. Nobody's going to tell them.'

'I'm an impoverished student,' said Daniel.

'Aren't you all?'

'I didn't do as much as Jason. I couldn't. I just wasn't as successful at it as he was.'

'Did you feel jealous?'

'I just wanted him to give it up. That's all.'

There was a momentary distraction as a punt sailed past with three teenage girls in it. One was having difficulty with the pole. The other two fought to grab it. One fell in. There was much screaming and laughing. Madden wished for a carefree day.

'Tell us about the drugs.' Madden returned to his earlier question.

'This isn't official?'

'No.'

'Cool. Okay. Jason took speed, E, a line of coke occasionally. We both did.'

'How occasional?'

'Weekends when we'd go clubbing in London,' Daniel said. 'Sometimes Jason and I would take a tab or two between us in my room.'

'How many tabs would he take when you went clubbing?'

'Maybe three or four. Five or six occasionally. Rarely more than that.'

Clara looked surprised. Madden tried not to be.

'And in your room, just one or two?'

'Yes. We just did it to get high. And have sex.'

'This is a world I don't know much about, Daniel. Educate me,' Madden asked.

'Okay, when you're coming down off E you get really horny. Even a table leg can turn you on. It's difficult to describe the feeling to someone who hasn't tried it.'

'Where did he get most of his drugs from?'

'That Greek guy.'

'Demos Panagoulis?'

'Apparently the guy was awash with them. That's the only reason Jason stayed around him, I'm sure.'

'So he got enough for you and for him?'

'We got them when we went clubbing, too. It's no problem when you're known. Jason and I always used to get up into the VIP suite where things were more private. You can get them off the bar staff.'

'Oh my God,' said Clara. She always said that when a cherished belief was shattered.

'Hundreds of teenagers don't dance until seven in the morning just getting their energy from bottled water,' said Daniel.

'You knew about Dimarco?' Madden asked.

'Roger Dimarco? Of course – Jason made hundreds of pounds a month out of him. Free trips abroad.'

'How did you feel about that?'

Daniel shrugged. He'd felt bad about it. Madden could tell.

'The money was great,' he said.

'I didn't ask you about the money. I asked you how you felt?'

'I told you. I wanted him to give it up.'

'Did you feel jealous?'

'Course I felt a bit jealous. Wouldn't you?'

Madden felt for him.

'One last question, Daniel. Where did you meet your clients?'

'Chat rooms mainly. Over the Internet. Once or twice Jason found a client for me.'

'You ever do a double act?'

'You mean a duo?' Daniel looked down at his thin freckled fingers. 'Once. It wasn't very successful.'

'Why not?'

'Jason was my boyfriend. I loved him. It's difficult to watch your boyfriend screw somebody else in front of you. He really enjoyed it, that was the trouble.'

'Who was it with?'

Daniel was shy of saying at first, but soon overcame it.

'Dimarco,' he said.

'You and Jason – Dimarco – together?' Madden tried to put it as tactfully as possible.

'I told you, it wasn't very successful. I was jealous and Jason thought that it might help me if I could watch the two of them together. Dimarco was for the idea and suggested I join in, but – well, like I said, it didn't work out.'

'You mean two's company, three's a crowd,' said Clara, perceptively.

'I don't think Dimarco enjoyed it when Jason and I were—' Daniel broke off.

'These things are always dangerous,' Madden told him. 'Two's definitely company.'

He looked at Clara, but she didn't meet his gaze.

'Thanks, Daniel. This must be as painful for you as it is for us,' he said.

'Sorry I'm no angel,' Daniel apologised.

Madden and Clara were driving back from Cambridge to London. He had just turned onto the M25. She had been silent for much of the journey. Clara was always silent when she was turning things over in her mind. Suddenly she turned to him and said, 'There's so much I didn't know about our son.'

'What parents know their children?' asked Madden.

'All that taking Ecstasy and stuff – having sex on it – I had no idea.'

'We never had any need of it.'

She looked straight ahead at the road in front.

'It was always good between us, Clara, wasn't it? Whatever else was bad. If we were good at something we were certainly good at that.'

'What did you think of Daniel?' She changed the subject, rather deliberately.

'A corrupting influence. You didn't answer my question.'

'I wasn't aware it was a question.'

'You happy?' he asked her.

'Of course I'm happy. And you, Steve, are you happy?'

The Golden Rule. Never show you're down.

'Until this happened, I was feeling great.'

'Have you got anybody at the moment?' she asked rather cautiously.

'Depends on what you mean by "got". It's nothing serious.'

'Oh.' She seemed somewhat surprised. 'Would I be prying if I asked who?'

'She's a friend. That's all. A colleague. We work together. You've met her, in fact. Detective Sergeant Jasmine Carol.'

Clara looked startled.

'The one who interviewed me?'

'The same one. Like I said, it's nothing serious. I don't want it to be and she doesn't want it to be.'

'She's Asian,' said Clara.

'Racism isn't one of my shortcomings.'

'Nor mine. You just surprised me, that's all. After you had that affair with a colleague last time, you swore you'd never get involved with anybody on the force again.'

'I'm not involved with her. And anyway, that was when we were married.'

'Remember the problems it caused for her? She didn't get the promotion she wanted because it got around she was sleeping with her superiors and you said—'

'With Jaz it's different. Nobody knows about it. We work together. And that's the way we play it. No one at the station suspects a thing. And that's the way we intend keeping it.'

'I'm relieved to hear it.'

'Clara, you've got your life and I've got mine. You've got to accept that.'

Rich coming from him, he thought. Was *she* jealous? He hardly dared speculate.

'We have to talk about Jason's funeral,' she said.

'I know. I've been thinking about that. I'd like it to be private but I don't want it to exclude Jason's friends. And I don't want it to exclude Jason, either.'

'What do you mean?'

Madden knew in his heart how it had to be. It could be no other way.

'We have to celebrate his life. We have to be honest about what he did. People will know, anyway. We mustn't hide it. That's what I mean about not excluding Jason.'

I'm happy, dad. I'm happy.

'I refused to face the truth once. I'm not doing it a second time.'

18

Nevertheless, Madden fell to rock bottom at the funeral. He tried
to pull himself up. There was a job to do and he was the only
one who was doing it. He looked around him in the church and
remembered the murder of a little Brighton schoolgirl called
Alison Betts. The service had taken place right here. Sitting at
the back was a twenty-eight-year-old hospital porter called George
Anthony Mooney. It had been he who had sexually assaulted the
girl, barely ten, strangled her, and hidden her body in a woodland
three miles away. The police had secretly taken photographs at the
funeral, and Mooney had been caught on camera, an unfamiliar
and unknown face among the mourners.

It was not unknown for murderers to attend their victims'
funerals and to visit their graves. Yet there was no police officer
taking photographs here. The killer was in jail, charged, and on
remand. Or so it seemed. Madden looked around at the faces. He
recognised most of them. Daniel Donoghue was there, wearing a
black suit that had the look and cut of Gucci or Hugo Boss, and
he wondered how an impoverished student could afford such a
suit. When you were a policeman, you wondered about things like
that. Or maybe it wasn't so mysterious.

Roger Dimarco was there, and his wife Celestine. Dimarco
looked ashen-faced, and Celestine was holding his hand. Madden
wondered about Dimarco. Here was a man well known in the
media, a millionaire many times over, attending the funeral of
a teenager he had paid for sex. Madden hadn't expected him
to come. Yet he was there, unafraid to be seen, unafraid to be
noticed. The papers had revealed the fact that Jason had been
working as a male prostitute. A horrible thought had flashed

through Madden's mind. Was it possible that Jason might have been blackmailing Dimarco?

He found it impossible to believe that his own son could have been a blackmailer. He found it impossible to believe that Dimarco, had he been the victim of blackmail, would have wanted to attend the funeral.

When you were a policeman, you wondered thoughts like that.

Then he saw Ming. She was dabbing her eyes somewhat theatrically, he thought, and wearing a bright purple dress and purple shoes. She carried a bunch of white and green lilies. One thought that had never occurred to him was that he would attend his own son's funeral and be sitting a few places away from a transsexual Thai prostitute.

His colleagues were there in force too, to show their respects, but not to hunt for a killer. Maybe they were right. Maybe the killer was already inside. He hoped so. Sometimes the end justified the means. Fieldhouse, built like an army barracks, had brought along his wife, a woman so tiny she looked as though she could fit in his pocket. A comical thought flitted across Madden's brain.

The Fieldhouse and the field mouse.

Millington was there, and Madden remembered that he was a Methodist. He couldn't rely on Fieldhouse, but he reckoned he could on Millington. Millington was an honest cop, had been all his life. There wasn't a stain on Millington.

Next to Madden stood Clara, the person he most wanted to be there. On the other side of her stood The Accountant From the Black Lagoon. It wasn't a day for animosity, and at least on this day he had the satisfaction of knowing that he had spent a few hours in Clara's company, unbeknown to the man who had taken her away from him. He still wondered what Clive had been doing in London until late that evening on the day when Clara had rung him at lunchtime to break the news that their son was dead.

When you were a policeman, you never stopped. Wondering.

On the other side of him was Jaz. Clara and Jaz had given each other a silent nod of recognition as they'd entered the church. He would introduce them properly after the service. A police interview wasn't a proper introduction. Jaz squeezed his arm, a gesture of emotional support.

Madden stood up and walked to the lectern. He addressed the hushed congregation.

'You will all have read things in the papers about Jason,' he began. 'It is painful to read in the papers about a son you should have known better than you did. Those who know their children are truly lucky. But we were lucky too.'

He looked at Clara. She looked at him. Clive looked down between his legs and tapped his fingertips together.

'We had a son who lived life to the full. He was happy, in his own way. It was maybe not a way that everyone here might accept, and there will be some among you who will think that the way Jason lived was morally wrong. I want to defend it. He chose it for himself. He did not choose it out of necessity, or greed, but as an alternative if unconventional lifestyle. There are many people who live in our city who live unconventional lives. We do have a reputation for being a somewhat bohemian place. Someone who knew Jason said to me that he was a decent boy. The two are not incompatible.'

He had no notes. He hadn't even known what he was going to say.

'We have to accept that our children will not always turn out the way we expected them to. Jason's tragic and premature death must be a lesson to us all that we can take nothing for granted in this world. Especially life. It is a precious gift, whatever we do with it, and I believe Jason did with his what was right for him. His reasons for choosing that life are still a mystery to me, but I hope that one day I will understand. I ask you to stand in memory of my son and not to judge him.'

The congregation stood. Madden returned to his place beside Clara. Ming was weeping and her sobs could be heard all over the church.

'That was beautiful, honey,' she said, outside in the sunshine.

'It was unplanned, believe me.'

'It was still beautiful,' she said.

Then came the burial. It seemed strangely anticlimactic after the service. With his words, Madden had put Jason where he belonged. Now he had to watch him put in the ground where no one belonged. Neither he nor Clara had favoured cremation. Jason had left no wishes, too young ever to contemplate the necessity to do so. It passed almost in a blur. Clara gripped his hand. They each threw a clod of earth onto the coffin lid. Ming threw a green and a white lily. Daniel Donoghue appeared emotionless as he dropped his handful of soil into the grave. Madden wondered at that. But then, people showed their grief in different ways. Some found it difficult to show it at all. Perhaps Daniel was one of those.

They drifted away from the graveside. Madden bottled up his grief. There would be plenty of time later to show it.

He was introduced by Ming to some gay friends of Jason's. One had punky green and orange spiked hair and a ring through his tongue, the sight of which made Madden squirm. He wore jeans and a white T-shirt. His name was Kevin. There was a tall willowy baby-faced boy called Marky who could have been no older than seventeen. A third boy had slight Spanish features and lips that looked as though they had been artificially inflated. He was called Joe and was a dancer, among other things. None of them had turned up formally dressed. Madden was quite glad. Convention was fine, but truthfulness was better. These lads had turned up to mourn Jason in the way they knew.

Madden guessed they were all escorts. That was the word they preferred.

'Hello, Mr Madden,' said Daniel. 'Mrs Madden.'

'Why don't you call us Steve and Clara?' Madden put a hand on his shoulder.

The suit was Armani. He caught a glimpse of the label.

'You were Jason's friend, almost one of the family.'

'Thanks. That's really cool.'

Madden walked up to the Dimarcos. They were about to get into their car. Celestine looked stunning in black, like one of those Scottish widows on the poster. She even had the ankles to go with it.

'Thanks for coming, Mr Dimarco,' he said.

'I thought you might object.'

'Why should I?'

'Obvious reasons. If you don't mind, we'll slip away now. I'm not sure you'd welcome me at the reception.'

'Everyone is welcome,' said Madden.

'All the same, we'll take our leave.'

'Whatever you prefer.'

'It was a lovely service,' said Celestine. 'You said some lovely things about Jason.'

'He was my son,' Madden reminded her.

The Dimarcos drove away. Madden noted they hadn't come in the Bentley that had been parked outside their house, but in an unostentatious Renault Mégane. He wondered if they'd hired it specially, so as to keep a low profile. He and Clara had asked for the press to grant them privacy, and the press had, perhaps only for once, complied.

He looked at Clara who was talking to Fieldhouse and Millington. Then he turned to Clive who was looking as though he wanted to leave.

'Thanks for coming, Clive,' he said. 'I appreciate it.'

Do you know I went to Cambridge with your wife two days ago?

'That's all right. I came for Clara's sake,' he replied, with a singular lack of tact.

'Look after her.'

'I do. I don't want you using this to keep seeing her. If you know what I mean.'

Madden felt his heart start to thump very fast. Was he hearing this man right?

'I know you've wanted to plan the funeral together, and that's only right and proper, but I don't want you hanging around her any more. You know what I mean?'

'No, I don't know what you mean.'

'I know you've parked near our flat. I know you've watched her. I want it to stop, Steve. I don't want any unpleasantness. Believe me. This is probably a good time to say it.'

'Why is it a good time? Because I'm vulnerable, is that it?'

'I just don't want you hanging around her. She's made a new life and – well, that's all I want to say, really.'

'Good,' said Madden. 'I'm only human, remember that.'

'Let's both try and behave like human beings then, shall we?'

'I was under the impression I was.'

Madden left Clive before being tempted to say other things he might have regretted. Jack Fieldhouse shook his hand.

'Glad this sorry business is over, Steve,' he consoled his colleague.

'It's never over.'

'You know what I mean.'

Madden knew what he meant. Fieldhouse had wrapped up the case, and quick. He didn't want prizes but he just wanted Madden to be aware of it. That was what he meant.

Finally, he took Jaz over to meet Clara.

'Jasmine, this is my ex-wife Clara. You've met, of course. Jasmine's my partner.'

'I heard,' said Clara, kissing her cheek. 'Pleased to meet you properly.'

'Pleased to meet you too, Mrs Westmacott.'

Westmacott, thought Madden. She really didn't suit that name. Then he saw Clive anxiously pacing, wishing it were all over. He and Clara had arranged the reception at the Albion Hotel. It wasn't over yet.

Madden left Clara and Jaz talking. Clara was saying how difficult it must be to break news of a death to relatives. Jaz replied that it was all part of the job they had to do.

There was a part of the job he still had to do.

'Sir, can I have a word with you in private?' he said to Millington.

'Sure, Steve, let's go and sit in the car.'

They sat in Millington's car and Madden spread his hands out on the dashboard.

'There's something I'm not easy about, sir.'

'Oh?'

'Have we got the right man?'

'The evidence is pretty straightforward. Motive, opportunity, forensic.'

'Certain people in Brighton would like to see Panagoulis put away.'

'You mean Frank Sullivan and his little empire? I'm aware of that. Villains are a bit like air, they rush in to fill a vacuum.'

'What if that vacuum's too convenient?'

'Are you implying that Panagoulis was set up? Framed?'

'No, sir. But an impeccable source informs me that Jack Fieldhouse met Sullivan between Panagoulis's arrest and his being charged.'

Millington took the suggestion stoically, even though it horrified him. When an officer came to you with this kind of information, it was never pleasant or easy.

'How impeccable a source?'

'One I have no reason not to trust.'

'Are you telling me one of my best officers is in league with Sullivan?'

'I'm telling you what my impeccable source said. I'm not drawing conclusions. Okay, Panagoulis might be our man, though there's a lot about it I don't like. Neither do I like the thought of a fellow officer egging the pudding and perhaps profiting from the recipe.'

Millington leant back and stared at the backs of his hands as though there was some solution etched on the back of them. It was evident that he didn't want to believe any of it.

'That's a very serious charge, Steve.'

'I'm not making it. I'm just stating facts.'

'Can you get me evidence?'

'Difficult.'

'Then my hands are tied. I can't do anything. We've charged a man and it's going to be pretty bad for the morale of the force if we suddenly decide that the charge was unfounded. Worse, that a fellow officer was involved.'

'This isn't any victim. This is my son.'

'I haven't lost sight of that.'

'I'm not going to allow anyone to play politics with Jason's death. And that includes you, sir. With respect. I want the truth and I'm going to find it.'

Millington bristled at his tone.

'And how do you propose to do that?'

'By making my own enquiries.'

'Then let me give you some advice, Steve. Be careful.'

'You mean, by not stirring up trouble?'

'Just be discreet.'

'I have your authority?'

'You don't have my authority. You've never spoken to me about this. I have no recollection of the conversation. What you do have is some leave, to get over this tragedy. Take as long as you like. Now, hadn't we better get to the reception?'

Madden opened the car door. He watched the mourners filing into cars to go to the hotel. He saw Ming, still clutching the rest of the green and white lilies to her bosom. The door of a black saloon was opened for her, and she got into the back, just like a real lady.

'Thank you, sir,' said Madden.

19

The call was unexpected. Whether or not it was unwelcome, Madden wasn't sure. It came through at five o'clock, just as he arrived home from the supermarket with a bag of groceries. The day following Jason's funeral was already beginning to feel pretty empty, pretty desolate. He had to admit that he didn't have a clue to work on. Just a gut feeling that something was wrong. And he'd had a bad night, replaying over and over again that evening when Jason had come home, and he'd thrown away the best chance he'd ever had to build a bridge between them.

He knew that was why he hated Clive so much. If he hadn't taken Clara away from him, she would have been there that night. They'd have spoken to Jason together. There would probably have been some soul-searching because no father wanted to be told he was never going to have grandchildren. But in the end it would have been all right. He would have come round. Jason could have had parents to whom he wasn't scared to take his problems.

'Mr Madden?'

'Yes, who's that?'

'This is Demos, Mr Madden. Demos Panagoulis.'

Demos was on remand. He was entitled to make phone calls.

'What do you want?'

'I didn't kill your son, Mr Madden. You've got to believe that. I went to the flat that night but I couldn't get in so I went away again. That's the truth. I swear on my mother's life.'

'Why should I believe you?'

'I know you have no reason to. But I don't know what else to do, who else to tell. I just hoped I could get through to you.'

'The evidence suggests that you were in the flat, Mr Panagoulis.'

'I swear I don't know how. I swear it!'

Demos could have torn into the police at that moment, accused them of planting evidence. He didn't. Madden wasn't sure whether to count that as a point in his favour.

'Neither do I,' said Madden. 'Unless you were there.'

Demos sounded as though he was crying. Even hard men became depressed and cried when they got banged up, especially if it was for something they hadn't done.

'Please help me,' he said. 'You want to find out who really killed your son, don't you?'

'The evidence points to you, Demos.'

'I never saw him that morning! I never hurt him in my life, I had no reason to! I rang him a few times, I went round there, but he never answered or wasn't in. I swear that's the truth.'

'You supplied him with drugs. You bought his body and paid him in cocaine and E, which he used. You call that not hurting him? He was nineteen years old, a teenager.'

'I don't feel proud of that, Mr Madden.'

'Good.'

'If I'd paid him in money, he would have just bought the drugs he wanted.'

'That's hardly the point.'

'The point is if I get life for this, Jason's killer is still out there.'

'Give me one good reason why I should believe you, Demos. Just one.'

They were cut off. Panagoulis's phonecard had probably run out. He didn't ring back.

Madden spent the next ten minutes putting away groceries into cupboards. He found himself doing it without even thinking about it. His mind was elsewhere. He didn't know whether to believe Panagoulis or not. Some criminals had an enormous capacity to swear that they were innocent, but not many phoned up the father of their victim and pleaded for justice. In his twenty-seven years in the force, he had never heard of it happening, not once. It had to count for something.

He made a few discreet and one or two less than discreet

inquiries and late that evening headed for the Red Planet, the newest and the biggest of the gay nightclubs in Brighton. It stood right on the front, halfway between the two piers, and had been a hotel until it was gutted by a mysterious fire, reckoned to be an insurance job but never subsequently proved. Now the phoenix had risen from the ashes. The queue stretched halfway round the block. A pair of bow-tied gorillas with shaven heads and barrel chests guarded the doors in time-worn intimidating fashion.

Madden produced his International Disco Card. That's what it was jokingly called. The warrant card had its misuses. He knew young DIs who went up to London, flashed them at the doors of clubs, and walked in ahead of the queue.

The gorilla nodded him in. The throb of music and the dry ice billowing out of the darkness assaulted his senses. He saw a group of kids who were obviously high on Ecstasy. They had their arms round each other and one was telling his friends how much he loved them all. Madden could tell what they were on just by looking at their eyes. One of the conditions of the International Disco Card was that you didn't interfere, you didn't make trouble. If there *was* any trouble, you helped sort it out, taking the side of the management. That was the way it went. You were expected to turn a blind eye while hundreds of kids destroyed their brain cells every night.

Madden went up the stairs to the manager's office. It was basic, but with heavy carpeting that complemented the people on it. Frank Sullivan was expecting him. There was a scene in every gangster movie that went like this: Mr Big sat framed behind a desk that was miles too large for any paperwork he was either interested in or expected to deal with. The desk itself was framed by two thugs, neither of whom spoke, one of whom was probably black and looked as though he could tear telephone directories in half, the other bald and flashing a gold tooth. Frank Sullivan had seen that movie. He had seen a lot of movies like it. And he liked that kind of movie. But there the resemblance stopped.

Frank Sullivan looked like most people's favourite uncle. In his fifties but prematurely white-haired, with a broad face and a genial smile and wearing a red blazer sprouting a silk handkerchief, he could have presided over a children's Christmas party without raising anyone's eyebrow. The only detail about his person that detracted from that image was the collection of rings on his fingers. They were no ordinary rings. In the room with him was the manager of the club, an insignificant and weaselly-looking individual whom Sullivan promptly dismissed, and a couple of apes in evening wear who were barely distinguishable from the others downstairs.

'Thank you for coming here to meet me.' Madden thought it best to be polite to start with.

'Not at all. I've moved to Brighton now. I like the sea air,' said Frank Sullivan, stepping forward and extending his hand – and then withdrawing it when Madden showed no sign of reciprocating. 'And it gives me a chance to keep my eye on my newest and most exciting club yet.'

'I'm sure you'll be a welcome addition to our growing business community.'

'The pink pound, Mr Madden. It's there for the reaping. Well, tell me: what do you think of the Red Planet?'

'Not my scene,' said Madden. 'Maybe twenty years ago.'

'Twenty years ago it was a different scene. I'm sure you remember. It's all love, peace and happiness now. The kids enjoy themselves, we enjoy ourselves, that's what life should be about. Enjoying oneself.'

'I had a son who was doing that until a week ago,' said Madden.

'I was really sorry to hear about that.' Sullivan lowered his head. 'Really tragic. You have my deepest sympathy.'

'Thank you.'

'Glad you locked up the bastard responsible, Mr Madden. Can't have people like that running around. Gives us business people a bad name.'

'Is that what you call yourselves? Business people?'

'I'm a businessman, Mr Madden. I can't speak for others, naturally.'

'That's what I came to talk to you about.'

'Anything I can do to help. I enjoy working with the police. I enjoy working with anybody who lets me get on with my business while they get on with theirs. Now I can't say fairer than that, can I?'

Sullivan's security personnel folded their arms and one grinned, showing enough gold to cause a rush. You didn't get past these guys unless you were wearing the right brand of trainers, Madden thought. Come to think of it, the right face probably helped as well.

'You were pretty quick to move in,' Madden said. 'I'm talking about your own security business.'

'I saw a gap in the market. That's good business. Demos Panagoulis, his outfit was stinking. Corrupt. Who is going to employ a company run by a man like that? I would rather handle the security in my own clubs and know that the job is being done properly.'

'Word is there are now quite a few gaps in the market. With Panagoulis out of the way.'

'All of them plugged, I'm pleased to say. Nature abhors a vacuum.'

'Human nature abhors an injustice.' Madden smiled.

'Are you accusing me of something, Mr Madden?' Frank Sullivan adopted an expression of choirboy innocence and opened his arms expansively.

'No. I'm just here as a father making a few inquiries. Making sure that the right man is inside for the murder of my son.'

'He's been charged, hasn't he?'

'Yes. But, as you know, an arrest is only a beginning. It's a long journey between suspicion and guilt beyond a reasonable doubt. A journey you've never made yourself.'

'Correct. And not a journey I think I'm ever likely to make.'

'Oh, I don't know, Mr Sullivan. I hear the travel agents are pretty busy this year.'

Sullivan chortled. 'I like you, Mr Madden. I like a man with a sense of humour.'

'I also have a sense of fair play.'

'Me too. Cigarette?'

He offered Madden one from a carved ivory box. Madden got the feeling he only wanted to show off his rings.

'No, thank you.'

'You see those rings, Mr Madden? Each tells a story. Would you like to hear one?'

He'd been right.

'So long as it's short.'

'Oh, it's very short. You see, these rings are all ancient. Perfectly genuine. They're all Roman. I have a penchant for antiquities.'

'Yes, I'd heard.'

As well as drugs, Sullivan was reputed to have both bought and smuggled ancient relics from various locations around the world. It wasn't so much a penchant as a passion. A man had to have a hobby.

'This one in particular—'

He twisted from his right forefinger a thick silver ring in which was set a piece of red glass. He held it out for Madden to inspect. There was a figure engraved on the glass.

'How old do you think that is?'

'Surprise me.'

'First century AD. Solid silver. The setting is just red glass but the figure engraved on it is a god.'

'Which god?

The God of Bullshit, perhaps.

'A Roman god. I don't know which one. But the point is, this ring was forged not long after Christ was crucified. It was excavated in Jerusalem. I've had it assessed by experts and it would have belonged on the finger of a person high up in the Roman army. Perhaps a general.'

'Really. How impressive.'

'And now –' he slid it back over the joint of his forefinger '– it is on my hand.'

'And the point, Mr Sullivan?'

'This ring is history. Ancient history. I am wearing a piece of the Roman Empire. The greatest empire the world has ever seen. An empire that gave the world democracy, trade, industry, roads, great cities. An empire that believed in fair play. Peace, prosperity. Do you know what it means to wear a ring like that?'

'I can imagine,' said Madden.

'I see myself as rather like that Roman general. Fair. Honest. Industrious.'

'Do you mind if we get back to the point of my visit, Mr Sullivan?'

'Not at all. You've listened to my little talk. Now the least I can do is listen to you.'

He sat back down behind his desk and waved his hand at his security personnel. They departed on cue. Perhaps, Madden thought, it had something to do with the power of the ring.

'I didn't come here so you could lecture me on your legitimacy,' Madden explained. 'I just wondered if Panagoulis's arrest perhaps sparked off a little opportunism.'

'Opportunism?'

'Yes. The opportunity to move in on his operations without having to remove him physically, which, as a law-abiding gentleman, you would be against.'

Frank Sullivan liked the law-abiding bit. You could tell.

'Like I said, Mr Madden, every businessman looks for opportunities. That's how the world goes round. A company in which I have a controlling interest now handles the security of this club, all the other ones I run, and many that I don't.'

'In Italy, where the Roman Empire began, I believe the business world goes round on bribes. Payments of money.'

'I wouldn't know,' said Sullivan.

'Payments of money to people who, let's say, just for example, help to put away inconvenient business rivals.'

'I think I get your point.'

'You wouldn't have had any help in getting Panagoulis put away, would you?'

'What kind of help?'

'I don't know. You tell me.'

'Are you accusing me of being involved in the murder of your son? Because if you are that's a serious accusation, Mr Madden. But I'm a reasonable man. I understand you've been under a lot of emotional stress because of this. And I'll tell you what I'm going to do. I'm not going to take offence.'

'That's very good of you.'

'I don't kill kids,' Sullivan said bluntly, and it was clear that he had stopped playing games.

'You just supply the stuff that destroys their brains.'

'I look after their safety. Their security. I let them dance till seven, eight, nine in the morning in the knowledge that no one's going to put a broken bottle into their face. That type doesn't get in here. If trouble breaks out, then we have a rapid-reaction force. It wasn't always like that. Twenty years ago you boys were called here almost every night to sort out trouble. Not any more.'

'All harmony now,' said Madden.

'Yes. I like to be where people are enjoying themselves. It makes me feel good. The world goes round. I'm a happy man when the world goes round.'

'Even if all that happiness is chemically induced?'

'I have ample supplies of serotonin, Mr Madden. I don't need drugs to increase it.'

'I'm talking about downstairs. And different kinds of supplies.'

'No drugs are sold in any of the clubs I control. You'll be aware I was once shut down because of an unfortunate business in North London?'

'You call the death of a teenager an unfortunate business?'

'What would you call it? Mr Panagoulis ran the security for me then. It was because of him I was shut down.'

'And now *he's* shut down. Revenge is sweet.'

Madden got up. The floor was throbbing with the music below. He felt queasy. He had to get out of Frank Sullivan's presence. The most dangerous kind of evil was evil that paraded good as its justification.

'Thanks for your time,' he said.

'Once again, please accept my condolences. I know it's not easy, losing a son. But I'm a great believer in natural human justice. It will always out.'

'Yes. It will,' Madden assured him.

He needed some fresh air. He left the club and walked down onto the beach, to the water's edge. The lights of ships blinked on the inky horizon. The throb and hum of Brighton on a Saturday night, like electricity coursing through wires, pulsated in his ears. A group of teenagers had lit a fire with some driftwood on the beach and were gathered round it. Couples meshed together like figures preserved in ash thrown out by a volcanic eruption, caught in the act, still as statues, under the night sky.

His mobile rang. It was Jasmine.

'Hi, Jaz.'

'Have you heard, Steve?'

'Heard what?'

'Demos Panagoulis is dead. He took his own life in prison. He managed to smuggle in a razor blade and slashed his wrists. They tried to save him but it was no good.' She paused. 'I'm sorry, Steve. I know what this means.'

Madden knew what it meant, too.

'It means he died technically innocent,' Madden declared.

The night closed in on him like a dark shroud. He felt a chill on the back of his neck. People were enjoying themselves, and yet he could not share their feelings. Justice seemed to retreat in all directions, and he was left with a strange, empty feeling of despair.

'Want me to come round?' she asked.

'Yeh. Make it quick. I need you,' he said.

20

They sat close together on the sofa; in the early hours of the morning. Madden felt an overwhelming sense of despair. Frank Sullivan had said justice would out, and he agreed with him. Platitudes aside, justice had cleared out. There was no way of knowing if an innocent man had died in prison or not. There was no way of knowing if a guilty man had got what he deserved. There was no way of knowing how the case could possibly be reopened now. It was all a mess. A bloody mess. When Fred West hanged himself in jail while on remand, the Crown still had Rosemary West to throw the book at. He had nobody.

'Do you really believe he was innocent?' Jaz asked him.

'Frankly, I don't know what to believe. He's the first prisoner who ever took the trouble to track down my number and ring me up.'

'Then you've got to go on, Steve. It's no use you just giving up. Suppose he was innocent? You've just to work on that theory until – until you find something else.'

'And if I don't find something else?'

'Then bring the crime back to Panagoulis. Prove it to yourself that he was guilty. And *for* yourself. The courts aren't going to be interested now. But if you give up you'll never know and you'll never forgive yourself.'

'What makes you think I could give up now?'

Madden went to his bedroom and brought out the jacket that he had worn a few days before. From the pocket he unfolded Jason's Arsenal scarf. He wasn't sure why but out of all his son's possessions that one seemed the most poignant. Perhaps it was because it reminded him of a time when they had the kind of father-and-son relationship that he wished they could have enjoyed for ever. A time of innocence.

He hung it over the mantelpiece. He vowed not to take it down until he had put a name to his son's killer.

'That says I have no intention of giving up,' he told Jaz.

'So where do we go from here?'

'Tell me about the alibis.'

'Whose alibis?'

'Anybody's. Everybody's. I haven't been going around asking that kind of question. Didn't want to put their backs up. Thought I might get more out of them that way.'

'Who do you want to start with?'

'The Dimarcos.'

'They alibi each other. The morning Jason was killed, they were two miles off Nice in a boat called the *Heraklion*. They'd gone out the previous morning and stayed out on the boat all night. Not returning until the next night.'

'That's strange. Wonder why Jason didn't go with him.'

'Maybe he wasn't asked.'

'Just the two of them?'

'Just the two.'

'Seems odd. From what I know about the Dimarco ménage. I take it the alibi's been checked? We don't just have their word for it?'

'They only alibi each other. I suppose theoretically one of them could have flown back secretly to England, committed the murder, and flown back again. But that's pretty unlikely. Then, of course, you have to entertain the possibility that they were both in on it together.'

'Let's entertain the possibility. Let's entertain every possibility. Check flights from Nice and also Marseilles back to the UK. Especially Gatwick. It's a short run from there down to the coast. Check the passenger lists of all flights. I want to know the flights they took out and the flights they came back on, and every other possibility in between. It just seems too convenient a boat trip.'

'You surely don't suspect Celestine Dimarco?'

'Just because she's a woman?'

'Her husband certainly would have a good motive.' Jasmine gave it as her opinion.

'Discovery?'

'A man in his position might not want it to get round that he was having a relationship with a nineteen-year-old male prostitute. He might go to any lengths to conceal it.'

'Only if he felt threatened,' Madden said. 'And don't try and tell me Jason was blackmailing him.'

'I wasn't going to. Only—'

'Only what?'

'Nothing.'

'Come on, Jaz. Only what? Say what's on your mind.'

'Okay. If you must know, Steve, it did cross my mind. But only because I'm thinking like a police officer. You're his father. You're not detached. You want to think the best about Jason and I don't blame you. I would if he'd been my son. But if he'd been anybody else's son and you were investigating the case, the first thing you'd consider would be blackmail.'

'Okay. It crossed my mind too. But Jason had already had everything he wanted out of Dimarco. Why would he throw away a good thing? By all accounts, he looked on the guy like a—'

He hesitated.

'Like a father,' he said, painfully.

'By whose accounts?'

'Dimarco and his wife.' He added, 'And I don't believe Dimarco would risk showing up at Jason's funeral if he didn't want to be connected with him. That goes against the grain.' Then, 'What about Daniel, the boyfriend?'

'Claims he spent the entire morning in his room at Cambridge, working on his dissertation.'

'Did he see anybody? Speak to anybody?'

'He claims that he had a webcam conversation with Jason at about half-past nine. You know, one of these where you talk face to face over the Internet.'

'What? He didn't tell me that.'

'They spoke for about half an hour, apparently.'

'What about?'

'I'd have to look at his statement. I don't have it with me right now. As far as I remember, it was nothing specific. Just lovers' talk. Jason didn't say he was expecting a client that morning, didn't mention Panagoulis. In fact, there was nothing that pointed to his killer.'

'All the same, Daniel was possibly the last person to talk to Jason before he was killed.'

'He didn't volunteer that when you met him?' she asked.

'No. Thought it might be something he would. What's his dissertation about?'

'Perec.'

'What or who the hell is Perec?'

'A French author. Apparently he wrote an entire novel without using the letter "e".'

'Sounds like we ought to arrest *him*,' Madden said.

'You mean Daniel?'

'No. This French guy. Before he does something *really* crazy.'

It was the first time she had seen him smile that evening. It was worth holding on to.

'You suspect the boyfriend?'

'I always suspect a lover.'

It was one o'clock in the morning.

'Do you want me to go home?' Jaz asked. 'Then we can continue this discussion in the morning.'

'Jaz, you don't have to go home if you don't want to.'

'It's late.'

'I know it's late, and it's been a difficult night for both of us. If you want to stay, do. I'm not pressurising you.'

'Okay,' she said. 'I'll stay.'

'And I promise not to think about Clara.'

'I promise to help you.'

Madden put his arms round her and held her to him. She didn't pull away. She rested her cheek against his shoulder. She was twenty years younger than him. What she saw in a forty-eight-year-old detective who was still hung up on his former wife, he could not imagine. Maybe it didn't do any good to probe too deeply. Sometimes the answers weren't what you wanted to hear. Neither was he sure why this night seemed right and others didn't. He wasn't about to ask.

They went to bed and made love for an hour on top of the sheets, both naked. He was true to his word and didn't think about Clara once. In the morning it would be business as usual, with each of them pretending that nothing had happened. It was the way they played it. Without any emotional attachment. He enjoyed the feel and the taste of her chestnut-coloured skin next to him, she enjoyed the warmth and the contours of his not-too-perfect body. And after bringing each other to climax, she fell asleep in a complex huddle, her head on his chest, her legs woven through this, and he lay awake for a few minutes longer, his arm wound round the small of her back.

Out in the Channel, a ship sounded its horn, a low, deep rasp reverberating through the night. Madden knew that moments like this were worth savouring. The greatest gift you could give somebody was the chance, no matter how fleeting, to forget pain.

21

Madden had only been asleep for half an hour when he heard the banging at the front door. For a few moments he thought that he was dreaming. Then he looked at the clock. 2.30 a.m. And someone was definitely banging on the front door. Not ringing the bell. But hammering on the panels with a fist.

Jaz was sleeping through it all, slumbering away sweetly in the crook of his arm. He gently slid it out from under her, got out of bed, pulled on his trousers, and ran down the stairs. The first thing he thought about was what he had read about communist countries when a bang on the door in the middle of the night signified an arrest and transportation to some place from which you never returned. It was a ridiculous comparison. Such things didn't happen in Brighton.

He pulled the door open, determined to give whoever it was a piece of his mind.

Jack Fieldhouse was standing there, looking like a zombie, staring straight in at him, his expression locked in a surly grimace. A wave of alcoholic fumes hit Madden full in the face. He was drunk. Blind drunk. He staggered forwards and all but fell into the house.

Madden caught him. Then he saw that his colleague had urinated on the front doorstep. Fieldhouse's trousers were soaked all down the front. Madden found in a cupboard an old sheet that had been used the last time the house had been decorated, threw it over the sofa, and let Fieldhouse fall down onto it. Under his colleague's weight, the sofa nearly went over backwards with the burly detective on it.

'You know what time it is?' Madden fired at him, deciding not to conceal his annoyance.

'Sorry to break in on you, Steve.' Fieldhouse slurred. 'You heard about it?'

'Yes. I heard about it.'

'I'm sorry.'

'I'm sorry, too.'

He thought of Jaz upstairs. And he saw her bag by the side of a chair. He kicked it gently, tucking it underneath. And then he remembered her car parked outside. That distinctive little purple number with the yellow upholstery and the cream-coloured dashboard. He hoped that Fieldhouse was too drunk to have noticed it. He cursed himself for not reminding Jaz to move it. They had never been that complacent before. The last thing he wanted was Jack Fieldhouse going back to the station, dropping all kinds of hints and making innuendos about the fact that Jasmine had stayed the night at his house. Fieldhouse was perfectly capable of it. Not only was he capable of it but Madden was convinced that he would enjoy it.

'Stay there, Jack,' he said to him.

Fieldhouse wasn't going anywhere. Not in that state. He wondered how he had found his way to his house. Surely he hadn't driven. He went to the front door again and looked out. The smell of the pool of urine on the front doorstep assaulted his nostrils. He looked up and down the street and couldn't see Fieldhouse's car. He felt a sense of relief in that he had probably walked. He doubted whether a taxi driver would have picked him up in that state.

He came back inside. Fieldhouse had his head thrown back and was talking to himself. Madden couldn't make out any structured sentences, just a few words. He thought he heard 'For you, Steve' and 'Did it for you'.

He hurried upstairs to the bedroom. Jaz had woken and was sitting up in bed.

'What's wrong?' she asked.

'Keep your voice down. Jack Fieldhouse is downstairs. He's drunk as a lord. He's pissed on the front doorstep and he's flat out on the settee right now.'

'What are we going to do?'

'He mustn't see you. Stay in here and keep the door shut. I don't know whether he saw your car. We should have moved it earlier.'

'How are you going to get rid of him?'

'I could put him in my car, take him home and dump him on his own front doorstep. I might just have to. That's if I can get him in there. He's not exactly a lightweight. But first I've got to make sure your car isn't outside. Even if he didn't notice it coming in, he might notice it going out. I'd better move it. Give me your keys.'

'They're in my bag downstairs.'

'Whatever you do, don't step out of this room.'

He kissed her, and closed the door. When he went back downstairs Fieldhouse was sitting with his eyes wide open, swaying back and forwards.

'Got to go to the toilet,' he said.

'Why don't you use the back garden, Jack? It'll save you going up the stairs.'

Fieldhouse managed to stand up on his own. Madden led him through the kitchen into the rear garden where he relieved himself on the grass. Madden looked up, hoping none of his neighbours would glance out at that moment. It was remarkable how noisy someone urinating in a garden at the dead of night could be. When Fieldhouse was finished, he made his own way back inside, staggering as he walked.

He fell over the sofa as he came back into the lounge and landed with a crash. There he stayed, his buttocks on the floor, his features twisted into an expression of remorse.

'Steve, I want you to know—' Fieldhouse said. 'We did it. We got him. You and me got him. Bastard's dead. Dead. Dead. Told you – I wouldn't let you down. Forty-eight hours. Forty-eight hours, Steve.'

Madden knelt down and surreptitiously removed the keys from Jasmine's bag.

'I know, Jack. Forty-eight hours.'

'I did it for you.'

'So you keep telling me.'

'I did it for you,' Fieldhouse told him again.

Madden had to move Jasmine's car but he didn't want Fieldhouse crashing about the house in the couple of minutes he would be out, and perhaps walking into the bedroom and seeing Jasmine. Still, it was a risk he had to take. Jasmine would be on her guard, though he doubted she could do very much to hold the door if Fieldhouse suddenly decided it led to the toilet and not the bedroom.

He slipped out of the front door without saying anything, unlocked Jasmine's car, slid inside and started the engine. He drove it twenty yards up the road, parked it round the corner, and walked back.

Jack Fieldhouse was still in the same position.

'I did it for you,' he said for the fifth time.

Then Madden had a better idea than driving Fieldhouse home himself. He didn't see why he should be burdened. Fieldhouse had done nothing for him. It would have been better if Fieldhouse had done nothing at all. He owed him zero favours.

He phoned Fieldhouse's home. His wife answered. Her name was Lesley.

'Lesley, Steve Madden here. Sorry to wake you up at this time of the morning but I've got your husband at my place. He's drunk out of his mind and I can't move him. I think he ought to be at home.'

He hoped she wouldn't say 'Leave him there.' Some detectives' wives would. He wasn't sure what Clara would have done. It had never happened to him.

'Don't worry.' She put him at ease. 'I'll be right round.'

The words were spoken not with anxiety but with gritty determination. Madden put down the phone. He smiled to himself. The field mouse had teeth.

'Your wife's on her way, Jack,' he said.

'I want you to know, Steve,' Fieldhouse babbled on, swaying again as he sat on the carpet with his back against the sofa, 'you and me – we'll always be friends. I did it for you.'

And then the big detective did something else for Madden. He vomited over the floor.

'Thanks, Jack,' said Madden. 'I really appreciate that.'

Lesley Fieldhouse arrived about twenty minutes later. When she walked in and saw the state of her husband and the pool of sick on Madden's carpet, she threw up her hands in anger.

'You bloody idiot! Look at the state of you!' she screamed at him. 'Get up off the floor and get into the car. And look what you've done to Steve's carpet. What a bloody state. I really am sorry, Steve, you've no idea how sorry I am.'

'That's okay.' Madden was only pleased to be seeing the back of his unwanted visitor. 'I'm just glad you're here to take him home.'

'This is not the first time,' she said.

'I'm sure it's not.'

'He was really distraught when that guy killed himself in prison. You must be, too.'

'It's a big setback.' Madden underplayed it.

'Still, there was no doubt about him being guilty, was there?'

'No, no doubt,' Madden lied.

'Off the floor, you big hunk,' she said, hauling at her husband's arm. Madden pulled at the other one. Fieldhouse got to his feet.

'See you, Jack.' Madden said goodbye. He meant good riddance.

'You want some help to clear that up?' Lesley asked him.

'Don't worry. What you're doing is already beyond the call of duty.'

Fieldhouse, his lower lip drooping, his eyes bloodshot, made one last long lingering leer at Steve Madden. 'I did it for you,' he said again.

And then he was gone. Madden watched just to make sure as the car pulled away. He fetched a bucket of water and a cloth and a dustpan from the kitchen and set about the unpleasant task of wiping up the mess.

He went upstairs where Jasmine was sitting up in bed, having been well out of it.

'Drama over,' he said, stripping off his trousers and getting back into bed. 'Had a bit of a mess to clear up downstairs. He threw up on the floor.'

'Oh Steve, I'd have helped you.'

'If you think you're staying round here and getting involved in that kind of thing, you're mistaken. Not exactly the best way to end a romantic night.'

'That was sex, Steve. I don't do romance.'

'Sorry. I forgot.'

'Do you think he saw my car?'

'I've no idea. I wasn't exactly going to ask him. The state he was in, I doubt it. We'll have to be more careful in future.'

'We will, won't we?'

She snuggled up next to him. He turned off the light.

'I don't think you'll have much trouble working with him tomorrow,' he told her. 'I doubt you'll see him much earlier than noon.'

'That's nice,' she murmured.

'Yes. Breakfast at eight?'

'Breakfast at nine,' she said.

In the morning they made love again. They were interrupted by the ringing of the telephone. Madden didn't answer it but let it go on the answerphone. He knew the caller. He wasn't in any mood to talk to a reporter from the local newspaper. Jasmine lay on top of him and took him inside her just as Clara had done.

'You're terrific,' he said.

'I try to please my superiors,' she quipped.

'Not too many of them, I hope.'

'I'd draw the line at Fieldhouse. And Chief Superintendent Millington.'

'I'm glad to hear that, Jaz. You're a girl with honour.'

He phoned back Graeme Cuthbertson at the *Brighton Argus*. Madden and Jaz were sitting in the kitchen, having breakfast. He knew Cuthbertson well. He was a canny Scottish guy with a good nose for the bizarre and the off-beam. He had once run a long-running story about a love affair between two bottlenose dolphins that had appeared one summer and taken up residence between the two piers – two bottlenose *male* dolphins, as it turned out. He'd given similar treatment to a local black-magic cult that had eventually put a hex on him. Murder was grist to Cuthbertson's mill.

He and Madden enjoyed a good relationship. Newspapers needed policemen. Policemen needed newspapers. That was the way it went.

'I'm sorry to intrude on you,' Cuthbertson said. That was newspaper man's parlance for *I want a story and I don't care how inopportune it is, I need it now.* 'I just wondered if you could tell me how you feel about Demos Panagoulis killing himself?'

From anybody else, Madden would've regarded it as a stupid question. But he knew that newspaper men had to ask obvious questions because their readers demanded equally obvious answers.

'How do I feel? I feel let down.'

'That he was never proved guilty?'

'There was no doubt in your mind, though, was there?'

Where was he coming from, Madden wondered.

'I wasn't involved in the investigation. I was shown the evidence against him. It'll never be proved now. That's all I can really say.'

'But was there any doubt in your mind?' Cuthbertson persisted.

'I was a victim in this case. I don't want to doubt it.'

'But do you have any doubts at all?'

When a newspaper man asked the same question three times, it was the question he would go on asking till he got the quote he wanted to print.

'Panagoulis died an innocent man. At least, he died innocent of murder. Does that answer your question?'

'You believe that?'

'I'm talking technicalities. The law. You get my meaning?'

'I get your meaning, Steve. Justice hasn't been done?'

'Justice hasn't been done,' said Madden. 'Theoretically the killer is still free.'

'It's just that we received a letter yesterday written by him. He said the same thing. Claimed the police had fitted him up.'

'A lot of criminals say that.'

'He was pretty passionate about it.'

'Don't ask me if I feel sorry for him, Graeme. I don't. He was an evil bastard who supplied my son with drugs. Whether or not he was his murderer is another story.'

'I'll be going with it tonight. Okay to quote you?'

'Feel free.'

Madden put the phone down. Jasmine glanced up at him, her fingers wrapped around a mug of steaming coffee.

'Something tells me the shit's going to hit the fan over this,' she said.

'Something tells me it's going to come back in my direction,' Madden commented.

It did.

That evening, the *Brighton Argus* carried the headline FATHER IN RENT-BOY MURDER CLAIMS KILLER STILL FREE.

'It hasn't hit the fan,' Jasmine told him when she rang.

'No?'

'The clouds just opened, Steve, and it rained down.'

22

By coincidence, the clouds did open the next day and it did pour down, culminating in a violent thunderstorm, high winds and twenty-foot breakers that smashed on the shore. Madden stood in Millington's office. He had never seen his superior in such a mood. He didn't know much about Methodists but had thought that they might be forgiving and understanding. He was wrong on both counts.

'What induced you to talk to the press? Millington raged.

'I didn't talk to the press, sir, they talked to me.'

'You should have talked to me first!'

'With respect, sir, I simply told them that Demos Panagoulis was innocent. Which is correct. Nothing was ever proved against him.'

'That isn't what's printed here!'

Millington slapped the paper onto his desk.

'I may have sounded ambiguous,' Madden explained.

'Ambiguous? There's nothing damned ambiguous about this! You're more or less suggesting that we arrested and charged the wrong man!'

'You know for a fact that we didn't, sir?'

'I know for a fact that there's no evidence that we did. And plenty of evidence that we didn't!'

'And if I find the evidence that Panagoulis was innocent?'

Millington sat down behind his desk and wiped his hand across his face. Torrents of water streamed down the outside of the window. The flash of lightning might as well have come from him clenching and unclenching his hands.

'You are referring to the conversation we never had.'

'I can't refer to a conversation we never had.'

'I know this isn't easy for you, Steve. No policeman likes to make an arrest and then never see it come to a trial. You feel cheated. So do I. So does everybody. This is particularly painful because Jason was your son and you're one of our own. But if we made a mistake, it means Panagoulis's suicide is our fault. We would be blamed for that.'

'So you're saying you wouldn't act on it? If it was a mistake?'

'I don't know what I could do.'

'Could do or would do, sir? You'd put the morale of the force above finding out who killed Jason?'

'Look at the position I'm in.'

Madden stepped forward and spread his hands out on Millington's desk.

'No, sir, *you* look at the position *I'm* in!' he thundered. 'Jason is dead and I have no way of knowing for sure who killed him. My own colleagues, you included, want to wrap it up in pretty pink paper and stamp it closed. Well, I don't. Why don't you take a look at Jack Fieldhouse's bank account and see if he got anything from a certain villain here in Brighton for tipping the scales and getting Panagoulis out of the way?'

'That's a serious accusation.'

'I'm making it.'

'If Sullivan wanted Panagoulis out of the way, it would have been easier for him just to arrange to have a bullet put through his head. Or have him run over one night. Or have any one of a hundred different things done to him.'

'That's murder, sir. Not quite so clever as taking advantage of one that someone else committed by getting your rival arrested for it. Look at this way. There was hostility between them, had been for a long time. Panagoulis was responsible for a club that Sullivan owned being shut down because Panagoulis let in some dodgy Ecstasy that killed a girl and sent three others to hospital. He's wanted the Greek out of his hair and out of his clubs for a long time. What better way?'

'You honestly believe he'd play that dirty?'

'I don't know what to believe any more. Or who to believe in.'

Madden took out his warrant card and threw it on Millington's desk. He reckoned on the action speaking louder than any more words.

'You can have this. I quit,' he said.

Millington gazed down at the card with a mixture of consternation and surprise. Madden wondered if anyone had ever thrown a warrant card down in front of him before in quite such a manner. But he felt aggrieved and there was no other way of driving home his point.

'Steve, think about this,' Millington pleaded.

'I've thought about it.'

'Rationally?'

'Rationally.'

'You can change your mind, you know.'

'Thank you for the option. But I've no intention of staying in a police force that puts saving its own face above finding my son's killer.'

Millington leant back in his chair, looked at Madden's warrant card again, picked it up and turned it between his fingers. He looked suitably penitent. Even chastised. *Just like a Methodist should*, thought Madden.

'Bring me the evidence. I will see what I can do. If there's been impropriety by another of my officers and an innocent man has died as an indirect result, then I promise you that I'll find a way to act on it.'

'Find a way, sir? Are you telling me there's a back-door method of reopening a case?'

'I would act on it,' Millington simply repeated.

'Even if it means destroying the morale of the force?' asked Madden.

'I don't want to go out of this job under a cloud. Nobody does,' said Millington. 'I won't have anybody saying I knew of an injustice and covered it up. If we're seen, even privately, to fail one of our own, it would be just as terrible. I hope you're wrong, Steve. I really, sincerely hope you're wrong.'

'So do I,' proclaimed Madden.

Millington tossed the warrant card back. Madden picked it up. *Point made.*

'Keep it. You might need it.'

'What I do from now on, I do as a father. Not as a copper,' Madden said, and left.

He passed Fieldhouse on the way out. He was looking a little the worse for wear. His eyes hadn't quite returned to their proper colour. Fieldhouse stared at him for a few moments as though he didn't quite recognise him.

Madden had heard that alcohol destroyed brain cells. Maybe this was the proof.

'How are you feeling, Jack?' he asked, as though he cared.

'Me? I'm feeling fine. Just fine.'

'No hangover?'

'Bit of one. Nothing I can't handle.'

'Glad you got home all right.'

'Oh, I got home okay.'

You could say sorry, you bastard, for throwing up on my carpet.

'How did you know?' Fieldhouse asked.

'Know what, Jack?'

'That I got home okay last night?'

'Well, I figured if you didn't you wouldn't be here now.'

'You weren't out with me last night,' Fieldhouse expressed bemusement.

'What do you mean, I wasn't with you? You sicked up all over my living room. I had to get Lesley to drive you home.'

'Don't remember a thing,' Fieldhouse maintained. 'Last night's a bit of a blur. Know how it is?'

'Yes, Jack. I know how it is.'

Madden shook his head and left the office. He was aware of Fieldhouse staring after him. He wouldn't put it past the bulky detective to save his face by pretending. Madden had never been so drunk he couldn't remember what he had done. He might have wanted to blot things out at times, but his success rate had not been good.

Jasmine was just getting out of her car outside. Madden told her about the conversation he had just had with Fieldhouse.

'If he's telling the truth we've got nothing to worry about,' he assured her.

'How could he just not remember a thing?'

'Let's just consider ourselves lucky. Have you got anything for me?'

'Yes. All the times you asked for.'

She passed him a note of flight times from Nice and Marseilles back to the UK and flight times in the opposite direction that might conceivably be relevant. The Dimarcos had travelled out to Nice on the morning of the day before Jason was killed and returned, the evening after the fatal day, from the same airport.

'There was no record of either of them on any flight,' she said. 'Frankly, I didn't expect there would be.'

'Why?' Madden studied the times.

'It doesn't fit in with the profile of this killer. They don't fit in with it.'

'Is this *your* profile?'

'Look at it logically. First, let's discount Celestine. No woman could do something like this. That leaves Roger. He's well known – people recognise his face. He can't just flit about Europe murdering people and not be noticed. And anyway, you said yourself that he had no motive. And then there's what was *done* to Jason. If you accept the scenario that Roger Dimarco somehow flew back to England to commit murder, he would want to get it over and done with as quickly as possible. Not hang around. Whoever murdered Jason was probably in the flat for about half an hour, searching for drugs.'

And cutting him up.

'The trouble is, Steve, there isn't really a profile of the killer at all. You said yourself, it's almost as though we're looking at two motives, one to do with a search for stolen drugs, the other connected with sex.'

'Could we be looking at two people?' He threw it open.

Jasmine appeared to have already considered it.

'Working *together*?' she speculated.

'One searches for the drugs, turns the flat upside down, while the other one gets nasty with Jason.'

'You want to believe Jason was a drug dealer as well, Steve? I thought you'd discounted that.'

'I'm ready to believe anything if it helps catch who killed him. I can forgive Jason. I can't forgive his murderer.'

'There's another possibility.' Jasmine put it to him: 'Suppose, let's suppose, that Panagoulis goes up to the flat, finds the door open. Finds Jason dead. Which really does put him at the scene. He turns the place upside down looking for the drugs, doesn't find them, leaves. Pretty unlikely, eh?'

'Pretty unlikely,' Madden agreed. 'Would Panagoulis stick around? I doubt it. I don't think he'd be that brave. And what were the drugs doing there, anyway? There's no evidence Jason stole them from him, or from anyone else. There's yet another possibility.'

'Which is?'

'That whoever killed Jason wanted us to go round the houses like this. That the whole thing was far simpler than it looks.'

'You mean the scene was set up?'

'Wouldn't be the first time.'

Clever killers made him think about Daniel Donoghue. Daniel had an excess of brain cells, at least of those that he hadn't destroyed with mind-altering chemicals. 'What did you find out about Daniel's computer?'

'Technical support said that it would be impossible to retrieve a webcam conversation from Daniel's computer unless Daniel had recorded it. There would be a record of the call but not of the actual conversation.'

'I take it there was a call? That Daniel was where he said he was?'

'There was a call. And Daniel was also alibied by another student who saw him in his room that evening. A young man called Aaron Webster.'

'Convenient.'

'You thought Daniel might have been the one?'

'Don't you think it's remarkable that the two people who might have had a motive for murdering Jason both have pretty unassailable alibis? The male lover who is miles away working on a thesis about a French author who leaves the letter 'e' out of his novels, and the possibly emotionally injured and jealous wife who is at sea with her errant husband?'

'I'm curious to know why you suspect Daniel,' Jasmine asked.

'Like I said, I always suspect a lover.'

23

Madden called the Dimarco household that afternoon. Roger Dimarco was in Paris on business, but Celestine Dimarco was there and answered the phone. Madden reckoned that if Jason had 'adopted' another couple as his mother and father, albeit under such bizarre circumstances, they were a pretty good place to start. He wanted to get under the skin of a woman who let her husband pay for sex with a nineteen-year-old boy.

'Is this official police business?' she asked – defensively, he thought.

'No. It's completely unofficial. Let me take you to dinner.'

There was a moment of hesitation, he thought. It did not surprise him.

'How can I possible refuse?' she answered, almost flirtatiously. 'May I choose the rendezvous?'

'Of course.'

She chose the best restaurant in Brighton. English's Oyster House.

It was unexpected, though Madden knew he shouldn't have been surprised. It was the sort of place she would automatically choose. Somehow he hadn't expected the Celestine Dimarcos of the world to settle for fish and chips and a bag of hot doughnuts on the prom.

'Is that all right?' She'd noted his silence.

'It's just that I was going to take Jason there the day he – he was murdered.'

'Oh, I'm sorry,' she said. 'I am so sorry.'

'Please don't be. English's it is.'

'I insist we go somewhere else.'

'And I insist we go there. Maybe it'll do me good. I don't know.'

'If you're sure?'

'I'm sure. I'll see you there at eight, then,' he said.

She arrived punctually. They sat at a corner table in a room with the intimacy of an Edwardian parlour. The seats were of plush red velvet and there were murals on the wall reminiscent of the paintings of Toulouse-Lautrec. One of Clara's favourite artists. Madden hadn't told Celestine that this was also the place where he had proposed to his wife twenty-two years ago. That memory was for him, and him alone. You couldn't live in a place like Brighton and not be reminded of something. The tablecloths were of starched white linen and the cutlery felt as heavy as lead. The wine list was leather-bound and encyclopaedic and had what looked like a curtain cord with a red tassel on the end as a page marker.

Celestine was as stunningly gorgeous as on the last two occasions he had seen her. The more he looked at her, the more he became convinced that Roger Dimarco should be charged with not appreciating a good thing when he had it. He was aware of it being a marginally homophobic thought. But they couldn't hang you for having thoughts.

'This must be painful for you,' she said.

'What would be more painful would be to pass by regularly and never come in and always remember. I don't believe in running away from things.'

He looked around him and thought how wonderful it would have been to have sat with Jason here. To have talked about both their lives. The conversation they would now never have. Their tongues perhaps loosened by a couple of bottles of good wine. *I'm glad you told me you were gay, Jason. It's better that I know. I'm sorry I behaved the way I did that night. You don't have to be scared of me. Any time you want to bring your problems to me and talk about them, you can do it. Your father has problems too. Maybe one day we can talk about them.*

Cool, dad.

I'll always love you, Jason. You're my son and you have a home here.

No, he couldn't run away. The things you tried to run from always caught up with you.

'Shall we order?' he said.

They chose mussels followed by grilled red mullet and a bottle of Sancerre.

'So this is unofficial?' She seemed in need of reassurance.

'Totally. I'm not working as a policeman for a while.'

'Why?'

'I have my own reasons. You'll know that the man we arrested killed himself while on remand while protesting his innocence.'

'Yes, I did read it in the papers. I also read that you are determined to track down the real killer.'

'The paper didn't exactly say that.'

She twisted a mussel out from its shell and forked it between ruby-red lips.

'I read between the lines,' she said. 'Though I'm not sure what I can possibly tell you that might help. Still, I'll do whatever I can, obviously.'

'Can I call you Celestine?'

'Of course you can.'

'When we last spoke you said that men make better prostitutes than women. I wonder if you could elaborate on that?'

'I'm not sure that I can,' she answered, obviously flattered that he should think her an expert on the subject.

'In solving a murder it's important to know the victim. I want to know about that side of Jason's life.'

'Ask Roger. I never went into the bedroom.'

'You and Roger must have talked about it?'

'They didn't do anything kinky, or strange, if that's what you're implying,' she said, shrugging as though it scarcely would have mattered to her if they had. 'Roger never had much imagination in that department. He was only interested in straight sex.'

She added, almost salaciously, he thought, 'If you know what I mean.'

'Who took the active role?'

'Jason did.'

'Roger told you that?'

'We don't have any secrets from each other.' Celestine eyed Madden curiously, as though he was a subject under her intense examination. 'I do not shock easily. In France, we regard sex as a private matter: if two people want to do whatever it is they want to do, then it is entirely up to them.'

'Even if one of them's your husband?'

'Why not? Everyone lives their life in a different way. We have a very unconventional lifestyle, Mr Madden, which is one of the reasons I'm here now, talking to you. It *is* rather unconventional, isn't it, for a policeman to invite someone out to dinner to question them?'

'I told you. I'm not here as a policeman. I'm here as a father.'

'And that's why I want to try and help you as much as I can,' she said. 'But I also want you to know that I'll say nothing against my husband. Neither of us had any reason to harm Jason. We loved him almost like a son. If you want to find his killer, look elsewhere.'

'If it's any comfort to you, I don't suspect either you or your husband of having anything to do with his death,' Madden assured her, making it sound as though he was easily convinced by her. 'I just need to know about Jason.'

Madden remembered what she had said at their last meeting, about finding vulnerable men sexy. Maybe it was because she could control them. He wondered if, in some subtle way, she had exercised a certain amount of control over her husband.

'I'm relieved to know that,' she said.

'You said Jason took the active role. Did he just do it . . . mechanically? Or was there passion?'

'These are questions you really must ask my husband.'

'I'm asking *you*, Celestine.'

'Jason was a professional. He took time to get to know what his clients wanted and believed in satisfying them.'

'He told you this?'

'Of course. We had many conversations about it, after dinner, during dinner. He'd talk about some of his other clients. I don't think Roger was very happy when he did that.'

'Why?'

'I just don't think he liked the fact that Jason advertised what he did with other people.'

'Did he name the other people?'

'A few. We gave all that information to the other officer.'

If this had been an official police interview, Madden would have pressed her on that point. A man in Dimarco's position would not want a nineteen-year-old male prostitute going around boasting about their relationship in an indiscreet manner. And it certainly seemed as though Jason had been indiscreet. Conversely, a man in that position would be unlikely to show himself publicly at the funeral and risk speculation. He didn't press her.

'So why do men make better prostitutes than women, Celestine?' He returned to his question.

'I suppose because they have the capacity to become friends as well. Roger was not looking for some sordid encounter in a backstreet brothel, or a one-night stand: he wanted a companion. Jason satisfied him sexually and yet became almost a son to him. He used to call Jason his "unconventional friend".'

'Pretty unconventional,' said Madden, masking his jealousy. 'Was Roger in love with him?'

Celestine tossed back her head. Madden glimpsed the soft down that glistened on the side of her neck. If his mind hadn't been concentrated on more important matters, he would have stared at it for longer.

'What is love?' she asked, almost with a laugh.

'It's when two people can't live without each other.' Madden sounded serious.

'Yes, I suppose Roger was in love with him in a kind of a way. I think in a kind of a way Jason loved Roger. Looked up to him.'

Madden found that more painful than anything she had said previously.

'I'm sorry,' she said, perceptively.

'That's all right.'

'This is not easy for you, is it?'

'To lose touch with your son, then find out he was selling his body to a man over forty years his senior and looked on him almost as a father? No, it's not easy.'

'I don't imagine for one moment it is.'

Madden finished his mussels. Celestine had already eaten hers. The waiter removed the plates of empty shells.

'Tell me about the boat trip.'

'Which boat trip?'

'The one Jason went on with you. Four people on a boat in the Mediterranean. A wealthy businessman and a nineteen-year-old boy, the businessman's wife and her lover. In my book that doesn't come under the heading of plain sailing.'

'We all got along, if that's what you mean,' she said.

'No jealousy?'

'We were all far too grown-up for that.'

'In my experience, it doesn't matter how grown-up you are. Jealousy can strike anyone at any age. You'll have to pardon me asking these questions but I've never been in a relationship like that.'

'It was a large enough boat,' she explained.

'All the same, you had to watch your husband at close quarters, and he had to watch you. I don't believe you felt nothing at all. I don't believe these open relationships are ever as happy and carefree as people make out.'

The red mullet arrived. The waiter topped up their wine from an ice bucket. Celestine pressed a fork into one of her potatoes and pushed it around delicately in a pool of butter. He could tell that he had touched a raw nerve.

'I suppose I did find it a little galling,' she confessed. 'But then, I did have Jacques, and he was always far more demonstrative with me than Jason ever was with Roger.'

Madden gave a little smile, but it was small enough for her not to notice. He had a habit of doing that when a picture became clearer.

'Didn't Roger mind that?'

'No. He positively encouraged me to be with Jacques. He used to suggest that we should go off by ourselves at every opportunity. He almost pushed him onto me. When he went ashore, he virtually begged me to go off with Jacques so that he could be alone with Jason.'

'Why was that? Because life on the boat had become maybe a little too oppressive?'

'I don't know. You would have to ask Roger that. I certainly did not find it oppressive.'

'When you say that Jason wasn't as demonstrative as Jacques, what do you mean?'

'Roger and Jason didn't sit and kiss, or put their arms round each other, or hold hands, or anything like that. Though Jacques and I did. Frequently.'

'And that didn't annoy Roger?'

'As I said, he positively encouraged it.'

'Pardon me asking this, but do you think he got some nefarious pleasure out of watching you and Jacques?'

'Do you mean, is my husband a voyeur?'

Madden was pleased to see that there was something here that ruffled and slightly shocked her, something she wasn't prepared to shrug off as being an acceptable eccentricity of the French nation.

'Yes, I suppose that was the question I was trying to ask delicately.'

'It's a very lucky woman who knows her husband,' she answered.

Madden took a mouthful of red mullet. *Good answer*, he thought. Then he decided the time was right to change the subject.

'How did you meet Jacques?' he asked.

'This sounds terribly like an official interrogation to me,' she said.

'Sorry. Force of habit.' Madden smiled. 'Ignore it.'

'I used to be a model,' Celestine explained. 'Jacques contacted me through the agency I worked for. He wanted to do a photo shoot for a French magazine, *La Classe*. Do you know it?'

'No. Sorry. Not exactly my type of reading.'

'Oh.' She seemed marginally disappointed. 'We spent three days together in Majorca. I spent most of it sitting naked under a fur on a beach with a platinum blonde wig on my head and a cocktail in my hand.'

'Sounds very avant-garde.'

'It was very uncomfortable. Some of the time.'

'But not all?'

'Not all.'

'How often do you see Jacques?'

'He flies over for two days a week. He's coming over tomorrow, in fact.'

'I'd like to meet him.' said Madden.

She looked surprised. Even vaguely unsettled.

'Pourquoi?'

'Because I'd like to meet everybody who knew Jason. No other reason. I failed my son when he was alive. I have no intention of failing him in death.'

'Very well,' she said. 'That is no problem.'

When they left the restaurant, Madden walked Celestine back to her car. It was a Saab Continental with pale grey leather seats. She slid into the driving seat as though the car had been especially designed for her legs.

'Can I give you a lift anywhere?' she said.

'No, thanks. I'll walk.'

The onion domes of the Brighton Pavilion seemed burnished by the setting sun. He watched her drive off and took a walk down the pier. He hung around until nightfall, when crowds started to gather. There was a crackle of fireworks in the air. He stood and watched as red and yellow and green explosions turned night back to day, and cascades of sparks drifted down into the sea. Two men, one of about thirty, with a shaved head and wearing a denim waistcoat over a muscly torso, the other pale and young and rather pretty, wearing floral Bermuda shorts and Nike trainers, held hands openly beside him.

Madden walked back along the promenade, past a black mono-lithic sculpture that at first glance appeared to be solid and purposeless. The climax to the fireworks display lit the evening sky up in a series of brilliant colours. The monolith, when illuminated from behind, turned out to be peppered with tiny holes that defined six pairs of faces, lips pressed together, one above the other. Men kissing women, women kissing women, men kissing men. It was a symbol of tolerance in a city that was known for its spirit of indulgence and toleration.

In that city of tolerance, somebody had sliced off his son's penis, cut his throat, and stabbed him twenty-seven times. Steve Madden had not failed Jason alone.

24

Jacques Romanet had the kind of body that Madden envied. Aged about thirty-eight or thirty-nine, and six foot in height, Jacques didn't have an ounce of fat on his lean, perfectly shaped torso. The body hair was all on his front, leaving his back as smooth and hard as marble. He had a boyish grin, almost impish, and his head hair, black and glossy, fell in locks about his neck. His nose and features, however, were unmistakably Gallic, and his accent was like raked gravel.

It didn't take a detective to work out why Celestine Dimarco and Jacques Romanet had got it together in Majorca on a three-day fashion shoot. It would have been a mystery if they hadn't.

'You wanted to interview me?' Jacques Romanet spoke in his gravelly accent. His English, however, was almost perfect.

He was standing by the pool, in a pair of pale blue briefs, shaking Madden's hand. In his other was a cocktail glass with a concoction of leaves and berries jutting out of it.

'Not officially. Not as a police officer,' Madden said. 'As Celestine must have told you, I'm Jason's father.'

'I was very sorry to hear of your son's death.' Jacques expressed his condolences, looking down at his feet.

'Thank you.'

Celestine came down from the house. Rather, she waltzed. She was wearing a bikini and carrying a pair of shorts. Her skin glowed with obscene health.

'I brought these for you in case you would like to swim,' she said to Madden.

'Thank you, but another time, maybe.'

'You said that last time.'

'I did, didn't I?'

'You swim?' said Jacques.

'Sometimes I take an early-morning dip in the sea. My father used to do it every day. He used to call it his therapy.' He added, 'I do it usually after I look in the mirror and feel guilty.'

'Would you like to do a length with me?' Jacques invited him.

'I'm not that fast,' Madden said.

'Let's do a length. Then we can talk.'

Madden undressed and put on the shorts. He held in his stomach, which wasn't the part of his anatomy he was most proud of. When he came to think of it, he wasn't really proud of *any* part of his anatomy. During his twenty-two years of marriage, he had, like most men, let his body go in the mistaken belief that he wouldn't need it again. Occasional visits to the gym, walking when he could instead of driving, and his early-morning dips in the surf hadn't exactly brought it back, though activity gave him a feeling of redemption.

'Ready?' asked Jacques.

'Ready.'

Jacques dived into the pool, Madden tumbled. Jacques swam, powering through the water with muscular arms, Madden splashed to keep up with him. Jacques got to the other end, Madden struggled to keep pace. Celestine watched as they hauled themselves out.

'I'm not as fit as I was,' said Madden, sitting on the edge of the pool with Jacques. It was a great place to conduct an interview. When a man was nearly naked, there was no place to hide anything.

'I'll leave you two to talk,' said Celestine, returning to the house.

Jacques could scarcely take his gaze off her.

'She is a beautiful woman, is she not?' Jacques appeared to solicit Madden's opinion.

'She's a very beautiful *married* woman.'

'You know the situation?'

'I know the situation. It's no concern of mine. All I'm interested in is Jason.'

'I don't know what I can tell you.'

'How many times did you meet him?'

'About a dozen times, maybe. Sometimes he was here when I was here, sometimes not.'

'Where do you live, Mr Romanet?'

'I live in Aix-en-Provence, which is near Marseilles. But I work in Paris a lot and abroad. I'm a freelance fashion photographer.'

'Would I have seen any of your work?' Madden asked.

'Do you follow fashion?'

'Not really.'

'Then maybe you haven't.' Jacques smiled, working his feet around in the water.

'I'm interested in the boat trip you all made together. In the Med. What was the name of the boat again?'

'The *Heraklion*. It's named after a sunken city off Crete.'

'Ah yes. The *Heraklion*. Two-berth?'

'Four.'

'I'm told Jason was learning to be quite a sailor.'

'Roger was teaching him. I suppose he did learn to sail quite a bit.'

'They were very close?'

'Very,' said Jacques. 'Like son and father.'

There was no flinching from Jacques Romanet, no awareness that he had said anything that might be hurtful.

'Did they ever argue?'

'I never *saw* them argue. If that's what you mean.'

'How long was the voyage for?'

'It lasted a week.'

'Did it appear to you that my son was enjoying his life?'

'He was enjoying life as much as anybody, I suppose.'

'Did the subject of drugs ever come up?'

Jacques's lips parted in a broad grin.

'All the time,' he said. 'We would be sitting on deck, enjoying dinner, and Jason would bring up the subject of some party he'd been to where Ecstasy was passed round, how it made him love everybody. We would argue with him but it was not much good.'

'What do you mean, argue? Who would argue?'

'All of us. Roger, Celestine and I. It was, like, we had a nineteen-year-old boy there. Another generation. We tried to tell him that abusing his body with drugs was going to damage his mind eventually, but he would argue that he knew lots of adults who had been taking drugs all their lives and that they were all right. Then he would say that cigarettes and alcohol killed more people than Ecstasy ever did. Who is right? I don't know.'

'Who was the most vociferous?'

'Pardon? I don't understand.'

'Who argued with Jason the most?'

Jacques nodded his understanding.

'Roger did. Almost certainly. But in a fatherly way. Roger hates drugs and was really concerned that Jason might come to some harm. There was one night—'

Jacques broke off, as though he felt he might be saying too much.

'One night?'

'Jason said that he had been to an LSD party. It had gone on for about three days. Roger went mad, called him irresponsible, demanded to know who had supplied him with the drug.'

'Who had?' Madden asked.

'I think it was Daniel, his boyfriend.'

Daniel hadn't mentioned LSD. Madden was not surprised, in the circumstances.

'Did you ever meet Daniel?' he asked the Frenchman.

'I think, once,' said Jacques. 'Jason brought him to the house to meet Roger. I think it was Daniel who introduced Jason to the drugs.'

'What makes you say that?'

Jacques Romanet shrugged his wet, naked shoulders and stared down into the depths of the swimming pool.

'This Daniel, he almost boasted that he had nearly poisoned Jason one night by introducing him to speed. It was a kind of joke with him. As though he deserved a medal for it. He struck

me as being a very arrogant and irresponsible young man. Have
you met Daniel?'

'Yes, I've met Daniel,' said Madden.

Madden felt the sun stinging on his back. He longed to slide
back into the water. He went on, 'So they did argue, Roger
and Jason?'

'Yes, but it was the kind of argument a father might have with
a son he cared about. Because Roger disapproved heavily of the
drugs. I remember that Jason sulked for a while and went and lay
on his berth.'

'He didn't like being told off?' Madden probed.

'Jason accused Roger of sounding just like his father. Like
you.'

'Really?' Madden wasn't sure whether a smile was appropriate.
He decided it wasn't.

'Don't misunderstand me,' Jacques said. 'Roger only did it
because he loved Jason. He did not want to see Jason come to
harm. Would you like to see some photographs I took on board
the *Heraklion*?'

'Yes, please.'

Madden towelled himself dry and dressed, while Jacques just
slipped a shirt on. They went up to the house. Celestine was
reclining in the cool of the lounge with a magazine and a cigarette,
creating a blue haze above her. She watched them come in.

'Did you learn anything new?' she asked.

'I learn something new every day,' said Madden. 'What I wonder
is, how will your relationship fare now that Jason is dead? Or will
Roger find himself a new boy?'

'I doubt that,' said Jacques, answering for Celestine, searching
in a desk drawer as though he owned the place, or at least used it
as a home in Roger's absence.

'Roger once said to me that no boy could ever replace Jason,'
Celestine told him. 'He had used escorts before, of course, but
Jason was—'

'Jason was special,' said Jacques.

Jacques showed him the photographs. Madden felt a lump in

his throat. Jason looked so happy in them all. They could have been family shots. They were all large-format and extremely professional.

'Taken with a Hasselblad.' Jacques felt the need to declare the information.

'May I have one?' Madden asked.

'Take them all if you like.' Jacques offered them to him. 'I can have copies made.'

Madden stopped his car on the promenade and looked again at the photographs. All of them had been taken on board the *Heraklion*. All of them featured a smiling Jason. In some his arm was around Roger Dimarco's shoulders, in one he was lying on deck in a pair of trunks with Roger sitting beside him, grinning broadly. In another, he and Roger were standing on the bow in a pose imitating that adopted by Leonardo de Caprio and Kate Winslett in *Titanic*. There were none in which Celestine appeared to be anything other than an appendage, and there was not one in which she was smiling.

Madden thought that was very interesting.

25

Jack Fieldhouse was waiting for Madden outside his house. He seemed to be breathing harder than usual. His weight and bulk looked threatening as he propelled himself like a large cannon ball into Madden's path. Madden was in no mood to be intimidated.

'What's this about you reopening the investigation?' Fieldhouse fired the question at him.

'Who told you that?'

'Come on, Steve, I'm not stupid. Do you think I don't know what's going on behind my back? You're tapping DS Carol for information.'

'She's my partner,' said Madden, half jokingly. 'She's only on loan to you, remember. And you'd better look after her because I want her back. As far as tapping her for information is concerned, I thought we were all in the same force.'

'You know what I mean. You're going over my head.'

'Jack, your head is so far up your arse a moonshot would find it difficult to get over it.'

'We got the right man, you know we did.'

'You seem to know *you* did, Jack. By fair means or foul.'

'What the hell do you mean by that?'

'What I said.'

Madden let himself in the front door. Fieldhouse barged in after him, over the front step on which he had relieved himself on his last visit. Madden wondered if it might bring his memory back. Fieldhouse gave no indication that it did.

'Demos Panagoulis had the lot. The means, the motive, the opportunity. And there was forensic to boot. The guy was selling Jason drugs for sex, there were drugs that Demos was searching for hidden in the flat. What more do you want, Steve? CCTV video?'

'That might help.'

'I wrapped this case up for you. I thought you'd be grateful.'

'I am grateful. Now get out.'

Fieldhouse wore a look of injured righteousness. For a moment it appeared as though no one had ever said 'get out' to him before. He sank onto the sofa, almost comatose with incredulity.

'Steve, I don't believe I'm hearing this from you.'

'If I ever find out you cut corners in the investigation of my son's murder, I'll have you, Jack.' Madden leant over him.

'Cut corners? Me?'

'I've known you demolish whole streets.'

'Panagoulis was guilty. We *knew* Panagoulis was guilty.'

'So you fitted him up? Great. He tops himself in prison? Great. We can all go home and watch *Blue Peter*.'

'That's a serious allegation, Steve.'

'I haven't made it. Yet.'

Fieldhouse got up, and Madden noticed that the sofa pad rose like a cake after him.

'You make it and see where it lands you. What we did, we did for you. Justice for you, and for Jason.'

'Just don't vomit over my floor again as you remind me.'

'Oh. That.'

'Memory come back, has it, Jack?'

'Sorry about that. Bit embarrassed I was, the other day. To admit it. No hard feelings. I was pretty gone that night.'

'You could say that.'

'Still, I do remember everything. I'm grateful for it.'

'Don't think about it. Was there anything else you wanted to see me about?'

'Like I said, I remember everything about that evening. Clear as a bell it all is. Funny how you can be drunk and sharp at the same time.'

'Yes. Hilarious.'

'Don't worry about a thing. I'll look after DS Carol for you,'

Fieldhouse said, patting Madden on the back. 'She's a good girl.'

'She's a young woman.'

'Nice little car she drives.'

Shit, thought Madden.

'Just don't go over my head, Steve. I don't like that kind of thing. I did my job and I got the man who killed Jason. If it had come to trial, we'd have seen the case come together. The evidence was all there. You think I could sleep soundly if I thought he was still out there?'

'I'm eternally grateful, Jack. Now, why don't you just go?'

Fieldhouse left. Madden poured himself a beer, then phoned Clara. She sounded agitated.

'Is the accountant from Hell there?' he asked.

'Steve, if you adopt that attitude, I'll put the phone down on you.'

'Sorry. Is Clive home yet? Can you talk freely?'

'No, he's not. And yes, I can.'

'Good. Want to pay another visit to Cambridge with me tonight? Few more questions I want to put to Daniel Donoghue. Then I thought we might have a punt down the river and a drink together.'

'I can't. Not tonight. I'm going up to London for a company dinner, meeting Clive.'

'Sounds exciting.'

'What other questions do you need to ask him?'

'Don't know yet. Just thought I'd fumble my way so he doesn't know he's being interrogated. I just have the feeling that he's the key to all this, or knows a damn sight more than he's telling.'

'I wish I could come. I can't.'

'I wish you could, too. Have a lot of fun,' he said.

Madden's next call was to Daniel. As it turned out, Daniel wasn't in Cambridge. He was at a party in Croydon. That was good news. Croydon was a commuter suburb south of London, and virtually just up the road from Brighton. Madden reckoned he could be there in an hour. The bad news was that Daniel began the conversation talking almost like a baby, or some cretin indulging in baby talk. When Daniel realised who he was talking to, he tried to talk normally. Madden reckoned he was high on something. Probably Ecstasy.

Daniel was hesitant. He agreed to meet Madden at ten o'clock that night at a pub up the road from where the party was being held. That way they could talk more freely.

Madden got into his car and started driving. He was at the Green Dragon public house half an hour early. He cruised up the road, which was full of detached houses with names like Little Orchards and Great Gables. From one came the high-octane thump of loud music. He parked a little way down the street and watched a young man with green and orange spiked hair winging his way along the pavement, carrying a bottle. He looked familiar.

Madden recognised him as Kevin, one of the rent boys who had come to Jason's funeral. He knew that he had struck gold.

Twenty minutes later, and after a number of other arrivals, Daniel left the house and started to make his way to the Green Dragon. Madden stepped out of his car and intercepted him.

'Mr Madden—' Daniel looked as though he had met the Grim Reaper on his way to church.

'Hello, Daniel. Want to invite me in to the party?'

'That wouldn't be a good idea. I mean, the other guests might not – you do know what I'm trying to say?'

'For a Cambridge undergraduate, you seem woefully short of vocabulary.' Madden smiled.

'They might not appreciate it. You do know what I mean?'

'You mean a copper at the party is a bit like a lion at the feast?'

'Exactly.'

'Tell you what. I'm coming in there as Jason's father. Not as a policeman. Nobody need stop what they're doing. If I see drugs, I'll turn the other way.'

'You might run out of ways to turn.'

'I can be cool,' said Madden. 'I think I can rely on you to assure everybody.'

They went into the house. The first thing that wafted under

Madden's nostrils was the smell of pot. Sitting smoking it in a candlelit parlour were George Adams, the one-time-brothel-keeper-now-honorary-Australian from the outback of Earls Court, and Kevin, Marky and Joe, the three boys who had all been at Jason's funeral. In the main living room across the passage there was a crowd of about thirty people of various ages, the younger of whom were dancing to a beat that made Madden feel as though he had just crawled out of a dinosaur egg.

'He's cool,' said Daniel.

'Hi,' said Madden.

The joint disappeared somewhere under the table nonetheless.

'Don't mind me. I'm here to enjoy myself, just like you. I want to get to know Jason's friends. Forget I'm a policeman. And somebody pass me a cigarette.'

Joe, the male prostitute with the big lips and the slightly Spanish looks, gave him a cigarette. Madden lit it from a candle flame, sat down. He thought it might be a good way of breaking the ice.

'There's a joint under the table,' he said. 'It's not doing much good there.'

The joint came out, but only Marky, the tall, willowy, baby-faced boy, had the courage to smoke it in front of him.

'What brings you here?' asked Adams.

'Just a social chat. With Daniel here. Trying to put right a few wrongs. Whose party is this?'

'Terry Hindland's. He's an old client of the agency that I used to run,' said Adams. 'He likes me to get as many boys together from the old days as I possibly can and bring them round. He invites a few friends.'

'I get the big picture,' said Madden.

'You only just got the trailer, dear,' quipped Marky, inhaling the marijuana smoke and falling back into the settee, legs lazily crossed like a twenties film star.

'So you haven't given up your old trade, then?' Madden asked Adams.

'You never really give it up,' explained Adams, rubbing the ring in his left ear lobe as though he expected something magical to happen. A genie to pop out, perhaps. There was more of the gypsy in him tonight than there was of the swashbuckler, thought Madden. 'You keep in touch with the boys, they come to you when they're hard up, you keep in touch with a few clients, they come to you when they're hard. You try to please everybody.'

'And sometimes you end up pleasing nobody,' said Joe, with a hoarse chuckle followed by a little laugh that trailed away into nothingness.

'Sorry if this sounds like a corny line –' Madden turned to Daniel Donoghue '– but what brings a boy like you to a place like this?'

'I used to work for George,' said Daniel, with some reticence.

'I see.'

'That's where I met Jason. That's how we met. I didn't do it all the time. Just at weekends. You know how it is, I'm sure. It was a way of making money.'

It became clearer. People never told you the truth straight away. It wasn't easy to admit to your boyfriend's parents that you'd met their son while working as a fellow rent boy in a male brothel. Madden reckoned that he could forgive Daniel for that. What he found hard to forgive was the fact that barely a week after his boyfriend's death Daniel was showing no sign of mourning. But then, thought Madden, maybe that was the old-fashioned streak in him.

'Mind if I have a few words with you in private?' Madden asked.

'Sure.'

Just at that moment, a man of about fifty, wearing tight jeans and a T-shirt and with a polished complexion and prematurely silvering hair, came into the room and hovered near Daniel, placing a hand on the younger man's shoulder. Daniel threw it off by pulling away sharply. The older man gave a nonetheless confident smile, and asked who his friend was.

'My name's Steve Madden,' Madden answered for him.

'He was Jason's father,' Daniel said. 'This is Terry.'

'Hello, Terry.' Madden shook his hand. The man looked familiar.

'I heard about your son. From Daniel. I'm so terribly sorry.'

Madden suddenly recognised Terry Hindland. The name as well as the guy's appearance had been familiar. He hosted a children's television quiz show – a popular one – in the afternoons. Sartorially, he was more usually associated with technicolour ties and ill-matching jackets, as well as with a catchphrase that Madden couldn't recall.

'I'm just going outside to have a word with Jason's dad,' said Daniel.

'Of course.' Terry beamed politely at them both. He squeezed Daniel's arm. Daniel looked embarrassed.

Madden and Daniel Donoghue pushed their way through the equally crowded kitchen into a secluded garden with wrought iron furniture and coloured lights. They sat down. Out here, the music was mercifully muted. Madden looked closely at Daniel's eyes.

'What are you on?' he asked.

'Just a tab,' said Daniel. 'E. I laid off it when I knew you were coming.'

'How do you know Terry Hindland?'

'He's a friend.'

Daniel, instead of meeting Madden's gaze, turned sideways and put his thumb in his mouth. It wasn't the first time Madden had seen him do it.

'You mean a client?'

'If you want to put it that way.'

'Let me put it *this* way, Daniel. I want to know the world Jason lived in. Square with me, don't hide anything. I'm not here to tell you how to live your life.'

'Okay.'

Madden saw a little boy under the adult exterior. A little boy who had grown up too fast and liked to think he was in charge of his life but wasn't.

'I was given the impression that Jason did a lot for you. Helped you out.'

'Who told you that?'

'Ming. The transsexual guy.'

'Ming's a girl.'

'Okay, girl. This world gets complicated.'

'Doesn't have to be,' said Daniel.

'Is it true? *Did* Jason help you out? Financially?'

'He did at times,' answered Daniel. 'He was lovely. I loved him. He'd buy me presents, chocolates, meals, that sort of thing.'

'Because he was earning more than you?'

'Yes.'

'What else?'

'What do you mean, "what else"?'

The thumb again. Madden saw it as a sign of retreat. The adult world suddenly got too much so Daniel had, if only for a second or two, to get out of it.

'I mean, anything else? Did he help you pay bills? Anything like that?'

'He helped me pay my phone bill once. And once he helped me pay off my credit card. As I said, he was lovely like that.'

'Ming got the impression you lived off him,' said Madden with a broad smile. 'That wasn't true, was it?'

'Course it wasn't.'

'Sour grapes?'

'I don't know.' Daniel shrugged. 'Jason was just lovely.'

'When we met at Cambridge, you didn't mention the fact you'd had a webcam conversation with Jason shortly before he was murdered.'

'Didn't I?'

'I thought it was something you'd have wanted his mum and I to know.'

'I must have thought you knew already.'

'I wasn't on the investigation, remember.'

'I'm sorry,' said Daniel. 'I didn't quite realise that at the time.'

'What did you talk about?'

'We just talked. Sometimes you don't talk about anything important.'

'He didn't give any hint that he was expecting somebody that morning? A client?'

'No. If he had done, I'd have told the police.'

'How long did you talk to him for?'

'About half an hour. Probably a bit longer. I can't remember.'

'I suppose when you're in love with somebody, half an hour seems like a few minutes,' said Madden.

'Yeh.' Daniel drew out the word almost ecstatically.

'You'll have to excuse me, I don't know very much about computers. This webcam conversation, you were actually face to face, talking?'

'Right.'

'You see what I'm getting at, Daniel? About ten minutes after you finished speaking with Jason, somebody came into his flat and murdered him. So anything he said to you in the course of that half-hour could be relevant, no matter how insignificant it appeared to you at the time.'

'I know.' Daniel drew it out in an almost babylike voice.

'The E making you talk like that?'

'I'm all right.' said Daniel.

'What I'd like you to do is write down as much as you can remember. I'm not going to ask you to remember it all now. Take your time. Every single thing, no matter how small it is, no matter how unimportant you think it might be, put it down on paper. Let me be the judge.'

'A lot of it was sexual,' Daniel admitted.

'I'm not easily shocked, Daniel. I hope you won't be easily embarrassed.'

'Okay.'

'Can we meet up again when you've done it?'

'I'm coming to Brighton for the Gay Pride weekend,' said Daniel. 'We'll be going to the Red Planet Club. Maybe we can meet up then?'

'Sounds like a good idea.' Madden smiled. 'Well, I'll let you enjoy the rest of your party. For God's sake, be careful.'

'I'm sensible.' Daniel sounded like a five-year-old who'd just been told off for stealing an extra slice of cake.

'Strikes me that's a relative term these days.'

'When you compare the number of people who die from Ecstasy with those who die from alcohol or smoking—' Daniel began.

'I didn't come here to spoil your fun. So spare me and don't deliver a lecture,' said Madden. 'And I won't ask you about how you introduced Jason to drugs in the first place. Or about other drugs like LSD. Do we have a deal?'

'We have a deal,' answered Daniel, gingerly.

'Can I use the toilet before I go?'

'It's upstairs. I'll show you.'

Madden went upstairs with some trepidation. From behind a closed bedroom door came what sounded like the sound of a belt on bare flesh, followed by cries of pain. He didn't feel inclined to ask what was going on. In the bath, a girl was lying, fully clothed and only semi-conscious.

'What's wrong with her?' Madden asked.

'She's a friend of mine.'

Good answer, thought Madden. Daniel deserved an honours degree for it.

'What's she on?'

'K. Short for ketamine. It's a horse tranquilliser.'

'Good grief.'

'Her name's Tamra. She's with me at university. She's a lesbian.' Daniel disposed of the facts as though they were somehow, in themselves, sufficient justification for lying in a bath stoned out of one's mind.

Driving home that night, Madden remembered a question he'd once read on a police recruitment poster. It went something like this. *You're off duty* (as though a policeman was ever off duty) *and you go to a party where your best friend is taking drugs. Do you (a) leave the party immediately and say nothing, (b) stay and ask your friend to desist and explain that he is compromising you, or (c) arrest him on the spot.* If you could answer that question, you were a better copper than most. The fourth option, that of joining in, was too cynical for the straight-faced bodies that designed police recruitment posters.

It wasn't until he stopped in a lay-by on the London to Brighton road, to make a call to Jasmine on his mobile, and became aware of another car slowing behind him and stopping at the far end of the same lay-by, that Madden realised he was being followed.

26

Madden momentarily forgot the call he was going to make to Jasmine, put the phone back in his pocket and waited to see if the other car pulled away. It didn't. He started his engine and pulled slowly out of the lay-by. The other car did the same. He jammed the gear lever into reverse and shot backwards into the lay-by again. The other car remained half out on the road, as though the driver didn't quite know what to do, while two other cars drove round it, the drivers sounding their horns angrily. Then it too crawled back sheepishly. Whoever was tailing him was no professional.

Madden got out and walked up to the other car. It was a ten-year-old Renault 5, dark green in colour and a bit rusty. At the wheel was Lucky Maynard. He wound down the window.

'Hello, Mr Madden,' said Lucky.

'Hello, Lucky.'

'Nice evening.'

'Yes, isn't it? Pity one can't see the stars. Still, you can't have everything.'

'I was just out for a drive,' said Lucky.

'You were following me. Why?'

'How did you know?'

'Lucky, you couldn't have made yourself more obvious if you'd been sitting on my bonnet taking notes. There's an art in tailing somebody and you haven't got it.'

'Sorry, Mr Madden.' Lucky sounded humbled.

'Sorry you're tailing me, or sorry you haven't got the art?'

'I can explain.'

'Let's go and sit in my car and you can do it.'

Lucky came with him and sat in his car. The lad was wringing his hands together grievously, guiltily.

'What's up, Lucky?'

'He asked me to do it, Mr Madden.'

'Who? Frank Sullivan?'

'I couldn't say no, could I?'

'Course you couldn't. Did he tell you why?'

'He doesn't like being associated with murder, Mr Madden. Drugs, yes, but not with murder.'

'He'll go to Heaven,' said Madden. 'I can see the pearly gates opening wide already.'

'You got a bit heavy-handed with him. He didn't like that. He thought you were trying to tie him in to your son's murder.'

'So he got you to follow me?'

Lucky looked down at his shoes. 'He trusted me to do the job properly,' he said. 'He doesn't have no idea about our relationship.'

'And he mustn't know, Lucky.'

Madden saw a notebook in Lucky's pocket. 'Can I see that?'

Lucky handed it to him. Madden looked at the last page on which he had written something.

'You spell Croydon with a Y, Lucky. You don't want your employer thinking you're uneducated, now, do you?'

'No, Mr Madden. I'll change it now.'

'Good. And you can record that at three minutes past eleven precisely, I stopped in a lay-by to make a telephone call. I spoke to my colleague Jasmine – that's Detective Sergeant Carol – for exactly nine minutes and told her about a party I went to. Mention some names – just make them up – he'll never know—'

'How do I know all this, Mr Madden?'

'Because I got out of the car and walked up and down the lay-by while making the call. You crept behind those hedges there and heard every word I said.'

'Then what?'

'I drove home. Got home at –' he looked at his watch '– twenty to twelve. You waited until you saw my lights go out. Assumed

I'd gone to bed. Oh, and you saw me watch television for twenty minutes with the curtains open. That's a nice touch. Choose whatever's on BBC-1 tonight at that time and that's what I was watching.'

'Couldn't I say something like – I heard you say on the phone that you didn't think Mr Sullivan was involved?' asked Lucky, clearly pleased with himself for dreaming up such a gem.

'No, no, no. Too contrived. He'd never believe it. Keep it simple, mundane. The stuff of everyday life. He might get bored and give you another job to do.'

'Okay. Thanks, Mr Madden.'

'Call me tomorrow, and I'll give you a rundown of my movements. They'll all be pretty boring too, I can assure you. Like the Queen's court diary. Or something the Prime Minister has said in order to get into the news bulletins. Stuff that no one will bother to read. Then you can have a day off.'

'That's really good of you, Mr Madden.'

'Don't mention it. Anything to help a friend.'

Madden put his arm round Lucky's shoulders and smiled warmly at him. Lucky looked terrified.

'What's wrong, Lucky?'

'Don't know, Mr Madden. Just that you never – well – seemed that friendly before.'

'What do you think, I'm making a pass at you?'

'You're not, are you, Mr Madden?'

'I'm fond of you, Lucky. But not *that* fond. I was thinking, you could do a little job for me instead. It involves tailing but the person you'd be tailing doesn't know who you are and isn't a police officer, so you should get away with it. Also, most of it will be on foot. Do you want the job? There's money in it.'

'Who do you want me to tail?'

'His name's Clive Westmacott. He's company accountant for a publishing firm called Cassiopeian Books.'

'What has he done?' asked Lucky.

'He stole my wife.'

Lucky just nodded. Madden wasn't sure if it had got through

or not. Or if it had, whether Lucky was bright enough to guess why Madden wanted him to do the job.

'I'd like you you to tail him in his lunch hour. And after he leaves the office. See where he goes, who he meets.'

'How will I know what he looks like, Mr Madden?'

'He's tall, bald, and looks like an eagle. You'll be at the Marina Village tomorrow morning at half-past seven, he'll come out of Tuscany Court about quarter to eight, get into a blue BMW convertible, registration number M40DRK. It's always parked in the same spot, by a sign that says No Ball Games. Got that?'

'No ball games,' said Lucky, writing it down.

'I want to know if he gets up to any.'

'Any—?'

'Ball games. Forget it, Lucky, Just a bad joke.'

'What, you think he's screwing around?' asked Lucky.

'They'll have you on *Mastermind* yet, my friend.'

Lucky beamed at that. Or, thought Madden, a quiz show called *The Master Maze*, hosted by one Terry Hindland who was, at this moment, probably snorting something and enjoying the company, if not the sexual services, of Daniel Donoghue. Madden wondered how long it would be before a Sunday tabloid got wind. He could almost see the headline. *TV Quizmaster in Gay Sex and Drugs Quiz.*

'I won't let you down, Mr Madden,' said Lucky, returning to his car.

'You'd better not.'

'I'd sooner work for you any day.'

'Thanks for the compliment.'

Lucky joined the flow of night traffic. Madden had a pee between the car and the hedge and headed for home. As Lucky would tell his bosses, he arrived there at exactly twenty minutes to midnight.

He didn't watch television, however. He drew the curtains, went into the kitchen, switched on the jug kettle, and made himself a cup of tea. He sat down with it and rang Jasmine.

'Not too late, is it?' he said.

'It's never too late to hear from you, Steve.'

'First the bad news. I had a visit from Jack Fieldhouse earlier tonight.'

'Drunk or sober?'

'Sober, unfortunately. I think he's had a cure for amnesia. I think he saw your car parked outside.'

'Are you sure?'

'Let's just hope he keeps any suspicions to himself and doesn't blab them round the station.'

'We're going to have to be more careful in future,' she sighed.

'Want to hear about a drugs party I went to up in Croydon?'

'You, Steve?'

'Yes, me, Steve. Load of kids taking E, K, you name it. It's an alphabetical jungle out there.'

'What did you learn?'

'Our Mr Daniel Donoghue is a young man on the take. Not content with selling himself to the highest bidder he even lived off the takings of his boyfriend. I suspect he's one of these guys who just uses people for what he can get out of them.'

'I hate that kind of person,' said Jasmine.

'And another thing. We've rattled Frank Sullivan's cage. Suddenly he's very interested in the investigation. Had me tailed tonight.'

'Steve, be careful.'

'Don't worry. I think he's just anxious that he doesn't get fitted up for murder like his erstwhile rival Panagoulis. What goes around, comes around.'

'All the same,' she said, 'we don't have an alibi for what he was doing when Jason was killed. It would be useful to know where he was.'

'Any alibi of Frank Sullivan's at this stage wouldn't be worth the Bible it was sworn on.'

He heard the sound of clunking dishes on the other end of the line.

'Just washing up a few things,' she said. 'It sounds like you've had a more exciting evening than I have.'

'Think I might ring Clara tonight,' he said. 'Keep her informed.'

'Steve, you're not using this as an excuse to keep – well – seeing her.'

'She was my wife. Jason was our son. I don't need an excuse to keep seeing her.'

'She's living with somebody else now, Steve. You've got to let go. You're only going to keep hurting yourself.'

'That's the second time tonight I've been lectured.'

'What was the first?'

'Daniel Donoghue tried to lecture me on the relative safety of hard drugs.'

'Go to bed, Steve,' she said. 'You're going to make yourself ill if you keep torturing yourself over her. I'm bloody serious. There are other women in the world, lots of them, just let her go. Unless you do that you'll never be free yourself.'

Then she threw in, 'Do you want me to come round tonight?'

'I don't want to keep using you in that way, Jaz.'

'You're not using me,' she said. 'I'm using you. I had a long telephone call from my mother tonight. She's met this nice boy that she wants me to meet too. She never gives up.'

'What parent doesn't want the best for their children?'

'She's still convinced I'm this nice virgin girl.'

'Don't disappoint me, Jaz. I am too,' he told her.

In the end, she thought it best that she didn't come round that night. Madden concurred. The amount of drugs he had passively inhaled at the party seemed to make him feel leaden. Neither did he phone Clara. Madden went to bed, but he couldn't sleep, and he couldn't let Clara go. Jason's death had brought her back into his life. And he kept thinking, out of pure compassion, about the kids he'd seen at that party. They weren't kids, they were young adults. If Jason had been alive, he might have been at that party with his friends. Selling his body, taking Ecstasy, collapsed in a bath tub with a skinful of horse tranquilliser. Madden felt old all of a sudden, out of touch. He wanted to reach out to all the Daniels of the world and shake them by the neck and tell them what they were doing to themselves. As he would have surely shaken Jason by the neck. In the old days, youth rebellion had been visible, it had screamed out from the clothes they wore and the music they listened to and the language they used. Now it was largely invisible, underground, unseen, off the streets. And insidiously dangerous.

'I'm sorry, I'm sorry,' he mouthed into the pillow for the son who had rebelled against him, out of fear, and who was now beyond his reach and compassion. And then he found himself crying into it, wetting the cotton with his tears, wishing that he could have a second chance at that night, the last night he had seen Jason. Would anything else he could have said have done any good? Prevented it happening? He didn't know, could have no way of knowing. But Madden would have cherished the satisfaction of having tried to understand.

Lucky Maynard delivered the goods less than twenty-four hours later. He and Madden met in a barely used, run-down amusement arcade a mile out of town, backed by a desolate stretch of shingle and alongside a children's ride that had long ago fallen into disrepair. They pumped coins into one-armed bandits that lived up to their names. Lucky had spent all day in London, but hadn't come back empty-handed.

'I followed him, like you said, Mr Madden,' Lucky said, cautiously weighing up the potential interest in his to-be-unfolded discovery.

'And?'

'I followed him to his office. All the way. He drove to the station, I parked beside him, he didn't know who I was. I got near enough to him on the train but sat so he couldn't see me and I couldn't see him.'

'You're learning, Lucky. And?'

'I followed him to his office, like I said. Then it was pretty boring because he didn't come out till lunchtime. I sat on a bench for three and a half hours, Mr Madden.'

'That's the cutting edge of surveillance for you. The really exciting part of undercover work.'

Lucky gave a modest grin, but from his expression it was pretty clear that he didn't get the irony in the remark.

'Anyway,' he carried on, 'he came out at lunchtime and got on the Underground, and that's when I lost him.'

'You lost him?' Madden felt deflated.

'Yeh, but only for a few minutes.' Lucky bristled with a kind of pride. 'I had to get change to get a ticket, and I caught up with him. He took the Piccadilly Line to Green Park.'

'Did he see you?'

'No. He was too busy reading his newspaper. He wouldn't have seen anybody. Anyway, he got off at Green Park and went to this little square called Shepherd Market. And he met this girl.'

'You're sure about that?'

'Yeh, I know a girl when I see one.' Lucky made a rare joke.

'No, that it was Shepherd Market – the name of the square?'

'I looked up and saw it.'

'Go on.'

'Anyway, he met this girl, and they talked for a few minutes, and then they went off for a drink. They went to a pub called the Lamb and Flag.'

'What was this girl doing when he met her?'

'She was just standing at the corner.'

'Did he just go up to her, or what?'

'I don't know. I got round the corner, and he was standing talking to her, and then they walked into this pub and had a drink.'

Madden hoped that Lucky had again been clever enough to have sat within hearing range without making himself obvious. But there his good fortune, and Madden's, had run out.

'I tried, Mr Madden, but the pub was too full and I couldn't get near them. And it was too noisy.'

'Did they appear intimate?'

'Well, they didn't kiss or anything like that.'

'You know what I mean, Lucky. This wasn't an accountancy forum.'

'Don't know what that is. But she wasn't any accountant.'

Madden smiled. Lucky was funniest when he didn't even know it.

'Was she pretty?'

'Yeh, she was a stunner.'

'Then what did they do?'

'They left and went up these stairs.'

Better and better, thought Madden. There was only one reason anyone met a girl in Shepherd Market and went up a stairway.

Then he checked himself. Better for whom? Better for Clara? He still loved her. He wouldn't wish this on her.

'Did you go up the stairs after them?'

'I didn't need to, Mr Madden. But I got the address.' He gave it to Madden. 'Her name was Mandy and she was a model.'

'How long did he stay up there?'

'About quarter of an hour.'

'That was a quick bit of modelling.'

'Then he came out and I followed him back to his office. And I followed him back to Brighton on the train.'

'An average exciting day for an average commuting company accountant. You've done well, Lucky.'

He gave him fifty pounds.

'There was a lot of hanging around, Mr Madden. Lot of shoe leather.'

Madden topped it up to a hundred. There were conditions attached.

'Don't go away – I've got another job for you. It'll take a bit longer but I'll make it worth your while. Plus the fact it's more important. I want you to go clubbing this weekend. Stick around a guy called Daniel Donoghue and his friends. Particularly Daniel Donoghue. I want to know what he does, how he behaves, who he sees. I want to know anything and everything.'

'How will I know him?' asked Lucky.

'I'll make sure you do. Don't worry about that. The only thing that might concern you is that you're going to have to spend a couple of nights in the Red Planet. Does that present a problem for you?'

'Why should it?'

'Well, your boss owns the place. Just thought he might get a little suspicious if you were to be – well – enjoying yourself there.'

'He doesn't mind, Mr Madden. My personal life is my own. I've hung around in these places before, anyway.'

'You surprise me, Lucky.'

'What's this Daniel done?' Lucky asked, in such a way that it was clear he half expected not to get an answer.

'He was a friend of my son,' Madden replied.

'I'll do my best for you, Mr Madden,' said Lucky.

'You've done well so far. As for today, you'll want to know my movements, so you can report back to your master. Tell him I went to the cemetery to visit my son's grave and that my wife came along with me. I spent most of the afternoon there.'

'You married again, Mr Madden?'

'My *ex*-wife. Sorry. Slip of the tongue.'

It had indeed been a genuine slip of the tongue. Just for a moment, it made him feel good.

He went to the cemetery with Clara that afternoon. It was a prearranged visit. The huge sprawling graveyard by Woodvale Crematorium, where Jason had been laid to rest, made you forget you were in a city. It was high up on the crest of a rolling valley, and from it one could look down to the spire of a more distant church nestling in a verdant green fold. A few yards away, on the other side of a wire fence, Brighton's organic gardening community went about their gentle, unobtrusive business in what had become a small shanty town of huts and allotments. Madden's own parents were buried up here. He still put flowers on their graves, twice a year.

Clara had vowed privately not to tell Clive that she was going with her ex-husband. Madden vowed privately not to tell her what he had found out from Lucky that morning. At least, not yet, anyway. No good could come of it. She would accuse him of spying. Worse, she might accuse him of making it up. He didn't want to risk them ceasing to be friends, now that Jason's death had brought about a fragile reconciliation. Better that it was swept under the carpet for the time being.

There were already fresh flowers on Jason's grave. Red carnations, about thirty of them, like a splash of blood against the white marble headstone. Tucked among them was a card on which was written: *'From your unconventional friend, Roger.'*

'What do you make of that?' he asked her.

'An understandable sentiment.' She shrugged.

'What exactly does he mean, *unconventional*?'

'Isn't it obvious?'

They laid down the flowers they had brought. Madden shoved aside the carnations. They weren't even damp, yet there had been a shower of rain only an hour earlier, which meant that Roger Dimarco hadn't long left the cemetery. Madden wondered how long he had spent sitting by Jason's grave.

'I had another chat with Daniel,' Madden told her.

'You don't think he's involved, do you?'

'I don't think he's telling the complete truth. I think he's keeping a hell of a lot back. But I'm not in any position right now to haul him in and drag it out of him.'

'He seemed such a nice young man.' Clara came to his defence.

'Even though he works as a prostitute and takes drugs?'

'You make that sound so seedy but he's not as bad as that. Lots of students take drugs, it's part of the culture. As for the prostitution, well, it is the world's oldest profession, after all.'

'Next to spying.'

'And there's a world of difference between a student doing it to help get through difficult times financially, and someone doing doing it full time.'

'Like Jason.'

'Like Jason.' She knelt down and arranged the flowers, almost obsessively.

'Do you know how they met?'

'Jason told me it was in a gay club.'

'It was in a London brothel. An escort agency. They were both working as rent boys. Jason wouldn't have told you that.'

Clara fell silent. She had been trying to shoulder the burden of truth, to come to terms with the son she had only partly known. But the truth kept falling on her in unpalatable chunks. Madden helped her to arrange the flowers. His hand touched hers briefly. For a moment she kept it where it was. Madden cupped his hand across the pale ridge of her knuckles. The sensation was good. Then she withdrew her hand slowly, but not before she had held him with a sympathetic glance.

'I'm pleased we could do that. Here,' he said.

'Me too.'

'Jason would have been pleased.'

'Steve, don't try to manipulate me.'

'I'm not. We're here, putting flowers on Jason's grave, united, as we should be. We brought him into the world and we failed him. We failed him because we didn't know him. We failed him because we got too tied up in our own lives and didn't take the time to find out about the life he was leading.'

'Would he have told us anyway?'

'I doubt it.'

'If we'd stayed together,' Clara reasoned, 'he would have done just the same, I'm sure. He was a nineteen-year-old boy. Neither of us could have kept him at home, controlled his movements. What parents can?'

'I'm fed up with people telling me that. I can't rid myself of the feeling that Jason became a rent boy just to – well, get back at us both.'

'Oh, come on,' she said.

'Can you give me another explanation?'

'Okay,' she answered, 'I will. You may not like it, Steve, but I've been thinking a great deal about this. I've seen Jason's website too. It's still on the Internet. From what you've told me and from what I've gleaned from our chat with Daniel, isn't it – well, just possible that Jason actually *enjoyed* what he was doing?'

'I never considered it.'

'It's not easy to, I know. But the evidence speaks for itself. You're a policeman, you should know all about evidence.'

'Go on.'

'It's not as though Jason needed to do it. And if he'd wanted to get back at us, he could have done it in a hundred different ways. Not by bringing his boyfriend to Brighton to meet me, as he did. He just wasn't the rebellious type.' Clara looked down at her hands, at the petals that had stuck to her fingers. 'Do you remember the time he made that friend when he was at school? When he was only fourteen?'

Madden remembered. It had worried them slightly at the time. Jason had joined a local football team and become friendly with the coach, a man in his early forties. The friendship had stretched beyond the pitch, to meeting up in cafés, and once they had gone to the cinema together. Madden had made discreet enquiries about the man, whose name was Alan Michaels, but he had no record, and Jason seemed unperturbed by their relationship. Once, they had challenged Jason. Apparently he had been to Alan Michaels's house, and they had watched a video together. Jason had protested that there was nothing 'odd' about it, and was upset that they should think there was. Alan was a 'really nice guy', in Jason's own words. He had never 'tried anything on' – his parents' words. They accepted Jason's word and the friendship went on for a couple of months until Alan Michaels left the area. Throughout the episode, their unease was diminished by Jason's anger that they should think anything was wrong. What did it matter that Alan wasn't a teenager his own age? He was an intelligent guy and Jason simply enjoyed his company. At fourteen, Jason knew his own mind.

'There was something I never told you about that time,' Clara said, and he could tell she was afraid of even bringing it up now.

'Oh yes? What?'

'You must promise me you won't do anything about it now.'

'That depends on what it what it is.'

Madden felt that he knew what she was going to tell him. Once again, a parent was the last person to know his child.

'I won't tell you unless you give me that promise. On our son's grave.'

'Okay, I promise.'

'Something *did* go on between them. I caught Jason sending an e-mail to him one day after he came back from school. He tried to delete it before I could read it, but – well, it was pretty explicit. Jason admitted to me that they'd had sex but begged me not to tell you. He didn't want anything to happen to Alan.'

Madden could hardly believe she was telling him this. After five years.

'And you just allowed this thing to go on?'

'No, I didn't. I spoke to him quite firmly about it. And I went to see Alan Michaels. I told him that at fourteen Jason was too young to know his mind and that they should – well, cool it a bit.'

'Just a bit?' Madden tried not to sound cynical but failed majestically.

'Jason had a crush on him. Alan was trying to distance himself but it wasn't easy. Jason kept turning up on his doorstep. Alan knew you were a policeman, and was terrified of you finding out. That's largely, I imagine, why he left the area.'

'He was scared you might tell me?'

'I promised him I wouldn't. And I promised Jason, too. What would have happened? Alan Michaels would have ended up in court, Jason would probably have had to give evidence, and about what? The fact that he pursued an older guy for sex? Jason wasn't innocent by any means.'

'He was fourteen, Clara.'

'I wasn't going to put him through that. Or destroy somebody's life and career.'

'Life and career? This guy could be doing the same to somebody else's fourteen-year-old son right now, or to some kid even younger.'

'It was a teenage infatuation,' Clara insisted. 'Don't you get the point I'm trying to make? Jason, our son, was attracted to older men. It happens.'

'And how do we know that he didn't stay in touch with this Michaels guy afterwards? How do we know he wasn't in touch with him when he died? How do we know Alan Michaels didn't kill Jason beacuse he was terrified that Jason would blow the whistle on him one day? If ever there was a motive for his murder, that's it.'

'Oh God.' Clara let out a deep sigh. 'I wish I hadn't told you.'

'You wish?' Madden remembered the promise he had made to her only minutes before. The promise on Jason's grave. 'I know I promised I wouldn't do anything, but you've just brought up the identity of somebody who might possibly be Jason's killer. Didn't you even consider that?'

Clara hadn't considered it. Not for one moment. All her life, Madden knew, she had tried to think the best of everybody, to give everybody a second chance. She had given *him* plenty of chances throughout their marriage. The fact that he had thrown them away was neither here nor there in the present inquiry. So Clara had met the man who was having sex with their fourteen-year-old son and had told him to cool it.

'I'm sorry,' Madden said. 'I have to pursue this angle. Don't you see?'

'Then promise me that if he has nothing to do with Jason's death you'll pursue it no further.'

'Why are you so keen to protect him?'

'Just promise me, Steve.'

She stood still on the cemetery path and stared at him with those large hazel-coloured eyes that had so often appeased him in the past. He realised how much he was still in love with her. She was still the same Clara. Leaving him for another man hadn't changed her. As a child, she had been forever finding injured birds and bringing them indoors and keeping them in cardboard boxes full of cotton wool and feeding them milk out of pipettes. It was typical of her to want to protect even someone like Alan Michaels, to give him the benefit of the doubt. Gentle, understanding Clara. There wasn't a cruel streak in her. Madden experienced in that moment a wave of regret. If he could have his time again with her, things would be different. He would learn to believe in her, not give in to wild imaginings simply because she was so beautiful. He would break the cycle of irrational jealousy. He would be kinder and more thoughtful to her. They would be even better friends than they were lovers, trusting each other and enjoying the fruits that trust brought. He would not work so hard. He would sacrifice anything, even his job, to make their marriage work. Pigs, indeed, would fly. But there was no harm in wishing for the impossible, either.

'Okay,' he conceded. 'If Alan Michaels had nothing to do with it, and he's living a blameless life somewhere, I'll take it no further. You have my word on that.'

Madden wished that he meant it.

28

It was the start of Gay Pride Weekend in Brighton. The city was gearing up for the influx. Madden couldn't escape it as he drove along the front, reading the banners that flapped in the breeze. The gay population of the city was swelling already. A mini-carnival of sorts, comprising an eight-foot-high fairy princess on stilts and an entourage of drag queens, made its way down the Old Steine to the Palace Pier. A lesbian steel band were thumping out Caribbean rhythms on the pavement outside one of the upfront gay bars on Marine Parade. There was a bohemian air about the place that was palpable. The circus was coming to town.

Madden met Jasmine in a Starbucks coffee house.

'Got two more jobs for you,' he said. 'Hope you don't mind.'

'You're the boss.' She shrugged.

'Glad you haven't forgotten it.' Madden grinned. 'See if you can trace an Alan Michaels who used to live at 45 Masons Terrace – he used to be a football coach for the Craven End Youth Club. He's since moved out of Brighton but might be working as a coach somewhere else. Be discreet, I don't want him knowing anybody's interested in him.'

'Want to tell me why?'

'Mind if I don't? It's personal.'

'And the second job?'

'I want you to use your International Disco Card. Pay a visit to the Red Planet tonight. You'll be accompanied by a young guy called Lucky Maynard. He's doing a job for me. I want you to seek out Daniel Donoghue and his mates and point him out to Lucky. Lucky will do the rest.'

'Doesn't he work for Frank Sullivan?'

'The same one.'

'Shit for brains, right?'

'His heart's the right consistency.' Madden smiled.

'Care to tell me what *that* is about?'

'Okay, if you must know. I just don't believe anything Daniel Donoghue's told me. The kid's slippery. He's also bright, and that's not a good combination. I just want somebody to keep an eye on him – see what he does, how he behaves, who he meets.'

'And Lucky Maynard is suddenly an expert in surveillance techniques?' Jasmine sipped her mocha through a straw and looked cynically at him.

'I'm taking an interest in his future career prospects,' said Madden.

'Can you trust him?'

'Right now, I trust him more than Jack Fieldhouse.'

Jasmine glanced around the coffee shop. It had filled up with gay people from London, down for the weekend. Two teenagers in Gap jeans who could have been no older than fifteen – one with a combat T-shirt, the other's proclaiming PRIDE in capital letters – stood next to them, arguing about the best place to go. One favoured this bar, one favoured another. Neither of them looked old enough to drink. Both were outrageously coquettish.

'The word is around the station that you're on a crusade that's going nowhere. Fieldhouse is adamant that Panagoulis was guilty. If he wasn't, then evidence was planted and that's unthinkable. They're closing ranks, Steve.'

'So it's just me and thee.'

The teens left, still arguing about which gay venue they should stop at first. Madden felt drawn to their openness, to the sheer exuberance with which they flaunted their sexuality.

'Jason would have been part of all this,' Madden mused aloud. 'If he was still alive. In my young days, you didn't even talk about it. Often wonder how my old man would have reacted if I'd turned round to him and said I was gay.'

'Didn't you once tell me he was a live-and-let-live kind of guy?'

'He was that. Doubt he could have envisaged the day when they would wear T-shirts advertising the fact, though. How about you and me doing it for good old-fashioned heterosexuality?' he suggested cheekily.

'Any time, Steve.' Jasmine slurped the last of her mocha through the straw and went on to a piece of carrot-and-marzipan cake. 'Any time you want to do it for heterosexuality is okay with me.'

There was a sadness in her voice. He knew something was wrong.

'What is it?' he asked.

'There's another kind of gossip around the station. Or rather it's the looks I'm getting. I'm sure that Jack Fieldhouse has been putting it around about us.'

'He didn't waste any time. You're sure you're not imagining it? You haven't actually heard anybody say anything?'

She looked down at her plate.

'When you're a woman, Steve, and two men look at you, you *know*. Well, I got that look this morning. Just sitting in the canteen, minding my own business.'

'It could be your imagination.'

'Fieldhouse made a comment,' she added. 'It was pretty obvious to me what he was referring to. He waited until I was in earshot and then said how he reckoned my new car would be a right goer. That wasn't my imagination.'

Madden felt angry. He wanted to go and smack Jack Fieldhouse in the face. Not only had the man fouled up the investigation into Jason's murder but now he was hurting Jasmine. The only thing that stopped him was that he knew it wouldn't do any good.

'I'm sorry,' he said. 'It's my fault.'

'Don't be stupid, Steve – I'm a grown woman and I know the risks. I can take a bit of banter, and I can give it back. What galls me is that here we are, sitting in the middle of Gay Pride, surrounded by people proud to be what they are, and we have to conduct our relationship in secret.'

'Me too,' said Madden.

*   *   *

Madden made an appointment to see Roger Dimarco that afternoon in London. Dimarco was one of those people you couldn't see in their office without an appointment made weeks ahead. Nevertheless, he had cancelled two other meetings at a moment's notice in order to accommodate Madden. Dimarco's executive suite at the top of the Dimarco Corporation Building in Canary Wharf was not one of those places where the buck stopped. It was the kind of place that the buck never reached. An eagle's nest with a stunning view up and down the Thames, it was furnished in a minimalist style, with two David Hockneys and an Andy Warhol on blindingly pure white walls.

Dimarco's secretary, a brisk and terrifyingly efficient middle-aged woman in horn-rimmed glasses who would have caused a stampede if let loose in Jurassic Park, showed him into the inner sanctum of the Dimarco Corporation.

'Mr Madden to see you, sir.' She announced his arrival in slightly disapproving tones. She had been forced to alter Dimarco's diary quite considerably, and at great inconvenience, in order to indulge him in the unusual peccadillo of seeing someone almost immediately, a situation that was new to her and practically unheard of.

Roger Dimarco strode towards Madden, clasping his visitor's outstretched hand in both of his.

'Good to see you.' He seemed to bask in the warmth of their meeting.

'Thanks for seeing me so quickly,' Madden said to be polite, though he hadn't expected any different.

'We don't want to be disturbed, Jennifer. Thank you,' he told his secretary. She left briskly. He showed Madden to a white leather sofa by a polished glass-top table where there was coffee already waiting.

'Terrific view,' said Madden.

'It has its aesthetic qualities. Not everybody wants to do their business at the top of tall buildings after September eleven but you can't let evil win, can you?'

'No, you can't.' Madden acknowledged the fact.

Dimarco pured him out some strong coffee.

'You like the Warhol?'

'An original?'

'You bet.'

'Jason ever mention to you a person called Alan Michaels?' Madden cut across the small talk.

'He did mention the name. Football coach or something, wasn't he?'

'Yes.'

Dimarco sank back into the sofa and crossed one leg over the other, exposing an expanse of white shin above a bright red sock.

'Jason said Michaels was a chap he had a relationship with when he was fourteen,' he elaborated, as though it was the most natural thing in the world.

'Were they still in contact?'

'He didn't say. I don't think so. He only told me about him one night on the boat.'

'How much did he tell you about the relationship?'

'It was just, like, part of his growing-up.' Dimarco resisted the temptation to shrug. 'I asked him how old he was when he first had sex and he told me about this guy.'

'Who instigated it?'

'I have no idea. I don't think Jason ever told me. He was certainly . . . certainly very attached to him. Teenage crush, sort of thing.'

There was more. Dimarco was holding back. Madden could tell. He decided to approach the most sensitive part of the interview in the way he knew best. Directly.

'Did Jason ever say my wife was involved?'

'I don't want to make problems here—'

'Just give me it straight, Mr Dimarco.'

'Okay.' Dimarco took a deep breath. 'Jason told me his mother found out but that she swore she would never tell you. They made a sort of pact because they were worried about your reaction. That's all. I think she was instrumental in ending the relationship.' He added, 'Jason seemed very attached to his mother.'

'Were you in love with Jason?' Madden threw the question at him suddenly. It was clear from Dimarco's response that it had pole-axed him.

'That depends how you define love.' He stumbled slightly over the words.

'We're both men of the world, Mr Dimarco. We know how to define love.'

'I suppose – in a certain way – yes, I was in love with him.'

'*Your unconventional friend.* Care to tell me where that came from?'

Dimarco's eyes glazed over. And yet he seemed prepared for the question. The flowers had been left there for Madden to see. It had only been a matter of time before they would have this conversation. A murder case – any case, in fact – was like an onion. You peeled and peeled away at the layers and there was always another layer underneath. You rarely ever got to the core. But you got as damned near to it as you could.

'Jason came up with the expression.' Dimarco explained. 'It's a long story. But if you want to know the truth—'

'I want to know the truth.'

Dimarco stood up, crossed to the window, and gazed down at the silvery-grey Thames that twisted serpent-like across the city. He was a man who had reached the pinnacle of his profession. Alongside the Hockneys and the Warhol were photographs of himself when he had been a reigning tennis champion in his early twenties. They depicted a handsome young man who not only held a silver cup but who had the whole world in his grasp. That early sporting promise had faded but Dimarco had a good business head on his shoulders. Now he was counted as one of the richest hundred men in Britain. But it didn't matter how high up you reached. There was always a way down.

'You can be a millionaire many times over, Mr Madden, have all the success that you crave, and yet still fall victim to the most . . . the most reckless emotions.'

Madden knew that. You didn't have to be rich to know it.

'As you know, with Jason and me it began as a purely financial thing. There was nothing wrong with that. He wasn't a cheap rent boy or however you want to describe that sort. He was an intelligent young man and he was doing it because he enjoyed doing it. I'm not trying to justify myself, Mr Madden, I don't think I have to. But I'm just trying to give you the picture.'

'Go on.'

Dimarco swallowed hard. It looked to Madden as though he was dredging up part of his soul.

'One day – Jason refused to take any money off me. He said he'd been thinking about it for some time, that it was starting to bother him. He said he thought it was wrong and that he liked me too much to do it. It was enough for him that I would take him on holiday, out on the boat, that sort of thing. Well, to be truthful, that kind of changed things.'

'How?'

'It changed our relationship. The way I felt about him. Paying for – what we did – kept a kind of distance between us. A professional detachment. I had a nineteen-year-old boy waking up with me in the morning and it was just—'

Dimarco struggled for the words to explain it. *Keep peeling the onion*, thought Madden.

'I'm sixty-one years old. Do you know how that made me feel?'

Do you know how it makes me *feel?* thought Madden.

'We're all human,' he said dryly. 'But with age comes responsibility.'

'I know that. You don't need to tell me about responsibility.' Dimarco dropped his cool facade for a moment. 'This is how it was. And I was taking a fatherly interest in him. I'm not explaining this very well, I know, but – it changed our relationship and I found myself falling in love with him. I didn't want to, believe me, I have enough responsibilities without having to cope with something like that.'

'You could have finished it.'

'I thought about that. I really did.'

'Was Jason in love with you?'

'That was the strange part of it, Mr Madden. Look – do you mind if I call you Steve?'

'I don't mind.'

He did, but it wasn't the moment to say so.

'"Strange" is the wrong word. I told Jason during one holiday how I felt. He said he felt the same way. And everything went fine for a few days until – one night he didn't want to do anything—'

'You mean, have sex?'

'Yes.'

'Why don't you just say these things outright?'

Dimarco turned to him and tried to explain. 'Because you're his father and I am finding this very, very difficult.'

'Not half as difficult as I am.'

'We had a big row about it. When I was paying Jason, there was never any problem, what we did was a straightforward business transaction, conducted between two people who were good friends. Being in love changed things.'

'It changed things,' said Madden, 'because love carries responsibilities.'

'*Both* types of relationship carried a great deal of responsibility,' Dimarco corrected him. 'Just because you're paying someone doesn't mean you don't feel responsible for them.'

'How big a row did you have?'

'Jason cried and said that he didn't want to be in love. He was . . . confused. I could see that. We flew back to London the next day and I suggested that we didn't see each other for a while, just to let things cool off.'

'Did they?'

'I wrote him a letter. Jason once remarked that our relationship was fantastic and unconventional. Those words stuck. In the letter I explained to Jason that it might be better if we broke off our friendship. I signed off with the words, *Your Unconventional Friend.*'

And there, thought Madden, *it should have rested*. But it hadn't. These things never did. For the first time, he began to realise exactly how much Jason had meant to Dimarco.

'I couldn't let it rest,' Dimarco confessed. 'I just missed him so much. And I was concerned about him. I didn't want him to be upset. So I phoned him up. He was overjoyed to hear from me. We talked about what to do – how to go forward.'

'And how did you?'

'I suggested we went back to the way we had been before. That we would continue to be good friends, that that wouldn't change, but that every time we had sex I would pay him, and there would be no arguments. He agreed.' Dimarco let a faint smile play on his lips for the first time. 'I remember saying something like: "Great, I've got myself a—" I didn't want to use the word "prostitute" or "escort". Jason said it for me. He said, you've got yourself an unconventional friend.'

Dimarco had finished talking. Madden got a sense of him having purged himself. As many layers of the onion as he could possibly have hoped for had come off.

'You played with his emotions. You're old enough to know better,' he said.

'I didn't play with them, Steve. Jason was looking for somebody older to relate to and he found that someone in me. I looked after him as best I could, tried to talk him out of taking drugs, took a real interest in his life. I remember what it was like to be nineteen. When I was that age, I wanted so much, I thrived on encouragement. The world was – was opening up for me. For Jason it was just opening up as well. I was prepared to take an interest in his future, help him in whatever career he chose for himself. He would perhaps have done another year of escorting at the most and learnt a lot of lessons from it.'

'He learnt a very hard lesson,' Madden reminded him bitterly.

Dimarco came and sat back down beside Madden. He rested his head on the back of the sofa, adopting a very unexecutive-like position.

'I don't expect you to like me,' he said. 'I don't expect you to understand what happened. But while Jason was with me he was as safe as he would have been with you.'

'And Celestine? Did she know you were in love with Jason?'

'I think so. I never told her. But she's not stupid.'

'I loved Jason too,' said Madden. 'I would give anything to have had half the love he seemed to give you.'

The jealousy and anger again. Madden tried to put a cap on it but couldn't.

'We never related properly.' He found himself suddenly opening up instead. 'I wanted to be a proper father, do things with my son that other fathers do.'

Indignation surged to the surface. He wanted to direct it at this man sitting next to him, but found in that very bleak moment that he couldn't. It turned inward, like a poisoned arrow, and pierced his own soul. This wasn't the reason he had come here. He wanted the truth. But the truth was worse than he could have imagined. The truth was that if he had been a more loving father to Jason, the boy might not have needed to look for – what was it Jason had been looking for? – the solace of older men.

'We must both find his killer, Steve,' Dimarco said. 'If you don't believe it was Demos Panagoulis, then I trust your judgement. You're the detective, not me. I could put up a reward of a hundred thousand pounds for information. And I don't say that or offer it lightly.'

'There's a problem there. Advertising it. The case is officially closed. I couldn't do it, the police couldn't do it. You would have to advertise it yourself.'

'That would be a problem.'

'I thought it would be.'

'Look at the position I'm in, Steve.'

'It didn't stop you coming to his funeral. You say you loved Jason. Now's the time to prove it. If you can lay flowers on his grave you can do something to catch his killer. Or perhaps Jason didn't mean as much to you as he did to me?'

'I have a reputation in the business world. I'm sure you appreciate that.'

'Perhaps you should have thought of that before.'

Dimarco thought about it now. 'My offer stands if I can find a way,' he said. 'But it must be strictly between us, Steve. An anónymous offer of a reward for information. If I can help find whoever killed Jason, then in some way it will expiate my guilt.'

'Your guilt?' Madden sounded surprised.

'The night he died, I was away with Celestine. I failed him too. He wanted to come with us but I – well, had to put other interests first. Celestine and I just felt we wanted some time to ourselves. Just wouldn't have done for Jason to be there all the time. I'm sure you understand. If I'd invited him along, he would have been with me and not—' He groped for the words. 'Whoever he was with.'

As Madden went to the door, he felt inclined to ask if Dimarco's offer of a reward extended as far as someone who might put the blame closer to his own front door than he liked, or could possibly imagine.

'Give my best to Celestine,' he simply said.

'I understand you two had dinner together. You would probably have got some of this from her eventually. I thought it best that you should get the full story from me.'

'I'm at least obliged to you for that.'

The two men shook hands.

'Keep me informed,' said Roger Dimarco.

29

Madden was awoken at six-thirty the following morning by the ringing of the telephone. News at that time of the morning was either very good or very bad. Usually it was very bad. Dimarco was on the other end of the line. His calm if emotional demeanour of the previous lunchtime had evaporated. In its place was a boiling rage. Madden wondered what had happened to transform the man. He was soon to find out.

'Did you tell them?' he hurled at Madden.

'Tell who?'

'You know damn well who. I made an anonymous offer of a reward for information – now I'm going to be out in the fucking open where I might as well make it public. Who else knows all the facts?'

'Mr Dimarco, why don't you calm down and tell me what all this is about?'

'The newspapers. That's what it's about. The *Mirror* phoned me late last night to tell me they're doing a story on me and Jason. They've got the lot. The fucking lot. They wanted my comments but wouldn't tell me who their source was.'

'It wasn't me,' said Madden.

'I don't know if I can trust you any more.'

'Trust me,' said Madden. 'It wasn't me.'

'Then who the hell was it? Who else knew all the facts?'

'Jason wasn't very discreet.' Madden tried to deflect Dimarco's ire. 'After all, he told you about his other clients, about Demos Panagoulis. The chances are that he told one of his other clients about you.'

'Jason wouldn't.'

'How do you know?'

'Because I trusted him.'

'Perhaps your trust was misplaced. You were taking him to the Med, out on your boat, treating him to a lavish lifestyle. You expect a nineteen-year-old boy to keep all that to himself? You said it yourself. You were nineteen once yourself. Imagine if it had happened to you. Would you have been able to resist going around telling everybody?'

'Shit,' said Dimarco.

'I'm sorry this has happened. I don't want it either. Do you think I want to see Jason's name all over the paper like this? What did you tell them?'

'I told them nothing.' Dimarco calmed down a little.

'They'll print it just the same.'

'I threatened to sue.'

'It's the truth. You might find that difficult.'

'It's the end,' said Dimarco. 'The fucking end.'

'I doubt it. Life goes on.' Madden tried to sound rational. 'Maybe thirty years ago you would be expected to fall on some kind of sword, but times have changed. You're a successful businessman, an entrepreneur. That stands you in good stead. What's one dalliance?'

'You think they'll write it that way?'

'No. Not for one minute.'

'They even knew that I'd attended Jason's funeral. They know the contents of the letter I sent to him. It wouldn't surprise me if they even had the letter itself. How do you suppose they got hold of that?'

'It might not be as bad as you think.'

'It might be worse,' said Dimarco.

'Believe me, I had nothing to do with it,' Madden reiterated. 'If I find out in the course of my inquiries, I'll let you know. I know it will be too late then, of course.'

'It's already too late.'

'I'm sorry,' said Madden. 'If there's anything I can do, I will.'

But Madden knew that there was nothing he could do.

He got up and went out for the papers. It was almost worse than Dimarco had described. The story had broken and the nation was waking up to the headline DIMARCO LINK IN RENT BOY MURDER and a further double-page spread inside with the banner MURDERED RENT BOY WAS DIMARCO'S LOVER – EXCLUSIVE. The paper quoted an anonymous but reliable source throughout.

Madden felt pretty hollow inside as well. To see Jason described in that way cut him up, made him feel as though his son would never be allowed to rest in peace.

'It's pretty devastating,' said Madden to Jasmine over a hasty lunch at the Cricketers pub. It was a cosy hostelry tucked away in the Lanes, one of the oldest in Brighton and a gem of Victoriana. Saturday was the day of the big Gay Pride parade and the city was packed, with visitors cramming into every venue, gay, straight and in-between. Three of them were talking about the news at the next table, relishing the ripping of yet another closet door off its hinges.

'It wasn't you, was it, Steve?' she asked him outright.

'Course it wasn't. Do you think that I'd want to see Jason's name plastered all over the paper like that? Curiously, I feel sorry for the guy.'

'How come?'

'Dimarco opened his heart to me yesterday. I can see how all this happened. The sooner I get it out of my head that Jason was abused by all and sundry the clearer I'll see into this thing. I wanted to know Jason and I'm finding out. I'm also jealous and I don't like that. I'm jealous because Dimarco had something I wanted: Jason's affection. Am I making sense?'

'Perfectly.'

'Did you find out anything about Michaels?'

'Haven't traced him yet. He doesn't have a record. That's the first thing I checked.'

'Keep looking.'

'It would help me a great deal if I knew why you were interested in him.'

Madden saw no reason to keep her in the dark any longer.

'Let's just say history has repeated itself. Alan Michaels was somebody Jason was attached to when he was fourteen years old.'

'How attached?'

'Scarcely matters. They were attached. I learnt about him from Clara.'

'And you think he might have wanted to kill Jason? In case Jason ever told anybody about him?'

'It's a distinct possibility. He might have been worrying about it for years. Who knows?'

'Your surveillance expert is settled in at the Red Planet.' She changed the subject. 'I pointed out Daniel to him. You sure he's up to this?'

'He hasn't let me down so far,' said Madden.

'Why Lucky Maynard? The boy's a villain.'

'He's given me good information over the years. Let's just say I feel kind of paternal towards him.'

Jasmine got the message. 'Let's hope you reform him.'

'I wasn't setting out to do that.'

'But it could be the end result?'

'Could be.'

The hubbub had been growing steadily. They heard the sound of whistles outside. Someone was banging a drum. The three gay men who had been gloating over the newspaper story at the next table hurried out, discarding the paper on a stool as they left for bigger and more important things. Tomorrow it would be the turn of the Sunday newspapers and the following week it would be yesterday's news – for most of the population, at least.

'Fancy going to see it?' said Jasmine. 'I'm off today. Let's make the most of it.'

They found that the parade had already started and was making its noisy, joyful way from the Peace Statue, the angel that presided over the holy union of Brighton and Hove, towards Preston Park in the north of the city where the festivities would carry on well into the night. Madden felt, as he watched the parade, that he knew

Jason better than ever. There was no escaping the exuberance of Pride. Floats passed them full of drag queens in increasingly outrageous attire, local gay youth groups, construction workers who had never seen a construction site, a tableau of the *Wizard of Oz* with a banner designating everyone on board as a Friend of Dorothy. The lesbian Caribbean band, which the day before had taken up an entire pavement, was now on wheels, pumping out steely rhythms as it rode past. Buckets jangled, full of coins for local charities and Aids hospices. Someone handed Madden a gladiolus. He waved it. Jasmine waved hers, too. The blowing of whistles was almost deafening.

'Smile, honey!'

Madden looked up. Ming was on one of the floats, dispensing confetti and free condoms from a cloud of evaporating dry ice.

'That's it – smile, honey!' Ming shouted again. She was wearing a cobalt-blue dress that shimmered in the sunlight like a burnished dragonfly. She waved frantically and blew an exaggerated kiss.

Madden smiled. He wondered which one Jason would have been on. Would he have been here, smiling, supporting him? Probably not. Yet here he was, a gladiolus in his hand, watching the parade and thinking of his son. He wished Jason could know that.

While a few miles away, in a millionaire's house in Hove, one gay man who didn't parade his sexuality was in all probability battening down the hatches and refusing to talk to the press who, Madden was sure, would now be camped at his gates. Madden wondered who the 'anonymous source' was. A client? One of Jason's friends?

He cared. A killer had taken Jason away from him and in so doing had almost destroyed his life. He didn't want to see anybody else's life destroyed. Even that of Roger Dimarco.

He and Jasmine followed the parade up to Preston Park. There was very little trouble. A couple of kids whose bravery probably deserved a medal if nothing else shouted a few derogatory words and were promptly chased up a side street by three transvestites and, Madden had no doubt, promptly handbagged. In the park there were marquees, a fairground with dodgems and bungee jumping, and a two-thousand-capacity dance tent. Within minutes of the parade descending on the park there was a tug-of-war between two teams that ended in utter disarray.

And then he saw Daniel who looked for all the world as though nothing bad had ever happened to him. He had a broad, beaming smile on his face and his arms were draped around the shoulders of people Madden didn't recognise. But he did recognise someone else on the edge of the group. Terry Hindland was herding them together.

Madden went over and spoke to Daniel.

'Hello, Daniel.'

'Hello, Mr Madden. How are you?' He sounded high on something. Nothing new.

'This is my colleague, Jasmine Carol. Daniel.' He introduced them. 'Having a good time?'

'Yeh. Terry's just getting us all into the VIP enclosure,' Daniel boasted.

'Well, enjoy yourself.'

'We will.'

Madden picked up a brochure and saw the VIP enclosure described. *Hobnob with the bright and beautiful people in the 'Royal Circle' VIP enclosure. Gourmet buffet. Champagne and cocktail bar, private garden and unparalleled views of the park and main stage.*

Typical Daniel, he thought. He wondered if the youth ever cultivated a friendship with someone who didn't buy him things or get him in somewhere. Then he considered that the same thing might have been said of Jason. The world went round like that. Money was power, and those who had it knew it.

'I just need to get some cash out,' Jasmine said.

She was sitting in the passenger seat of Madden's car as he drove her home. Home for Jasmine was in Coldean on the outskirts of the city where she shared a semi-detached house with two other Asian women. Madden thought it would be a nice idea if they got out of Brighton that night and had a quiet supper somewhere further along the coast, or perhaps at some village pub on the Sussex Downs. He missed working with her. It continued to stick in his craw that she was now attached, even if it was temporary, to Jack Fieldhouse. It still rankled that in the heat of Gay Pride they had to keep their relationship a secret because of a male-dominated culture that branded young unmarried policewomen as 'bikes' if they slept around. Jasmine hadn't slept around but it scarcely mattered. The impression was all-important.

And with a bastard like Fieldhouse pumping fuel into the gossip engine, there was no telling where her reputation might end up. He remembered years back when he'd had his brief affair with a young female detective sergeant who wasn't his partner. Her name had been Caroline and she *had* slept around, though only with a couple of more junior officers before him. It was a big mistake, and he regretted it. The affair was one of a number of catalysts that had eventually precipitated the end of his marriage. It had also hastened the end of Caroline's career because she was turned down for promotion and promptly left the force. She always maintained it was because she had acquired a reputation. No one could know for sure.

What Madden knew for sure was that he didn't want the same fate befalling Jasmine. She was a good cop and the force needed women like her.

'Can you stop just here for me, Steve?'

He pulled up and she got out and went across the road to a cash machine. Madden switched on the local radio station. There was a live broadcast from Pride. He leant back and at first only registered marginally the white Ford Escort pulling up on the other side of the road.

Two youths leapt out. One remained in the car. Madden caught the movement out of the corner of his eye and turned his head swiftly. The passenger-side window was down. He heard the voices before he could see anything because the other car was blocking his view, but it was enough to spur him into immediate action.

'Give us that, you fucking Paki black bitch.'

Madden was legging it across the road. He almost collided with a van travelling too fast. Jasmine brought her knee up into the groin of one of the attackers. The other twisted her arm and seized the money.

Madden ran across the pavement. He dragged off the one with the money while Jasmine beat at the other with her fists.

'Police.' Madden produced his ID card.

The lad in the driving seat blasted on his horn and at the same time decided to make the proposed getaway fast – and without his two companions. He screeched off, tyres smoking, up the road, while the two left behind quickly surrendered.

'Snap,' said Jasmine, bringing out her own card.

'Fuck, man,' swore the one whom Jasmine had kneed in the groin and who was still smarting with the pain. 'That's fucking assault, man.'

'Dead right, my friend,' said Madden. 'You're both under arrest.'

'You black *cunt*.' The stricken scumbag delivered the obscenity with the viciousness of a cornered animal straight into Jasmine's face as Madden seized the shoulder of his jacket. 'How come *you*'re a fucking policewoman? Of all my *fucking* luck.'

They were a choice breed, Madden thought. Unmistakable South London accents. They certainly weren't local.

The two detectives hauled the unsuccessful muggers over to Madden's car and within minutes had reinforcements on the scene. It didn't take long to trace and stop the third member of the little party. They were all in their twenties and, as Madden had rightly guessed, they weren't from Brighton. It would later emerge that they had driven down to Brighton looking for 'a few poofs' to set upon but had decided that they were spectacularly outnumbered. While driving back through the outskirts they had chanced upon what they'd thought was a far easier target, a lone Asian woman standing at a cash machine on a street corner. It had clearly not been their day.

'You okay?' Madden said to Jasmine after they had both finished making their statements.

'Where were we?' She tried to pretend that nothing had happened.

'I was driving you home. You still want to go there?'

'I think I'd like that very much,' she answered.

He took her home, and they abandoned their plans to have something to eat that night. Jasmine had phoned her mother who was driving down to be with her daughter. Madden decided not to stick around. Racist yobs he could cope with, mothers he wasn't sure about. He felt aggrieved that three animals – there was no other way to describe them – had ruined his evening with her.

It was a mild night. It had also been a disturbing one. Police officers rarely got attacked in such an unprovoked way. Jasmine had just been unlucky. But she had held up well. He was proud of her. It was the second time in her career that she had whipped out her warrant card and brought someone down to size. The knee to the thug's groin had been a pretty quick response, too. Madden wouldn't have wanted to be on the receiving end of *that*.

He went home and tried to piece together the evidence about Jason. He thought of driving along to the Dimarco house and offering his support. It would be an excuse to see Celestine again, but he felt that the Dimarcos, like Jasmine, probably needed some time on their own.

Celestine. He couldn't get her out of his mind. Tolerant partner or jealous wife? Neither could he stop thinking about Daniel Donoghue. Jealous boyfriend or just a crackhead who cared about no one but himself? And Roger Dimarco. What was he? Surrogate father or just a man who knew what money could buy him?

Madden went down to the nudist beach, stripped off down to his shorts, then took them off too and waded into the icy-cold water. He wasn't alone on the beach. There was someone with a metal detector who seemed oblivious to the fact that there were naked people around at eleven o'clock at night. Madden splashed out until the buoyancy of the water threw him off his feet, and a wave tossed him back towards the shore. He hung there among the breakers, weed softly gathering around his ankles like gentle threads softly caressing him. *Ferapy*, his old man had called it.

Being in the sea, naked, at one with nature. Though Madden Senior had never done it at night. Night was for the pub. Night was for the beer and his fags and his mates. *Come in and enjoy the ferapy.*

Madden vowed, in that moment, that he would not rest until he had found Jason's murderer. If it took days, weeks, or even years, he would do it.

There was really nothing else he could do.

30

'Steve, get over here right away. The Red Planet. Three kids are dead. They were all friends of Jason's.'

At first Madden couldn't believe the words he was hearing. It was Jasmine's voice coming down the line at two a.m. He'd only been asleep for an hour, but it took him less than a second to comprehend the urgency of her message. He swung his legs out of bed and sat on the edge, gripping the phone.

'Just repeat that,' he said. 'Just so I get it right.'

'Three friends of Jason's – and Daniel's – are all dead at the Red Planet.'

'Who?'

'Kevin Martin, Mark Thomas and Joseph Conolly.'

It was as though a computer hard drive in Madden's not-yet-functioning brain suddenly booted up. Kevin, Marky and Joe. The three rent boys who had come to Jason's funeral, and whom he had spoken to only two days before at the party in Croydon.

'All three? How?'

'Ecstasy,' said Jasmine. 'Or at least that's what it looks like.'

Madden dressed quickly and was at the Red Planet in fifteen minutes. The streets of Brighton were deserted. Gay Pride had gravitated to the numerous city clubs, of which the Red Planet was the biggest, the newest and the most popular. Jasmine was waiting for him outside. There was a steady trickle of clubbers out into the street, faces marred with grief and shock. Three ambulances were parked outside the door, blue lights pulsating. They had arrived too late.

'Who's taken charge?' he asked her.

'Fieldhouse,' she said. 'And he's treating this as a murder inquiry. You'd better come in and see.'

Madden walked into the cavernous room in which three or four hundred clubbers stood miserably, some clearly spaced out of their heads, others shedding tears over the fact that death had come to the biggest and most spectacular night of the year. A sizeable chunk of the Brighton police force was there, taking statements and names and addresses, and releasing people a few at a time. A huge Gay Pride banner was slung across from wall to wall, streamers and helium-filled balloons floated about, sad remnants of the night, and there was the unmistakable and all-pervasive sweet sickly smell of amyl nitrate, the 'poppers' that Madden knew increased the heart rate. Lying on the floor, in contorted positions and with agony etched on their young faces, were the bodies of three boys whose heartbeats had stopped. The local pathologist was kneeling by one of the corpses, shining a torch into lifeless eyes.

'Ecstasy did this?' Madden sounded sceptical.

'They all took it a few minutes before they died,' Jasmine said. 'One tablet each. One of the boys had six more in his pocket. They've gone away for analysis.'

'Never knew Ecstasy to kill people dead on the spot like that.'

'Witnesses say they just collapsed and started writhing. A few said their backs seemed to arch.'

'Christ.' Madden thought of the waste of three young lives. And for what? A few kicks. A high. And then he saw Daniel Donoghue. He was sitting nervously in a corner, talking to Jack Fieldhouse. Gone was his cheerfulness from the previous afternoon as he'd breezed towards the VIP enclosure in Preston Park in company with his friends. He was wearing a tight black vest that was soaked with sweat and a thin gold chain round his neck. His lean arms looked skeletal. His pale, almost bloodless face and his black-dyed hair were covered in glitter, as were his clothes. He looked like a Hallowe'en ghost that had been dusted down and dressed up for Christmas. The party had stopped suddenly.

Madden walked over to them. Fieldhouse looked up. A tub of

shit in a suit. That was how Fieldhouse always looked to Madden.
He almost felt sorry for Daniel, who'd drawn the short straw.

'Hello, Daniel,' he said.

'Hello, Mr Madden.' Daniel's voice was shaky and pleading.

'Thought you were taking time off,' Fieldhouse said.

'Couldn't stay away from the job. You finished with him yet?'

'Why?'

'Because when you are I'd like to talk to him.'

'They didn't get the E off me, Mr Madden.' Daniel had tears
in his eyes. 'Honestly. I had two tablets of my own and I've taken
one and the other one's still in my pocket.'

Actually, it wasn't still in his pocket. Fieldhouse had taken it,
bagged it up, and sent it off to Forensics. But Madden got the
message.

'They all just fell down on the floor,' Daniel cried. 'They were
in agony. I tried to help them. Marky died in my arms!'

Daniel sobbed. Fieldhouse looked irritated. Madden wanted to
put a hand on Daniel's shoulder. He didn't like him but nobody
deserved to see three friends die like this.

'Mind if I finish this interview?' Fieldhouse asked pointedly.

'Be my guest, Jack.'

Madden went with Jasmine over to where the bodies of the three
boys were now being put into bags for transportation to the city
mortuary. It was his first opportunity to get a closer look at them.
It was hard. Hard looking at their changed faces, hard thinking of
the sheer agony that had taken their features and twisted them into
ugly masks, tough contemplating the thought of three teenagers
who had come out for a night of fun and ended up dying horribly.
Marky wore a pair of baggy trousers and designer trainers and
a tank-top vest exposing a navel with a stud in it. Joe had white
tracksuit bottoms and a black polo neck. Kevin had his hair in
spikes. Madden could imagine without difficulty all three of them
spending time in front of the mirror, unaware that they had only
hours to live. He blinked back a few tears. The day he became
immune or desensitised to death would be the day he gave up
being a policeman.

'Anyone know yet where they got the Ecstasy from? Or are we in stupid-question land?'

'The kids get searched at the door by security and any drugs are taken off them. But it's a pretty safe bet they get recirculated inside – though no one's admitting to it.'

'Three kids are dead!' Madden shouted. 'What do you mean, no one's admitting to it?'

'Don't shoot the messenger, Steve.'

'Sorry.' He brushed her arm gently. 'How are you?'

'I'm fine,' she said. 'Still a little shaken but unstirred.'

'That's my Jaz.'

'Then, of course, there are the drugs supplied under the counter by Sullivan's own security personnel. Nobody right now is admitting to that, either.'

'Je – sus.' Madden felt like despairing.

'I've spoken to a few of the kids who smuggled drugs in,' she said. 'Your friend Daniel brought in two Ecstasy tablets, or so he says, in the heel of his shoe. So it's not impossible they were brought in by someone from the outside.'

'Ecstasy didn't do that.' Madden looked down at the faces of the boys.

'Something did. You think there's a connection with Jason?'

'They all knew Jason. They all knew Daniel. Daniel was Jason's boyfriend. You work it out.'

'Even if it was an accident?'

'Is that what you believe? That this was an accident?'

'No, sir,' she said. 'I don't.'

'Nor do I.'

A familiar figure strode towards Madden, wearing crocodile-skin shoes and a camel-hair coat. He was not smiling. Even the rings on his fingers seemed to have lost their lustre. Frank Sullivan had been dragged out of his bed and now surveyed the appalling scene with his own eyes. There were dark bags under them. Before the night was out, they would get a lot heavier, Madden reckoned.

'All love, peace and happiness now,' Madden said to him. 'The kids enjoy themselves. That's what life should be about.'

He grabbed hold of Frank Sullivan by the lapel and twisted his head to make him look at the three teenage corpses.

'Well, look at them! Is *that* what life should be about?'

'Not my fault,' Sullivan said, lamely.

'Not your fault? You run this club and you control the drugs that are sold in it!'

'No drugs are sold here.' Frank Sullivan stared him straight in the face, almost defying him to believe it.

'What do your security staff do? Give them away for Oxfam?'

'No drugs are sold here,' Sullivan repeated in a calm and measured tone.

'Take a good look at those kids. None of them are twenty-one yet. They had everything to live for. Everything. Till they came in through these doors.'

'Ecstasy kills relatively few people.' Sullivan sounded like a token apologist for a pro-drugs lobby. 'It's a well-known fact.'

'Let me tell you another well-known fact, Mr Sullivan. You've already presided over a club where one Ecstasy death took place. Now you've got three on your hands. Your days as a club owner are finished. When this enquiry is over, I'll see to it with everything in my power that this place is shut down and that you are not only finished in this city but everywhere else. Do you want me to make that any plainer?'

'I think you've made your point.' Sullivan turned away.

'You've become like these rings on your fingers. History,' Madden threw in for good measure. Sullivan did not appreciate the joke.

Madden had no doubt that Sullivan knew that what he'd told him was true. No club survived something like this. No club operator did. It was one of the hazards. Ecstasy deaths *were* few and far between but when one came along, blind eyes that had been shut for years were suddenly prised wide open.

'You can't keep your eye on every youngster,' said Sullivan lamely and in his own defence. 'You should know that as a father. You couldn't keep one son on the rails, Mr Madden – you expect us to look after the welfare of eight hundred kids? Don't make me laugh.'

Madden felt rage swelling up inside him. That this piece of human detritus had actually referred to Jason in justification for what had happened in his club was more than he could humanly take. Luckily, Jasmine intervened before his fist could connect with Frank Sullivan's face. Which was just as well. He had never punched anybody in his life and this wasn't a good place to start.

In that moment – Madden thought he caught it – a look passed between Fieldhouse and Sullivan. He felt like taking Fieldhouse aside as well. That wouldn't have been a good idea, either. Chief Superintendent Millington had just turned up.

Millington, who had witnessed his confrontation with Sullivan, put a gentle but restraining hand on his shoulder.

'Steve, can I have a word, please?'

Madden retreated, but his eyes still blazed with anger.

'I want you out of here,' Millington said coldly.

Jasmine looked on, then turned away. Madden thought it best not to involve her.

'I want you off this investigation. I know you feel aggrieved but this isn't the time to take it out on the likes of Sullivan,' Millington continued.

'Aggrieved, sir? That's an understatement.'

'Look at me. I want you to go home and *rest*.'

'Rest? You have to be kidding. These boys were all friends of Jason's!'

'I know that.' Millington lowered his voice and drew Madden aside. He said tersely, 'And if you start drawing connections with his murder, this could blow it wide open.'

'Blow what wide open?'

Millington sighed deeply, looked down at his feet, then glanced about him to make sure that no one else was listening. When his gaze met Madden's again, there was deep forewarning in it. He spoke in a deeply hushed but nonetheless angry tone.

'The fact you think that we got it wrong. Every time there's an

Ecstasy death in this country, the papers go to town. With three, God knows where they'll stop. Your association might make them think there's some cover-up. I can't risk that.'

'These weren't Ecstasy deaths,' said Madden, pushing the point hard.

'Whatever they were, those kids believed they were taking Ecstasy tablets.'

'And you stand there and tell me you don't believe this has something to do with Jason's murder? Because you don't want this case contaminated with the shambles that you allowed Jack Fieldhouse to make of the last one?'

'Don't tax my patience, Steve.'

'Don't tax mine.'

'Our agreement still stands. You find me evidence that we were wrong about Panagoulis and I'll act on it. Until then, keep out of this.'

Madden watched Daniel get up and move away from Fieldhouse. Fieldhouse glared over at him like a bull about to charge at a red cloak. Daniel disappeared down the stairs, probably glad to be out of his presence.

'You won't even know I'm there,' Madden said cryptically.

31

Death had come to Mardi Gras. The dancing had stopped and the laughing with it. The clusters of people who were hanging about on the street outside the Red Planet looked as though they had nowhere else to go. Daniel Donoghue stood limply in the shadows, his head lowered. Ming had her arms around him.

Madden walked up to them.

'Okay, honey?' said Ming desperately. The mascara on her face had run into black rivulets that she attacked with a tissue drawn from a sequinned handbag.

'I'm okay,' said Madden.

'They were good kids,' Ming blurted out, holding back more tears. 'They didn't harm anybody.'

'I know that, Ming.'

'You know that expression, *Don't piss on my parade*? Well, some-body certainly came along tonight and pissed on our parade.'

'For what it's worth, Ming, you look gorgeous,' he compli-mented her.

'Thank you, darling. Maybe you prefer that to "honey".'

He smiled.

'Daniel, can we talk privately?' he asked.

Daniel kissed Ming and she gave him a tight, rapturous hug. Then he went down onto the beach with Madden. The sea looked ink black under a moonless sky. Had it only been four hours ago he was swimming in it, unaware of the drama that was unfolding and that would claim three more lives? The lights of vessels winked far out at sea. The roll of surf on the shingle was the only sound. They sat down. Even though it was milder now, Daniel shivered. The sweat on his black vest was starting to make it stick coldly to his skin. Madden took off his jacket and draped it over the young man's shoulders. Daniel looked up.

'It's okay,' Madden said. 'I've got a jumper on underneath.'

'I'll never take Ecstasy again,' Daniel stated. If his one remaining tablet had not already been taken away from him for analysis, he would, Madden felt sure, have flung it into the sea. 'I swear it, I swear it!'

'Not a bad idea.'

'I never saw anybody die like that. It was horrible.'

'How did they die? Tell me.'

'I only had one tablet left. We were all dancing together. Kevin went off to get some more. He came back and handed them out, though I didn't take one because I still had one of my own. It happened so quickly.'

'Describe it.'

'I think it was Joe first. He seemed to have trouble breathing. Though he was still smiling. Like you do on E. But it wasn't the same kind of smile. Then it was just like he had a seizure. He fell on the floor and his body went all stiff. His back kept arching, like this.'

Daniel gave a demonstration, pushing out his birdlike chest and bending his back.

'Then Kev and Marky seemed to follow a few minutes later. They were lying on the floor and they couldn't breathe! I knelt down and held Marky but it seemed to make him worse. He just kept – seizing up, and he was frothing at the mouth. I think he was in my arms when he died.'

Madden put a hand on his arm, which was trembling.

'It's okay, Daniel,' he said. 'Just take your time.'

'I never saw it do that to anyone before.'

'Do you know where Kevin got the E from?'

Daniel shook his head. 'He came back, we were dancing, he just handed them out. I don't know where he got them from.'

'Where would he normally have got them?'

'One of the bar staff. Or the security personnel. You had to be known. They wouldn't just give it out to anybody.'

'Names, Daniel.'

'I don't know any of the names. I've never been down to this club before. Kevin had been. He was known, he knew everybody.'

'Who else might he have bought the drugs from?'

'He could have bought them from anybody. Okay, they search you at the door but there are always ways. I'm sure you know.'

'I hear you smuggled yours in in the heel of your shoe?'

'Old trick of mine,' said Daniel.

'How many did he come back with? Do you know?'

'I don't know.'

Even under Madden's jacket, draped about his shoulders like a cape, Daniel was still shuddering. The terrifying images of that night continued to play in his mind. He would probably never forget them.

'This may not seem like the right time, Daniel. But did you give any thought to our last meeting? You were going to draw up a list of all the things you and Jason talked about the morning he died.'

'You don't think this is connected, do you?'

'Do you?'

'I can't see how,' Daniel said, almost furtively.

He put his hand into his pocket and pulled out his wallet. From that, he unfolded a sheet of paper. He passed it to Madden.

'I was going to contact you tomorrow. Let you have this. It's all I can remember.'

Madden glanced over it. On half a side of an A4 sheet of paper had been printed a series of disconnected thoughts. He would study them later. But one sentence stood out.

'There was nothing really important,' Daniel said. 'Just chat.'

'Says here you asked Jason when he was going to give up escorting.'

'That's right.'

'Sounds pretty important to me.'

'It's something we talked about all the time.'

'You wanted him to give up but he wouldn't? Were you willing to give up yourself?'

Daniel seemed to retreat inside himself for a few moments.

'I would have done if he had,' he answered.

'Is that the truth?'

'Of course it's the truth. The morning he was killed, when I was having that webcam conversation with him, he said he was tired of it. He said that Greek guy had phoned him four times and had been to the door but he didn't want to see him. Then he changed his mind and said he might see him because the money was good.'

'You didn't tell me this before, Daniel.'

'I just assumed he had changed his mind like he said and let Panagoulis in.'

'Panagoulis claimed he never went back. If that's true, then someone else knocked on Jason's door and Jason let him in.'

'Maybe,' said Daniel, 'he thought it was Panagoulis.'

'Maybe. You're absolutely certain he didn't say he was expecting anyone else?'

'Absolutely certain,' Daniel assured him.

Daniel picked up a handful of pebbles and slung them into the breaking surf. The sound of them plopping into the sea was barely audible above the rush of white water as it clawed at the shingle. Daniel flung another handful, and then another. Four of his friends had died in the space of a few days. Madden reckoned that nothing Daniel Donoghue learnt at Cambridge would stand him in better stead for the future than the lessons he had learnt that night. If Daniel had taken one of the tablets, he too would be on his way to a mortuary right now.

'Are you staying down here in Brighton tonight?'

'Yes. At George Adams's flat. We were all going to stay there.'

'I'll drive you back there. If you like.'

'I'd like that very much.'

They stood up.

'Mr Madden,' asked Daniel, still shivering under the jacket, 'do you think whoever sold Kevin these tablets intended to kill all of us?'

'It looks that way.'

'I thought so,' Daniel said, sounding almost as calm as the night, and for one strange, unfathomable moment, seemingly relieved.

32

Madden drove Daniel Donoghue back to the flat where it had all begun. It was a difficult journey to make. Etched in Madden's brain were the images that still haunted him. His son's severed penis. The mouth stuffed with excrement. The many stab wounds. Jason's face, pressed into the carpet, surrounded by a puddle of blood. How many times had he tried to blot the memory out? How many times had it come back?

He wondered if he ought to go upstairs with Daniel, to see the flat again, to see the place. He knew he had to. The first and only time he had entered that flat, he had rushed out of it, unable to face the horror of knowing it was Jason's corpse in there. He hadn't taken in the crime scene. Others had done that. By now, of course, it would have changed, been altered, but nonetheless he had to go up there and see the room again.

'Stop for a coffee,' said Daniel as they climbed the stairs.

'Thanks,' said Madden, though coffee was the last thing on his mind.

George Adams was in the flat, with Ming. He hadn't been to the club, but Ming had told him everything. She was still red-eyed, still reeling from shock. Her shoes were kicked off, lying like little broken toys on the carpet. From between her trembling fingers a cigarette protruded, the ash from which fell onto her tights. Her mascara had run until her face looked like the Nile Delta.

George Adams was nursing a can of lager, his shirt unbuttoned to the waist. He was hunched forward, rocking slightly. He looked up as Madden and Daniel Donoghue came in.

Ming burst into tears again and disappeared into a bedroom from where Madden heard the sound of uncontrolled sobbing.

'I heard everything,' said Adams, stony-faced.

'You weren't at the club?' Madden asked. 'Why?'

'Too old for that kind of thing. Too past it. Just want a quiet domestic life nowadays. Put my feet up, enjoy the television. Have a few beers.'

'Do a bit of pimping on the side?'

'You summed it up.'

'Did they all used to work for you? In that brothel you ran in London?' Madden asked.

'Yup. They all worked for me. They were good kids.'

'Know why anyone would want to kill them?'

'No,' said Adams. 'I don't.'

Madden looked at the floor. The bloodstained carpet had been removed. In its place was a Chinese rug, thrown hastily over bare floorboards. Other than that, the flat had changed little. The table on which the smashed computer had stood now boasted a horrendous pink plastic head of David with a lamp inside, the ultimate in gay kitsch. Madden got the feeling that it was there just to fill a space. He wondered about the smashed computer. He had seen computers smashed before, usually after domestic arguments, but none quite so thoroughly as this one had been. Did the killer expect to find two grands' worth of Ecstasy hidden inside? Or was it just a way of showing that he meant business? Either way, it was excessive.

'Coffee?' asked Daniel.

'No, thanks.' Madden changed his mind. He didn't want to stay in this flat any longer than was necessary.

Daniel slumped into a chair, sullen and withdrawn, and folded his bare freckly arms in front of him. As hard as he tried, Madden could not rid himself of the thought that Daniel regretted not so much the fact that three of his companions had died but that his evening of entertainment had been curtailed. It was an unpleasant thought, a deeply uncharitable one. But sometimes human nature at its worst shone through like a beacon. The Daniel Donoghues of this world were out for themselves, for what they could get. Sex, drugs, money, a fun time, and no reckoning.

There was always a reckoning.

'You're bound to be questioned, Mr Adams,' Madden warned him.

'I wasn't there,' said Adams.

'Maybe not, but the three boys who are dead all have one thing in common. They all worked as male prostitutes in your brothel in London once upon a time.'

'That was a long time ago,' said Adams.

'Motives for murder sometimes don't go away. They hang around for a long time. Fester. Obsess people. Like jealousy, anger, resentment.'

'I looked after them,' said Adams defensively.

'I'm not saying you didn't.'

Daniel shrunk even more morosely into his chair.

'Tell him, Daniel. Tell him I looked after all of you.'

'He looked after us,' said Daniel.

Ming's sobs came from the other room, voluble, hysterical. Adams got up.

'I've got to go to her,' he said.

'You go.'

Adams went through to the bedroom. Madden caught a glimpse of him comforting Ming, holding her in his arms. He sat on the bed and she buried her face in his chest. He stroked her hair. There was more than just friendship there.

'They used to be a couple,' Daniel told him.

'I know.'

'Before Ming became a woman.'

Adams got up and closed the door, protecting their privacy.

'Who did it hit harder?' Madden asked.

'Both of them. Ming wanted George to love him as a woman, but George only likes men. They're still close, though. Like brother and sister.'

Madden looked once again at the sheet of paper that Daniel had given him on the beach. If this was the extent of half an hour of conversation between two people who professed to be in love, then Madden despaired for the young. He could have dealt with everything on the list in about five minutes. Or were there just lots of lovers' silences? It wasn't as though he had never been in love himself.

'You sure this is everything you can remember? There's nothing else?'

'Everything,' answered Daniel, turning his cricket-like head away in a gesture that convinced Madden he was not only lying, but lying to save himself.

Madden was returning to his car when his mobile rang. It was Lucky Maynard. Lucky might be ten chips short of the full fish supper, thought Madden, but at least he was solid and reliable.

'Mr Madden, I've got to see you tonight,' he said.

'What's the urgency, Lucky?'

'I've just got out the club. I was there tonight like you asked, watching that guy. The police questioned me but I didn't tell them anything. I thought I'd better tell you first.'

'Tell me what, Lucky?'

'I saw the bloke who sold one of these boys the tablets.'

'You what?'

'I saw the bloke who—'

'I heard you the first time, Lucky.' Madden cut him short. 'Where are you right at this minute?'

'I'm at the entrance to the West Pier.'

'Wait there. Don't move. I'm coming to pick you up.'

Within thirty seconds, Madden was at the wheel of his car, steering it towards the seafront. It was now three-thirty a.m. The streets were almost deserted. He jumped a red traffic light, took a corner so recklessly that he almost split his front left tyre, and pulled out in front of a rumbling pantechnicon that had come all the way from and was presumably heading back to the Czech Republic via Dover. The driver blasted at him with his horn. Madden made a very English gesture. The driver of the pantechnicon gave him what Madden assumed was a very Czech one.

He looked for Lucky and saw him loitering, miserable and cold, like a lost wraith, in front of the locked up and derelict shell of the West Pier. The lorry was looming up behind him, almost bearing down on him. Madden envisaged the irate Slav lorry driver, sitting in his cabin, spitting and cursing and thumping his horn. He drove on, pulled up and waited for the lorry to overtake, which it did with a final rasp that seemed loud enough to carry across the Channel. Madden checked that the road was clear, did a U-turn and started heading back towards Lucky.

He saw Lucky walking towards him.

Madden slowed down and pulled up by the kerb.

Lucky got within five yards of the car. And then Madden heard it. The unmistakable sound of a gunshot. Lucky leapt at the passenger door. The gunshot was almost simultaneous with what sounded like a ricochet.

'Get in!' Madden yelled at him.

Who had fired the shot and from which direction it had come was impossible to ascertain in that split second. Lucky scrambled into the passenger seat and shut the door. Madden spun the car round.

'Keep your head down!'

Lucky's head was already down. Madden lowered his own. No one had ever shot at him in all his years in the police force. It wasn't something he knew instantly how to deal with. All he knew was that on that lonely Brighton promenade there was someone with a gun, and that for as long as he stayed around, both he and Lucky were possible targets. He put his foot down and accelerated.

'They could have killed me!' Lucky screamed, his hands now covering his slumped head.

'They?'

'I've never been shot at before, Mr Madden.'

'I'm a member of that club myself.'

Madden drove in the direction of home, checking all the time that no one was following them. When he was satisfied that they were safe, he pointed the car towards Queen's Park and to his house, pulled up outside, and turned to Lucky – who was still cowering.

'It's okay, Lucky. You lived up to your name tonight.'

'Where are we, Mr Madden?'

'We're at my house. We'll be safe here.'

Madden took him indoors. It was the only thing he could do. He poured him a large Scotch to calm his nerves. Lucky Maynard was shaking as he drank it. Madden had one himself. He didn't normally drink whisky. In fact, the bottle had been there and untouched since before Clara had left him. Tonight seemed a good time to awaken it from hibernation.

'Suppose you tell me now who that was?'

'I don't know who it was, Mr Madden. I don't know. Honest. I was just waiting for you, then, bang. It was like the bullet went right past my ear.'

'If you hadn't started walking towards my car at that precise moment, it might have gone between the two of them.'

Lucky seemed to go faint at that thought.

'Was it Sullivan?'

Madden wasn't sure why that thought should have crossed his mind so quickly, but it did.

'Mr Sullivan?' Lucky seemed surprised at the suggestion.

'Yes. Mr Sullivan. Mr Frank Sullivan. The guy you drive around and do odd jobs for and who trusts you to keep your mouth shut. *That* Frank Sullivan.'

'He wouldn't try and kill *me*, Mr Madden.'

'You have a lot of trust in human nature, Lucky.'

'I trust him, Mr Madden. He's been kind of like a father to me. He wouldn't see any harm come to me.'

'Suppose he knew you were talking to me, Lucky? Suppose someone tipped him off. Suppose he found out you've been giving me information for a long time.'

'He thinks I'm too stupid.'

'But you're not, Lucky. You said you saw who sold these kids the Ecstasy tonight?'

'Yeh, I did.'

'Was it someone connected to Sullivan? One of his staff? His bouncers?'

'No. It was a customer.'

'How do you mean, a customer? You mean just somebody who was in the club?'

'Yeah.'

'Did he see you?'

Lucky thought about that for a moment. 'Yes,' he said.

'Not so lucky, Lucky.'

'I was watching that guy Daniel like you said, sticking near him all night. He was out of his head, Mr Madden. Anyway, one of the blokes he was with, he goes off to the toilet, and I needed it myself so I followed him. I went into this cubicle and when I came out, this other guy is handing him a lot of tablets and the bloke's paying him. They both saw me, and I don't think the guy with the tablets was very pleased. At least, that's the impression I got.'

'The boy who bought the tablets, which one was he?'

'He kind of had hair done in spikes – like this.' Lucky gestured.

That was Kevin. Daniel had volunteered the information that Kevin had bought the tablets the group had shared. The story held.

'The seller, what was he like?' Madden probed.

Don't let me down now, Lucky, he thought. *Please don't let me down now.*

'He was about forty, Mr Madden. An older guy,' Lucky recounted. 'Quite a well-built kind of bloke. Had wavy black hair. Good-looking, I suppose you'd say.'

'Could you identify him again?'

'Yeh, easily.'

'His hair, describe it a bit more.'

Don't lead him.

'Well, it was black. Kind of curly at the front. Shiny.'

'Build?'

'Quite strong. Muscular. I could draw him for you, if you like.'

'You *draw*?'

Lucky seemed momentarily overcome by a fit of modesty.

'You *draw*?' Madden repeated.

'Whose are the pictures?' Lucky asked, looking at the paintings on the walls.

'My ex-wife's. She's an artist. She has a studio and shop in the North Laine where she puts on exhibitions.'

'I used to be good at art at school,' Lucky volunteered.

Madden gave him a sheet of paper and a pencil.

'Take your time,' he said. 'Don't hurry it. I'm not letting you go home tonight, Lucky. You'll sleep here.'

'I can't ask that of you, Mr Madden.'

'You didn't ask. I just offered. One thing still puzzles me, Lucky. You weren't embarrassed spending all night at a gay club owned by Sullivan?'

Lucky shrugged, looked down into the depths of his glass.

'No, why should I be?'

'You weren't worried he'd get to hear about it? Maybe wonder what you were doing there. I know I asked you about this before.'

'He knows me, Mr Madden. Like I said, he doesn't mind.'

'What are you telling me?'

'Just that – what's the expression when you like boys and girls?'

'You swing both ways?'

'That's it, Mr Madden.'

'Which sex do you have most luck with?'

Lucky did a brief calculation.

'I don't have much luck with either,' he admitted. 'The girls think I'm too thick and the boys don't think I've got enough class.'

Madden tried to resist smiling. He failed.

'You've got to have a bit of class.' Lucky smiled back. 'Especially now. Them gay blokes with all their fancy clothes – okay, they might like a bit of rough sometimes but I reckon I'm too rough even for them. They don't look twice at me. Then the girls come along and they just laugh at me. Still, you got to keep trying.'

'You're in a class of your own, Lucky,' Madden said to him.

Lucky's face lit up, like the sun expelling the darkest of nights.

'Thanks, Mr Madden.' He sounded more than sincere. Madden doubted that anyone had ever flattered him before.

'Want to draw me that guy?'

'I'd find it difficult with you standing over me. Know how I mean?'

'I know how you mean. Clara used to hate it when I stood over her while she was painting. She said I made her nervous.'

Madden took Lucky upstairs to the room that had been Jason's bedroom, and gave him a clean towel. As he did so, he looked at Jason's football scarf, still draped across the mantelpiece. It felt strange, putting someone else to sleep in Jason's old room. And so soon.

He felt he had got to know Lucky Maynard, that it hadn't taken much time or effort. It hurt deeply that he hadn't done something similar for Jason. He wasn't a bad father. Just a repentant one.

'Hope you sleep well,' he said. 'This was my son's room. Before you turn in, do me that drawing and I'll take a look at it in the morning.'

'Not sure I'm going to sleep. After tonight.'

'You're safe here. Nobody's going to hurt you. I promise you that. Sleep with the light on if you want. I'll be just next door.'

'You don't mind what I told you, then, Mr Madden?' said Lucky, stripping off his shirt. Madden noticed for the first time that he had the tattoo of an eagle on his scrawny arm.

'You mean about you swinging both ways?'

'Yeh.'

'Why should I mind?' Then, 'Where did you get the tattoo?'

'Had it done up London,' Lucky answered.

'My old man was a tattooist. Had a shop in Trafalgar Street. He was quite famous on the South Coast.'

'Didn't you ever think of following him into the business?'

'I wasn't artistic,' said Madden.

Madden closed the door. He went back through to the lounge, sat down and contemplated his next move. He phoned Millington at home. He knew it would do the trick. Millington had just returned and was preparing to go back to bed.

'Steve, do you know what time it is? Didn't I tell you to go home and rest?' Chief Superintendent Millington almost hissed down the telephone.

'I just thought you'd like to know someone took a shot at me tonight down by the West Pier,' he said.

'*Someone did what?*'

'Took a shot at me. Fired a gun. Whoever it was will be long gone by now, but you could try mobilising a team to search for the bullet.'

'Is this some kind of a joke?'

'I wish it was, sir. Oh, and if you want a full statement, it'll have to wait until the morning because I'm going off to bed. West Pier. It's my guess you'll find it somewhere around the locked-up souvenir shop. I think it ricocheted against the wall. Goodnight, sir.'

'Just a minute—'

Madden put the phone down. Then he took it off the hook. He spun round, aware that Lucky Maynard was standing in the doorway. For a brief moment, he thought that Lucky had done the sketch already and had brought it out to show it to him. But Lucky was not holding the sheet of paper. Instead, he was clutching one of the photographs that Jacques Romanet had taken aboard the *Heraklion*. Madden had put them on the table in Jason's old bedroom and had forgotten that they were there. Lucky's jaw hung open.

'Mr Madden,' he said, 'that's the man. The man who sold the Ecstasy. This one here, in the photograph.'

Madden stepped forward, his heart racing. Lucky pointed to the figure in the photograph.

'Are you sure, Lucky? Are you absolutely sure, beyond any doubt?'

'I'd swear my life on it.'

Lucky's finger hovered over Jacques Romanet, the lover of Celestine Dimarco.

33

Madden did not go to bed that night. He made a pot of strong black coffee and drank it slowly. After about an hour, he looked in on Lucky. Incredibly, Lucky was asleep. Not only that, but he was snoring. He could almost have been Jason in that bed. Madden closed the door gently, and continued to formulate his next move.

He feared that if he told his police colleagues what he knew about Jacques Romanet, the combination of Millington's spinelessness and Fieldhouse's need to play down any connection with Jason's murder might tip things the wrong way. Jacques Romanet could be allowed to escape back to France, if he wasn't already on his way. However, Madden doubted very much that, having failed to kill Lucky and knowing that he had been identified, Romanet would attempt to leave the country by the next available train or plane – at least, not if he was using his own passport. He tried to second-guess what Romanet might do. He had no idea if Romanet had recognised his car, or seen him. If he was Romanet, he would lie low for a while on the South Coast, and then have another go at the one person who could identify him.

Then there was the question of motive. *Why* should Romanet want to kill Jason's friends? And did Celestine Dimarco have anything to do with it? Overriding both of these questions was the one that now boiled to overflowing in his fevered quest for the truth. *Did Romanet kill Jason?*

The doorbell rang. Madden knew that Millington would not let the matter rest until morning. Jack Fieldhouse and Jasmine Carol stood on the path, faces as impassive as concrete, as though Madden had called them out to help him mend a plug.

'Turning out to be one of these nights,' he said.

'There's a report that you were shot at,' Fieldhouse muttered disbelievingly.

'You'd better come in,' Madden said.

Jasmine and Fieldhouse entered. Madden remembered the last time all three of them had been in his house together. He was going to make sure that Fieldhouse remembered this one. Jasmine, he could sense, was dying to ask him a few questions privately but felt restrained by Fieldhouse's presence.

'Is this some kind of a joke?' Fieldhouse levelled the question at him accusingly.

'I'm not in the habit of making practical jokes at this time of the morning,' Madden replied curtly.

'Why didn't you report it straight away?'

'There was someone shooting at me. I wasn't going to hang around.'

Jasmine furrowed her delicate brow in a way that told Madden she didn't seem to believe a word of it either. Perhaps he was making too light of it. But what else could he do? He didn't want Fieldhouse knowing that it was Lucky who'd been shot at, that it was Lucky Maynard who'd only just got away with his life. He didn't want Lucky being dragged in and questioned. Lucky was his. For the moment, his colleagues would have to content themselves with the knowledge that there was somebody out there with a gun.

'Look, we've got three kids dead from taking Ecstasy tonight, and you're saying that two hundred yards from the club where it happened somebody took a shot at you. When was this?'

'About three-thirty this morning.'

'That was half an hour before you called Millington!'

'I had things to do. Like saving my skin. The bullet will be lying around the entrance to the West Pier somewhere. I suggest you start looking for it before the street sweepers come round.'

'What were you doing there?' asked Jasmine.

'Taking the air. I'd just driven Daniel back to the flat he was staying in. Couldn't sleep. Came back to the front for a walk. Bang.'

He could hear Lucky snoring, even through two closed doors and up a staircase. So could Fieldhouse. So did Jasmine. How Lucky could sleep after all he had been through was beyond him. For the second time, it struck him, he was keeping Fieldhouse in the dark about a visitor.

'Somebody else here?' asked Fieldhouse.

'I've got a guest,' said Madden.

Jasmine raised her eyebrows. He looked across at her and tried to pass her a surreptitious message to the effect that she needn't worry, but it had been too long a night for her.

'What kind of a guest?' Fieldhouse insisted on knowing.

'A family friend. Nobody who has anything to do with this.'

'*Female* family friend?'

'That's my business, Jack.' He hoped it might dispel Fieldhouse's other suspicions.

'Something doesn't ring true about this story of yours, Steve.' Fieldhouse shuffled around stiffly, like a turtle trying to cast off its shell.

'Are you trying to tell me that you think I made it up?' Madden poured himself some more coffee. 'That I'm suffering from Munchausen's syndrome, perhaps?'

Jasmine grinned. She could see he was playing with Fieldhouse.

'You *have* been under a strain,' he said.

'If that's the most useful comment you have to make, then I suggest you let me go to bed,' Madden told him. 'Are you going to mount a search for the bullet or not?'

Fieldhouse came close to blowing his top.

'Steve, we've got twenty-four officers interviewing hundreds of fucking fairy clubbers about three deaths in a nightclub! Do you think I'm going to waste more fucking manpower searching for a bullet that may or may not exist? You can't even tell me where it was fired from!'

'The grassy knoll, perhaps?' said Madden.

Jasmine let out a chuckle. Fieldhouse glared at her. Then he loomed over Madden. When Fieldhouse loomed, it was pretty scary.

'I'm tempted to have you for wasting police time, Steve,' he snarled.

'That would be pretty unique. A policeman wasting police time.'

'Do you mind if I go to the toilet?' asked Jasmine.

'Of course not. It's up the stairs and second on the left.' Madden spelt the directions out as though she had never been to his house before.

'Up the stairs and second on the left,' she repeated.

'Oh, and go quietly in case you disturb my visitor.'

'I wouldn't dream of doing that,' she said.

She went upstairs, leaving Fieldhouse alone with him. Fieldhouse was furious at being played with.

'What's going on?' he asked Madden.

'I told you. I was shot at. That's what's going on. And I'll tell you something else that's going on. The deaths of those three boys tonight were no accidents. They were murder.'

'You don't have to tell me that.'

'They also have some connection with Jason's death.'

Fieldhouse turned away, not wanting to hear this. Madden was determined that he should, and would.

'Don't you dare turn away from me, Jack. You'll listen. They're connected. They were all friends. Four male escorts who know one another don't just get murdered in this city within days of one another by coincidence.'

'Different modus operandi,' said Fieldhouse.

'Maybe. But that counts for nothing in this case.'

'I'll consider it.'

'You'll do more than consider it, Jack. You'll look for the evidence that connects them. And the moment you find any evidence you bring it to me. You don't keep it to yourself. Do we have that agreement?'

'We don't have any agreement.' Fieldhouse brazened it out.

'What are you so afraid of?'

'I'm not afraid of anything. You listen to me for a change, Steve. I have every sympathy with what you've been going through.

I really have. I worked thirty-six hours without sleep to bring Panagoulis in. The fact that we can never put him on trial and prove it isn't my fault. I did my best. If you don't think so, tough.'

'Forty-eight hours on this one, then?'

'Forty-eight hours. That's my limit.'

'Perhaps you should start by investigating Frank Sullivan,' Madden suggested.

'Oh? Why?'

'He owns the club where it happened. You might get a lot of information out of him. Just a thought.'

'I'll make a note,' said Fieldhouse.

'Good. You do that, Jack.'

Jasmine came back downstairs.

'Are we ready to leave now?' she asked.

'I'm ready,' said Fieldhouse. 'I've been ready for a long time.'

Jasmine turned to Madden as he showed them out of the front door.

'Oh, and I didn't disturb your guest.' She smiled sweetly at him. 'She's sleeping peacefully.'

Fieldhouse simmered. Madden watched them get into the car and drive off. He knew, of course, that Jasmine would not have been able to resist the temptation to open the bedroom door and look in. What he didn't know was what she must now be thinking.

It was the only trivial thought that he allowed himself that night.

34

Madden met Jasmine down by the shoreline and they went for a stroll. He had not been mistaken. The first thing she had done was glance into the bedroom. It was not, she said, because she had been forbidden to do so but because he had almost invited her to do it. She knew he was up to something. She hadn't recognised the figure in the bed with the light off but could tell that it was male.

'It was Lucky Maynard,' he told her.

'He's a family friend, is he?'

'I just said that to put Jack Fieldhouse off the scent.'

'He thought you had a woman up there.'

'Let's let him go on thinking that. It may make him think less of me and more of you.'

'Very civil of you.' She smiled. 'And just what was Lucky Maynard doing sleeping at your house?'

'It was Lucky who was shot at last night.'

Jasmine stopped in her tracks.

'You said *you* were shot at.'

'That was my cover story.'

'Steve, I was worried.'

'I only said that because I didn't want to tell Fieldhouse the truth. Lucky wanted to meet me last night because he saw who sold one of the lads the Ecstasy in the club last night. Not only did he give me a pretty good description of him, he even identified him as someone we know.'

'Who?' she asked breathlessly.

'Jacques Romanet.'

'Celestine Dimarco's *lover*?'

'Lucky picked him out of a photograph I'd left lying in Jason's bedroom. He wasn't in any doubt. He's equally convinced that Romanet spotted him.'

'And you think Romanet shot at Lucky?'

Madden shrugged.

'At first I thought it might have been Frank Sullivan, or somebody connected with him. But it would seem more logical if it was Romanet.'

'But why? Why should Romanet want to kill them?'

'We don't know yet what he intended to do. We don't know what was in the Ecstasy tablets. Yet. I confess, Jaz, I'm as mystified as you are.'

'You think he had some connection with Jason's death?'

It was an appalling thought but Madden had to consider the possibility. That a woman as young and as beautiful and who had as much as Celestine Dimarco did should stoop to asking her own lover to murder her husband's 'kept' boy for whatever reason – jealousy, perhaps? – was by no means inconceivable. Frenchwomen had done some terrible things, and some Englishwomen had been capable of them, too.

'I'd like you to contact the French police and find out all you can about Jacques Romanet. He lives in Aix-en-Provence but works as a fashion photographer in Marseilles. Be discreet. I don't want Fieldhouse or anyone else to know anything about this.'

'Steve, we could both swing for withholding information, you do know that?'

'Then, Detective Sergeant Carol, it will be a privilege to go to the gallows with you.'

'I found out something about Alan Michaels, the football coach,' she told him. 'He's not the killer, unless he came back from the dead. He committed suicide two years ago in Blackpool while under suspicion by the parents of a fifteen-year-old boy. He'd taken him on holiday, apparently. Couldn't face the prospect of going to prison.'

'Clearly he didn't have my wife as an ally on that occasion,' said Madden, a note of sarcasm in his voice.

'I don't understand.'

'I was out of the loop a few years ago. My wife and my son decided that I shouldn't be in on the fact that my son was intimate with a paedophile.'

'When exactly did she tell you about him, Steve?' Jasmine became curious.

'The other day. At Jason's graveside. She was afraid of what I would do. She sorted the matter out in her own sweet way. With a minimum of fuss.'

'What would you have done?'

'I've wondered about that ever since. Probably I'd have gone round there and confronted him. Threatened him with prosecution if he ever saw Jason again. Jason would probably have hated me, been even more afraid of me. Maybe Clara had the right idea. I don't know.'

'Mothers see things differently,' said Jasmine.

'Some mothers do. Yours still with you?'

'She thinks I need her moral support after that business yesterday.' Jasmine gazed down at the shingle at her feet. 'She never liked me joining the police force, she didn't think it was a suitable job for a woman. She was horrified that when I heard about the deaths at the Red Planet I wanted to rush out and contact you so soon after being attacked. I told her, it's the job I do. She remembers the police in Pakistan where she grew up – I'm sure she thinks the British police are the same. Now there's this Hindu boy called Gautam who she thinks will make me into a "very good wife". And you won't believe what he does.'

'Surprise me.'

'He's an accountant.'

Madden suddenly felt protective towards her.

'Don't do it, Jaz.' He grinned.

'It's strange,' she said. 'What happened yesterday. It's the first time anything like that has ever happened to me.'

'You're over it?'

'I'm over as much of it as I'll ever get over, I suppose.'

'What do you mean by that?'

'Being attacked was like – well, it was something you accept in this job. You learn to defend yourself. Even if it didn't happen in the course of duty. And the sexual innuendoes you learn to put up with. It's part of the police culture.'

'Not my culture.'

'But it's still part. I can give just as good back and I'm good at my job and that makes it easy to deal with. What's hard is when somebody you've never met before and who has never met you and to whom you've never given offence suddenly attacks you over the colour of your skin. That hurts.'

'That guy yesterday was a yob. An animal. You don't want to let something like that get to you.'

'It wasn't just him and his mates. It was symptomatic, Steve.'

Madden guessed what was in her in mind.

'Maybe you should have reported that copper years ago. You'd have felt better.'

'Maybe,' she said. 'Yesterday just brought it all home in a way. Don't worry. I'm all right. And I won't be marrying an accountant.'

Jasmine looked up at Madden as the tide raced over their feet and they stepped back hurriedly.

'What do you intend doing about Lucky?'

'That's something that's been on my mind,' he confessed. 'I'm still thinking about it. I daren't let him out on his own in case Romanet or whoever it was takes another shot at him. And he can't stay at my place.'

'Would you like me to put him up?' Jasmine offered.

'That would be over and above the call of duty.' He beamed at her. 'I have one or two ideas. In the meantime, I need to pay a visit to our friends the Dimarcos.'

'Suppose Romanet's there.'

'I'm counting on it,' said Madden.

35

Madden went back to see how Lucky was. The lad was sitting watching television, a cheese sandwich in one hand, a can of beer in the other and his feet up on a kitchen stool. Madden had told him to make himself at home and Lucky was taking him at his word.

'Comfortable?' he asked.

'Yes, thanks, Mr Madden. Slept really well last night.'

'You surprise me. I've got to go out again. Will you be okay?'

'Okay if I go out myself for a while?'

'No, Lucky. You stay here. And keep the curtains drawn. I don't want you stepping outside at all. Not until I've decided what we do with you.'

'It's just that Mr Sullivan phoned me this morning and he wants to know where I am.'

'Sullivan *what*?'

'He phoned me. On my mobile. He says he's got a job for me. I don't like to turn him down, Mr Madden.'

'Did you tell him where we you were? Lucky? Did you?'

'No. Course not. I said I was at a friend's house, that's all.'

'Where's your mobile?'

'Upstairs. In the bedroom.'

Madden went upstairs and got it. He switched it off. He put it down beside Lucky.

'Listen, Lucky. You keep your mobile switched *off*. You hear? You don't talk to Frank Sullivan, you don't talk to anyone except me. It might have escaped your attention but somebody tried to kill you last night.'

'They didn't get me,' Lucky boasted.

'They might next time.'

'What am I supposed to say to him? He's expecting to meet me at the end of the pier tonight. At ten o'clock.'

'You don't say anything to him. You don't contact him. You've disappeared and you can't be contacted. I can't put it much plainer than that.'

'He said he had something very important to tell me.'

'Did he say what?'

'No. Just that it was something in my best interests.'

'At the end of the pier at ten o'clock at night? Lucky, can you swim?'

'Never tried, Mr Madden.'

'Well, you might just end up having a quick lesson if you go out there tonight. I know what's in your best interests and your interests are best served by staying here. I want you to promise me on your word of honour that you will not leave the house. And you don't open the door to anyone, not even if they keep ringing the bell.'

Lucky stared at the television screen and took a bite out of the cheese sandwich.

'Okay, Mr Madden,' he said. 'Whatever you say.'

Madden considered taking Lucky's mobile phone with him just in case, but decided against it. He couldn't lock Lucky in the house. He would have to trust him.

Madden drove to the Dimarcos' house in Hove. On the way, he tried to think about what Frank Sullivan would consider to be in Lucky Maynard's 'best interests'. The best interests of no one were ever served, he felt sure, by meeting a man like Frank Sullivan at the end of any seaside pier at ten o'clock in the evening. He didn't care how much Lucky trusted him. Misplaced trust had, in his experience, got more than a few people – some deserving and some undeserving – an early grave. Sullivan had little left to lose. His empire would be crumbling right at this moment. No authority in the land would ever grant him a licence to own another club. He was finished. And like a lot of people who had nothing to lose, he might not worry unduly about taking somebody else with him.

Madden arrived in Tongdean Avenue. The gates were locked against the world, though the world had now retreated. He rang the bell. After a few moments the unmistakable sound of Celestine Dimarco's velvety voice came through the speaker panel.

'Who is it?'

'Steve Madden.'

'My husband doesn't want to see anybody today,' she said.

'*I* want to see *him*. Open the gates.' Madden made it clear that he wasn't in a mood for compromising.

The gates swung open. He drove through. Celestine Dimarco opened the door to him in a rose-pink negligee. Her hair was down, uncombed, and she had no make-up on, but she was still beautiful. Madden stepped inside.

'Sorry to intrude,' he said. 'How's Roger taken it?'

'Badly, as you'd expect.'

'The Mr Clean image somewhat tarnished? Well, that's what happens in this world. The cleaner you squeak, the more dirt they enjoying throwing at you.'

'He's not entirely convinced you had nothing to do with it.'

'Suppose I swear on my son's life?'

'That,' said Celestine, 'is certainly good enough for me. But I don't know if anything would be good enough for Roger right now.'

She led him through to the drawing room where Roger Dimarco, still in dressing gown and pyjamas, was sifting through a pile of the morning papers. He looked as though he hadn't slept, either. Madden spotted a headline in the *Sun*. DIMARCO'S RENT BOY SECRETS – EXCLUSIVE. They had dug up a few choice individuals from the past, boys with heartfelt stories to tell with honour and dignity – for the right price.

'Good morning,' said Dimarco through gritted teeth.

'Good morning,' Madden responded, casually scanning the rest of the papers. 'I shouldn't worry about it too much. A man like you can ride out the storm, I'm sure.'

He sat down without being invited. Celestine went and seated herself by her husband. She put her hand in his. It was a touching moment. He had reckoned Celestine Dimarco to be many things, but the dutiful wife standing by her husband in a time of crisis was not one of them. He wondered how and when and why the transformation had taken place.

'This is the worst country in the world to be a millionaire in,' Dimarco grumbled. 'If you're a millionaire in America, they admire you. In this country, they just like to pull you down. Destroy you. To see the mighty fall.'

'A few of the mighty have fallen in America,' Madden reminded him. 'At least you're alive. Three friends of Jason's aren't.'

'I don't know what you mean.'

'Those three Ecstasy deaths that the papers are reporting this morning. The names haven't been divulged yet because we're still trying to trace next of kin, but they were all friends of Jason's.'

'Good God. I didn't know,' said Dimarco.

He appeared to be genuinely surprised. Presumably he had been so preoccupied with reading about his own indiscretions that he hadn't stopped even to wonder at the coincidence of three more young gay people dying in Brighton.

'The young are so foolish,' opined Celestine. 'They never learn.'

'The young sometimes just go out enjoying themselves. They think there's plenty of time to learn. They don't expect to suffer an agonising death on a dance floor. They don't expect their night of fun to end in a mortuary,' Madden asserted.

There was no evidence of Jacques Romanet's presence. Madden thought it wiser not to ask, or at least not in a direct fashion. He didn't want to alert the Dimarcos to what he knew. He was aware of how carefully he had to tread. One hint and he could blow the whole thing. If Romanet had been responsible for taking that shot at Lucky, the chances were that he might still be around and would try again. On the other hand, he might have decided to cut and run after an obvious failure and make good his escape across the Channel.

All the time Madden kept thinking to himself *why*? And was Sullivan somehow involved?

'Have you got whoever sold them the Ecstasy?' asked Dimarco.

'Not yet. Inquiries are ongoing. The trouble is, one of the poor kids who bought the tabs is dead and nobody saw who sold them to him.'

'That's tragic. Really tragic.' Dimarco shook his head.

Celestine nestled in closer to her husband. He clasped her hand tightly, played with her slender fingers as though almost counting them.

'What did you want to see us about?' she asked.

Do I really need an excuse to see Celestine Dimarco? But of course Madden could not say it. Think it he did. And a lot of other things besides. He felt almost guilty for thinking that she might have wanted Jason's murder. He looked into her eyes, trying to see what was going on there. You could tell a lot about people from their eyes.

It was time to lie, outrageously. To put them off the scent.

'I came to tell you that I think the motive for Jason's death and for the murder of his three friends was somebody's hatred of male prostitutes. We have no idea whose.'

'You said murder?'

'The Ecstasy deaths were murder. But whatever killed those boys wasn't Ecstasy. We'll know what it was soon enough. I take it you never met any of Jason's friends, other than Daniel. He didn't introduce you to them for duos, or orgies, or anything like that?'

'No. Most certainly not,' said Dimarco.

Roger seemed affronted by the suggestion. Madden thought it was time to remind him.

'It's just that my son's friend Daniel told me that the three of you once – well, need I say any more?'

'If you came here just to rub salt in the wound, you're on your way to succeeding.'

'I'm sorry,' he apologised – for nothing. 'Just a policeman's questions, the kind that have to get asked. I'm sure you understand.'

'I'm trying to.'

'It might be a good time to say – well, in the grander scheme of things – thank you for taking an interest in my son. Believe me, this is hard.'

It wasn't hard. But they swallowed it.

'Hard for me to say as his father,' Madden went on, continuing the performance of his career. 'Apart from the sexual side of your relationship, it seems that the two of you took a real interest in his welfare. I never talked to him about drugs and never talked to him about his life. I should have done. If I could have my time again on this earth, I'd do all these things, and more.'

'It was a pleasure.' Celestine all but purred out the words. 'We adored your son.'

'I only wish we could have prevented what happened,' said her husband.

Now, thought Madden. *And don't make it sound as though you've been building up to this question. Play it so casually that they don't suspect a thing.*

'Me too.' He glanced around. 'Your French friend not about?'

'Jacques is in France,' said Celestine. 'He's joining us in a day or so.'

Said so casually, almost thrown away. There wasn't a flicker of guilt. She betrayed not an iota of nervousness. She didn't even meet his gaze as though to return the challenge of a question she had been expecting. Perhaps she was as good at acting as he was.

'I'm glad to see you both so clearly love each other. In spite of everything.' Madden smiled.

'Roger's still my husband. In spite of everything,' Celestine responded.

As Madden left, he quietly congratulated himself on an Oscar-winning performance. He thought he knew the reason for Jason's murder, and who was behind it. But there were many more pieces to gather in first.

He phoned Jasmine as soon as he got back into his car.

'Can you talk?' he asked.

'For a moment,' she said. 'I'm waiting on an Inspector Charrier from Marseilles to call me back in about ten minutes. Apparently he's worked on Jacques Romanet's file and knows all about him.'

'What do you mean, *file*?'

'When did you leave the police force, sir?' She sounded almost lippy. 'You *do* know what a file is?'

'You're telling me that Jacques Romanet has a criminal record?'

'I think that's putting it mildly.'

'Jaz, you are a—' He searched his vocabulary for the right word. 'An angel.'

He wondered if Hindus believed in angels.

'If you don't get off the line, he won't be able to get through to me. Neither will God.'

'I'm getting off now.'

The next half-hour was the longest that Steve Madden had ever spent. He spent it in Hove, wandering around aimlessly. He went into Hove Park and found himself staring at a bowling match. There was something about watching a bowling match when you were wound up as tight as a spring. It was like looking at a bunch of people indulging in some strange ritual in another dimension where time seemed not to exist. Madden kept studying his watch. Twenty-two minutes had passed since he called Jasmine. Twenty-three, twenty-four. He wanted to call her again but checked himself.

Then, as he was walking back to his car, his mobile rang.

'Yes, Jaz.'

'Can't talk over the phone,' she said. 'Meet me in half an hour? Say the Heart and Hand?'

'What have you got for me?'

'Dynamite,' she said.

36

Madden drove back to Brighton and went to the Heart and Hand pub which was in the North Laine area, quite near to where Clara had her shop and studio. Like the Cricketers, it was a real Brighton local. He had often met his ex-wife in there in happier days. He wondered if by chance she would use it today. It was still, he assumed, very much her local. In fact, Brighton had so many pubs that felt like locals that at times the city seemed just like one big village. As he walked in, Marvin Gaye was playing on the jukebox, which was full of such blasts from the past. Madden bought a pint and waited.

Jasmine arrived five minutes later.

'I appreciate this,' he told her.

'I'm not sure you'll really want to hear everything I've found out,' she said.

He bought her a half of lager.

'Try me,' he said.

'I had a long talk with this Inspector Charrier. Your Jacques Romanet is connected to the Marseilles Mafia.'

'Jes-us.'

'He married a girl called Denise Gentien who was the daughter of a certain Pierre Gentien. He's pretty high up in criminal circles down there, runs a property company, apparently he's behind loads of development on the Côte d'Azure. Your Jacques Romanet – wait for this, Steve – was suspected of carrying out a couple of hits on Gentien's rivals.'

'No evidence, I take it?'

'Right. These hits happened before he married the daughter. As well as being a fashion photographer, Romanet has another string to his bow. He's a hired killer, Steve.'

Madden could hardly believe what he was hearing. She may not be an angel, he reckoned, but she deserved ten brownie points for this.

'Got any details? Of the murders?'

'One was a supposed suicide. One of Gentien's rivals in the property business fell to his death from the twentieth floor of an office building in Marseilles. The official verdict was suicide, but Charrier's convinced it was murder and that it was Jacques Romanet who carried it out. The other is even nastier. Want to hear it?'

'You bet.'

Madden's stomach was churning. The whole scenario was beginning to fit into place. The reason for Jason's murder. The person who had carried it out. The person who was behind it. The only thing he couldn't yet figure was the Ecstasy that palpably wasn't, and why some of Jason's friends had had to die.

'The second murder was of Gentien's wife,' Jasmine went on breathlessly. 'She walked out on him and went to live with another man called Paul Dubourg, an architect. They fled to Brazil. About three months later, Gentien's wife was found stabbed to death in their apartment in Rio. Fifty-eight stab wounds, Steve – she was ripped up dreadfully. Initially, the Rio police thought that Dubourg had done it but when they caught him he had a cast-iron alibi. Inspector Charrier had some evidence that Jacques Romanet had been in Brazil at that time, but as in the other case there just wasn't enough.'

'Sounds like a pretty ruthless merchant, this Jacques Romanet. But surely a hired killer doesn't stick around to stab someone fifty-eight times? I always thought these guys were supposed to do the job and get out fast without getting caught.'

'That's Romanet's speciality,' she said almost excitedly, checking herself a little. 'He kills without making it look like a hired killing. Classic hired kills have a certain signature about them, they're obvious. The police still look to the person who had the motive. They're rarely fooled. Romanet can make a hired murder look like a suicide, or a dreadful accident, or a – a sex murder.'

The image of his son's slashed-up body flashed suddenly across Madden's mind. *Eight-inch uncut dick.*

'He'd have to be one hell of a sadistic bastard to do a job like that,' he said.

'Inspector Charrier has no doubt that he is. There's a story about Romanet that when he was a boy at a boarding school in Lyons he and a group of classmates used to bite the heads off swans so that they could see the blood spurt out.'

'Oh, lovely.'

'There's more, Steve.'

'Can we stand it?'

'There's a third string. To the bow.'

'Oh?'

'As well as being a professional fashion photographer and part-time hired killer, Jacques Romanet is a professional gigolo.'

Madden nearly spilt his beer.

'He's reputed to have slept with over a hundred women for money,' Jasmine said.

'Some people have all the luck,' Madden commented.

'And this is where ours runs out, Steve. Charrier made a few discreet enquiries as to Jacques Romanet's whereabouts last night. He wasn't in the UK. He was at a restaurant in Marseilles with three people.'

'He couldn't be. He was here in Brighton.'

'Three people alibi him, Steve.'

'I don't care if he was taking tea with the French President, he was here in Brighton. And probably still is. Does your source have any idea where he is now?'

'No.'

'I thought not. It wouldn't be hard for a guy like Romanet to fix up an alibi for himself, with his contacts. He'd be a fool not to.'

'Suppose your source is wrong?' Jasmine suggested.

'Lucky identified him. He saw Romanet's photograph.'

'Did you show it to him? That could prejudice our case.'

'No. He just saw it. Accidentally.'

'If Lucky ever has to get up in court and give evidence—' She collected her thoughts.

'If Lucky ever gives evidence in court,' said Madden, 'they'll take him apart anyway. He wouldn't stand up to one minute of cross-examination. Let's find Romanet first.'

And then, suddenly, there was Clara. He and Jasmine drew back from their conversation. She was with a man. Madden didn't need to be a detective to spot that the guy was an artist. He was about six and a half feet tall, had a mop of unruly ginger hair, and carried a canvas wrapped in brown paper under his arm.

Clara saw him. Then she saw Jasmine.

'Hello,' she said. 'You two look cosy.'

'Working,' he said.

'I'm glad to hear it.'

Clara introduced them to the artist. He was one of her new 'finds'.

'Well, I don't really want to bother you while you're working,' she said. 'We'll find another pub. Wouldn't like to cramp your style.'

'We are rather tied up in conversation at the moment.'

'Yes, I can see that.' She sounded almost rankled. 'Well, it was nice meeting you again, Sergeant Carol.'

'Call me Jasmine,' she said.

Clara made a show of remembering the pub she had meant to take her new protégé into, and all but herded him out of the door. It was yet another indication of how impossible it was to live in a place like Brighton and not be continually reminded of people you were trying or ought to forget. Not that Madden ever wanted to forget Clara. He'd spent months painfully reminding himself of her. Now it seemed, through Jason's death and minor accidents such as this, that she was drifting back into his life piece by piece. He didn't know whether that was a good thing or not. He only knew that he wouldn't be able to stand it if he was never to see her again.

Jasmine returned quickly to their discussion.

'Steve, we've got to make this official!'

'No. This is still our show.'

'You've got enough to put in front of Millington now.'

'We've got nothing. A man who wasn't here, whose where-abouts are still unknown. An identification made at night, uncor-roborated, in my house, by a known villain. That's all we've got.'

'We have got something else,' she told him, having kept her most dramatic piece of information for last. 'The lab's report on those Ecstasy tablets. They were from the same batch that were found in the flat where Jason was murdered. Only this time there was one extra ingredient.'

'What was that?' asked Madden.

'Strychnine,' she said.

37

Madden was driving up the M3 towards London. Next to him, in the passenger seat, sat Lucky Maynard. Madden had bought him some spare underwear, a few pairs of socks, a change of clothes and a newspaper. He'd have bought him some books, but Lucky didn't read. Madden wasn't sure if Lucky *could* read that well. He perused the newspaper as they drove, but turned the pages so quickly that he couldn't possibly have taken very much in. The important thing was that Lucky was safe. Safe with him. He hadn't allowed Lucky to go home. Romanet could be anywhere, waiting in a car somewhere, waiting to get his second shot at Lucky. Madden had to get Lucky somewhere that Romanet wouldn't think of looking for him.

They arrived in Earl's Court. Madden rang the bell to the flat, and Ming answered the door. She was expecting him.

'Hello, honey,' she said.

'Hello, Ming. Thanks for doing me the favour.'

'If it helps, I'll do you ten.'

'Busy?'

'Quiet kind of day.'

'This is Lucky. Lucky Maynard. Lucky, meet Ming. She's from Thailand.'

If Madden could have captured Lucky Maynard's expression for all eternity, he would have done. The lad stood open-mouthed, so much so that it seemed his lower jaw was about to go into free fall. Before him stood a tall and gorgeous woman, tightly shoehorned in a bottle-green suit, smelling of exquisite perfume. Ming, on the other hand, was not fazed by Lucky in the slightest. She met all sorts. It was the nature of her profession.

'I saw you at the club. That night,' Lucky said.

'I'd have been mortally offended if you hadn't. Noticed me, that is,' she said, with a coquettish turn of her head.

Lucky grinned, a mixture of excitement and nervousness.

'Do you smoke, honey?' she asked.

'Er – yes.' Lucky tripped over his tongue as he spoke.

'That's good. At least we have something in common.'

'I don't want him going out, Ming. Not until I resolve a few things.' Madden gave Ming his mobile number and told her to ring him if there were any problems. 'Lucky, let's see you continue to live up to your name.'

'Who called you Lucky?' Ming offered him a cigarette. Lucky's hand shook as he took it. He couldn't take his gaze off her.

'Can't remember,' said Lucky. 'Just always been called that.'

'You must have a real name, honey. What is it?'

'I've got to split,' said Madden. 'I'll leave you two to get to know each other. Ming works from home, Lucky, so I trust you won't get under her feet too much.'

Not unless you pay her first, he was tempted to add.

'I'll put him in the spare room,' said Ming. 'He'll be comfortable there.'

Madden went to the door. Lucky ran after him, like a dog unwilling to leave its master.

'Mr Madden,' he said, 'I want to say thank you.'

'Thank me when I've finished the job.'

'You think this guy would try to kill me again?'

Madden considered Jacques Romanet's record. A murder in Marseilles that went down as a suicide. A murder in Rio, brutally executed and doubtless as painstakingly planned. The murder of Madden's own son. The deaths of three teenagers by yet another agent. A killer who crossed continents, who used different methods, who arranged alibis in advance. Romanet was no bungling amateur.

'Let's just say, Lucky, that that night in Brighton you really did live up to your name.' Madden smiled.

'What about Mr Sullivan? Can't he know where I am?'

'Absolutely not. You keep your mobile off. No contacting anyone.'

'But Mr Madden—'

'Look, Lucky, I've brought you up to London for one reason. To get you away from Brighton. As far as I know, Sullivan could be wrapped up in all this somehow.'

'Wrapped up in what?' Lucky sounded incredulous. 'Trying to kill me?'

'The guy isn't Francis of Assisi.'

'Who's Francis of Assisi?'

'A fucking saint,' he heard Ming mutter from the next room. 'There aren't many of them around.'

Madden returned to his car. He had just turned on the ignition when the glint of something metallic caught his eye. It was embedded in the carpet in the well of the passenger seat and clearly didn't belong there. He stretched down, picked it up, and gently turned it over in his hand. He smiled. It was his lucky day, too.

Madden went to the Dimarco building, having first checked that Roger Dimarco was still there. It was the early evening of his first day back after the scandal and his secretary was fielding all callers. Madden reminded her he wasn't just any caller. She wasn't having any of it. Even the police were *persona non grata* in her book.

'Unless it is vitally important,' she said, 'Mr Dimarco is not seeing anyone today. If you wish to tell me the purpose of your visit beforehand, I'll put it to Mr Dimarco and ask him if he wishes to meet you.'

Madden thought that she would make a very good solicitor.

This time, Dimarco was not so welcoming. Gone were the open arms with which he had greeted Madden a few days before, when he had opened up about the unconventional friendship between Jason and himself. He looked harassed, troubled, inconvenienced.

'Sorry to butt in again,' Madden said. 'But I've recently learned some new information that makes it vital that we speak. Confidentially, that is.'

'You'd better make it quick.' Dimarco glanced at his watch. 'Celestine is in London tonight and she's meeting me for dinner. We would invite you but three's a crowd.'

Madden pretended to look hurt.

'It's good to see how devoted she is,' he said, sitting down and studying the man who could so coolly go out to dinner with his wife the day after being outed in the press as a user of rent boys.

'She's been incredibly supportive.' Dimarco remained at his desk.

'I take it that doesn't surprise you?'

'What do you mean by that?'

'What do you think your wife intends to do about *her* lover?'

'I have absolutely no idea. I don't rule her life and she doesn't rule mine. And frankly, Steve, I don't think it's any of your concern. I've had enough invasions into my private life lately. I don't need any more.'

Madden gazed out of the window. He wasn't enjoying this one. But things had to be said.

'Mr Dimarco, there are things I know which, if I was to make them official, would create a great many more invasions into your privacy as well as a full-scale police investigation. You either let me address them now, uncomfortable and unpalatable as they might be, or face that consequence. Which is it to be?'

Dimarco sat back in his chair, stretched out his fingers, looked up squarely at Madden and let out a deep sigh of vexation.

'All right,' he said. 'Fire away.'

'How well do you know Jacques Romanet?'

'What do you mean by *how well*?'

'Do you know of his criminal connections, for instance?'

Dimarco was stopped in his tracks.

'What criminal connections?'

'The fashion photographer who was put in touch with your wife, and who took her on a photo shoot to Majorca, and has been her lover ever since, is also connected to the Marseilles mafia. He's suspected of two murders by the French police and is – I'll try and put this delicately – a hired killer.'

'You're mad.' Dimarco turned away.

'He also makes his living as a gigolo. What I mean by that is, he sleeps with women for money. Society women, women who want a bit of fun away from their husbands without the danger of having an affair. Women who want a bit of discretion with their excitement.'

Dimarco got up from behind his desk. This was clearly more than he could take.

'I don't know anything about this and I don't see what the hell it has to do with anything.'

'Look at it this way, Roger. Don't you find it extraordinary that a husband should be paying for sex with a rent boy when his wife suddenly turns up with a full-blooded heterosexual male who makes his living in exactly the same way?'

'I'm afraid I don't see what you're getting at.'

But he did. He was seeing it very well, Madden knew.

'If you're suggesting that my wife was paying Jacques to be her lover just to get back at me—' he began.

'Yes, that's exactly what I'm suggesting.'

'My wife doesn't need to pay. Men would queue up to have her.'

'*You* didn't.'

'That's totally irrelevant.'

'I don't see why it should be. She didn't get from you what most women want. Why shouldn't she want a bit of similar excitement on the side?'

'She could have affairs if she wanted.'

Madden had heard some callous remarks in his time but that topped them. Not even his worst moments with Clara had thrown up such cold-blooded sentiments.

'Money is power,' Madden said. 'No complications. No risk that Jacques will run off with somebody else. No risk that he'll tire of the whole ménage. No rows. No jealousy. He's there, doing a job, and she holds all the cards in the relationship. Every single one.'

'Celestine wouldn't do something so . . . so cheap,' Dimarco almost spat out.

'That's pretty rich, coming from you – if you don't mind me saying so. And I don't think Jacques Romanet comes that cheap. I take it that Celestine has her own bank account? Her own money?'

'Of course.'

'Do you ever check it? Look at it?'

'No,' he said. 'Celestine does as she likes and I don't interfere.'

'I suggest you do. A little surreptitiously, I would advise. Just to see if there are any regular payments.'

'My God, you sit there and have the effrontery to accuse my wife of paying a prostitute—' Dimarco broke off suddenly.

Madden thought to himself, *Yes, I have the effrontery*. The saying about geese and ganders sprang to mind again.

'Aren't you just a mite curious?' Madden asked him.

'You are asking me to spy on my wife? Well, I've got a better idea. Why don't you ask her outright when she arrives? Why don't you put your suspicions to her? I'm sure she'll oblige you with the truth. Neither of us have had anything to hide up until now.'

'I don't think that would be wise,' said Madden.

'Why not?'

'Because of the possibility that your wife may have paid her lover to do more than just sleep with her. I'm putting it no higher than that.'

Dimarco could not have reeled more in shock if a window had opened and a bolt of lightning had struck him. The colour drained from his face, and then Madden saw the sweat on his brow. It wasn't easy to turn a man against his wife, to make him think the unthinkable. The more Madden thought about it, the more he felt he knew what Jason's murder had been about. It had not been about drugs. Those had been planted to throw any investigators off the scent. Neither had it been about sex. The mutilation of Jason's body, like the drugs, had been to blind them to the real motive.

Madden knew all about that motive. He'd been there, experienced it for himself. The nights spent sitting outside his ex-wife's home, staring at the curtains. The pang in his stomach when the lights went out. Long lonely nights, his entire energy concentrated on a desire to win her back, a pit of emotional anguish out of which it was impossible to climb. Blinded by suffering, there had been moments when his own perception of reality had been heavily distorted. He could never have crossed the line and killed. Or could he? How could anyone tell what they would do, driven to that limit? To have a rival for your affection under your nose, to have that nose constantly rubbed in your rival's presence – that was ten times worse than torturing yourself with your imagination.

'That,' said Madden, 'is why I am talking to you like this. If I'm wrong, and it's not true, then my suspicions remain strictly between us. And I apologise unreservedly for the distress I've caused you. All I'm suggesting you do, Roger, is look at your wife's bank statements, her financial dealings over the last year. Satisfy yourself. And satisfy me. We both loved Jason in our own ways.'

'I can't – can't—' Dimarco sat down and buried his head in his hands. 'Oh God, I can't believe she would do such a thing.'

'Jealousy's a powerful emotion. What does Celestine have now? You, back to herself.'

'The . . . other boys. The Ecstasy deaths. You're not for one minute suggesting that they have something to do with her?'

'No. Those killings were committed by Jacques Romanet to ensure his own survival. Only the plan went wrong—'

They were interrupted by Dimarco's secretary. She walked in on a scene that would have had most normal people apologising and walking out tactfully. Dimarco was slumped in his chair, his head still in his hands, while Madden stood over him, one hand gently resting on the other man's shoulder. But Dimarco's secretary was not a normal human being.

'Your wife is here, Mr Dimarco,' she said.

And into the office, like a piece of fine silk blowing on a breeze, wafted Celestine Dimarco. She had been shopping. She wore a white skirt that showed off the pinkness of her legs, and a blouse that hugged her breasts. She immediately saw the state Roger was in, and rushed to take him in her arms. Once again, Madden was touched.

It touched him so much that he wanted to be sick.

She looked up at him, and this time he saw real fire in her eyes.

'What are you doing to him?' she said.

'Just talking,' answered Madden.

'Can't you leave him alone? Can't you leave *us* alone?'

'I guess it's a bad habit of mine. Not being able to leave people alone.'

'*Mon cheri, mon cheri.*' She held Dimarco in her arms.

'I'm all right.' Dimarco gently pushed her away. 'I just got a little emotional for a moment but I'm all right now. It's been a difficult time.'

'I have news for you,' she said, but addressed the remark to them both. 'I'm getting rid of Jacques. I don't need him any more. He was an amusing diversion for a while but I've left a message at his home in Aix, asking him not to come over. I know what I want from my marriage now.'

Dimarco looked up and seemed to smile. But the expression was lost somewhere in a mass of confusion on his face.

'Do you know what you're saying?' he asked her.

'Of course I do. Is it unreasonable for a woman to want her husband back? Is it remarkable that I should want to love only the man I married?'

Celestine kissed Dimarco. Madden caught a trace of perfume on the air, something so exquisite and so delicate that it seemed to emanate from inside her. Celestine Dimarco was a woman who didn't *wear* expensive perfume – she *breathed* it through every pore of her being. She looked genuinely startled that two men should think it extraordinary that she wanted to be a happily married woman. In that moment she was superbly, breathtakingly, seductively French.

'Have I said something that is so surprising?' she asked.

'No,' answered her husband.

'Good. When this is all over, Mr Madden, I'm taking Roger away for a long holiday. There will be just the two of us and no one else. We must rediscover our marriage, how much we mean to each other. The past is dead.'

She seemed to have buried it already. Six feet down.

Madden turned to the door and looked back at them both. His gaze met that of Roger Dimarco. Dimarco, more than at any other time during any of their previous meetings, looked scared.

'Enjoy your dinner,' Madden said.

38

Ming's voice was frantic. At first Madden could hardly make out what she was trying to say. The signal kept cutting out. He gunned the car into a farm turn-off and braked sharply. The signal was better now but Ming was still distraught.

'I was out with a client,' she said. 'When I came home he was gone.'

Madden gripped his mobile so tightly that he was almost crushing it.

'Ming, are you telling me that Lucky's vanished?'

'Vanished, yes.'

'And he didn't say where?'

'I was out with a client. When I came home he—'

'Yes, I know. You just said. How long ago was this?'

'I just got home. A few minutes ago.'

'How long were you out? How long was it since you last saw him?'

The signal cut out again. Madden dialled her back. He was driving back to Brighton over the Sussex Downs and it was already dark. He got out of his car to try and get a better signal.

'Ming, it's me again. When did you last see Lucky?'

'About four hours ago.' She seemed almost in tears.

Four hours. If Lucky had left soon after Ming went out to see her client, he would have had ample time to get back to Brighton on the train. Madden figured that Lucky wouldn't go anywhere else. Lucky would have been lost in London. Brighton was his home.

'Did he give any indication of where he might go?'

'He didn't say anything. I left him watching the television.'

'Did he contact anybody? Did anybody phone him?'

'Not that I'm aware of, honey.'

'Has he taken his phone?'

'It's not here.'

'Okay, Ming. Phone me the moment you hear anything, if he gets in touch.'

'I will. I'm really sorry, Mr Madden. Really sorry.'

'It wasn't your fault. Believe me.'

Madden tried to get Lucky on his mobile. It was switched off. He was fifteen minutes away from Brighton. He got back into his car, reversed out of the farm track, and headed as fast as he could for home.

What did it take to get through to Lucky? Of course he was afraid of Frank Sullivan. That was the root of it. He was terrified that in severing all connection with the club owner he was drawing some fate worse than merely being shot at down on himself. Madden wondered if Lucky realised the seriousness of what had happened. Lucky, without doubt, was a dangerous name to have.

Madden cruised along the front, hoping he might catch sight of Lucky. He considered it too dangerous to go in person to Lucky's flat. He would never do such a thing. Lucky was an informer and technically still was. If he wasn't a corpse.

Madden passed the Red Planet night club. The doors were shut and a notice outside read CLOSED UNTIL FURTHER NOTICE. It might as well have read 'closed permanently'. He had been trying Lucky's number but without success. Then suddenly Lucky rang him.

'Mr Madden?'

There was a cacophony in the background. Madden could hardly hear him.

'Lucky, where are you?'

'I'm—'

There was a crash followed by screams and the sound of people shouting.

'Lucky! Answer me!'

A girl shrieked. Madden heard music. He knew the music. He'd heard it countless times before. It came from the funfair at the end of Palace Pier.

It had gone ten o'clock. And Lucky's 'best interests' were being served.

Madden turned his car off the road onto the tarmac at the entrance to the pier, jumped out, and started legging it down the boardwalk, past crowds of people eating hot doughnuts and candyfloss and fish suppers, past the clairvoyants' booths and the souvenir shops and the noisy amusement arcades and the Dolphin Derby where punters rolled red balls into holes and made model dolphins race along tracks. He arrived at the funfair. He tried phoning Lucky back. The phone rang but there was no reply. The noise on the other end had been so loud that he was convinced Lucky had been very near to where he was standing now, by the dodgems. He could hear the same music. He gazed round the crowds, sick with worry. Sometimes you could be most at risk in a crowd. He ran over to the edge of the pier and looked down into the choppy grey water.

If anything had happened to Lucky, he would feel responsible.

Madden was hurrying back round the edge of the dodgem enclosure when he saw Lucky. He had to look twice. He didn't quite believe what he was seeing.

Sitting in a dodgem car together were Lucky and Frank Sullivan. The car stopped at the edge of the boardwalk and they climbed out. Sullivan had his hand pressed on Lucky's back. They were smiling at each other. Madden's mind went into overdrive.

'Hello,' said Lucky, surprised to see him there.

'What the hell's going on?'

'I tried to phone you but I couldn't hear for the noise.'

Sullivan turned to Lucky.

'Why don't you go for a walk, Lucky? I'll catch up with you later.'

'Hang on. Lucky's not going for a walk anywhere. Someone took a shot at him yesterday not a million miles from here and that person is probably still around somewhere.'

'You thought it was me?' asked Sullivan.

'I would like an explanation.'

'So you'll have one. But first we should find somewhere safe for Lucky.'

Madden couldn't believe he was hearing this. It was out in the open now. His relationship with Lucky. Everything. And here was Frank Sullivan behaving to both of them with concern and civility. It didn't make sense. Nothing that crazy night was making sense at all.

The Dolphin Derby was in full swing. A dozen punters were seated out front in numbered aisles, rolling balls into holes. As each ball dropped, the corresponding dolphin lurched forward. The winner was the person whose dolphin reached the finishing post first. It wasn't difficult to guess the prizes.

Madden knew the proprietor slightly. He asked if Lucky could remain inside, at the back, out of sight. There was no problem. If Romanet had been bold enough to take a shot at Lucky late at night on the promenade, he was bold enough to be mixing with the evening crowds outside right now, still looking for his target. Madden was taking no chances.

'Now, suppose you tell me what this is all about?' he asked Sullivan.

'I came, I saw, I conquered,' this nightclub operator replied.

'Cut the bullshit.'

'You were right, Mr Madden. I'm a finished man tonight. I'm thinking of getting out of the club scene altogether.'

'You don't have any choice, the way I see it.'

'I shall probably explore other avenues. Meanwhile, you'll probably want to know about Lucky. Don't think I haven't known for some time about his meetings with you. I never let Lucky overhear anything I didn't want you to hear. He's given you bits and pieces of information, I know, but always against erstwhile associates or rivals of mine. People who are – let's say dispensable.'

'People you *wanted* to dispense with.'

'Inconvenient people. One makes a lot of enemies in this life.'

Madden wondered where this was going, what game Sullivan

was playing. Sullivan had pulled a fast one on him. He didn't like that.

'Tonight is a kind of conversion for me,' Sullivan continued. 'I don't like to see teenagers die any more than you do. It cuts me up.'

Forget St Francis of Assisi, thought Madden. *This is the conversion of Paul on the road to Damascus.*

'Twenty-five years ago I had a relationship with a young woman. Not a very promising specimen, unfortunately. She became an alcoholic. Actually, she was one when I met her – though I didn't realise it. Anyway, she became pregnant and had a son by me. She drank her way through the pregnancy, which had a not very beneficial effect on her unborn child. In fact, the child nearly died. Luckily, it didn't. She brought the child up single-handed for about five years. He wasn't the brightest boy and had a propensity to get into trouble. Unfortunately, his mother died and the boy was put into a children's home.'

'You didn't pay for his upkeep?' Madden guessed where this was going.

'I helped out, through the years. I kept an eye on the boy's progress. He never knew that I was his father and – well, until tonight, the truth about his parents had always been a mystery to him. Nobody wanted to adopt a troublesome five-year-old so he stayed in the children's home until he was old enough to go out into the world and fend for himself. Then, one day, our paths fortuitously crossed and I offered him a job.'

'How fortuitously?'

'A little manipulation on my part.' Sullivan smiled.

'Lucky Maynard is your son?'

'Maynard was his mother's name. Lizzie Maynard.'

'And this is what you had to tell him? In his best interests?'

'Tell me what is in the best interests of any son.' Sullivan leant against the pier railings and played with the ring of a Roman general, twisting it so that the god in the red glass faced upward. 'To know his father?'

Madden took a photograph from his pocket. It was the one of

Jason and the Dimarcos and Jacques Romanet on the boat, the *Heraklion*. He pointed to Jacques Romanet.

'You ever seen this man before?'

'No. Should I have?'

'I've reason to believe he was in the Red Planet that night and that he sold the Ecstasy that killed the three boys.'

'I'm sorry. I don't recognise him.'

Madden put the photograph away. He was becoming increasingly nervous. He didn't know how far he could trust Sullivan. Or believe him. Romanet might still be out there somewhere. If Jasmine's information was correct, he was a vicious killer who would stop at nothing. And Madden had swum a length with him.

'Was Demos Panagoulis one of those inconvenient rivals you just wanted out of the way?'

'You want me to admit that he's on my conscience?'

'Do you have one?'

'I have a sense of public duty.'

'Don't give me that crap, Sullivan. You? Public duty?'

'I'd known for some time that Demos was seeing Jason. I didn't know then, of course, that Jason was your son. Who would ever have thought that? My spies had just informed me that Demos had this – shall we say, unorthodox relationship with a nineteen-year-old male prostitute. It was well known in certain circles what Demos was into. The Marquis de Sade certainly has a lot to answer for. When Jason was murdered, I felt it was my public duty to inform the police.'

'*You* informed us?'

'I contacted your Mr Fieldhouse. He came to see me. I tipped him off about Demos. I presume that's what put him on his trail.'

'There was no other incentive?'

'No other incentive. What do you think I am, Mr Madden?'

'A corrupt, evil, degenerate bastard.'

Sullivan seemed only to grow in confidence as the words rained down on him.

'For what it's worth, I don't believe now that Demos would have been capable of committing that murder. I always make a rule. Know your rivals and your enemies better than you know yourself.'

'That didn't stop you fingering him.'

Lucky emerged tentatively from behind the relative safety of the Dolphin Derby.

'Is it safe?' he asked. 'I'm getting hungry.'

'I'll buy you fish and chips on the way back to the car.' Madden took his arm. He turned to Sullivan. 'You've no objection if I take him back somewhere I consider safe?'

'None at all,' said Sullivan.

Lucky approached him and swung his arm round so that it rested loosely about his waist.

'Thanks for what you told me tonight, Mr Sullivan.' Lucky expressed himself in the only way he knew how. Not very well.

'You don't need to call me Mr Sullivan.'

'Well, whatever you want me to call you, mate. Thanks a lot.'

'Come on, Lucky.' Madden pulled at the young man's arm.

They walked back along the pier. Sullivan remained by the Dolphin Derby, watching them go. He raised his hand in a half-wave. Madden had a drive ahead, back up to London, back to Ming's flat. This time, he felt certain, Lucky would stay there.

'What did I tell you about talking to strangers, Lucky?'

'Mr Sullivan isn't a stranger.'

'So tell me. I'm dying to know. What was your real name? Or rather, what *is* your real name?' Madden asked.

Lucky didn't answer.

'Something you're embarrassed about?'

'It's not that, Mr Madden. Mr Sullivan did tell me but I've forgotten.'

'He told you your real name but you've forgotten?'

'Yeh. I'll have to ask him next time.'

39

The wind blasted across the stunted grass of Beachy Head, blowing away the last vestiges of the mist that had settled in the night. The high sea cliff, a drive of thirty minutes east along the coast from Brighton, and a place long popular with lovers and suicides, was lit suddenly by shafts of coral-coloured light as the sun broke over the horizon. A body sprawled in the passenger seat of Celestine Dimarco's grey Saab, which was parked in a lay-by. Most of the head and the face had been blasted away by a single gunshot. Pieces of brain and one chunk of human flesh containing an eye lay scattered on the ground behind the car, the eye staring upwards as though seeing some greater reward in Heaven. Jacques Romanet's other eye had been pulverised by the shot. The only thing that could safely be said at first was that he had died instantly.

Fifty yards away, at the very edge of the cliff, lay a revolver.

Later that day – much later – at the foot of the cliff, thrashed by five-foot-high waves backed by all the fury of the English Channel, the body of Celestine Dimarco was discovered being tossed and pitched onto some rocks, dragged out again, and repeatedly deposited in a variety of ungainly positions back among the weed-strewn boulders. Death knew no dignity. The blood that had seeped from her broken, buffeted body still stained the sea red around her corpse.

The evening newspapers called it THE DOUBLE TRAGEDY AT BEACHY HEAD. For Steve Madden it went way beyond tragedy. It was a mischance. He had longed for the opportunity to confront his son's killer and had played a skilful game so as not to alert Jacques Romanet or Celestine Dimarco to his quest. Not skilful enough. The two people who had conspired to murder his son were dead and beyond his reach. He felt no pity for either of them. All he felt that evening, standing looking out over Beachy Head, with the sun going down on a long day of agonising and soul-searching, was anger.

Chief Superintendent Millington was in no mood for discretion. Not now. Madden stood with him near the edge of the cliff and told him about his confrontation with Roger Dimarco. He also explained to him what had happened the previous night.

'You knew about Romanet but you didn't pass it on!'

'I didn't have enough evidence. I was gathering it. Like you asked me to do.'

'By your own admission you had a witness who identified him at the Red Planet nightclub. As the person who sold the Ecstasy tablets.'

'Strychnine tablets, sir.'

'Whatever! You had a witness! And after four hundred man-hours of interviews, we had nothing. We wasted our time while you sat on the one most invaluable piece of evidence!'

Then came the inevitable question.

'How much did DS Carol know?'

'She found me pieces of information, sir. But she wasn't in on the big picture.'

'I'd like to believe you, Steve.'

'Jacques Romanet's record was there for anyone to find out,' Madden said. 'Jack Fieldhouse could have looked into it after Jason was murdered. You could have looked into it. Anyone of a hundred people could have looked into it. A woman jealous of her husband, a hired killer as a lover, money for sex – all the ingredients were there.'

'Is there anything else you're keeping from me?' Millington demanded. 'For instance, why did Jason's three friends have to die at the Red Planet?'

'That's still a mystery to me,' Madden lied. He thought he knew, but it wasn't time yet to put all his cards on the table.

'I only hope we get more out of Roger Dimarco than I'm getting out of you right now!'

'He's the man to tell us what happened here.'

'You actually confronted him with your suspicions that Celestine Dimarco paid her lover to kill Jason? And asked him to spy on her?'

'It was the only way of getting evidence, sir.'

Millington was by now almost apoplectic with rage. He didn't like his officers running around like loose cannons. He liked things done by the book. But he couldn't deny that he had been instrumental in setting this up. Madden knew it.

'You gave me the lead. You said gather evidence. Put it on your desk. I was doing just that. Even then there was no guarantee that you'd reopen the case. What I had wasn't yet evidence. An identification made under less than perfect conditions, a man I couldn't find, and a motive for three more murders I couldn't fathom. You'd just have thrown that back at me.'

'Two more people are dead, Steve! Instead of having suspects who can answer questions, we have two dead bodies! If that's the only way you can gather evidence then you'd better be out of this job, and fast!'

Madden chose his words carefully.

'I collected my evidence, sir. I didn't create it. Perhaps you should bear that in mind when you consider who should be out of a job, sir.'

Roger Dimarco sat forward on the settee in his drawing room, flanked by an antique globe of the world and a marble bust of himself that was an exercise in sheer vanity. His elbows were planted on his knees and his forehead was buried in his hands. He was no longer the rich, powerful entrepreneur. He was a destroyed man. He had played around with the fruits of life and ignored the thorns that lay in wait. He had tried to have it all ways, and had ended up with nothing. His reputation was in ruins, his wife was dead, as was his 'unconventional friend', the young man he had loved. Madden's own son. The words of a song came to Madden's mind. *Love laughs at a King/Kings don't mean a thing.*

Madden tried to feel sorry for him but couldn't. Feeling sorry could wait. What was more important was to discover what had taken place that night at Beachy Head. Madden thought he knew, but he wanted it from the mouth of the man who had started it all. A casual meeting over the Internet, and seven people had died. Dimarco had started one hell of a ball rolling.

Chief Superintendent Millington, Steve Madden and Detective Sergeant Jasmine Carol waited for him to speak. When he did, he looked and sounded like a man haunted.

'I might as well tell you the truth.' He looked squarely at Madden. 'But first, let me tell you what happened last night.'

'You mean you didn't tell me everything before?' Madden asked.

'No. I couldn't. I felt you were starting to like me, to empathise with me.'

'That,' said Madden, 'gives full credit to your imagination, if nothing else.'

'I'll come to that. I'll come to the truth in a minute. God help me, I started this thing, I don't deny it. Just – just give me a moment. Could I please just get a glass of water?'

Millington nodded. Jasmine went to the kitchen, poured him one and came back with it. He drank it in one.

'When you left yesterday, Steve, I was convinced you were right. Sometimes in a marriage you pretend not to see things. Things that you know are there, but . . . I did think Celestine and I were happy. Until—'

'Just tell us what happened last night,' said Millington.

'When you left, Steve, I went out and had dinner with Celestine. She was behaving pretty differently towards me. Telling me she was getting rid of that Frenchman, that she wanted us to start anew. That we didn't need anybody else in our relationship. I told her that things weren't as simple as that, that – well, I had my needs that she – by the very nature of them – couldn't satisfy. She seemed angry at that. I told her that I still loved her, that I didn't want to spend my life with anybody else but her. Even that didn't seem to satisfy her. She wanted my total commitment or nothing.'

'Not a lot for a wife to ask,' said Madden.

'A lot to ask of *me*,' Dimarco retorted. 'I'm no paragon of virtue. I never pretended to be, in my private or public life. Anyone who sets himself up as such is just asking for trouble. The press painted me as one and I can't be held responsible for that.'

He had strayed a little from the events of the previous day. Jasmine brought him back round to them.

'So how did your dinner end?'

'That was the stupid thing,' said Dimarco. 'But I had to know. I told her what I knew about Jacques Romanet's reputation. And in her eyes, you know, I could tell that she knew. That's why we lived such an open relationship, because each of us found it impossible to lie to the other. I could tell she knew. That she knew he was a murderer. Then I asked her directly if she'd had anything to do with Jason's death.'

'What did she say?' asked Madden.

'She said I was sick, asking her such a thing. And she got up and left. Later last night I heard her on the phone to somebody. She put it down and wouldn't tell me who it was. I asked her about Jacques, where he was. She told me he was in France and that she'd called him and told him not to come over. I asked her again, and again, and she just kept telling me the same thing. I said to her, "I don't believe you, I think he's in this country. I think he's in Brighton." She said to me that I could think that if I wanted to.'

'Could you tell if she was lying?'

'She was lying. I asked her how she could take as a lover a man wanted for murder and she just said he was suspected of murder but there was no evidence against him. I said to her, this man works for the Marseilles mafia, for Christ's sake, as a hired killer – these guys don't go around leaving evidence!'

He broke off briefly. Somehow Madden felt that it wasn't the end of the story.

'I then did something I am heartily ashamed of. I told her that if she was behind Jason's murder, I would be prepared to forgive her, to make sure that she didn't go to prison. But that somehow Jacques Romanet had to face justice. Can you understand that?'

'Did you mean it?' asked Madden.

'I meant it.'

'You'd forgive her? For murdering my son?'

'She was my wife! I loved her!' Tears broke from Dimarco's eyes. He appeared to brush them out with his knuckles. When he looked up they were streaming down his cheeks. 'What was I supposed to do? Turn her in? Watch her go to prison? I couldn't do that. I was prepared to do anything to keep her. Even lie for her.'

'Even though the person who'd really killed Jason would go free?'

'Hasn't the end satisfied you?' Dimarco sobbed. 'Hasn't it? Celestine stormed out on me last night and never came home and I knew she was going to meet him. Beachy Head was one of the places where they used to go. To watch the sun set, and do other things that lovers do.'

Madden was once again touched. He could see how it might have happened. Celestine put the gun to her lover's head, blew his brains out, then threw herself off Beachy Head to her death, unable to face the fact that her husband knew. It was the noble thing to do.

'You said there was something else. That you hadn't told me the whole truth.'

'That's what I meant when I said that I started this whole thing. You see, when you go into Celestine's finances, bank statements and the like, you won't find that she paid Jacques Romanet to be her lover. She didn't.'

He vacillated for a moment.

'I did,' he said.

'Why?' asked Millington, astonished.

'I set up everything. The photo shoot. I arranged their love affair. I got Jacques Romanet's name through a female business colleague in the south of France. I paid him to come to England, to be my wife's lover, to accompany us on holidays abroad. I did it because – well – I thought it would make it easier for Jason and me. That having a lover of her own would curb her jealousy.'

Madden had met all types in his job. But Roger Dimarco

transcended even the worst. He had tried to buy everything with money. Sex, love, even a happy marriage. He had brought into the ménage the very seeds of its own destruction. Seven people were dead because a millionaire thought he could buy everyone he came into contact with. Money was power, Celestine Dimarco had said. Money was the king. But in the end, money didn't buy you control over your life. It bought you misery, unhappiness, death. Money always had its price.

'My son looked up to you as a father figure,' Madden said.

'I know.' Dimarco knew what was coming.

'I'm glad he didn't live to see what a total and utter shit you really are.'

Madden spread his arms across the roof of his car, looked across at Jasmine and said, 'How much of that do you believe?'

'Story sounds pretty convincing to me. On the surface.'

'Come on, Jaz. Woman's intuition. What would you do? Dig under that surface.'

'You mean if I'd been Celestine?'

'Yes.'

'I'd probably have denied it with my last breath. Said how could he possibly believe such a thing. She doesn't strike me as the martyr type.'

'Nor me,' said Madden. 'You think she'd really shoot her lover in the face before killing herself? Would a woman do that kind of thing? Why not through the heart? Pumping a bullet into his head doesn't sound – well, very feminine.'

'You're right. It isn't.'

'What if Romanet told her that Dimarco had been paying him to be her lover?'

'That might make her blow her top. And his.' Jasmine tried to create an instant profile of a woman caught up in such a scenario. 'I think I might have done the same thing under the circumstances.'

Madden smiled. He couldn't see Jasmine killing anybody.

'Go on,' he said. 'She shoots her lover and decides to take her own life. Why not just turn the gun on herself? Instead of suffering the protracted death of jumping off the cliff.'

'Women don't often shoot themselves,' Jasmine stated, as though she was an authority on the subject.

'You mean, it's too messy?'

'And it lacks the drama. Maybe she contemplates it. She walks out to the edge of the cliff. Her life is in ruins. She has two choices. I think I'd jump, having just witnessed the horror of one head blowing apart.'

It was all conjecture, of course. One comment Jasmine made kept nagging at him, like a refrain. Celestine Dimarco wasn't the martyr type. Why not deny it with her last breath? She had what she wanted.

'There's always the possibility Romanet was blackmailing her,' Jasmine threw in.

'Why? He's a professional hit man, a hired killer. He was getting paid to do a job, to be her lover. How could he blackmail her without endangering himself? Sorry, Jaz, but you're way out there.'

'I tender my sincerest apologies,' she said. 'Of course, you're quite right.'

'But I think somebody *was* being blackmailed. And it wasn't Celestine Dimarco.'

Millington approached them. He appeared deflated by events that had overtaken even his capacity for understanding.

'Something still stinks about this, Steve.' He gave his own opinion.

'Yes, sir. DS Carol and I were just exercising the same sense of smell.'

'Well, don't take too long about it. There will be a full impartial enquiry into this when all is done. That I promise you. When Forensics complete their examination and we have a fuller picture, the truth will come out.' Then Millington added, 'Are you certain you're not keeping anything else back?'

'Just one thing,' Madden said.

He passed Millington an evidence bag from his pocket. In the bag was a bullet.

'I think you'll find a match between this one and the one that was used at Beachy Head to blow Romanet's head apart.'

Even Jasmine looked nonplussed. Millington stared at the object.

'It's the bullet,' said Madden, 'that was fired at Lucky Maynard near the Red Planet nightclub. If they were fired from the same gun, it ties in Jacques Romanet to the club killings. And all we have to do is find out the motive for them.'

'Where did you get it?'

'I found it in the passenger-seat well of my car. The night I picked up Lucky, I opened the car door for him to get in. The bullet was fired across the street. It must have ricocheted off the wall and lodged in the carpet on the floor of my car. Only discovered it when I got into the car yesterday. Lucky break, eh?'

Millington took the bag containing the bullet. He didn't see the joke.

'This is withheld evidence,' he stated.

'I only discovered it last night. Events rather took over, sir.'

Still unsmiling, Millington returned to his car.

'Glad we didn't waste time on our hands and knees looking for it,' said Jasmine.

'Glad you didn't have to waste time visiting a Munchausen syndrome sufferer in the local mental hospital,' Madden added.

'You *do* know more. Don't you?'

'Yes, Jaz. I now know who killed Jason, and why. And I'm going to have the personal satisfaction of confronting him.'

'But—'

'You thought it was Celestine Dimarco?' Madden shook his head.

'Isn't that what we're all thinking? That she hired Romanet to do it?' Jasmine asked.

'The person who killed Jason is a cunning, lying cheat and a coward who thinks he's got away with it,' said Madden. 'By God, he hasn't.'

40

Madden took Jasmine with him to Cambridge. He would have liked to take Clara to have had her in on the uncovering of the truth about Jason's death, but he needed a fellow officer to bear witness to his treatment of Daniel Donoghue. He wasn't entirely sure that he trusted himself. No officer, in his experience, had ever done anything entirely by the book. Few major crimes would ever have been solved if that had been the case. Criminals didn't obey any rules, yet policeman were expected to. Murderers who showed no restraint were expected to be treated with such by their interrogators. The book was there to remind people like him how far you could go beyond it.

'When did you work it out?' Jasmine asked him, stunned by what he had just told her.

'The significance of the smashed-up computer in Jason's flat didn't strike me until just now. My deepest regret – after the loss of Jason, that is – is that Celestine Dimarco died because I got the right motive but the wrong person. I could have prevented her death. I didn't. I'll have to live with that as well.'

Jasmine put her hand on Madden's knee as he drove. He took one hand off the wheel and held hers tightly. He wanted to say so much, but matching his intent with the right words was difficult. She had stayed much more of a good friend than a lover. He preferred it that way. Friendship was less of a strain.

Holthouse College, Cambridge was a lofty Victorian red-brick building set in its own grounds and entered via a large stone archway. Madden and Jasmine parked in the visitors' bay and went to the porter's lodge. There, by arrangement, but not alerted to what they knew, was Daniel Donoghue. He was wearing blue jeans and a black polo neck, and round his neck was a silver chain. As far as Daniel knew, this was just another social visit, maybe with a few more searching questions thrown in.

'Hello, Daniel,' said Madden. 'Good of you to meet us again. You've met my colleague, Detective Sergeant Carol.'

'Anything further I can do,' answered Daniel, rather sullenly. 'Come on up to my room.'

They followed Daniel through cloisters, along a vaulted corridor and up a series of staircases to a set of rooms connected by a common hallway. The place reeked of tradition and furniture polish. Mahogany banisters ended in ornate curves and portraits of luminaries adorned the walls. Madden hadn't been to a boarding school, but he imagined it would feel something like this.

A cleaner was hoovering his room as they went in.

'It's all right, the gyp will be gone in a minute,' said Daniel.

'Gyp?'

'That's what we call the cleaners up here at Cambridge.'

The cleaner smiled at him. She looked East European.

'I'd like it if she could go now,' said Madden.

'Anita, do you mind?' Daniel asked.

'No, Meester Donoghue.' She switched off the Hoover and prepared to leave the room. 'I leave you now at peace.'

She smiled at Madden. Jasmine mustered a polite smile in return. Madden wasn't in any mood for such pleasantries. He was impatient to get on with it. He scanned the room quickly. Daniel Donoghue's domain was probably little different from that of any other third-year student. There was a single bed, alongside which stood an ice bucket with an empty bottle of cheap champagne leaning inside it. His computer and books were in the other corner. The computer was on, displaying a screen-saver of leaf-eating caterpillars. It was oddly hypnotic to watch. This time Madden wasn't there to be hypnotised by Daniel Donoghue.

'Would you like a cup of coffee?' asked Daniel.

'No, thanks, Daniel. We didn't come here for that. We came here to find out the truth. That's all.'

Daniel cleared his throat for a moment. 'I've told you all I know,' he said.

'Far from it – you've told us nothing. From the beginning you've lied to us. We're not leaving until you tell us why Jason died. Because you know.'

Daniel suddenly looked afraid. He tried to cover up his fear.

'I don't know what you mean,' he said, directing his gaze to the floor.

'Oh yes, you do!' Madden grabbed him by the shoulder and pushed him against the wall of his room. 'Make no mistake about this, Daniel: you are facing arrest, and in your third year at Cambridge I don't think that's something you or your parents will want.'

'Arrest for what?' Daniel almost squealed.

'You might as well tell us the truth,' said Jasmine. 'Don't you think we already know it, Daniel?'

'Then if you know the truth, why do you need me to tell you?' Daniel became cocky.

Which wasn't a good idea. Perhaps it had something to do with the cloistered atmosphere in which he had been living for so long. An environment that had given him an inflated opinion of his invulnerability, shielding him in part from a real world that held far more dangers than he realised. Madden wanted to hit him. He wanted to strike him so hard that he would fall on the floor. He desired nothing more that to wipe the arrogant smile off that self-assured smug little insectile face. But instead he showed restraint.

He glanced over at Daniel Donoghue's computer. On top of it was a webcam.

'You were having a conversation with Jason the morning he died. A webcam conversation on that computer. Only it didn't finish when you said it did. You were still talking to him when he went to the door and opened it to the person who killed him. *You saw everything that happened!*'

Daniel didn't respond. He tried to wriggle out of Madden's grasp, but Madden kept him pressed against the wall. If necessary, he would *nail* him to it and keep him there until he told everything.

'That's why the murderer smashed up the computer so thoroughly at Jason's end. He saw you on the screen. And you recognised him, didn't you?'

'I don't know what you're talking about.' Daniel tried to bluff it out, but in vain.

'Jason had introduced you to the Dimarcos. You met Jacques Romanet. It was him you saw, wasn't it?'

'I didn't see anyone.'

'It was Jacques Romanet, wasn't it! And you knew that one of the Dimarcos had put him up to it! And you kept that information to yourself while another man went to prison and died.'

'You don't have any proof of this.' Daniel sounded increasingly like a child caught with stolen sweets in his pocket.

'Where's the record of that conversation?' asked Jasmine.

'There's no record.'

'Yes, there is. You saved it and you've got it on a disc somewhere, and we want it.'

'I told you, there's no record. It would take a huge amount of computer memory.'

Madden slung him onto the bed. Daniel stared up at him, breathing hard, scared of what he might do next. Madden thrust his finger at Daniel's face. He could feel his own temples throbbing. His blood was up now. And he wanted Daniel's.

'What did Jason tell you that night?' he asked.

'I told you everything.'

'No, you didn't! You wanted Jason to give up escorting. Is what you discussed? Is that what he'd decided to do?'

Jasmine came and sat on the bed beside Daniel. The boy was afraid. His breathing was erratic. His small eyes darted from each of them to the other. Beneath Daniel's almost feminine lashes, they betrayed how deeply exposed he was. There was no way out, and he knew it.

'You knew it was Roger Dimarco who had put his wife's lover up to killing Jason, didn't you?' Madden pressed on. 'And you also knew why. It's my guess Jason did as you wanted him to do. He was going to give up escorting, wasn't he?'

'Yes,' said Daniel.

'And he told Dimarco that?'

'Yes.'

'Had you discussed it before that night?'

'Yes.'

'Tell us the truth, Daniel. That's all we want.'

'Will I get into trouble?'

'You *are* in trouble. There's only one reason, Daniel, why you held on to the truth about that night. Did you attempt to blackmail Dimarco?'

'I've contacted him,' said Daniel.

'Did you attempt to blackmail him?'

'I've contacted him,' Daniel repeated.

'With what purpose if not blackmail?'

'Don't you have to caution me?' Daniel wised up to his predicament.

Madden cautioned him. Jasmine breathed a sigh of relief. She was wondering when he was going to.

'There,' he said. 'Now you have two options. Say nothing more. Or start talking.'

Daniel started talking.

'I thought I could make some money out of him,' he confessed. 'And then tell the truth about what had happened.'

'You bloody, shit-stirring little liar.' Madden swore at him. 'Tell the truth? You would have done that? Don't make me laugh. You were out for yourself. And because of what you did, you nearly got yourself killed. Those Ecstasy tablets laced with strychnine – one of them had your name on it. *You* were the intended victim that night at the club. Romanet sold them to one of your friends, intending that he'd share them round the group. Only you had a supply of your own and didn't take one. That's how near you came to dying.'

'I didn't realise,' said Daniel.

'You didn't realise? *You didn't realise!* Three of Jason's friends died because of your little game! And you didn't realise? Don't give me that.'

'I'll tell you the truth.' Daniel sniffed up the tears that now trickled down the edges of his thin, aquiline nose.

'That's all we want.'

'Jason told Roger that he was giving up escorting, that he was doing it for me because we were lovers. Roger was jealous of us, almost insanely so. He couldn't bear to think of Jason and me together. When Jason told him he couldn't see him any more, it was more than he could stand.'

'Was it Jason's decision? Or yours?'

'Mine,' said Daniel. 'He was my boyfriend. Do you think I liked him going off and cruising in the Mediterranean with Dimarco? Having sex with him? Okay, it was great that we had the money, and if it hadn't been for the money—'

'That's why you tolerated it for so long?'

'I suppose so.' Daniel shrugged, trying to pretend that it had been a minor part of his decision.

'Did Dimarco ever threaten Jason?'

'No. He just broke down in tears. Begged him not to end their friendship. He'd got too close to Jason. He was in love with him. It was a big thing in his life. I think he got really jealous of us when Jason used to tell him about how we took E together. How it made sex a thousand times more fantastic. He wanted Jason all to himself.'

'And if he couldn't have him, he was going to kill him?'

'I didn't know he was going to do that.'

'Jealousy can drive people to do things they would never do in normal circumstances,' said Madden. 'When it takes a grip, there's very little one can do about it. Except find a way out.'

Madden knew all about that. The motive for Jason's murder had been as old as the hills. He had been nursing similar feelings for months. But he hadn't crossed the line. Dimarco had.

He picked up Daniel's mobile phone, which was sitting by the side of the bed.

'You're going to phone Dimarco now, Daniel,' he explained. 'And you're going to say exactly what I'm going to tell you to say. You're going to offer to meet him, and you're going to demand a substantial sum. In cash.'

'That's blackmail,' said Daniel.

'You'll probably face charges for intent to commit blackmail, and for withholding evidence. What you do from now on is for me. I'll take full responsibility.'

'What will I get?' Daniel's hand shook as he took the phone.

'I'm not a judge. But yes, you'll probably go to prison.'

'Oh Christ!' Daniel squeezed his eyes shut. 'I couldn't stand that!'

'You should have thought of that before.'

'My parents saved up to send me to Cambridge—'

'Waste of their good money, wasn't it?'

'I'm sorry,' Daniel sobbed. 'I just saw it as a way to get rich.'

'Yes, most blackmailers do. And in seeing it as a way to get rich, you let six more people die. Don't expect any sympathy from me, Daniel. The only thing I feel glad about right now is that Jason didn't live to make you his partner. Frankly, my son is better off dead than committed to a worm like you.'

Daniel put his hand into the table by the side of his bed, and pulled out a white envelope. Inside was a floppy disc.

'They're saved on there,' he confessed. 'Screenshots I took . . . with Romanet in them . . .'

Jasmine took it from him.

'I guessed you would have saved something as important as that,' she said.

So Daniel had taken pictures. Pictures of Romanet and his son. Pictures, perhaps, that showed the struggle before Jason was dragged to the bedroom and murdered. Madden knew he could never look at them.

'Was it you who tipped off the newspaper about Dimarco and Jason?' he asked sharply.

'I don't know what you mean.'

'Come on. You were the source. You made money out of that too, didn't you? Trying to destroy a man's career. Was *anything* sacred to you?'

'Probably not much,' Daniel confessed sullenly.

'If you want just one iota of help from me, Daniel, then you'll do exactly what I tell you now,' Madden ordered him. 'You'll demand to meet Dimarco tomorrow at midnight under the West Pier at Brighton. Tell him to have with him fifty thousand pounds in a carrier bag, tied up in five-hundred-pound bundles. He's to have his mobile phone with him and to await instructions. That should be enough to satisfy a poor struggling student.'

'Will I have to be there?' asked Daniel, nervously.

'As tempting as that would be, no,' said Madden.

'Why tempting?'

'Because Dimarco would probably try and kill you.'

'What happens to me now?'

'You're coming back with us.'

Daniel held his mobile phone and stabbed out Roger Dimarco's number with his finger.

'I can't do this,' he said.

'You can, and you will,' Madden told him. 'You'll help us get the evidence to bring him to justice. Consider it as the only decent thing you've got left to do.'

41

In the waxen glow of the moonlight, the West Pier looked like some ghostly ethereal structure that had somehow strayed from another dimension. Long closed, having fallen into disrepair, it was a hollow, rotting edifice, open now to the elements. Soulless and spiritless, its skeletal framework seemed almost to have been stripped of its past. Memories of summer nights and lovers' trysts no longer clung to it. Only barnacles and weed did that. When one stood on the seafront between the West Pier and the living, thriving incandescent pendant of its easterly neighbour, it was almost as though the westernmost one was a dark wraith, a sinister and malevolent shadow of the other.

Roger Dimarco was on time. Madden had not expected any less of him. Under his jacket he carried a large bundle. He plodded across the pebbles, his feet crunching, until he was beneath and between the round metal supports of the pier. It was a lonely spot at night. The beach descended steeply in a series of startling dips and the powerful breakers had to claw their way up the banks of pebbles. Overhead was a disused gangway, while behind were long-closed-up Portakabins advertising cycles for hire and seaside souvenirs. The neglect that had sucked the life out of the West Pier had also siphoned the life out of its surroundings. At night, this was a place of ghosts.

Dimarco's mobile phone rang almost immediately he arrived under the pier.

'Yes?' said Roger into it.

'Mr Dimarco, you know who this is?'

'I know who it is. Where are you?'

'I'm watching you, Mr Dimarco, that's all you need to know,' said Daniel. 'Among the pebbles in front of you, you'll see a large piece of wood sticking up. I want you to go over to where that piece of wood is, pull it out and in the same spot, under the pebbles, bury the bag with the money. Is it all there?'

'Of course it's all there,' said Roger Dimarco.

'If it isn't, then I'll tell the police what I know. When you've buried it, I want you to walk away. I'll be watching you so don't try anything.'

'Daniel—' Roger Dimarco began.

'We don't have anything to discuss. Just do it.'

'Daniel, listen, this can't go on. Let's talk about it, face to face.'

'So you can kill me, like you did the others? Do you think I got into Cambridge by being stupid?'

'I know you're not stupid. And neither am I. I promise you, Daniel, I'm unarmed. I only want to meet you and talk with you.'

There was silence for a moment on the other end of the line.

'Just do as I say,' said Daniel.

'Listen, this will just go on. You'll want more and more money. It's what happens in situations like this.'

'How many situations like this have you been in?' asked Daniel.

'This is the first time.'

'Then what makes you think I'll want more money?'

'Daniel, listen to me. If you had really loved Jason, really cared about him, you would turn me over to the police right now. I know that the only reason you tolerated us was because Jason spent the money I gave him on you. I can keep you amply supplied with that money. For life, if you want. But it doesn't have to be like this. It doesn't have to be so – clandestine.'

'What are you suggesting?' There was a quiver in Daniel's voice.

'An arrangement. A properly set up financial arrangement.'

'Are you trying to buy me?'

'No. I'm trying to do this in a businesslike way. But we've got to talk.'

'No way.'

'What I'm going to suggest is this, Daniel. You write a letter describing everything, and place it with a solicitor, the letter to be opened only in the event of your death. That way, your safety is assured. I shan't come after you and I shan't send anyone else after you.'

'You already did.'

'Yes, and I'm sorry. The deaths of your friends were unfortunate. But again, if you really cared, you wouldn't be attempting now to profit from their deaths.'

Daniel paused once again.

'Are you still there, Daniel?'

'I'm still here.'

Roger Dimarco moved his head around, looking along the beach both ways, up onto the deserted promenade, around the locked-up Portakabins. He could see no one. What he did not know was that Daniel Donoghue was standing in the courtyard of a police station two miles away.

'So let's meet and talk, shall we? I don't have any means of harming you. Look.' He opened his jacket, revealing the bag of money. He threw it onto the pebbles. 'I'll even come up and meet you somewhere more public if you prefer.'

'Why should I trust you? You even killed your wife and made it look like suicide so the blame would be attached to her.'

'Daniel, let's not make this difficult.'

'I'm not making it difficult. I'm making it easy for you. Leave the money where I told you to leave it.'

'No,' said Roger Dimarco. 'We're doing it my way. You come down here and talk or there's no deal. I can afford to pay you much more than fifty thousand. Would you throw away a fortune? You and I have a lot in common, Daniel. Who knows, we might even become friends.'

'Unconventional friends?'

The words did not come over the telephone, or from Daniel.

They came from Steve Madden's lips. He stepped out from behind one of the pier supports. Roger Dimarco was stricken with panic. He dropped his mobile phone.

Then Madden saw the revolver in Dimarco's hand. The metal barrel of the gun reflected the moonlight.

'I wouldn't,' said Madden.

'That boy tricked me.' Roger Dimarco was consumed with rage.

'You had my son killed so nobody else could have him.' Madden walked towards him.

Dimarco held the gun out in front of him. Madden had waited so long for this moment, to confront his son's killer, that the satisfaction he felt overrode his natural fear.

'I wouldn't,' he said again. 'I'm not alone. Kill me and you just add one more miserable notch to your career.'

'You're bluffing,' said Dimarco.

'How did you fake your wife's suicide? Did you knock her unconscious, carry her to the edge of the cliff and throw her off? Knowing that the injury would never be noticed among the others she suffered in the fall.'

'You have an overactive imagination.'

'It's served me well. You killed my son out of pure jealousy and sacrificed your wife to save yourself.'

There were the sounds of car doors slamming up on the promenade, and of feet coming down the steps onto the beach. The doors of one of the Portakabins burst open. Figures appeared. Black-uniformed figures. Roger Dimarco spun round. Madden took advantage of his distracted state and wrestled the gun from him. It went off, the bullet sailing upwards and clanging against a metal strut under the West Pier.

Madden swung Dimarco back round and hit him with his fist. He reckoned he had less than a minute. He wasn't going to waste a second. Again and again, he slammed his tightly clenched and already bloodied fist into Dimarco's face. Dimarco fell backwards onto the hard pebbles. Madden sat astride him and continued pounding his face. Blood gushed from Dimarco's nose.

'That's for Jason!' Madden wept, losing control.

And then hands restrained him and he was dragged off.

'Give me more time!' he yelled.

'You've had your time,' said Chief Superintendent Millington. Jasmine took his arm.

'You've done enough,' she said.

'I haven't done enough. I wanted to kill him.' Madden struggled against the hands holding him back.

'Enough,' said Millington.

Roger Dimarco was led away. He could scarcely walk and had to be dragged. His face was a mass of blood. Madden shook his fist as though to rid it of the contamination. He looked up and saw Fieldhouse staring at him.

'You okay now?' asked Fieldhouse.

'They shouldn't let dogs onto the beach,' said Madden. 'I just put my hand in one heap of shit and if I'm not careful I'm going to do the same again.'

Fieldhouse shifted uneasily in his ill-fitting suit, as though he was trying to get out of it.

'I owe you an apology.' He even seemed to be wrestling with the words.

'Keep it. Stick it where I don't have to listen to it.'

Madden turned away and started walking down towards the sea.

'Steve, we'll make this up to you.' said Millington. 'I promise you. We failed you, I admit that. You did a good job. A very good job.'

'I did a lousy job,' Madden corrected him. 'As a father, as a husband, I did a lousy job. All I did was try to put that right. That's all.'

'You put it right.'

Madden carried on walking. Jasmine followed him, keeping her distance. She knew that that was what he needed now more than anything else. Some distance. A lot of distance. He waded into the sea until it rushed over his shoes and soaked the bottoms of his trousers. He walked out further, put his hands in the air and seemed to grasp something invisible. Then he fell to his knees, with the sea lapping round his waist.

'Sir.' Jasmine spoke softly. Rank reasserted itself almost as naturally as her urge to show her concern.

He felt he wanted to say something to her, but didn't know what.

'Sir?' she said again, wading in after him. She was aware that they had an audience.

'What?'

'If you want me to leave you on your own, sir, just say so. But you're going to get pretty wet out there.'

'Detective Sergeant Carol, I don't want you to leave me on my own.'

She braced herself against the almost glacial sensation of the sea on her bare legs, and closed the distance.

42

Madden walked with Clara along the metal walkway that circum-navigated Brighton Marina. It was a mild, breezy day and the clashing of the masts of the yachts rang out. There was a soft engine purr as someone took a motor boat out to sea. Gulls cried out greedily as two children tossed morsels of bread into the air. Clara was looking as she always had looked, the most beautiful woman he had ever known, and lost.

It was two days now since Madden had felt like killing Roger Dimarco under the West Pier. He was glad he hadn't. In spite of his wealth and business connections, it was unlikely that Dimarco would be able to buy off the justice that was his. Perhaps in America, thought Madden, the Dimarcos of this world could summon up enough power and persuasion to sway juries, but this was England. Death would have been a far kinder fate than what he had coming to him. Disgrace and dishonour would be the least of his just deserts. The most he could hope for was a young man, a fellow prisoner, to ease his solitude. Madden hoped that he wouldn't find even that.

'I sold my painting of *The Two Piers* today. For six hundred pounds,' she told him.

Clara had painted the piers from every direction and in every mood and at every time of the day. Bathed in bright sunlight, veiled in mist, cloaked by twilight. Every artist who lived in or came to Brighton painted the piers.

'That's good,' said Madden.

'The customer wants to commission me to do another painting. This one will be of his house and land in Tunbridge Wells. And his horses.'

'I didn't think you could do horses.'

'Of course I can do horses.'

'If you say so. But I just never thought that you were very good at horses.'

'Well, that just goes to show how little you remember,' she chided him.

They stopped at the edge of the marina. A breeze whipped at Clara's strands of red hair, sending them across her face. She pulled them aside.

'Clara.' Madden faced her, 'I don't want you to do anything you don't want to do, but I thought, occasionally, you know, we might meet for lunch. Have a drink. Put the past behind us, for Jason's sake.'

'Steve, I'm with Clive now,' she reminded him.

'He works all day in London, doesn't come home till late at night sometimes, leaves you living in this soulless concrete place.'

'I like living here. And I love Clive.'

'Don't doubt it. Don't doubt it at all.'

'Then why are you trying to turn me against him?'

'I'm sure he's a really good provider.'

'Stop it, Steve,' Clara said. 'I don't mind us keeping in contact but I won't have you trying to make out I'm not happy – because I am. Frankly, I'd rather keep up normal contact than have you wandering up and down here late at night like some . . . lovesick cat.'

'I'm over that stage,' said Madden.

'Good. Jealousy is a very destructive emotion.'

'Don't I know that? I saw what it did to Dimarco. Sometimes it's scary when you see in another human being something that's in yourself. We're all capable of letting something go too far and of losing touch with reality as a result. I suppose that's what separates people sometimes. Those who pull themselves back from the brink and those who don't.'

Madden gave an involuntary shudder. Dimarco's love had amounted to an obsession, an infatuation that the man hadn't been able to control. The demon had been in both of them. In

Dimarco's case it had driven him inexorably towards a conclusion that allowed for no other outcome than the complete destruction of the cause of his torment. Like many men who had come before him and many who would come after, he had killed the thing he loved.

Madden turned to Clara.

'So are we friends?'

'I don't see why not. But I'd rather Clive didn't know.'

'Clive needn't know. Besides, he has his own diversions.'

She looked at him sharply.

'What the hell do you mean?' she asked.

'What was he doing up in London that was so important on the day Jason died that he couldn't come home? To be with you?'

'He had a meeting.'

'Does his business ever take him to Shepherd Market? You know, where the prostitutes hang out?'

'I'm not listening to any more of this.'

'I had him followed, Clara.'

'You bastard!'

'You'd want me to tell you, wouldn't you? A few days ago, he met a girl in Shepherd Market, went up to her room with her and stayed there for quarter of an hour. That's not including the drink they had beforehand. Her name was Mandy. Hardly original, I know. But I just thought you ought to know. For – well – a few obvious reasons. I'm sure you know what they are.'

'How dare you?' she shouted. 'How dare you have my husband followed?'

'I'm sorry.'

'I don't believe it. I don't believe one word of it.'

'Okay, don't. But if I knew and I didn't tell you, I wouldn't be much of a friend, would I?'

'You could be making it up.'

'What kind of friend would do that? I still love you, Clara, I'll always love you in a kind of a way. Not in any stupid possessive way, I've finished with all that. I've got to get on with my life. But I couldn't carry on as your friend and not tell you what I'd found out. I'm sorry if it shocks you. I'm sorry if you think I'm a heel for doing it. Shit, maybe I am. Maybe I should have just kept my big mouth shut.'

Madden started to walk away. He hoped that Clara would say something to make him come back. She did. She had made her token protest. Now she made a not-so-token concession that took the wind completely out of his sails.

'Steve, I always suspected it,' she said.

Madden stopped. He turned.

'You know how it is?' she begged.

'No, I don't know how it is.'

'In a marriage, you sense things. Pick up hints. But you try to pull the wool over your own eyes.'

'Like you sensed in our marriage?'

She angled her head seaward. He took her hand and softly caressed it.

'Steve,' she said, 'you've been hurting so much. Haven't you?'

'You could say that. I just couldn't bear the thought of you two together.'

'Oh God, I wish I could explain.' Clara clearly had something she wanted to tell him.

'Try,' he asked her.

'You've been screwing yourself up with jealousy over me and Clive. It wasn't necessary. Any of it.'

Madden's hand froze on hers. She looked back at him. He tried to extract some meaning from her gaze. Was she trying to tell him she was still in love with him?

'I don't understand. *Why* wasn't it necessary?'

'Because I don't have a sexual relationship with Clive. We never have had. Not really.'

It was as though a steel ball had suddenly hit him in the stomach.

'Clive and I really just began as a good friendship. I had to get away from you, that's all. We don't even sleep together, for Christ's sake.'

'You mean – all those nights—?'

'All those nights, with you prowling up and down. Would you like to know what I was probably doing? Lying in bed reading, with a mug of hot chocolate, while Clive did the accounts that he brings home.'

'You mean all those nights when I lay awake jealous of you and him and—'

'You were torturing yourself needlessly.'

Madden let out his breath in a sudden gasp.

'Why did you never tell me?'

'Oh, how could I? And why should I? It was none of your business! I love Clive, that's all there is to it. Love doesn't have to be about sex. Sometimes when it isn't life is far simpler.'

'You mean you left me for a man you don't even sleep with?'

'I needed to be with someone who didn't make demands on me, Steve. Someone I didn't end up arguing with all the time. I wanted calm in my life. Someone whose . . . arms I could lie in and just feel there was no pressure there.'

'I never felt so happy,' said Madden, smiling.

Clara frowned suddenly. If she had found calm, it was about to be replaced by a brief squall.

'Well, I'm glad you're happy. I find out that Clive's going with prostitutes. Yes, that makes me very happy. Why don't we have a party, Steve, and tell all our friends how happy we are!'

Just like Clara. In the middle of making up, she could be mercurial.

'I'm sorry.' He toned down his elation. 'It's just that we were so good together, it was like – well – you were never meant for anybody else but me. And I thought that you and Clive would be just the same as we were. That was what was so difficult.'

'Is it easier now?'

'Much easier.'

'Because you missed the sex but not me?'

'It was all part and parcel,' said Madden, finding it hard to explain. 'Course I miss you. I'll always miss you. We had twenty-two years, after all, and that's a lot of time.'

'Yes. It is, isn't it?'

'I'm sorry I behaved like a bloody fool.' He bared his soul.

'I think I'd like to handle this in my own way,' Clara said. 'Just leave me now.'

'Okay. So shall we meet for lunch soon?'

'Soon.' She spoke though lips that hardly moved.

He took her hand again, pressed it, then put it lightly to his own lips and kissed her fingers.

'Take your time,' he said. 'No rush. I'm not going anywhere. And good luck with the horses.'

Madden had suggested that they meet, but it was actually Lucky who asked to meet Madden in the Queen's Arms in George Street. Why Lucky should have offered to meet him in a gay pub was a mystery to him. Lucky had never suggested that before. When he got there, the mystery was soon cleared up. Sitting next to Lucky, in a corner of the empty pub, was Ming. She looked altogether more feminine than at any other time he had seen her. She smoked a long cigarette.

'Hello, Mr Madden,' said Lucky. He was beaming broadly.

Madden noticed that they were holding hands.

'Hi, honey.' Ming blew a kiss. 'Well, you just wouldn't believe what's happened.'

'I've been around.' Madden smiled. 'I can believe anything.'

'I'm just crazy about her,' Lucky admitted. 'Okay, I know she used to be a he, but that doesn't matter to me. It's what you are now that matters, isn't it?'

'Yes, Lucky. It's what you are now.'

'And I'm giving up the game, honey,' said Ming. 'This tranny's found love and is holding on to it.'

'I'm glad to hear that.' Madden looked from one to the other. They made an odd pair. The word 'unconventional' came to mind. He dismissed it. 'Well, let me buy you both a drink and let's celebrate.'

He bought a round. He had a large whisky for himself. He felt he needed it.

'Happened just like it does in the movies,' Ming explained.

'There we were, just sitting round the fire talking, late into the night, weren't we?'

'Didn't think we had much in common,' Lucky stated.

'You know, you can go through life looking for somebody and not finding them, and there, suddenly, under your nose, is the very person you're looking for,' said Ming.

'I know that feeling well,' Madden stated.

'She's just so – different.' Lucky looked up into Ming's eyes with an innocent chuckle.

'And he's just so normal. And straight. Much more straight than gay, and I like that. A bit rough at the edges but nothing a hammer and chisel can't cure.'

'Oh yeh? Thought you didn't have your tool kit any more.' Lucky nudged her.

'Listen to that! Shy as a fucking church mouse she was when you brought her to me, now she's got a mouth on her that carbolic wouldn't clean out.'

'Less of the "she",' said Lucky.

Madden wondered if he truly belonged in this conversation.

'We're thinking of going into business together.' Ming stubbed out her cigarette.

'What kind of business?'

'We don't know yet. But Brighton needs its entrepreneurs,' she said. 'I've put aside quite a lot of money over the years. Was saving it up for my old age but what the hell. Maybe we could be seaside landladies.'

The thought of Ming and Lucky taking in paying guests stretched Madden's imagination somewhat.

'Or run a pub,' Lucky threw in. 'Or open a shop.'

'The world's our oyster.' Ming defined a wide arc with her cigarette.

Madden reckoned he ought to make some verbal contribution that fitted the occasion.

'Well,' he said, 'it's not often one finds an oyster with a pearl and a rough diamond together inside it.'

'Honey, for a policeman you say the sweetest things.'

Madden drank up. It was time to go.

'I wish the two of you well,' he said.

'It's thanks to you, Mr Madden.' Lucky raised his glass to him.

'I was just doing my job. That's all.'

With that, he left the pub. He turned the corner, and walked down St James's Street, onto Old Steine. Then he headed for the pier. The sun was low in the west and the sea was a sparkling, shimmering sheet. It looked as though it was burning, like white-hot metal. He leant on the railings and looked out, blinded to the point of being mesmerised by the light. No wonder so many artists came to Brighton. A cold breeze coming in off the Channel made him shiver slightly. He thought about Lucky and Ming and wondered how long it would last. In any other city, a relationship like that would invite comment. Brighton was just bohemian enough to let them pass. The city had long enjoyed a history of acceptance.

He started walking, past throngs of weekend visitors who came whatever the season. He didn't know where he was going. It scarcely mattered. He had not failed Jason in the end. There was no way he could ever put it right, because Jason was dead and he could not bring him back. But given time, he could learn to forgive himself.

That, considered Steve Madden, would be the hardest thing of all.